Kelley Armstrong is the author of *Bitten, Stolen* and *Dime Store Magic*. Her fourth book in the series *Industrial Magic* is published in November 2004. She lives in Ontario with her husband and two children.

Also by Kelley Armstrong

Dime Store Magic

KELLEY
ARMSTRONG

An *Orbit* Book

First published in Great Britain by Orbit in 2004

A CIP catalogue record for this book is available
from the British Library.

ISBN 1 84149 323 6

Printed and bound in Great Britain by
Clays Ltd, St Ives plc

Orbit
An imprint of
Time Warner Books UK
Brettenham House
Lancaster Place
London WC2E 7EN

www.orbitbooks.co.uk

To my father, for all his support
and encouragement

Contents

Prologue ❖

TODD ADJUSTED HIS LEATHER POWER seat and smiled. Now, this was the good life—driving along the California coast, road stretching empty before him, cruise control set at fifty, climate control at sixty-eight, Brazilian coffee keeping warm in its heated cup-holder. Some might say it'd be even better to be the guy lounging in the back seat instead of his driver, but Todd liked being where he was. Better to be the bodyguard than the guy who needed one.

His predecessor, Russ, had been the more ambitious type, which may explain why Russ had been missing for two months. Odds around the office water-cooler were split fifty-fifty between those who assumed Kristof Nast had finally tired of his bodyguard's insubordination and those who thought Russ had fallen victim to Todd's own ambitions. Bullshit, of course. Not that Todd wouldn't have killed to get this job, but Russ was a Ferratus. Todd wouldn't even know *how* to kill him.

Todd figured the Nasts were behind Russ's sudden disappearance, but that didn't bother him. When you signed up with a Cabal, you had to know what to expect. Give them your respect and your loyalty, and you had the cushiest gig in the supernatural world. Double-cross them and they'll wreak their revenge right into your afterlife. At least the Nasts weren't as bad as the St. Clouds. If the rumors were right about what the St. Clouds did to that shaman? Todd shivered. Man, he was glad—

Lights flashed in the side mirror. Todd looked to see a state patrol car behind him. Christ, where had that come from? He checked his speedometer. Dead-on fifty. He made this trip twice a month and knew the speed limit didn't change along this stretch.

He slowed, expecting the police car to whiz past. It stayed on his tail. He shook his head. How many cars had zoomed by in the last hour, going seventy or more? Oh, but they hadn't been custom-designed Mercedes limos. Better to pull over someone who looks as if he might pass you a few twenties to avoid the hassle of a ticket. If so, they'd picked the wrong car. Kristof Nast didn't bribe mere highway patrolmen.

As Todd put on his signal and pulled over, he lowered the shield separating him from his passenger. Nast was on his cellphone. He said something, then held the phone away from his ear.

"We're being pulled over, sir. I had the cruise set at the speed limit."

Nast nodded. "It happens. We have plenty of time. Just take the ticket."

Todd raised the shield and rolled down his window. Through his side mirror he watched the patrolman approach. No, make that patrol*woman*. A cute one, too. Slender, maybe thirty, with shoulder-length red hair and a California tan. Her uniform could fit better, though.

It looked a couple of sizes too large, probably a hand-me-down from a male colleague.

"Morning, officer," he said, taking off his sunglasses.

"License and registration."

He handed them over with a smile. Her face stayed impassive, eyes and expression hidden behind her shades.

"Please step out of the vehicle."

Todd sighed, and opened his door. "What seems to be the problem, officer?"

"Broken tail light."

"Aw, shit. Okay, then. Write me up and we'll get it fixed in San Fran."

As he stepped onto the empty road, the woman turned and marched to the rear of the vehicle.

"Can you explain this?" she asked.

"Explain what?"

As he walked toward her, his heart beat a little faster, but he reminded himself that there couldn't be a serious problem. The Nasts never used their family cars for anything illegal. Just in case, though, he flexed his hands, then clenched them. His fingertips burned hot against his palms.

He glanced at the patrol car, parked a mere two feet behind his. It was empty. Good. If things went bad, he'd only have to worry about the woman.

The officer stepped into the narrow gap between the cars, bent, and checked something just to the right of the left tail light. She frowned, eased out of the gap, and waved at the bumper.

"Explain that," she said.

"Explain what?"

Her jaw tightened and she motioned for him to look for himself. He had to turn sideways to fit between the cars. Couldn't she have backed up? She could see he was a big guy. He bent over as much as he could and peered down at the bumper.

"I don't see anything."

"Underneath," she said curtly.

Bitch. Would it kill her to be polite? It wasn't like he was arguing with her.

He lowered himself to his knees. Christ, was this gap narrower than he'd thought or had he been packing on the pounds? The front bumper of the patrol car pressed against his mid-back.

"Ummm, do you think you could back your car up a little? Please?"

"Oh, I'm sorry. Is this better?"

The patrol car pitched forward, pinning him. The air flew from his lungs. He opened his mouth to yell for her to put it into reverse, then realized she was still standing beside the car . . . which wasn't running. He grabbed the limo's bumper and pushed. The smell of burning rubber filled the air.

"Oh, come on," the woman said, leaning over him. "You can do better than that. Put some real firepower into it."

When he swiped at her, she backpedaled out of reach and laughed. He tried to speak but could only get enough air to grunt. Again he pushed against the bumper. The rubber stripping melted against his fingers, but the car didn't budge.

"Only an Igneus?" she said. "The Cabals must really

be hard up for half-demons. Maybe there's an opening for me after all. Sit tight, now, and I'll be right back."

Leah opened the driver's door and climbed into the limo's front seat. She looked across the rows of buttons on the dash. Talk about electronic overkill. Now which one—

The shield between the seats whirred. Well, that saved her the trouble.

"Did everything go—" Nast began. He saw her and stopped. His hand lifted, just off his lap, fingers moving as his lips parted.

"Now, now," Leah said. "No spellcasting."

Nast's seat belt jerked tight, taking up the slack so fast he gasped.

"Hands out where I can see them," Leah ordered.

Nast's eyes blazed. His fingers flicked and Leah shot backward, hitting the dash.

"Okay, I deserved that," she said, grinning as she righted herself. She looked at the seat belt. It loosened. "Better?"

"I'd suggest you seriously consider what you're doing," Nast replied. He adjusted his suit jacket and eased back into his seat. "I doubt this is a road you wish to take."

"Hey, I'm not stupid or suicidal. I didn't come here to hurt you. Didn't even hurt your bodyguard. Well, nothing a few weeks of bedrest won't cure. I came here to make you a deal, Kristof—oops, sorry—Mr. Nast, I mean. It's about your daughter."

His chin jerked up, eyes meeting hers for the first time.

"And now that I have your attention . . ."

"What about Savannah?"

"Been looking for her, haven't you? Now that Eve's gone, there's no one to stop you from taking what's yours. And I'm just the person to help you do it. I know exactly where she is."

Nast shot his sleeve up and checked his watch, then looked at Leah. "Is my driver in any shape to resume his duties?"

She shrugged. "Questionable."

"Then let's hope you can talk and drive at the same time."

Bewitched, Bothered, and Bewildered ❧

I WAS IN TROUBLE with the Elders. Again.

I'd been a trial to them all my life, and now, at twenty-three, no longer a precocious child or a rebellious youth, they were running out of excuses for me.

"Something must be done about Savannah." The speakerphone added a not inappropriate whine to Victoria Alden's voice.

"Uh-huh." My fingers flew across the keyboard, hammering out the next line of code.

"I hear typing," Victoria said. "Are you typing, Paige?"

"Deadline. Enhancements to the Springfield Legal Services website. Due in two days. And counting. Look, can we discuss this later? I'll be at the Coven meeting next week and—"

"Next week?! I don't think you're taking this seriously, Paige. Pick up the telephone, stop working, and talk to me. Where did you ever learn such manners? Not from your mother, rest her soul."

I lifted the receiver, gripped it between my shoulder and ear, and tried to type quietly.

"It's about Savannah," Victoria said.

Wasn't it always? One of the few perks of having custody of thirteen-year-old Savannah Levine was that my rebellions paled in comparison.

"What's she done now?" I asked. I flipped to my file-list of JavaScript functions. I was sure I'd written a function for this last year. Damned if I could find it now.

"Well, I was talking to Grace last night and she expressed concern over something Savannah told Brittany. Now, Grace admits Brittany may have misunderstood the details, which I can certainly see. We don't expose Coven neophytes to this sort of thing, so I'd be shocked if Brittany did understand what Savannah was talking about. It seems—" Victoria paused and inhaled sharply, as if it pained her to go on. "It seems Brittany is having trouble with a few girls at school, and Savannah offered to . . . to help her make a potion that would result in these girls being unable to attend the school dance."

"Uh-huh." Ah, there was that function. A half-day's coding saved. "Then what?"

"What do you mean, 'then what'? Savannah offered to show Brittany how to make these girls sick!"

"She's thirteen. At her age I would have liked to make a lot of people sick."

"But you didn't, did you?"

"Only because I didn't know the spells. Which was probably a good thing or there'd have been some serious epidemics going on."

"See?" Victoria said. "This is exactly what I've been talking about. This attitude of yours—"

"I thought we were talking about Savannah's attitude."

"There. That's it exactly. I'm trying to bring a serious matter to your attention and you brush it off with quips. This flippant attitude will never make you Coven Leader."

I stifled the urge to remind her that, as of my mother's death, I *was* Coven Leader. If I did, she'd "remind" me that I was Leader in name only, and this discussion would turn from irritating to ugly in a heartbeat.

"Savannah is my responsibility," I said. "You Elders have made that very clear."

"For good reason."

"Because her mother practiced dark magic. Oooh. Scary. Well, you know what? The only scary thing about Savannah is how fast she's outgrowing her clothes. She's a kid—a normal, rebellious teenager—not a black witch. She told Brit she could make her a potion. Big deal. Ten to one she can't even do it. Either she was showing off or trying to shock us. That's what adolescents do."

"You're defending her."

"Of course I'm defending her. No one else will. The poor kid went through hell last summer. Before my mother died, she asked me to take care of Savannah—"

"Or so that woman told you."

"That woman is a friend of mine. You don't think my mother would have asked me to take Savannah? Of course she would. That's our job: to protect our sisters."

"Not at the risk of endangering ourselves."

"Since when is it more important—"

"I don't have time to argue with you, Paige. Talk to Savannah or I will."

Click.

I slammed the phone down and stalked from my office, muttering everything I wished I'd said to Victoria. I knew when to hold my tongue, though sometimes knowing and doing were very different things. My mother was the political one. She'd spend years working to effect one small change to Coven Law, soothing every rumpled feather and arguing her point with a smile.

Now she was gone. Murdered nine months ago. Nine months, three weeks, and two days. My mind performed the calculation unbidden, springing open the stoppered well of grief. I slammed it shut. She wouldn't have wanted that.

I was brought into this world for one reason. At fifty-two, after a life too busy for children, my mother looked around the Coven and saw no worthy successor, so she found a suitable "genetic donor" and, using magic, conceived me. A daughter born and raised to lead the Coven. Now that she was gone, I had to honor her memory by fulfilling that purpose, and I would, whether the Elders wanted it or not.

I abandoned my computer. Victoria's call had chased all interest in programming from my brain. When I got like this, I needed to do something that reminded me of who I was and what I wanted to accomplish. That meant practicing my spells—not Coven-sanctioned spells but the magic they forbid.

In my bedroom, I pulled back the area rug, unlocked

the crawl-space hatch, and tugged out a knapsack. Then, bending down and reaching farther into the hole, I undid a secret latch, opened a second compartment, and pulled out two books. My secret grimoires. After putting the books into my bag, I headed for the back door.

I was slipping on my sandals when the front door-knob turned. I checked my watch: 3:00 P.M. Savannah didn't get out of school until 3:45, which is why I figured I had nearly an hour to practice before making her after-school snack. Yes, Savannah was too old for the milk-and-cookies routine, but I did it every day without fail. Let's be honest, at twenty-three I was ill-equipped to parent a teenager; being home for her after school was one thing I could manage.

"What happened?" I asked, hurrying into the hall. "Is everything okay?"

Savannah backpedaled, as if fearing I might do something rash, like hug her. "Teachers' meeting today. Early dismissal. Remember?"

"Did you tell me?"

She rubbed her nose, trying to decide whether she could get away with a lie. "I forgot. But I would have called if I had a cellphone."

"You'll get a cellphone when you can pay for the airtime."

"But I'm too young to get a job!"

"Then you're too young for a cellphone."

Old argument. We knew our lines, never wavered from them. That's one advantage to being a mere decade older than Savannah—I remember pulling the same crap with my mom, so I knew how to handle it. Maintain the routine. Give no sign of wearing down. Eventually she'd give up . . . not that I ever did.

Savannah peered over my shoulder to look down at my backpack, a feat she could easily manage, being two inches taller than my five foot two. Two inches taller and about thirty pounds lighter. I could explain the weight difference by pointing out that Savannah is very slender, but to be truthful, I'm about fifteen pounds over what most women's magazines list as the ideal weight for my height.

Savannah, by contrast, is very tall for her age; tall, thin, and coltish, all awkward angles and jutting limbs. I tell her she'll grow into her body, as she'll grow into her oversized blue eyes. She doesn't believe me. Like she didn't believe me when I advised her that cutting off her waist-length black hair would be a mistake. Now she had a straight, wispy bob that only made the angles of her face even more prominent. Naturally, she blamed me, because I didn't forbid her to cut her hair instead of just cautioning against it.

"Heading out for spell practice?" she asked, pointing at my knapsack. "What are you working on?"

"Making you a snack. White milk or chocolate?"

Dramatic sigh. "Come on, Paige. I know what kind of stuff you practice. I don't blame you. Those Coven spells are for five-year-olds."

"Five-year-olds don't cast spells."

"Neither does the Coven. Not real spells. Oh, come on, we can work together. Maybe I can get that wind spell working for you."

I stared at her.

"You wrote in your journal that you were having trouble with it," she said. "Sounds like a cool spell. My mom never had anything like that. Tell you what—you teach me that one and I'll show you some real magic."

"You read my journal?"

"Just the spell practice journal. Not your personal one."

"How do you know I have a personal one?"

"Do you? Hey, you know what happened at school today? Mr. Ellis told me he's sending two of my paintings to get framed. They're going to hang them at graduation next week."

Savannah headed for the kitchen, still talking. Should I pursue the journal comment? I considered then rejected the idea, hefted my knapsack, and went to my room to return the bag to its hiding spot.

If Savannah did read my personal journal, at least it meant she was taking an interest in me. Which was good. Well, unless she was snooping in hopes of finding something she could use to blackmail me into buying her a cellphone. Which wouldn't be so good. What exactly did I have in my journal, anyway . . . ?

While I was locking away my bag, the doorbell rang. Savannah shouted, "Got it," and thundered into the hallway, making enough noise for someone three times her size. When I walked into the living room a few minutes later, she was standing in the hall doorway, lifting a letter to the light and squinting at it.

"Testing your psychic abilities?" I said. "A letter opener works much faster."

She jumped, jerked the letter down, hesitated, and held it out.

"Ah, for me. In that case I'd advise steaming it open."
I took the letter. "Registered mail? That bumps it up
from simple mail fraud to mail fraud plus forgery. I hope
you're not using that skill to sign my name to any notes
at school."

"As if," she said, walking back toward the kitchen.
"What would be the good of skipping school in this town?
No mall, no Starbucks, not even a Mickey D's."

"You could hang around outside the hardware store
with the rest of the kids."

She snorted and disappeared into the kitchen.

The envelope was standard letter-size, no unusual
markings, just my name and address handwritten in
clean, exact strokes and a return address preprinted in
the upper left corner. The sender? A California law firm.

I tore it open. My eyes went straight to the first line,
which requested—no, demanded—my presence at a
meeting tomorrow morning. The first thing I thought
was, Oh, shit. I suppose that's the normal reaction for
anyone receiving an unexpected legal summons.

I assumed it had something to do with my business.
I created and managed company websites for women
tired of male web designers who thought they'd want
nothing more technically challenging than floral wall-
paper. When it comes to the Internet, the issue of copy-
right is as murky and convoluted as a celebrity prenup,
so, seeing a letter filled with legal jargon, I assumed I'd
done something like design a Flash sequence that inad-
vertently bore some passing similarity to one on a
website in Zaire.

Then I read the next line.

"The purpose of this meeting is to discuss our client's petition for custody of the juvenile, Savannah Levine . . ."

I closed my eyes and took a deep breath. Okay, I'd known this could happen. Savannah's only living relative was one of the Coven Elders, but I always assumed Savannah's mother might have friends who would be wondering what became of Eve and her young daughter. When they discovered that a great-aunt had taken custody of Savannah and handed her over to me, they'd want answers. And they might want Savannah.

Naturally, I'd fight. The problem was that Savannah's Aunt Margaret was the weakest of the three Elders, and if Victoria insisted Margaret relinquish custody, she would. The Elders hated trouble, broke into collective hives at the mere prospect of drawing attention to the Coven. To secure their support I'd need to persuade them that they'd face graver personal danger by giving up Savannah than by keeping her. With the Elders, it always came down to that—what was best for *them*, safest for *them*.

I scanned the rest of the letter, sifting through the legal jargon to find the petitioner's name. When I saw it, my stomach dropped to my shoes. I couldn't believe it. No, strike that—I believed it only too well. Cursed myself for not seeing it coming.

Did I mention how my mother died? Last year, a small group of humans learned about the supernatural world and wanted to harness our powers, so they kidnapped a sampling of powerful supernaturals. One of those had been Savannah's mother, Eve. Savannah had the misfortune to be home from school that day and was taken as well.

Eve, however, quickly proved more dangerous than her captors expected, so they killed her. As a replacement they targeted my mother, the elderly leader of the Coven. She was taken, along with Elena Michaels, a werewolf. There they met another captive, a half-demon who would later kill my mother and blame Savannah, part of an intricate plot to take control of Savannah and so gain access to a young, malleable, and extremely powerful neophyte witch.

That half-demon's name? Leah O'Donnell. The same name that now stared up at me from the custody petition.

Home Security 〰

LEAH WAS A TELEKINETIC HALF-DEMON of the highest order. A half-demon is the offspring of a demon and a human. Half-demons always look human, taking after their mother. What they inherit from their father depends on what kind of demon he is. For Leah, that power was telekinesis. That means she could move things with her mind. Only don't think sideshow spoon-bending. Think of a woman who can mentally hurl a steel desk into a wall—literally *into* a wall, with such force that the desk embeds in the plaster and obliterates anything in its path.

Not surprisingly, then, the first thing I did upon reading this letter was rush around securing the house. After fastening the door locks and pulling the blinds, I moved to less conventional security. At each door I cast a lock spell, which would hold them closed even if the deadbolts failed. Next I used perimeter spells at all the doors and windows. Think of perimeter spells as supernatural security systems; no one could enter the house without my knowing it.

All of these were Coven-sanctioned spells, though a few months ago one witch felt it her duty to point out that a lock spell could be used for evil, if we ever took it upon ourselves to lock someone *in* a room instead of keeping them out. Would you believe the Coven actually convened a special meeting of the Elders to discuss this? Worse yet, the Elders voted two to one to outlaw the second-level spell, leaving us the first-level spell, which could be broken with a strong twist on the doorknob. Fortunately, my vote carried extra weight, so the motion failed.

Savannah walked in as I was casting the perimeter spell across the bottom of our unused fireplace.

"Who are you trying to keep out?" she asked. "Santa Claus?"

"The letter—it's from Leah."

She blinked, surprised but not concerned. I envied her that.

"Okay," she said. "We expected this. We're ready for her, right?"

"Of course." Was it my imagination, or did my voice just tremble? Inhale, exhale . . . now once more, with confidence. "Absolutely." Oh yeah, that sounded about as confident as a cornered kitten with three broken legs. I busied myself casting perimeter spells at the living-room windows.

"So what was in the letter?" Savannah asked. "A threat?"

I hesitated. I can't lie. Well, I can, but I'm lousy at it. My nose might as well grow, my falsehoods are so obvious.

"Leah . . . wants custody of you."

"And?"

"There's no 'and.' She wants to take custody of you, legally."

"Yeah, and I want a cellphone. She's a bitch. Tell her I said so. And tell her to fuck—"

"Savannah."

"Hey, you allowed 'bitch.' Can't blame me for testing the boundaries." She shoved an Oreo into her mouth. "Go—gi—geen."

"The correct sequence is: chew, swallow, talk."

She rolled her eyes and swallowed. "I said you know what I mean. 'Witch-slave' wasn't my choice at career day last week. Tell her I'm not interested in what she's selling."

"That's good, but it might take more than that to change her mind."

"And you can handle it, right? You sent her packing before. Do it again."

I should have pointed out that I'd "sent her packing" with lots of help, but my ego resisted. If Savannah thought I'd played a significant role in beating Leah last time, there was no need to enlighten her now. She needed to feel secure. So, in the interest of ensuring that security, I returned to my perimeter spells.

"I'll go do my bedroom windows," she said.

I nodded, knowing I'd redo them when she wasn't looking. Not that Savannah lacked proficiency in level-two spells. Though I hated to admit it, she'd already surpassed me in all levels of Coven magic. I'd redo her spells because I had to, for peace of mind. Otherwise I'd worry that she'd missed a window or rushed through the incantation or something. It wasn't just Savannah; I'd do the same with any other witch. I'd feel better knowing I'd done it myself.

By seven Savannah was in her room, which might have worried me except that she disappeared after dinner almost every night—before I could ask for help clearing the table—and spent the next few hours in her bedroom, ostensibly doing homework, which somehow involved ninety-minute phone calls to school chums. Group home-work—what can I say?

Once Savannah was in her room, I turned my attention back to the letter. It demanded my presence at a ten o'clock meeting the next morning. Until then, I could do little but wait. I hated that. By seven-thirty I resolved to do something, anything.

I had one lead to pursue. The letter was from a lawyer named Gabriel Sandford, who worked at Jacobs, Sandford and Schwab in Los Angeles. Odd. Very odd, now that I thought about it. Having an LA lawyer would make sense for someone living in California, but Leah was from Wisconsin.

I knew Leah hadn't moved; I made discreet biweekly inquiries at her station. By "station," I mean police station. No, Leah wasn't in jail—though I know of few people who belong behind a stronger set of bars. Leah was a deputy sheriff. Would that help her custody case . . .? No sense dwelling on that until I knew more.

Back to the LA lawyer. Could it be a ruse? Maybe this wasn't a real legal case at all. Maybe Leah had invented this lawyer, placing him in a huge city as far from Massachusetts as possible, and assumed I wouldn't investigate.

Though the phone number was on the letterhead, I called 411 to double-check. They provided a matching address and phone number for Jacobs, Sandford and Schwab. I called the office, since it was only four-thirty on the West Coast. When I asked for Gabriel Sandford, his secretary informed me that he was out of town on business.

Next, I checked out Jacobs, Sandford and Schwab on the Web. I found several references on sites listing LA law firms. All mentions were discreet, none encouraging new business. It didn't seem like the kind of firm a Wisconsin cop would see advertised on late night TV. Very strange, but I'd have to wait until tomorrow to find out more.

With morning came a fresh dilemma: what to do with Savannah. I wasn't letting her go to school with Leah in town. I certainly wasn't taking her with me. I settled for leaving her with Abigail Alden. Abby was one of the very few Coven witches to whom I'd entrust Savannah, someone who'd protect her without question, and without telling the Elders.

East Falls was only forty miles from Boston. Yet, despite its proximity, people here didn't work in Boston, they didn't shop in Boston, they didn't even go to concerts or live theater in Boston. People who lived in East Falls liked their small-town ways and fought viciously against any encroachment from the big bad city to the south.

They also fought against incursions of another sort. This region of Massachusetts is overflowing with beautiful villages, replete with gorgeous examples of New England architecture. Among these, East Falls took its place as one of the best. Every building in the downtown area dated back at least two hundred years and was kept in pristine condition, in accordance with town law. Yet you rarely saw a tourist in East Falls. The town didn't just fail to promote tourism, it actively worked to prevent it. No one was allowed to open a hotel, inn, or bed and breakfast in town, or any sort of shop that might attract tourists. East Falls was for East Falls residents. They lived there, worked there, played there, and no one else was welcome.

Four hundred years ago, when the Coven first came to East Falls, it was a Massachusetts village steeped in religious prejudice, small-mindedness, and self-righteous morality. Today, East Falls is a Massachusetts village steeped in religious prejudice, small-mindedness, and self-righteous morality. They killed witches here during the New England witch trials—five innocent women and three Coven witches, including one of my ancestors. So why is the Coven still here? I wish I knew.

Not all Coven witches lived in East Falls. Most, like my mother, had moved closer to Boston. When I was born, my mother bought a small two-story Victorian on a huge corner lot in an old Boston suburb, a wonderful, tight-knit little community. After she died, the Elders insisted I relocate to East Falls. As a condition of my taking custody of Savannah, they wanted me to move where they could keep an eye on us. At the time, blinkered by grief, I'd seen their condition as an excuse to flee painful memories. For twenty-two years my mother and I had shared that house. After her death, every time I heard a footstep, a voice, the closing of a door, I'd thought, It's just Mom, then realized it wasn't and never would be again. So when they told me to sell, I did. Now I regretted my weakness, both in surrendering to their demand and in giving up a home that meant so much to me.

Leah's lawyer was holding the meeting at the Cary Law Office in East Falls. That wasn't unusual. The Carys were the only lawyers in town, and they made their meeting room available to visiting lawyers for a reasonable fee— the Carys' typical blend of small-town hospitality and big-city business sense.

The Carys of East Falls had been lawyers for as long as anyone could remember. According to rumor, they'd even been around during the East Falls witch trials, though the gossipmongers are divided over which side the Carys served on.

Currently, the office had two lawyers, Grantham Cary and Grantham Cary Jr. My sole legal dealing in East Falls had been the title transfer on my house, which had been handled by Grant Jr. The guy had invited me out for a drink after our first meeting, which wouldn't have been so bad if his wife hadn't been downstairs manning the reception desk.

For as long as the Carys had been lawyers, they'd practiced out of a monstrous three-story colonial house in the middle of Main Street. I arrived at the house at 9:50. Once inside, I noted the location of each employee.

Grantham Jr.'s wife, Lacey, was at her main-floor desk, and a polite inquiry confirmed that both Granthams were upstairs in their respective offices. Good. Leah was unlikely to try anything supernatural with humans so near.

After engaging in the requisite two minutes of small talk with Lacey, I took a seat by the front window. Ten minutes later, the meeting-room door opened and a man in a tailored three-piece suit walked out. He was tall, dark-haired, late thirties. Good-looking in a sleek, plastic, Ken doll kind of way. Definitely a lawyer.

"Ms. Winterbourne?" he said as he approached, hand extended. "I'm Gabriel Sandford."

As I stood, I met Sandford's eyes and knew exactly why he'd taken Leah's case. Gabriel Sandford wasn't just an LA lawyer. No, it was worse than that.

A Brilliant Strategy Four Centuries Too Late ❧

GABRIEL SANDFORD was a sorcerer.

I knew this the moment I looked into his eyes, a gut-level recognition that registered before I could have told you what color those eyes were. This is a peculiarity specific to our races. We need only look one another in the eye and witch recognizes sorcerer, sorcerer recognizes witch.

Witches are always female, sorcerers male, but sorcerers aren't the male equivalent of witches. We are two separate races with different yet overlapping powers. Sorcerers can cast witch spells, but at a reduced potency, just as our ability to use sorcerer spells is handicapped.

No one knows when sorcerers and witches originated, or which came first. Like most supernatural races, they've been around since the beginning of recorded history, starting with a handful of "gifted" people who grew into a full-fledged race, still rare enough to hide from the human world but plentiful enough to form their own micro-society.

The earliest references to true witches show that they were valued for their healing and magical skills, but in

Medieval Europe women with such powers were viewed with growing suspicion. At the same time, the value of sorcerers was increasing, as aristocrats vied to have their own private "magician." The witches didn't need weather-forecasting spells to see which way the wind was blowing, and they devised for themselves a fresh role in this new world order.

Until this time, sorcerers could cast only simple spells using hand motions. Witches taught them to enhance this power by adding other spellcasting elements—incantations, potions, magical objects, and so on. In return for these teachings, the witches asked that the sorcerers join them in a mutually advantageous covenant. If a nobleman wanted help defeating his enemies, he'd consult a sorcerer, who would take the request to the witches. Together, they'd cast the appropriate spells. Then the sorcerer would return to the nobleman and collect his reward. In turn, the sorcerer would provide for and protect the witches with his wealth and social standing. The system worked for centuries. Sorcerers gained power, in both the human and supernatural worlds, while the witches gained security, through protection and a guaranteed income.

Then came the Inquisition.

Sorcerers were among the first targeted by the Inquisition in Europe. How did they react? They turned on us. The Inquisitors wanted heretics? The sorcerers gave them witches. Freed from the moral restrictions imposed by Covens, the sorcerers turned to stronger and darker magic. While witches burned, sorcerers did what they did best, becoming rich and powerful.

Today, sorcerers rule as some of the most important men in the world. Politicians, lawyers, CEOs—search the ranks of any profession known for greed, ambition, and a distinct lack of scruples and you'll find a whole cadre of sorcerers. And witches? Ordinary women leading ordinary lives, most of them so afraid of persecution they've never dared learn a spell that will kill anything larger than an aphid.

"Figures," I muttered, loud enough for Sandford to hear.

If he knew what I meant, he gave no sign of it, only extended his hand and broad smile. I declined both with a level stare, then brushed past him and strode into the meeting room. Inside sat a red-haired woman, average height, lean, thirtyish, with a blossoming tan and a ready smile. Leah O'Donnell.

Sandford flourished a hand in my direction. "May I present the esteemed leader of the American Coven."

"Paige," Leah said, rising. "Don't you look—" Her eyes took in every one of my excess pounds. "—healthy."

"Any more insults?" I said. "Get them off your chests now, 'cause I'd hate for you to be lying in bed tonight thinking of all the zingers you'd failed to get off."

Leah dropped into her seat.

"Oh, come on," I said. "Go ahead. I won't even retaliate. Cheap one-liners were never my style."

"And what is your style, Paige?" Leah waved at my dress. "Laura Ashley, I presume. How very . . . witchlike."

"Actually," Sandford said, "from what I hear, most

Coven witches prefer polyester stretch pants. Blue, to match their hair rinse."

"Want to take a few minutes to think up something more clever? I can wait."

"Oh, let's get on with it," Leah said. "I have things to do, places to be, lives to ruin." She bared her teeth in a grin and rocked back in her chair.

I rolled my eyes, sat, and turned to Sandford. "She's right, let's get this over with. It's simple. You're not getting Savannah. By arranging this absurd 'custody' meeting, all you've done is put me on the alert. If you thought you could wave phony custody papers in my face and scare me into handing her over, you've got the wrong witch."

"Oh, but they aren't phony," Sandford said.

"Uh-huh. On what grounds could you possibly challenge me? My age? Leah's not much older. Because I'm not related to Savannah? Well, neither is she. I have a prosperous business, a house with no mortgage, a solid record of community service, and, most importantly, the blessing of Savannah's sole surviving relative."

Sandford's lips twitched in a smile. "Are you sure?"

"Yes, I'm sure. Is that your plan? Persuade Margaret Levine to relinquish custody?"

"No, I mean, are you sure Miss Levine is Savannah's sole surviving relative? Just because her mother is dead doesn't make the child an orphan."

It took me a second to realize what he meant. "Her father? Savannah doesn't even know who her father is. Oh, let me guess. You somehow managed to track him down, and persuaded him to cast his vote behind Leah.

How much did that cost?" I shook my head. "Never mind. Take that route. It'll still be my suitability versus Leah's, a battle I'm willing to fight any time."

"Who said I'm the one who wants custody?" Leah asked from her end of the table. "Did you say that, Gabe?"

"Of course not. Clearly, Paige is leaping to conclusions. It says right here—" He raised his copy of the letter he'd sent me and feigned a deep frown—about as believable as smacking himself in the forehead. "I don't believe this. That new secretary of mine. I told her to include your name as a witness. What does she do? She puts you down as the plaintiff. Unbelievable."

Both shook their heads, then left me dangling in silence.

"Who is the plaintiff?" I asked.

"Savannah's father, of course," Sandford said. "Kristof Nast."

When I didn't react, Leah leaned toward Sandford and said in a stage whisper, "I don't think she knows who that is."

Sandford's eyes widened. "Could it be? The leader of the all-powerful American Coven doesn't know Kristof Nast?"

Beneath the table, I dug my fingers into my thighs, willing my tongue to stay still.

"He's heir to the Nast Cabal," Sandford continued. "You do know what a Cabal is, don't you, witch?"

"I've heard of them."

"Heard of them?" Sandford laughed. "Cabals are billion-dollar corporations with international interests.

The crowning achievement of sorcerers, and she's 'heard of them.'"

"This Nast, he's a sorcerer?"

"Naturally."

"Then he can't be Savannah's father, can he?"

Sandford nodded. "Admittedly, it is difficult to comprehend how any sorcerer, particularly one of Mr. Nast's stature, could demean himself by sleeping with a witch. However, we must remember that Eve was a very attractive young woman, and brutally ambitious, so I can understand how she might have seduced Mr. Nast, in spite of the repugnance of such a union."

"Don't forget," Leah said, "Eve wasn't just a witch. She was also a half-demon—a true supernatural."

"Really?" I said. "A supernatural who can't pass on its powers to its children? More an aberration than a race, wouldn't you say?" Before she could answer, I looked over at Sandford. "Yes, I agree that I cannot conceive of any witch screwing around with a sorcerer while there was anyone else with a dick on the planet, but beyond that, there's the biological impossibility. A sorcerer sires only sons. A witch bears only daughters. How could they reproduce? It can't happen."

"Is that a fact?" Sandford said.

"Of course it is," Leah said. "Paige knows everything. She went to Harvard."

Sandford snorted. "The most overrated school in the country, and now they even admit witches. How the mighty have fallen."

"You couldn't get in, huh?" I said. "Sorry to hear it. However, if you do have proof that a witch and sorcerer can bear children together, please fax it to my place. Otherwise, I'll assume I *am* right."

"Mr. Nast is Savannah's father," Sandford said. "And now, with her mother gone, he wants to ensure she has the kind of power she deserves, the kind of power Eve would have wanted for her."

"Good argument," I said. "Like to see you take that one before a court."

"We won't need to," Sandford said. "You'll surrender custody long before we reach that point."

"And how do you intend to make me do that?"

Leah grinned. "Witchery."

"What?"

"You give us Savannah or we'll tell the world what you are."

"You mean—" I sputtered a laugh. "You plan to accuse me of practicing witchcraft? Oh, that's a great plan. Or it would have been, four hundred years ago. Witchcraft? Who cares? It's old news."

"Are you sure about that?" Sandford asked.

"The practice of witchcraft is a state-accepted religion. You cannot discriminate against me on the basis of my religious beliefs. You should have done your homework, counselor."

"Oh, but I did."

He smiled and, with that, they walked out.

❧ The Furies Descend

WE WALK A FINE LINE, as supernaturals in a human world. Human rules and laws often have little meaning in our lives. Take Savannah's case: a young girl, a witch, immensely powerful, pursued by dark factions who would kill to woo her to their side while she was still young and malleable. Her mother now dead, who will protect her? Who *should* protect her? The Coven, of course—sister witches who can help her harness and control her power.

Now look at it from the perspective of human law and social services: a thirteen-year-old child, her mother missing, turned over to a great-aunt whom she's never met, who in turn pawns her off on an unrelated woman barely out of college. Try going before a judge and explaining those circumstances.

To the rest of the world, Eve was only missing, and would remain so, since no one would ever find her body. This had made it easier to take de facto custody of Savannah because, technically, I was only caring for her until her mother returned. So long as I provided a good home for Savannah, no one was about to argue that she should be handed over to child services and enter the foster care system. To be honest, though, I wasn't sure how well my claim would hold up in court.

The idea of battling a telekinetic half-demon, while daunting, was well within my sphere of understanding. But fighting a legal case? My upbringing prepared me for no such thing. So, faced with this custody suit, I naturally chose to research, not the legal side, but the supernatural aspect, starting with learning more about Cabals.

I had heard of Cabals, but my mother always downplayed their existence. According to her, they were the supernatural world's equivalent of the bogeyman, a seedling of truth that had been twisted and blown out of proportion. They were unimportant, she said. Unimportant to witches and to the supernatural interracial council.

As Coven Leader, my mother had also led the interracial council, and as her heir I'd been sitting in on meetings since I was twelve. Some wits liken the council to a supernatural United Nations. That's not a bad comparison. Like the UN, we're supposed to keep the peace, to end injustice in our world. Unfortunately, also like its human counterpart, our power lies more in a semi-mythical reputation than in reality.

Not long ago I'd overheard my mother and fellow council member Robert Vasic arguing over the importance of Cabals. These days Robert acted more as a resource for the council, as he ceded his delegate duties to his stepson Adam, who, like Robert, was a half-demon. Though Robert claimed he was backing off because of declining health, I often suspected that he was frustrated with the council's limited sphere of influence, its inability to fight the true evil in our world. In the argument I'd overheard, he'd been trying to convince my mother that we needed to pay more attention to Cabals. Now, suddenly, I was ready to agree.

Once I got home, I called Robert. No answer. Robert was also a professor of Demonology at Stanford, so I tried his office there and left a message on his machine. Then I almost dialed Adam's old number before remembering that he'd moved back home last month, after enrolling at Stanford to take his second shot at a bachelor's degree.

A year older than me, Adam has also been attending council meetings since adolescence, preparing for his role as delegate. We've been friends for almost as long— discounting our actual first meeting, where I called him a dumb ox and he roasted me for it, literally, leaving burns that lasted for weeks, which might give some idea what kind of half-demon he is.

Next I prepared to make a far tougher call: to Margaret Levine. If Leah and Sandford were serious about this custody suit, they'd have to contact her. I should have thought of this yesterday, but my knee-jerk reaction had been to *not* tell the Elders.

I was still dialing when Savannah emerged from her room, cordless phone in hand.

"You called Adam?" she said.

"No, I called Robert. How'd you know?"

"Redial."

"Why are you checking the redial?"

"Did you tell Adam about Leah? I bet he'd like another shot at her. Oh, and how about Elena and Clay? They'd come too, if you asked. Well, Clay wouldn't. Not if *you* asked. But Elena would come, and he'd follow." She thumped down beside me on the sofa. "If we got everyone together again, you guys could kick ass, like back at the compound. Remember?"

I remembered. What I remember most was the smell— the overwhelming stench of death. Corpse upon corpse, littering the floors. Although I'd killed no one, I'd participated. I'd agreed it was necessary, that every human who had been involved in kidnapping supernaturals had to die, to guarantee that our secrets would not leave those walls. Yet I still jolted awake at least once a month, bathed in sweat, smelling death.

"For now, let's see if we can handle this ourselves," I said.

"You haven't told the Elders yet, have you?"

"I will. It's just—"

"Don't. They'll only screw things up. You're right, we can handle this. All we need to do is find Leah. Then we can kill her."

Savannah said this with a nonchalance that took my breath away. Before I could respond, the doorbell rang.

It was the Elders. All three of them, standing on my porch, their expressions ranging from vapid confusion (Margaret) to worried concern (Therese) to barely contained fury (Victoria).

Margaret Levine, Therese Moss, and Victoria Alden had been the Coven Elders for as long as I could remember. They'd been my mother's friends and, as such, part of my life.

Therese fit the image Gabriel Sandford ascribed to

witches, right down to the blue rinse and polyester stretch pants—the stereotypical grandmother with a wide lap and a purse that held enough supplies to see her through a three-day siege. Savannah's aunt, Margaret, was, at sixty-eight, the youngest of the Elders. A beauty in her youth, Margaret was still strikingly attractive but, unfortunately, fulfilled another stereotype, that of the dim-witted beauty. And Victoria Alden? She was the model twenty-first-century senior, an impeccably groomed, energetic woman who wore suits to church and khakis on the golf course, and sniffed at less active seniors as if any physical or mental impairment they suffered was due to self-neglect.

I undid the perimeter and locking spells and opened the door. Victoria barreled past and strode into the living room, not bothering to remove her shoes. That was a bad sign. Rules of Coven etiquette—which bore a disquieting resemblance to those by Emily Post, *circa* 1950—dictated that one always removed one's shoes at the door as a courtesy to the housekeeper. Walking in with your shoes on treaded the border of insult. Fortunately, Therese and Margaret did take off their orthopedic slip-ons, so I knew the situation wasn't critical.

"We need to talk," Victoria said.

"Would you like some tea first?" I said. "I should have fresh muffins too, if Savannah hasn't finished them."

"We aren't here to eat, Paige," Victoria said from living room.

"Tea, then?"

"No."

Turning down baked goods was damning enough, but to refuse a hot beverage? Almost unheard of in the annals of Coven history.

"How could you have kept this from us?" Victoria said as I joined them in the living room. "A custody battle is bad enough. A legal custody battle. But—"

"It's not a legal custody battle," Savannah said, slipping around the corner. "Taking custody means kidnapping, like breaking in at midnight and dragging me away kicking and screaming. That kind of custody battle."

Victoria turned to me. "What is she talking about?"

"Savannah, how about you take your aunt downstairs and show her your artwork."

"No."

"Savannah, please. We have to talk."

"So? It's about my life, isn't it?"

"See?" Victoria turned to Therese and Margaret, and waved a hand at Savannah and me. "This is the problem. The girl has no respect for Paige."

"The girl has a name," I said.

"Don't interrupt. You aren't ready for this, Paige. I said so right from the start. We should never have let you take her. You're too young and she's too—"

"We are fine," I said, teeth gritted so hard they hurt.

"Wanna see my art, Aunt Maggie?" Savannah asked. "My teacher says I have real talent. Come see." She bounced off, wearing a "good girl" grin that looked as painful as my clenched teeth. "Come on, Aunt Maggie," Savannah called back, her voice a high-pitched singsong. "I'll show you my cartoons."

"No!" I yelled after her as Margaret followed. "The

oils, please. The oils." Somehow I doubted Margaret would see the humor in Savannah's dark cartoons. They'd probably give the Elder a heart attack—just what I needed.

Once they were gone, Victoria turned on me. "You should have told us about this."

"I just got the notice yesterday, after we spoke on the phone. I didn't take it seriously, so I didn't want to upset you. Then, when I met with them this morning, I realized it *was* serious, and I was just about to call Margaret—"

"I'm sure you were."

"Now, Victoria," Therese murmured.

"Do you know what they're threatening to do?" Victoria continued. "Expose you. Expose us. They're alleging you're an unfit guardian because you're a practicing witch."

"So are thousands of mothers in this country," I said. "It's called Wicca, and it's a recognized religious choice."

"That's not what we are, Paige. Don't confuse the issue."

"I'm not. Every person who reads that custody challenge will jump to the conclusion that by 'witch' they mean 'Wiccan.'"

"I don't care what they'll conclude. I care about protecting the Coven. I will not allow you to risk exposing us—"

"That's it! Of course. Now I get it. *That's* why she's accusing me of witchcraft. Not because she thinks it'll win the lawsuit. She wants to scare us. A witch's worst fear—exposure. She threatens us with exposure, and you force me to relinquish Savannah."

"A small price to pay—"

"But we can't let her win. If this ruse succeeds, they'll use it again. Every time a supernatural wants something from the Coven, they'll pull the same scam."

Victoria hesitated.

I hurried on. "Give me three days. After that, I promise you won't hear anything more about witches in East Falls."

After a moment, Victoria gave a curt nod. "Three days."

"There's just one other thing. And I'm telling you this not because I believe it, but because I don't want you to hear it from someone else. They say Savannah's father is a sorcerer."

"Wouldn't surprise me. There is definitely something wrong with the girl."

"There is nothing—" I began, then cut myself short. "But it's not possible, is it? For a witch and a sorcerer to have a child?"

"How should I know?" Victoria said.

As Victoria snapped at me, I thought of how my mother would have responded. No matter how many questions I asked or how silly they seemed, she always found the time to answer, or to find an answer. I stifled the sharp pang of grief and pushed on.

"Have you ever *heard* of it happening?" I asked.

"Of course not. Coven witches would never do such a thing. But I'd believe it of Eve Levine. You remember Eve, Therese. She'd do such a thing simply because it *was* unnatural."

"What does Savannah say?" Therese asked.

"She has no idea who her father is. I haven't mentioned the paternity suit. She thinks Leah's the one suing for custody."

"Good," Victoria said. "Let's keep it that way. I don't want anyone in the Coven knowing of this. I won't have them thinking we allowed a witch with sorcerer blood to join our Coven or worrying that a sorcerer might come to East Falls."

"A sorcerer? In town?" Therese fairly squeaked with terror.

Victoria's eyes narrowed. "He isn't in town already, is he?"

"As far as I know, Kristof Nast is still in Los Angeles," I said, deciding not to complicate the situation by mentioning Sandford. "I'll take care of the witch accusation, and the custody challenge."

Therese nodded. "You need to handle it properly, dear. Get a lawyer. The Carys are good."

Bring a human lawyer into this mess? Not likely. Wait—maybe that wasn't so crazy after all. It gave me an idea.

❦ The Beauty of Science

ONCE THE FRONT DOOR HAD CLOSED behind the Elders, I cast fresh lock and perimeter spells, then grabbed the phone book. Savannah walked in.

"It's a real custody battle, isn't it?" she said, taking a seat on the sofa.

"I thought you knew that."

"When you said Leah wanted custody, I figured you meant she wanted you to just hand me over."

"It doesn't matter. They don't have a case—"

"So Leah has a lawyer and everything? What is he? A sorcerer, I bet."

"Yes, but there's no need to worry."

"Oh, I'm not scared of any sorcerer. Or any lawyer. You know, we should get one."

"I was just about to call Mr. Cary."

"I meant a *sorcerer* lawyer. They're really good at it. All the best sorcerers are lawyers. Well, until they get older and become politicians. That's what my mom always said."

Here was the perfect opening for a query that might help answer the question of Savannah's paternity, something like, Did your mother, uh, know a lot of sorcerers? Of course, I didn't ask. I never asked anything about Eve. If Savannah wanted to tell me, she would.

"Witches don't work with sorcerers," I said.

"Oh, please, that's for Coven witches. A real witch works with anyone who can help her. A sorcerer lawyer could help, as long as we picked carefully. Most of them are real jerks—they won't have anything to do with witches—but Mom knew a few who'd take a case like this if you paid them enough."

"I'm not hiring a sorcerer. I'm getting a human lawyer."

"Don't be stupid, Paige. You can't—"

"Why can't I? They won't be expecting it. If I get a human lawyer, Leah will need to handle this case by the books. The *human* law books. No secret meetings discussing sorcerers and Cabals—"

"What about the Cabals?"

"I'm just saying, they can't talk about that kind of thing in front of a human lawyer. If they want to play by human laws, let them. I'll play right along."

She leaned back into the sofa cushions. "That might not be such a stupid idea after all."

"Glad you approve."

Friday morning started off feeling very familiar. Once again, I decided to keep Savannah home from school, picked up her assignments, took her to Abby's, then returned to the Carys' law office for another ten o'clock meeting.

This time my meeting was with Grant Cary Jr. Yes, I chose Grant Jr. Despite my misgivings about the guy's moral compass, he was a good lawyer. He knew me . . .

well, not as well as he'd like, but well enough. When I spoke to him on the phone the day before, he seemed interested in the case. We'd arranged to meet at ten, then I'd set up a conference with Leah and Sandford for eleven.

I'd been sitting in Cary's office for twenty minutes now, gazing out the oversized window behind his desk while he read through my papers. So far everything had gone well. Other than a lingering look at my boobs when I walked in, he hadn't done anything untoward. I'd probably been too harsh on the guy. I seem to attract a lot of Cary-types, forty-something married guys who see me, if not as a gorgeous blonde who'd look great on their arm, as a young woman who might enjoy and appreciate the attentions of an older man.

From what I'd seen of Grantham Cary II, he likely hit on every woman he met. You know the type: All-American boy of 1975, the town's brightest star, every girl in town wetting her pants if he so much as looked at her. Fast-forward to 2001. His weekly golf game no longer keeps his love handles in check, he's recently resorted to a slight comb-over to cover that growing bald spot, he squints to avoid wearing the bifocals he hides in his desk drawer, and he spends his days in an office filled with decades-old sports trophies. Still a good-looking guy, but these days more likely to be coveted for his bank account than his biceps.

"Well," Cary said, returning the last sheet to the stack. "This certainly is unusual."

"I—I can explain," I said. I could?

"Let me guess," Cary said. "You're not really a witch and this is simply a ploy to gain custody of Savannah by dredging up an uncomfortable element of East Falls' past and playing on the historical paranoia of this particular region of New England."

"Uh, yes," I said. "Something like that."

Cary laughed. "Don't worry, Paige. It's a very transparent scheme, obviously dreamed up by folks who don't know much about modern-day Massachusetts. You say this man Kristof Nast has no proof that he's Savannah's father. But I assume he's willing to submit to a DNA test?"

"DNA?"

"We can't just take his say-so on the matter."

Of course they couldn't. This was a human court, which played by human rules. Any supernatural knew that we couldn't risk having humans study our DNA, but to a judge it was evidence so easily given that to refuse would be tantamount to an admission of fraud.

"He won't give DNA," I said.

Cary's brows shot up. "Are you sure about that?"

"Absolutely," I said, breaking into a grin. "Is that good?"

Cary leaned back in his chair and laughed. "That's better than good. It's wonderful, Paige. If Sandford's client refuses to submit DNA, he has no case. I'll see to it."

"Thank you."

"Don't thank me yet," he said. "You haven't seen my bill."

He laughed loudly, as if unaware that this was a very old joke, and I was in the mood to be generous, so I laughed along. We spent the next thirty minutes discussing the case. Then we wrapped it up and prepared for the meeting with Leah and Sandford. I hadn't told them Cary was representing me. They thought they were coming for a private conference with me.

I do love surprises.

I was sitting in the meeting room alone when Lacey ushered in Sandford and Leah on the dot of eleven o'clock. Cary had agreed to wait a few minutes before joining us.

Leah fairly bounced in, like a kid on Christmas morning. Sandford followed, trying—but not very hard—to conceal a self-satisfied smirk.

"Do you have the papers?" I asked, injecting a quaver into my voice.

"Of course." Sandford slid them across the table to me.

For a few minutes I stared down at the pages that would relinquish my custody rights to Savannah. I inhaled deeply, then I said, "I can't do this."

"Yes, you can," Sandford said.

"No, really, I can't." I shoved the papers back to him, with a grin to mirror his. "I'm not giving her up."

"What?" Leah said.

"Oh, it was a clever plan, I'll give you that. Threaten me with exposure and make sure the Elders hear about it. If I don't cave, they'll force me. Well, you underestimated the Coven. With their support, I'm fighting this petition."

The look on their faces provided a memory to cherish forever.

"What does Margaret Levine say about this?" Leah asked.

"You want to know?" I lifted the phone. "Call her. I'm sure you have the number. Call all the Elders. Ask them if they support me."

"This is bullshit." Leah aimed a glare at Sandford, as if it was his fault.

"No," I said, "it's not bullshit. I assure you, I understand that this is a serious legal matter and, as such, I'm treating it very seriously. To that end, I've hired legal representation."

I walked to the door and waved in Cary, who'd been waiting in the hall.

"I believe you've met Mr. Cary," I said.

Their jaws dropped. Okay, they didn't actually *drop*, like in the cartoons, but you get the idea.

"But he's—" Leah began before stopping herself.

"A damn fine lawyer," I said. "And I'm so glad he's agreed to represent me."

"Thank you, Paige." Cary's smile held a bit more personal warmth than I liked, but I was too happy to care. "Now, let's get straight to the heart of the matter. About the DNA test—may I assume your client is willing to submit to one immediately?"

Sandford blanched. "Our—my client is a . . . a very busy man. His business interests make it quite impossible to leave Los Angeles at the moment."

"Otherwise he'd be here now," I said. "Hmmm, doesn't that seem odd? He's so interested in regaining custody of his daughter yet can't find a few days to fly out and meet her."

"He could provide the sample in California," Cary said. "Our firm may be small, but we have contacts in San Francisco. I'm sure they'd be happy to oversee the testing."

"My client does not wish to submit to DNA testing."

"No DNA, no case," Cary said.

Sandford glared at me.

"Checkmate," I said. And grinned.

When Sandford and Leah left, Cary turned to me and smiled.

"That went well, don't you think?"

I grinned. "Better than well. It was perfect. Thank you so much."

"With any luck, it's all over. I can't imagine them pursuing the case without DNA." He checked his watch. "Do you have time for coffee? We can discuss the final details before my next appointment."

"Details? But if it's over . . . ?"

"We hope it is, but we need to cover every contingency, Paige. I'll let Lacey know we're leaving."

❖ Shot Down

CARY AND I WALKED to Melinda's Bakery on State Street. Even by my jaded big-city standards, Melinda's was a first-rate bakery. The coffee alone almost made living in East Falls bearable. And the scones? If I ever persuaded the Elders to let us move, I'd be making weekly runs to East Falls for Melinda's raisin scones.

I would have preferred a window table, but Cary selected one near the back. Admittedly, even the main street of East Falls has little to offer in the way of people-watching and since we were discussing confidential legal matters, I understood why Cary picked a more private seating arrangement.

When we sat down, he pointed at my scone. "I'm glad to see you're not one of those girls who's always on a diet. I like women who aren't afraid to look like women."

"Uh-huh."

"The girls these days, dieting until they're so thin you can't tell if they're a boy or a girl. You're different. You always look so—" His gaze dropped to my chest. "—put together. It's so nice to see a young woman who still wears skirts and dresses."

"So you think they'll drop the case?"

Cary added three creamers to his coffee and stirred it before answering.

"Reasonably certain," he said. "There are a few more things I need to do."

"Like what?"

"Paperwork. Even in the simplest case, there's always paperwork." He sipped his coffee. "Now, I suppose you want to hear how much this is going to cost you."

I smiled. "Well, I can't say I want to hear it, but I should. Do you have an estimate?"

He pulled out his legal pad, ripped off the top sheet, and started tallying figures on a clean page. As the list grew, my eyes widened. When he wrote a total at the bottom, I choked on a mouthful of scone.

"Is that—please tell me there's a decimal missing," I said.

"Legal expertise doesn't come cheap, Paige."

"I know that. I have legal work done for my business all the time, but my bills don't look like that." I pulled the legal pad toward me and flipped it around. "What's this? Nine billable hours accrued? We only met today, from ten until—" I checked my watch. "—eleven-forty."

"I did need to review your case last night, Paige."

"You reviewed it this morning. In front of me. Remember?"

"Yes, but last night I was researching similar cases."

"For seven hours?"

"'Billable hours' is a complex concept that doesn't necessarily correspond to actual time spent."

"No kidding. And what's this? Three hundred dollars for photocopying? What did you do? Hire Franciscan monks to transcribe my file by hand? I can make copies at the 7–Eleven for ten cents a page."

"We're hardly dealing with the straight cost of copying. You have to take into consideration the cost of labor."

"Your wife does all your secretarial work. You don't even pay her."

"I understand it may not be easy for you to pay this, Paige. That's one of the fundamental problems with the practice of law: those who are most deserving of our help often can't afford it."

"It's not that I can't afford—"

He held up a hand to stop me. "I understand. Really I do. It's a difficult burden to place on someone who's only trying to do what's best for a child. Making you pay this much wouldn't be fair. I only wanted to show you how much something like this could cost."

I eased back into my seat. "Okay. So—"

"Unfortunately, this is how much my father and Lacey will expect me to charge you. What we need to do is discuss this further, see how we can reduce the cost." He checked his watch. "I have a client in twenty minutes, so we can't do this now. How about I finish the case, then we can meet over lunch and discuss the bill." He took out his Daytimer. "Say Monday?"

"I guess so."

"Good. We'll go someplace nice—someplace in Boston. Do you still have that dress you wore to the Memorial Day picnic? Wear that."

"Wear—?"

"And find a sitter for Savannah after school. We probably won't be back until evening."

"Evening—?"

He smiled. "I like long negotiation sessions. Very long. Very intense." He leaned forward, leg rubbing against mine. "I know how difficult it must be for you, Paige. Living in East Falls. Caring for a child. Not a lot of eligible young men in town, and I doubt you get many opportunities to get out and meet someone. You're a very attractive young woman. You need someone who can appreciate your . . . special needs. It could be a very profitable alliance for you, and I'm not just referring to free legal help."

"Oh, I get it—you're saying you'll waive your fees if I have sex with you."

Half the people in the restaurant turned. Cary leaned forward to shush me.

"But the bill's only a couple grand," I said. "For that you'd be lucky to get a hand job."

He motioned me to silence, eyes darting from side to side, trying to see who might have overheard.

"Does Lacey know about this creative financing arrangement?" I continued. "How about I call and ask her? See if she's willing to forgo this much profit so her husband can get laid."

I took my cellphone from my purse. Cary grabbed for it, but I waved it out of his reach. I hit a few buttons. He flew across the table, hands out like a wide receiver lunging for the game-breaking pass. I shoved my chair out of his reach, then leaned over and dropped the phone back into my purse. Cary lay stretched across the table for a few seconds, slowly raised himself up, adjusted his tie, and glanced around, as if trying to convince himself that not everyone in the bakery was watching.

"I hate to eat and run," I said, standing, "but I have to go pick up Savannah. In case you didn't guess, the answer is no. Don't take it too hard. It's not just because you're married. It's because you've been married longer than I've been alive."

A snicker sounded behind us, followed by an ill-stifled giggle. As I passed the counter, Nellie, the cashier, shot me a discreet thumbs-up.

Savannah went to bed at nine-thirty without protest, after spending the evening helping me with some graphic work for a website contract. Yes, we not only spent quality time together, but she lent me her artistic expertise without even a joking request for compensation. It was one of those perfect one-in-a-million days, a karmic reward for the crap I'd endured.

At ten o'clock, I carried a cup of tea into the living room, preparing to curl up with a book for a much-deserved mental holiday. As I settled into the sofa, I noticed a wavering light on the front porch. I set aside my mug, then leaned over, pulled back the curtains, and peered into the night. Someone had placed a burning candle on the far corner of the porch railing. Witches, candles—get it? Next thing you knew, they'd be hanging crystal unicorns from my mailbox. Kids.

I was inclined to ignore the candle until I finished my tea, but if my neighbor across the street, Miss Harris, saw it, she'd probably call the fire department and accuse me of trying to torch the neighborhood.

As I stepped onto the porch, I saw the candle clearly

and my breath caught. It was in the shape of a human hand, each fingertip glowing with a tiny flame. The Hand of Glory. This went beyond an innocent child's prank. Whoever did this knew something about the occult and had a very sick turn of mind.

I marched toward the candle. As I snatched it up, my fingers clamped down not on hard wax but cold flesh. I yelped and jerked back, throwing the thing to the ground below. A flame flared and a puff of smoke billowed up. I raced down the steps and grabbed the hand, but again, as I touched the icy flesh, my brain balked and I dropped it.

Lights flickered in Miss Harris's house. I dropped to my knees, hiding the hand from view, and whacked at the small fire burning through dead grass clippings that Savannah had shoved under the porch. The flames singed my palm. I stifled a yelp and kept smacking the pile until the fire was out.

I closed my eyes, caught my breath, and turned to look at the thing lying in the grass. It was a severed hand, skin grayish-brown, a nub of sawn bone sticking from the bottom, the flesh wrinkled and stinking of preservatives. Each finger had been coated in wax and fitted with a wick.

"The Hand of Glory."

I jumped and saw Savannah leaning over the railing.

"Is Miss Harris watching?" I whispered.

Savannah glanced across the road. "She's looking through her blinds, but all she can see is your butt sticking up in the air."

"Go inside and get me something to wrap it in."

A moment later, Savannah tossed me a hand towel. One of my good hand towels. I hesitated, then bundled the hand. This wasn't the time for worrying about linen. Any minute now Miss Harris would venture onto her porch for a better look.

"Must be the sorcerer," Savannah said. "Leah wouldn't know how to make one of those. Is it preserved or dried?"

I didn't answer. I stood, hands trembling around the bundle. Savannah reached over the railing for it. Motioning her back into the house, I hurried up the steps.

Once inside, I shoved the towel-wrapped hand under the kitchen sink, then ran to the bathroom and turned on the hot water full blast. Savannah came in as I was scrubbing.

"I'll bury it later," I said.

"Maybe we should keep it," Savannah said. "They're tough to make, you know."

"No, I wouldn't know," I snapped.

Silence. In the mirror, I saw Savannah behind me, her expression unreadable, eyes shuttered.

"I didn't mean—" I began.

"I know what you meant," she said, then turned, went into her room, and shut the door, not slamming it, just closing it softly behind her.

The Hand of Glory is a thief's tool. According to legend, it's supposed to prevent the occupants of a house from waking up. Criminal, to be sure, but neither harmful nor dangerous. So was Leah planning to break into my place tonight? If so, why leave the hand on my porch railing in mid-evening? Or did she just put the macabre candle there to attract attention and cause more trouble for me? That also didn't make sense. By placing it outside my front window, chances were good that I'd see it and get rid of it before anyone noticed.

I lay in bed trying to figure out Leah's motivation, but all I could think about was the hand itself, wrapped under my sink. The stink of it seemed to permeate the house. I couldn't shake the memory of touching it, couldn't forget it was still in my house, couldn't stop worrying about how to dispose of it. I was spooked. And maybe that, after all, was Leah's goal.

I'd set my alarm for 2:00 A.M., but I needn't have bothered. I didn't sleep, only lay there, counting the minutes. At 1:30, I decided it was late enough.

Initiate Phase Two

I COVERED MY SILK CHEMISE with the matching kimono before leaving my room. For some reason this seemed to make more sense than getting dressed. From the hall closet, I selected the old rubber boots my mother used for gardening. I'd kept them in the dim hope that someday I'd sprout a green thumb.

I slipped out the back door, casting a perimeter spell in my wake. I'd left the hand under the sink, so if someone caught me digging, at least they wouldn't see what I was burying. Yeah, like that was going to help matters if anyone saw me in the forest after midnight, digging a hole while dressed in a red silk kimono and black rubber boots.

Once outside, I caught a whiff of smoke. As my stomach clenched, I cursed my fear. In first-year psychology I'd read a theory that all the major phobias are the result of hereditary memory, that our distant ancestors had good reason to fear snakes and heights, so evolution passed those fears on to future generations. Maybe that explains witches' fear of fire. I fight against it but seem unable to overcome the fear completely.

Struggling against instinct, I sniffed the air, searching for the source of the smell. Was it smoke from a fireplace extinguished hours ago? Smoldering embers from an evening trash-burning? As I scanned the darkness, I noticed an orange glow to the east, in the forest behind my back fence. A bush party. With the weather warming, local teens must have found something better to do on a Friday night than hang out in the hardware store parking lot. Great. Now the hand would have to stay in my house until tomorrow night. I didn't dare bury it with a potential audience looking on.

As I turned to go back into the house, I noticed the silence. Complete silence. Since when did partying teens sit silently around a campfire? I considered other excuses for a late night fire. East Falls was too small for a homeless population. Could a dropped match or cigarette have ignited the undergrowth? Could someone be secretly burning hazardous material? Either required action.

I tiptoed across the grass, wondering whether I'd have another fire to put out. Two in one evening—coincidence? Please don't let this be a second Hand of Glory. I took a breath and pushed past my revulsion. If it was, at least I'd seen it before anyone else had.

As I reached the fence, I was glad I hadn't done anything so foolish as calling the fire department. There, laid out in the grass, was a ring of lit black candles surrounding a red cloth embroidered with a goat's head. A Satanic altar.

With an oath, I raced to put out the candles. Then I saw that they encircled a blood-covered heap. For one terrible, endless moment I thought it was a child's body. Then I saw the face and realized it was a cat. A skinned cat, a lifeless mass of blood and muscle, teeth bared in a lipless snarl.

I twisted away from the sight. Something slapped me in the face, something cold and wet. Frantically shoving it away, I stumbled back, but my hand was caught in a loop of spongy elastic. I bit back a shriek. I looked up and I saw what I'd hit: another skinned cat, this one hanging from a tree, its belly sliced open, guts spilling out. A loop of intestine was wrapped around my hand.

I yanked free barely in time to bring my hands to my mouth to stifle my scream. I fell to my knees, chest heaving, struggling for breath. My hands were covered in blood. My stomach lurched and I spilled my dinner into the grass. For several minutes I crouched there, unable to move.

"Paige?" Savannah's whisper floated from the backyard.

"No!" I hissed, springing to my feet. "Stay there!"

I ran and grabbed her as she rounded the corner. Her eyes widened and I knew she'd seen everything, but I still pushed her away.

"Go—go back in the house," I said. "I—I have to clean it up."

"I'll help."

"No!"

Silence.

"I'm sorry. I didn't mean—" I realized I was getting vomit and blood all over her bathrobe and pulled back. "I'm sorry. Go inside and clean up. No, wait. Put your robe in a bag. I'll burn it—"

"Paige. . ."

"T—take a shower," I stammered. "But leave the lights off. Don't turn on any lights. No radio, no lights, nothing. Don't open the blinds and—"

"Paige!" Savannah said, grabbing my shoulders. "I can help," she said, enunciating each word as if I might not understand her. "It's okay. I've seen this kind of stuff before."

"No, you haven't. Get in—"

"Yes, I have. Goddamn it, Paige—"

"Don't swear."

Savannah blinked, and for a second she looked as if she might cry. "I know what that stuff is, Paige. Like I know what a Hand of Glory is. Why do you keep pretending I don't?"

As she tore off, I started going after her, but a light flicked on next door and I froze. I looked from Savannah's retreating back to the glow of the candles behind me. I didn't have time to go after her—not now. Leah had devised this horrific tableau for a reason, and I doubted she went to all that trouble just to spook me. The police would receive an anonymous phone call: Go look behind Paige Winterbourne's house. I had to clear this away before anyone followed up on that tip.

To the left of the altar, smoke rose from a blackened mound, carrying with it the stench of burned meat. I closed my eyes to compose myself, then approached the smoldering heap and bent to look at it. At first glance I couldn't tell what it was, or what it had been. I wanted to walk away then, get a shovel and bury it without ever knowing. But I had to know. If I didn't, I'd lie awake at night wondering what I'd buried.

I took a stick and prodded at the mound. At the first sharp jab it fell apart, exposing a sawed-open rib cage. I pressed the back of my hand to my eyes and took a deep breath. The very taste of it filled my mouth and I lurched forward, spilling whatever was left in my stomach.

Oh god, I couldn't—I just couldn't. No, I had to. This was my problem, my responsibility.

I forced my gaze back to the charred bones, struggling to study them with a scientist's eye. From my few years of biology I could differentiate between a biped and quadruped rib cage. This was quadruped. To be sure, I poked the stick near the end of the spine, revealing a tail. Yes, definitely an animal. Probably another cat. Okay, I could handle this now. Observe without truly seeing, that was the trick.

I stood and surveyed the site. My brain processed the details, making no judgments, allowing no reactions. There was a chalice beside the dead cat on the makeshift altar, filled with blood. Yes, that was to be expected. Black Mass was an inversion and perversion of the Catholic Mass. In a university folklore course, I'd done my term project on Satanic cults, debating whether they fit the standard definition of a contemporary legend, so I knew what to look for, what I needed to find and clear away.

There should be an inverted crucifix . . . yes, there it was, hanging from the tree. I strode over and pulled it down. Pentagrams? No, it appeared they'd overlooked . . . wait, there, drawn in the dirt. I started to erase it with my boot, then grabbed a handful of brush instead, so I wouldn't leave footprints. The black candles were on the altar. Okay, that seemed to be everything.

Next I needed to bury the corpses. I turned to look toward the eviscerated cat in the tree. I willed my gaze past the poor beast, to study the hanging device instead, so I'd know what I needed to cut it loose, but I couldn't help seeing the body swaying in the breeze.

What kind of people could bring themselves, not only to kill a cat, but to— My gorge rose and I doubled over, retching. This time, nothing came but a thin string of acid. I spat to clear the taste from my mouth, then, still bent over, wiped my face and took a deep breath of the foul air. I marched to the shed to find a shovel.

Twenty minutes later, I'd buried the cats and started dismantling the altar.

"Paige?"

Savannah's whisper sent me a foot into the air. I spun to see her jogging across the lawn.

"There's a car circling the block," she said. "I've been watching from the front window."

Her eyes were red. Had she been crying? Why did I make such a mess of everything? Before I could apologize, she grabbed my arm and dragged me across the yard.

As we stepped through the back door, I glimpsed myself in the hall mirror. Blood, vomit, and dirt streaked my face, hands, and kimono. Just then, lights flashed through the living-room sheers. A car engine died.

"Oh god," I said, staring into the mirror. "I can't—"

"I'm clean," Savannah said. "I'll answer it. You go wash up."

"But—"

The doorbell rang. Savannah shoved me into the living room. I ducked below window level and ran for the other side of the house.

The local sheriff, Ted Fowler, stood at my door. Leah hadn't settled for placing an anonymous call to the station's overnight answering service. No, she'd called Fowler at home, babbling hysterically about strange lights and screams coming from the woods behind my house.

Fowler had thrown on clothing that looked like it came from his bedroom floor and drove straight over. In reward for his haste, he found the remains of a Satanic altar a scant ten feet beyond my backyard.

By dawn, my house and yard were crawling with cops. By disposing of the cat corpses, I'd only made things worse. When Fowler saw traces of blood and no bodies, his imagination leaped to the worst possible conclusion: murder.

Since East Falls wasn't equipped to deal with homicide, the state police were called in. On the way, the detectives woke up a judge and got him to sign a search warrant. They arrived shortly before five, and Savannah and I spent the next several hours huddled in my bedroom, alternately answering questions and listening to the sound of strangers tearing our home apart.

When I heard the oven door open, I remembered the Hand of Glory under the sink. I bolted for the hall, then checked my pace and strolled into the kitchen. One officer rifled through my cupboards as another waved some kind of light-wand over the contents of my fridge. They glanced at me, but when I didn't speak, they returned to their work.

Heart thudding, I waited as the cupboard-searcher moved to the cabinets under the counter. When he reached to open the sink cupboard, I whispered a spell under my breath. It was a form of cover spell that would distort the appearance of an object. While it wouldn't have worked on the entire Satanic altar site outside, it would do fine for the wrapped bundle under the sink.

As he threw open the cupboard, I said the last words and directed the spell at the object to be hidden. Only there was no object there. The hand and the towel were gone. The officer did a cursory search, then closed the cupboard door. I hurried back to the bedroom.

"What did you do with it?" I whispered.

Savannah looked up from her magazine. "With what?"

I lowered my voice another notch. "The Hand of Glory."

"I moved it."

"Good. Thank you. I completely forgot. Where'd you put it?"

She rolled onto her stomach and returned to her magazine. "Someplace safe."

"Ms. Winterbourne?"

I spun to see the lead detective from the state police in my bedroom doorway.

"We found cats," he said.

"Cats?"

"Three dead cats buried a short distance from the scene."

I motioned toward Savannah and lifted a finger to my lips, indicating that I didn't want this discussed in front of her. The detective moved to the living room, where several officers were lounging on my sofa and chairs, muddy shoes propped on my antique coffee table. I swallowed my outrage and turned to the detective.

"So it was cat's blood?" I said.

"Apparently, though we'll run tests to be sure."

"Good."

"Killing cats might not be on the same scale as murder, but it's still a serious offense. Very serious."

"It should be. Anyone who'd do that. . ." I didn't have to fake my shudder, remembering the sight of those maimed bodies. "I can't believe someone would do that—stage a Satanic altar behind my yard."

"Stage?" the detective said. "What makes you think it was staged?"

"It looked real to me," one of the officers said, waving a cookie that looked suspiciously like ones in my cupboard.

He had scattered crumbs across my ivory carpet. I looked at those crumbs, at the muddy bootprints surrounding them, at the bookcase with my books and photos and mementos shoved into haphazard piles, and I felt a snap. Just a small one.

"And you say that based on witnessing exactly how many Satanic altars?" I asked.

"We've seen photos," he muttered.

"Oh, right, the photos. There's probably one genuine

photo circulating endlessly around the entire country. Attention all units: Beware of Satanic cults. Do you know what Satanic cults are? The biggest hoax ever perpetrated by the American media. Do you know who builds all those so-called Satanic altars you hear about? Kids. Bored, angry teenagers. And the occasional homicidal moron who's already planning his defense: The devil made me do it. Satanic altar, my ass. What you saw out back there is a prank—a very, very sick prank."

Silence.

"You sure seem to know a lot about this stuff," one officer said.

"It's called a university education." I wheeled on the detective. "Are you charging me with anything?"

"Not yet."

"Then get the hell out of my house so I can clean up your mess."

After a tersely worded admonition against leaving town, and a suggestion that I "may want to retain legal counsel," the police left.

❦ Black Mass Pizza

THE POLICE WERE BARELY out the door when Savannah appeared from her room and dropped down beside me on the sofa.

"Black Mass," she said. "I can't believe they still believe in that stuff. Humans are so stupid."

"You shouldn't say that," I replied, without much conviction.

"It's true. About the Satanism stuff, at least. They just get all weird about it. You try to tell them the truth, that Satan's just one of tons of demons and that he doesn't give a crap about us, and they still figure you can conjure him up and he'll give you anything you want. As if." She sank back into the sofa cushions. "My mom had this friend, a necromancer, who used to make really good money selling Black Masses."

"Selling Black Masses?"

"You know, setting them up for people. He ran this business Satanic Rites by Jorge. His real name's Bill, but he figured he could charge more with 'Jorge.' He'd supply all this fake stuff, set it up, give them scripts, the whole thing. If he did a full Black Mass, which cost a lot, he'd buy us pizza. Black Mass pizza, we called it.

We tried eating it upside down, but the toppings fell off, so we settled for eating it backward." She sat up. "There's still pizza left from last night, isn't there? That's what I'll have for breakfast. Black Mass pizza. You want some?"

I shook my head.

Savannah trotted off to the kitchen, still chattering. I collapsed back into the sofa.

Two hours later I was still on the couch, having ignored eight phone calls and three answering machine messages, all from reporters dreaming of a "Satanism in a Small Town" scoop. Like the police, these people knew nothing about true Satanism—not to say that I agree with that belief system either, but at least it has nothing to do with mutilated cats and bloody pentangles.

The Satanic cult scares that crop up periodically are just a new form of witch hunt. People are always looking to explain evil, to find a rationale that places the blame outside the realm of human nature. The scapegoats change with remarkable ease. Heretics, witches, demonic possession, the Illuminati—they've all been targeted as hidden sources of evil in the world.

Since the sixties, Satanic cults have been the favored group. The damn tabloids publish so much crap on the subject that it's a self-perpetuating cycle. They print one story, some psycho reads it and copies the methods described, so they print his story. And on it goes. In 1996, the government spent $750,000 to reassure the American public that Satanic cults weren't operating in the nation's daycare facilities. Whew, I sleep so much better knowing they cleared that up.

With this new development, I'd have been reluctant to send Savannah to school. Fortunately, it was Saturday, so that wasn't an issue. After lunch, she went down to the basement to work on her art. Yes, I know, most artists like big airy studios filled with natural light and soothing silence. Not Savannah. She liked the semi-dark basement and blaring music.

When the doorbell rang, I suspected it was one of the reporters trying something more proactive than making phone calls. I ignored it and continued emptying the dishwasher. The doorbell rang again. I realized then that it might be the police come to renew their search. The last thing I needed was cops busting down my door; they'd done enough damage already.

I hurried to the front hall, undid the spells, and flung open the door to see a young man. He was about six foot, thin, with a face so average I doubted anyone remembered him five minutes after meeting him. Short dark hair, clean-shaven, Hispanic. Presumably, dark eyes behind his wire-frame glasses, but he wouldn't meet my gaze. He stood there, eyes downcast, clutching an armful of papers, with a beat-up satchel slung over one shoulder. Oh, did I mention he was wearing a suit? On a Saturday? Wonderful. Just what I needed—a Jehovah's Witness.

"Lucas Cortez," he said, shifting the papers to his left hand and extending his right. "Your new legal counsel."

"Look, I'm not interested—" I stopped. "Did you say 'legal counsel'?"

"I'll be taking your case from here, Ms. Winterbourne." Despite his lowered gaze, his voice was confident. "We should step inside."

He brushed past me without waiting for an invitation. As I stood momentarily dumbfounded, Cortez took off his shoes, walked into the living room, and surveyed his surroundings as if assessing my ability to pay for his services.

"I assume the disarray is from the search," he said. "This is unacceptable. I'll speak to them about it. I presume they had a warrant? Ah, here it is."

He picked up the warrant from the coffee table, added it to his papers, and walked into the kitchen.

"Wait a second," I said, hurrying after him. "You can't just take that."

"Do you have a copier?"

I swung into the kitchen. He'd already established himself at the table, moved my things aside, and started spreading his papers.

"I take my coffee black."

"You can take your coffee down at the donut shop unless you tell me who sent you here."

"You are in need of legal services, are you not?"

I hesitated. "Oh, I get it—no one sent you. What do they call you guys? Ambulance chasers? I'm not interested. And if you try to bill me for this visit—"

"I'll do nothing of the sort. This visit is entirely free, a sample of my services. I've taken the liberty of acquainting myself with your case, and I've devised a strategy for defending you." He moved two papers across the table and turned them to face me. "As you'll see, this is a simple contract stating that, by agreeing to speak to me today, you are in no way committing yourself to retaining my services and will not be charged for this meeting."

I scanned the contract. For a legal document it was surprisingly straightforward, a simple statement relieving me of any obligation for this initial consultation. I glanced at Cortez, who was busy reading the warrant. He couldn't be more than late twenties, probably just out of law school. I'd once dated a newly graduated lawyer, and I knew how tough it could be to find work. As a young entrepreneur myself, could I really blame this guy for hard-selling his services? If, as the police suggested, I did need a lawyer, it certainly wouldn't be someone this young—but there was no harm in hearing him out.

I signed the contract. He added his signature and handed me a copy.

"Let's start by discussing credentials," I said.

Without looking up from his papers, he said, "Let me assure you, Ms. Winterbourne, there is no one more qualified to handle your case."

"Humor me, then. Where'd you go to school? Where do you practice? How many custody cases have you handled? What percentage have you won? Any experience handling defamation of character? Because that may be a possibility here."

More paper gazing. Some paper shuffling. I was two seconds from showing him the door, when he turned to me, eyes still downcast.

"Let's get this over with, then, shall we?" he said.

He looked up at me. I dropped the contract. Lucas Cortez was a sorcerer.

❄ Spell-Boy

"GET OUT OF MY HOUSE," I said.

"As you can see, I'm quite qualified to handle your case, Paige."

"So now it's 'Paige'? Did Savannah hire you?"

"No." He said this without surprise, as if the thought of a child witch hiring a sorcerer lawyer wasn't at all peculiar.

"Then who sent you?"

"As you've already determined, no one sent me. You called me an ambulance chaser, and I didn't argue the point. Though, admittedly, I find the phrase reprehensible, the motivation it implies can be accurately applied to me. There are two ways for a lawyer to rise in the supernatural world: join a Cabal or gain a reputation for successfully fighting them. I have chosen the latter route." He paused. "May I have that coffee?"

"Sure. Just go out my front door, make a left at the end of the road, and look for the big neon donut. You can't miss it."

"As I was saying, being a young lawyer seeking to make a name for myself outside the Cabals, I must, unfortunately, chase down my cases. I heard of Mr. Nast's intent to seek custody of Savannah and, seeing an opportunity, I followed it. I understand Mr. Nast has not yet abandoned his challenge?"

"He refuses to submit to DNA testing, meaning he can't prove he's Savannah's father, meaning I don't see a case, so I don't need a lawyer. Now, if you'd like those directions again—"

"While his refusal to surrender a DNA sample may seem advantageous, let me assure you, it doesn't eliminate the problem. Gabriel Sandford is an excellent lawyer. He'll find a way around this, likely by bribing a medical laboratory to provide phony test results."

"And willingness to bribe officials makes one an excellent lawyer?"

"Yes."

I opened my mouth, but nothing came out.

Cortez continued, "If he does attempt such a maneuver, I will insist that the court supervise the testing." He returned to his papers. "Now, I've prepared a list of steps we should take to—"

Savannah walked into the kitchen and stopped short, sizing up Cortez and his accouterments.

"What's with the salesman?" she asked. Then she looked Cortez in the face. She didn't even blink, only tightened her mouth. "What do you want, sorcerer?"

"I prefer Lucas," he said, extending a hand. "Lucas Cortez. I'm representing Paige."

"Repres—" Savannah looked at me. "Where'd you find him?"

"The Yellow Pages," I said. "Under *U*. For unsolicited, uninvited, and unwanted. He's not my lawyer."

Savannah sized Cortez up again. "Good, 'cause if you

want a sorcerer lawyer, you can do much better than this."

"I'm sure you can," Cortez said. "However, since I am the only one who's here, perhaps I can be of some assistance."

"You can't," I said. "Now, if you've forgotten the way to the door—"

"Hold on," Savannah said. "He's pretty young, so he's probably cheap. Maybe he'll do until we can get someone better."

"My services are extremely reasonable and will be agreed upon in advance," Cortez said. "While it may seem at this point as if Nast doesn't have a case—"

"Who's Nast?" Savannah asked.

"He means Leah," I said, shooting Cortez a "don't argue" glare. "It's O'Donnell, not Nast."

"My mistake," Cortez said without missing a beat. "As I was saying, Leah has not withdrawn her petition for custody and shows no signs of doing so. Therefore, we must assume that she plans to pursue that endeavor. Thwarting her efforts must be our primary purpose. To that end, I have drawn up a list of steps."

"The twelve-step program for un-demonizing my life?"

"No, there are only seven steps, but if you see the need for more, we can discuss making the additions."

"Uh-huh."

"Who cares about lists?" Savannah said. "All we have to do is kill Leah."

"I'm glad to see you're taking such a keen interest in this, Savannah. However, we must proceed in a logical, methodical manner—which, unfortunately, precludes running out and murdering anyone. Perhaps we should begin by going over the list I prepared for you. Step one: Arrange to have your homework brought to the house by a teacher or student known to both you and Paige. Step two—"

"He's kidding, right?" Savannah said.

"It doesn't matter," I said. "I'm not hiring you, Cortez."

"I really do prefer Lucas."

"And I'd prefer you found your way to my front door. *Now.* I don't know you and I don't trust you. You might very well be what you say you are, but how do I prove that? How do I know Sandford didn't send you here? 'Hey, Paige's lawyer quit, let's send her one of ours, see if she notices.'"

"I don't work for Gabriel Sandford or anyone else."

I shook my head. "Sorry, no sale. You're a sorcerer. No matter how hard up you were for a job, I can't believe you'd offer to work for a witch."

"I have no quarrel with witches. The limitations of your powers are hereditary. I'm sure you endeavor to use them to their full potential."

I stiffened. "Get out of my house or I will show you the limitations of my powers."

"You need help—my help—both as legal counsel and added protection for both you and Savannah. My spellcasting is not outstanding, but it is proficient enough."

"As is mine. I don't need your protection, sorcerer. If I need help, I can get it from my Coven."

"Ah, yes, the Coven."

Something in his voice, a nuance, an inflection, snapped the last restraint on my temper.

"Get the hell out of my house, sorcerer."

He gathered his papers. "I understand you've had a difficult day. While we must go over this list soon, it's not necessary to do so immediately. My advice would be to rest. If you'll allow me to listen to your telephone messages, I can return calls from the media, after which we can review this list—"

I grabbed the paper from his hands and ripped it in two.

"If that makes you feel better, by all means, go ahead," he said. "I have copies. I'll leave you a new one. Please add any concerns that may have escaped my—"

"I am not going through any list. You are not my lawyer. Want to know when I'd hire a sorcerer to represent me? Ten minutes after being hit by a transport and declared brain-dead. Until then, scram."

"Scram?" His eyebrows rose an eighth of an inch.

"Leave. Go. Get lost. Beat it. Take your pick. Just take it with you."

He nodded and returned to his writing.

"Listen," I said, "maybe I'm not making myself clear—"

"You are." He finished his note, put the papers into his satchel, and laid a card on the table. "In the event that you reconsider . . . or experience an unfortunate collision with a large trucking conveyance, I can be reached at my cell number."

I waited until he was gone, then cast fresh lock spells at all the doors and vowed never again to answer the bell. At least not for a few days.

After Cortez left, Savannah decided to watch TV, so I slipped downstairs for some spellcasting. After what happened last night, I could hardly let my neighbors catch me sneaking into the woods to cast spells. The forest is my preferred location for spell practice. Nature not only offers peace and solitude, but something about the very primordiality of it seems to provide an energy of its own. From the earliest times, shamans and spell-casters have trekked into the forest or the desert or the tundra to reconnect with their powers. We need to. I can't explain it any better than that.

My mother taught me to spellcast out of doors. Yet, as strongly as she believed in this practice, she was never able to impose it on the Coven. For several generations now, the Coven has taught its children to practice indoors, preferably in a locked room with no windows. By forcing the young into locked rooms, it seems to me that they're validating the idea that we are doing something wrong, something shameful, an idea that is only underscored in neophytes by the way the Coven handles their first menses ceremony. First menses marks the passage into true witch-hood, when a witch comes into her full powers. A witch's powers increase automatically at this time, but she must undergo a ceremony on the eighth day to fully release her powers; skip the ceremony and you forever forfeit that extra power. The Coven's stance on this was that if a mother wished her daughter to go through the ceremony, she had to find the ingredients, study the rituals, and perform them herself.

Understandably, few did. My mother had performed it for me, though, and when the time came, I would do the same for Savannah.

I headed down to the basement. It's a large, unfinished, single room that stretches the length of the bungalow. The far corner, under Savannah's bedroom, was the spot she'd staked out for her art studio. So far I'd only thrown down an area rug for it, but eventually I planned to finish it into a separate room for her.

I won't say I understand Savannah's art. Her dark-themed paintings and cartoons tend toward the macabre. When her choice of theme began to worry me last fall, I talked to Jeremy Danvers, the werewolf Pack Alpha, who's the only artist I know. He looked at her work and told me not to worry about it. In that, I trust his judgment, and I appreciate the encouragement and help he's been giving Savannah.

This past year has probably been a nightmare for her, and she's been so strong about it that sometimes it worries me. Perhaps here, on canvases covered with angry splotches of crimson and black, she finds an outlet for her pain. If so, then I must not interfere, however strong the temptation.

When I spellcast in the basement, I do it in the laundry area, right near the bottom of the steps. So I settled myself on the floor, laid the grimoire before me, and leafed through the yellowed pages. I had two such spellbooks, ancient and ripe with the stink of age, a smell that was somehow simultaneously repulsive and inviting. These did not contain Coven-sanctioned spells, although they were Coven property. It might seem like the Coven was asking for trouble, having these books around where any rebellious young witch could get hold of them. But the Coven wasn't worried about that. Why? Because according to them, the spells didn't work. And I feared, after three years of tinkering with them, that the Coven was mostly right.

Of the sixty-six spells contained in these tomes, I'd managed to cast only four successfully, including a fireball spell. With my fire phobia, I'd been nervous about the fireball spell, but that made it all the more alluring, and made me all the more proud of myself when I'd mastered it. That bolstered my determination to learn the rest, convinced me that all I needed to do was find the right technique.

Yet, in the ensuing two years, only one other spell had shown any sign of working. Sometimes I wondered if the Coven was right, that these were false grimoires, passed down only as historical oddities. Still, I could not put the books aside. There was so much magic in here, magic of true power—elemental spells, conjuring spells, spells whose meaning I couldn't even decipher. This was what witch magic should be, what I wanted it to be.

I worked on the wind spell Savannah had seen mentioned in my practice journal. That was the spell that had shown signs it might eventually work. It was actually a spell to "wind" a person, that is, deprive them of oxygen. A lethal spell, yes, but my experience in the compound last year had taught me that I needed at least one lethal spell in my repertoire, a spell of last resort. Now, with Leah in town, I needed it more than ever.

After thirty minutes I gave up, still unable to get the spell working. Knowing Savannah was alone upstairs, even if she was protected by security spells, played havoc with my concentration.

Savannah was watching television in the living room. I paused in the doorway, wondering what she could have found to watch on a Saturday afternoon. At first I thought it was a soap opera. The woman filling the screen certainly looked like a soap opera actress—a sultry redhead in her late thirties who'd been outfitted in glasses and an upswept hairdo in a laughable attempt to make her look scholarly. When the camera pulled back, I saw that she was walking through an audience with a mike clipped to her blouse, and revised my assessment: an infomercial. No one smiles that much unless they're selling something. From the way she was working the crowd, it almost looked like a religious revival. I caught a few sentences and realized she was selling a different kind of spiritual reassurance.

"I'm getting an older male," the woman said. "Like a father figure, but not your father. An uncle, maybe a family friend."

"Oh, please," I said. "How can you watch this crap?"

"It's not crap," Savannah said. "This is Jaime Vegas. She's the best."

"It's a con, Savannah. A trick."

"No, it's not. She can really talk to the dead. There's this other guy who does it, but Jaime's way better."

A commercial came on. Savannah picked up the remote and fast-forwarded.

"You have it on tape?" I said.

"Sure. Jaime doesn't have her own TV show. She says she prefers traveling around, meeting people, but *The Keni Bales Show* has her on every month and I tape it."

"How long have you been doing this?"

She shrugged.

"Oh, hon," I said, walking into the room. "It's a con job, don't you see that? Listen to her. She's making guesses so fast that no one notices when she's wrong. The questions are so open—did you hear that last one? She said she had a message for someone who had a brother die in the past few years. What's the chance that nobody in the audience has recently lost a brother?"

"You don't get it."

"Only a necromancer can contact the afterworld, Savannah."

"I bet *we* could do it if we tried." She turned to look at me. "Haven't you ever thought of it? Contacting your mother?"

"Necromancy doesn't work like that. You can't just dial up the dead."

I walked into the kitchen and picked up the phone. Lucas Cortez's visit had one positive outcome in that it reminded me about my Cabal questions—which in turn reminded me that Robert hadn't returned my call. It wasn't like Robert not to call back, so when I made the rounds again—phoning his house, phoning his office, checking my e-mail—and got no response, I began to worry. It was now nearly four, so I phoned Adam's work again, though I doubted the campus bar would be open at one in the afternoon. Silly me—of course it was.

When I spoke to one of the servers, I learned that Adam was away for the week at some conference. This sparked a memory flash and a big mental "duh!" I returned to my computer and checked my recent e-mail, finding one from two weeks ago in which Adam mentioned going with his parents to a conference on the role of glossolalia in the Charismatic movement. Not that Adam gave a damn about Charismatics or glosso-lalia (a.k.a. "speaking in tongues"), but the conference was being held in Maui, which had more than its share of attractions for a twenty-four-year-old guy. The dates of the conference: June 12 to 18. Today was June 16.

I thought about tracking them down in Maui. Neither Robert nor Adam carried a cellphone; Robert didn't believe in them and Adam's service had been disconnected after he'd failed to pay yet another whopping bill. To contact them I'd need to phone the conference in Hawaii and leave a message. The more I thought about this, the more foolish I felt. Robert would be home in two days. I'd hate to sound like I was panicking. This wasn't critical information, only background. It could wait.

Lucas Cortez's visit had, in fact, prompted me to remember two things I needed to do. Besides contacting Robert, I had to line up a lawyer. Though I hadn't heard back from the police, and doubted I would, I really should have a lawyer's name at hand, in case the need arose.

I called the Boston lawyer who handled my business legal matters. Though she did only commercial work, she should be able to provide me with the names of other lawyers who could handle either a custody or criminal case. Today being Saturday, there was no one in the office, so I left a detailed message asking if she could call me Monday with a recommendation.

Then I headed to the kitchen, grabbed a cookbook, and looked for something interesting to make for dinner. As I pored over the possibilities, Savannah walked into the kitchen, grabbed a glass from the cupboard, and poured herself some milk. The cupboard creaked open. A bag rustled.

"No cookies this late," I said. "Dinner's in thirty minutes."

"Thirty minutes? I can't wait—" She stopped. "Uh, Paige?"

"Hmmm?" I glanced up from my book to see her peering out the kitchen door, through to the living-room window.

"Are there supposed to be people camped out on our front lawn?"

I leaned over to look through to the window, then slammed the cookbook closed and strode to the front door.

Hell Hath No Fury
Like a Middle-aged
❖ Man Scorned

I THREW OPEN THE FRONT DOOR and marched onto the porch. A camcorder lens swung to greet me.

"What's going on?" I asked.

The man with the camcorder stepped back to frame me in his viewfinder. No, not a man, a boy, maybe seventeen, eighteen. Beside him stood another young man of the same age, swilling Gatorade. Both were dressed in unrelieved black, everything oversized, from the baggy T-shirts to the backward ball caps to the combat boots to the pants that threatened to slide to their shoes at any moment.

On the opposite side of the lawn, as far as they could get from the young cinematic auteurs, stood two middle-aged women in schoolmarm dresses, ugly prints made into unflattering frocks that covered everything from mid-calf to mid-neck. Despite the warm June day, both wore cardigans that had been through the wash a few too many times. When I turned to look at the women, two middle-aged men appeared from a nearby minivan, both wearing dark gray suits as ill-fitting and worn as the women's dresses. They approached the women and flanked them, as if to provide backup.

"There she is," one of the women whispered loudly to her companions. "The poor girl."

"Look," I said, "it's no big deal. I appreciate your support, but—"

I stopped, realizing they weren't looking at me. I turned to see Savannah in the doorway.

"It's okay, sweetie," one man called. "We won't hurt you. We're here to help."

"Help?" she said between cookie bites. "Help with what?"

"Saving your immortal soul."

"Huh?"

"You needn't be afraid," the second woman said. "It's not too late. God knows you're innocent, that you've been led into sin against your will."

Savannah rolled her eyes. "Oh, please. Get a life."

I shoved Savannah back into the house, slammed the door, and held it shut.

"Look," I said, "not to deny you folks your right to free speech, but you can't—"

"We heard about the Black Mass," the boy without the camera said. "Can we see it?"

"There's nothing to see. It's gone. It was a very sick prank, that's all."

"Did you really kill a couple of cats? Skinned them and cut them all up?"

"*Someone* killed three cats," I said. "And I hope they find the person responsible."

"What about the baby?" his camera-wielding friend asked.

"B-baby?"

"Yeah, I heard they found some parts they couldn't identify and they think it's this baby missing from Boston and—"

"No!" I said, my voice sharp against the silence of the street. "They found cats, nothing else. If you want more information, I'd suggest you contact the East Falls or state police, because I have nothing further to add. Better yet, how about I call them myself? Charge you with trespassing? That's what this is, you know."

"We must do as conscience dictates," the second man said in a deep, orator's voice. "We represent the Church of Christ's Blessed Salvation and we have committed ourselves to fighting evil in every form."

"Really?" I said. "Then you must have the wrong address. There's no evil here. Try down the street. I'm sure you can find something worth denouncing."

"We've found it," one of the women said. "The Black Mass. A perversion of the most sacred rite of Christianity. We know what this means. Others will know. They will come. They will join us."

"Oh? Gee, and I'm fresh out of coffee and donuts. I hate to be a bad hostess. If they don't mind tea, I'll put on the kettle. I make a really wicked brew."

The boy dropped the camcorder. For a second I thought it was the tea comment. Then, as he stumbled forward, I glanced up to see Savannah peering through the front curtains. She grinned at me, then she lifted her hand and the boy jerked backward, falling to the grass.

"That's not funny," I said, glaring at the teen as he struggled to get up. "I won't stand here and be mocked with pratfalls. If you have something to say to me, contact my lawyer."

I stormed into the house and slammed the door.

Savannah lay collapsed on the sofa, giggling. "That was great, Paige."

I strode across the room and yanked the curtains shut. "What the hell did you think you were doing?"

"Oh, they won't know it was me. Geez, lighten up." She peeked under the curtain. "He's checking his shoelaces, like maybe he tripped or something. Duh. Humans are so stupid."

"Stop saying that. And get away from that window. I'm just going to ignore them and make dinner."

"Can we eat out?"

"No!"

We ended up eating out.

Savannah didn't railroad me into it. As I was defrosting chicken for dinner, I kept thinking of the people on my lawn, and the more I thought about them, the angrier I got. The angrier I got, the more determined I was not to let them upset me . . . or at least, not to let them know they'd upset me. If I wanted to go out to dinner, damned if they'd stop me. Actually, I didn't really want to go out to dinner, but after I made up my mind, I decided to proceed, if only to prove my point.

No one stopped us from driving away. The teenagers filmed our exit, as if hoping my car would transform into a broomstick and take flight. The Salvationists had retreated to their minivan before we made it to the corner, probably grateful for the excuse to sit down.

Savannah decided she wanted takeout from the Golden Dragon. The local Chinese restaurant was run by Mabel Higgins, who'd never set foot outside Massachusetts in her life and, judging by her cooking, had never cracked open an Asian cookbook. Her idea of Chinese cooking was American chop suey—that is, macaroni and ground beef. Unfortunately, other than the bakery, the Golden Dragon was the only restaurant in East Falls. The bakery closed at five, so I had to buy my dinner from the Golden Dragon also. I decided on plain white rice. Even Mabel couldn't screw that up.

I parked on the street. Most parking in East Falls is curbside, particularly in the village core, where all the buildings predate the automotive age. I've never mastered parallel parking—I'd rather walk an extra block than attempt it—so I pulled over in the empty stretch in front of the grocer's, which had closed at five as well.

"Geez, can't you park a little closer?" Savannah said. "We're, like, a mile away."

"More like a hundred feet. Come on, get out."

She launched into a moaning fit, as if I were asking her to trudge twenty miles through waist-high snow.

"Wait here, then," I said. "What do you want?"

She gave me her order. Then I warned her that I was locking her in and did so, with both the car remote and spells.

❧

As I headed back to the car, I noticed an SUV parked behind my Accord and quickened my pace. Yes, I was being paranoid. Yet, considering there were no other cars within a half-dozen spaces of mine, it did seem odd, even alarming. As I jogged toward my car, I saw the face of the SUV driver. Not Leah. Not Sandford.

Grantham Cary Jr.

"Great," I muttered.

I slowed to a quick march and yanked my keys from my purse. Under my breath I undid the locking spells, then I hit the remote unlock, so I could hop into my car without stopping long enough for him to approach me. As I drew near, I heard the soft rumble of his engine idling. I kept my gaze fixed on my car, listening for the sound of his door opening. Instead, I heard the clunk of his transmission shifting into gear.

"Good," I said. "Just keep going."

Out of the corner of my eye I saw him reverse to pull out. Then he drove forward—straight forward, hitting my car with a crash. Savannah flew against the dashboard.

"You son of a bitch!" I shouted, dropping the takeout bag and running for the car.

Cary veered out and tore off.

I raced to the passenger door and yanked it open. Inside, Savannah cupped a bloody nose.

"I'm okay," she said. "I just hit my nose."

I grabbed a handful of tissues from the box behind her seat and passed them to her, then examined the bridge of her nose. It didn't feel broken.

"I'm okay, Paige. Really." She glanced down at her

blood-streaked T-shirt. "Shit! My new Gap shirt! Did you get a license number? That guy's paying for my shirt."

"He's paying for more than your shirt. And I don't need a license number, I know who it was."

I pulled out my cellphone, called the operator, and asked for the police.

"I'm not doubting it was Cary," Willard said. "I'm asking if you can prove it."

Of the three East Falls deputies, Travis Willard was the one I'd hoped they'd send. The town's youngest deputy—a few years my senior—he was the nicest of the bunch. His wife, Janey, and I had served at several charity functions together, and she was one of the few townspeople who'd made me feel welcome. Now, though, I was questioning the wisdom of phoning the police at all.

Although Willard was considerate enough to sit in my car instead of making us stand on the sidewalk, everyone who passed did a double take. Only twelve hours ago the police had found a Satanic altar at my house, news of which I was sure had flown through the town before noon. Now, seeing me pulled over talking to a deputy, tongues would wag with fresh speculation. If that wasn't bad enough, I was quickly realizing that accusing a respected town member of intentional hit-and-run was no easy sell.

"Someone must have seen it," Savannah said. "There were people around."

"None of whom stuck around to do their civic duty," I added. "But there's bound to be evidence. He didn't do a lot of damage, but the paint's scratched. Can't you check his truck?"

"I could," Willard said. "And if I find silver paint on his bumper, I can ask Sheriff Fowler to requisition a lab test and he'll laugh in my face. I'm not trying to give you a hard time, Paige. I'm suggesting maybe this isn't the way you want to pursue this. I heard you had a run-in with Cary at the bakery yesterday."

"You did?" Savannah said. "What happened?"

Willard turned to the back seat and asked Savannah to step outside the car for a moment. When she was gone, he looked back at me.

"I know he hit on you. The guy's a—" Willard cut himself short and shook his head. "He hits on every cute girl in town. Even made a pass at Janey once—after we were married. I could have—" Another head shake. "But I didn't. I didn't do anything. Some things are more trouble than they're worth."

"I understand that, but—"

"Don't worry about the car. I'll write it up for your insurance company as a hit-and-run. And maybe I'll pay Cary a visit, drop a hint that he should pay the deductible."

"I don't care about the damage—it's a car. I'm upset because Savannah was inside. She could have gone through the windshield."

"Do you think Cary knew she was there?"

I hesitated, then shook my head.

"That's what I figure too," Willard said. "He wouldn't

have seen her over the headrest. He was driving by, saw your car, and pulled in behind, thinking it was empty. When he saw you walking up, he slammed into the rear end. An asshole, like I said. But not a big enough asshole to intentionally hurt a kid."

"So you won't do anything."

"If you insist, then I have to make the report, but I'm warning you—"

"Fine. I get the idea."

"I'm sorry, Paige."

I fastened my seat belt and waved Savannah into the car.

Next stop: 52 Spruce Lane, home of Mr. and Mrs. Grantham Cary Jr.

The Carys lived in one of East Falls's finest homes. It was one of five stops on the annual East Falls garden walk. Not that the gardens were spectacular—quite mundane, in fact, tending to over-pruned shrubbery and roses with fancy names and no scent. Yet each year the house made the tour, and each year the people of East Falls paid their fee to troop through the house and gardens. Why? Because every year Lacey hired a top-notch decorator to redo one room in the house, which then set that season's standard for interior design in East Falls.

"Do you think this is a good idea?" Savannah said as I stalked up the front walkway.

"No one else is going to do it for us."

"Hey, I'm all for putting the boots to the guy, but

there are other ways, you know. Better ways. I could cast a spell that'll—"

"No spells. I don't want revenge. I want justice."

"A good case of body lice would be justice."

"I want him to know what he did."

"So we'll send him a card: 'Cooties courtesy of Paige and Savannah.'"

I tramped up the steps and whammed the cherub knocker against the wooden door. From inside came the scuffling of shoes. A curtain fluttered. Voices murmured. Then Lacey opened the door.

"I'd like to speak to Grantham, please," I said with as much courtesy as I could muster.

"He isn't here."

"Oh? That's odd. I see his SUV in the lane. Looks like he scraped up the front bumper."

Lacey's surgically tightened face didn't so much as ripple. "I wouldn't know about that."

"Look, could I please talk to him? This doesn't concern you, Lacey. I know he's in there. This is his problem. Let him handle it."

"I'm going to have to ask you to leave."

"He hit my car. On purpose. Savannah was inside."

Not a flicker of reaction. "I'm going to have to ask you to leave now."

"Did you hear me? Grantham hit my car."

"You're mistaken. If you're trying to get us to pay for damages—"

"I don't care about the car!" I said, pulling Savannah over and waving at her bloodied nose and shirt. "This is the damage I care about! She's thirteen years old."

"Children get bloody noses all the time. If you're hoping to sue—"

"I don't want to sue! I want him to come out here and see what he's done. That's it. Just bring him out here so I can speak to him."

"I'm going to have to ask you to leave."

"Stop covering for him, Lacey. He doesn't deserve it. The guy chases—"

I stopped there. My quarrel was with Grantham, not Lacey, and as good as it would have felt to tell Lacey what else her husband was doing, it wasn't fair. Besides, she probably already knew. I'd only be lowering myself to cheap shots.

"Tell him this isn't finished," I said, then turned and stomped down the steps.

As I approached the car, I realized Savannah wasn't behind me. I turned to see her in front of the house. Inside, the lights flickered on and off. A television soundtrack blared, then faded, then blared again.

"Savannah!" I hissed.

A main floor curtain drew back. Lacey peered out. Savannah looked up and waved her fingers. Then she jogged toward me.

"What do you think you're doing?" I said.

"Just a warning," she said, grinning. "A friendly warning."

When we got home, the teens were filming my neighbor's black cat. I ignored them and pulled into the garage.

While Savannah reheated her dinner, I listened to my messages and returned calls to several Bostonian friends who'd seen my plight on the news. My Satanic altar made the Boston news? They each assured me it had been only a cursory mention on one channel, but that didn't make me feel better.

The teenagers left at 9:45, probably to make curfew. The older quartet stayed, taking turns sitting in the minivan and standing vigil on my lawn. I didn't phone the police; that would only have called more attention to myself. If I didn't react, the Salvationists would tire soon enough and go home, wherever home was.

I went to bed at eleven. Yes, sad but true. I was young, single, and going to bed at eleven on a Saturday night, as I had almost every night for the past nine months. Since Savannah's arrival, I've had to struggle to maintain even friendships. Dating is out of the question. Savannah is very jealous of my time and attention. Or, perhaps more accurately, she dislikes not having me at her convenience. Like I've said, stability was one of the few things I could offer her, so I didn't push it.

Before retiring for the night, I peeked out the front curtain. Two men still stood on my front lawn, with two women in a nearby car, but the faces and the vehicle had changed. Replacement workers? Great.

I spent way too much time that night brooding about Cary. As if dealing with a custody battle and a Satanic altar wasn't enough, now I had a maturity-challenged lawyer stalking me. How did I get myself into these messes? Maybe publicly humiliating Cary wasn't my brightest idea ever, but how was I to know the guy would retaliate like a sixteen-year-old turned down for a prom date?

Then there was Travis Willard. I liked Willard, which made his cop-out only that much worse. If he wouldn't support me against Cary, who would? I could say East Falls was a typical small town, insular and protective, but I grew up in a small community and it hadn't been like this at all. If the Elders would only let me move . . . but that led into a whole new area of brooding, and I already had enough to last me the entire night.

All was quiet the next morning—not surprising, given that it was Sunday and this was East Falls. At 9:00 A.M. the phone rang. I checked caller ID: private caller. Whenever someone doesn't want you to know who they are, it's a good bet they aren't someone you care to speak to.

I let the machine pick up and set the kettle on the stove. The caller hung up.

Ten minutes later, the phone rang again. Another mystery caller. I sipped my tea and waited for the hang-up. Instead, the caller left a cellphone-static-choked message.

"Paige, it's Grant. I want to speak to you about last night. I'll be at the office at ten."

I grabbed the receiver, but he'd already hung up. "Star sixty-nine" didn't work. I considered my options, then dumped my tea in the sink and walked down the hall to Savannah's bedroom.

"Savannah?" I called, rapping at the door. "Time to get up. We've got an errand to run."

Flying Through the Air with the Greatest 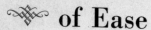 of Ease

WHEN WE ARRIVED at Cary's office, the reception desk was deserted. No surprise there; I doubt Cary wanted Lacey to overhear this conversation. Our footsteps echoed through the emptiness as we crossed the hardwood floor.

"Hello!" Cary's voice drifted from his second-story office. "I'll be right with you!"

I headed up the stairs, Savannah behind me. A rustling of paper erupted from Cary's office, followed by the squeak of his chair.

"Sorry about that," he said, still hidden from view. "No reception on a Sunday, I'm afraid. The wife doesn't—" He stepped from his office and blinked. "Paige? Savannah?"

"Who were you expecting?"

He disappeared back into his office. I followed and waved for Savannah to do the same.

"New client," Cary said. "Not until ten-thirty, though, so I guess I can spare a few minutes. Lacey tells me you stopped by the house last night. Apparently I bumped your car on State Street. I did go downtown to pick up some dry cleaning. I can't say I recall hitting anything, but I noticed a scratch on the front bumper. Of course, I'm extremely sorry—"

"Cut the crap. You know what you did. If you called me here to make excuses, I don't want to hear them."

"Called you here?" He frowned as he settled into his chair. I studied his face for any sign of dissembling but saw none.

"You didn't call me, did you?" I said.

"No, I . . . well, of course, I was *going* to call—"

"Where's Lacey?"

A deeper frown. "At church. It's her week to help Reverend Meacham set up."

"It's a trap," I murmured. I looked at Savannah. "We have to get out of here. Now."

"What's going on?" Cary said, rising from his desk.

I pushed Savannah toward the door, then thought better of it and yanked her behind me before starting forward. She grabbed my arm.

"Careful," she mouthed.

Right. Barreling out the door probably wasn't the best idea. I had too little experience with running and fighting for my life. Savannah already had too much.

After motioning Savannah back, I inched around the doorway, pressed myself against the wall, and peered into the hallway. Empty.

"Is something wrong?" Cary asked.

I reached for Savannah. Tugging her behind me, I ventured into the hallway. We sidestepped along the wall, moving toward the stairs. Halfway there, I stopped and listened. Silence.

"Are you in some kind of trouble?" Cary's voice fluttered from his office and echoed down the hall.

I slipped back to the office and closed the door, then cast a lock spell to seal him inside. I needn't have bothered. Cary obviously had no intention of risking his neck, choosing instead to sit behind his big desk and play dumb.

The hallway was fully enclosed, flanked by rows of shut doors, with the stairs along the left wall. Motioning Savannah to follow, I quickstepped across the hall and wheeled around so my back was against the other wall. Again I slid sideways, this time stopping two feet from the stairs.

"Wait," Savannah whispered.

I waved her to silence and leaned toward the stair opening. Savannah grabbed my sleeve and jerked me back, then gestured for me to crouch or bend before looking out. Okay, that made sense, instead of sticking my head out exactly where someone would expect to see it. I crouched and glanced down the stairwell. Empty. I scanned the waiting room below. Also empty. Five feet from the base of the stairs lay my goal: the front door.

As I pulled back, I caught a glimpse of reflected sunlight, froze, and checked again. The front door was open an inch or two. Had Savannah left it ajar when we came in?

I turned to Savannah. "Cover," I mouthed.

Her lips tightened. Defiance flashed in her eyes. Before she could open her mouth, I locked glares with her.

"Cover now," I hissed.

Another flare of anger, then she lowered her eyelids.

Her lips moved, and when they finished, she was gone. Invisible. So long as she didn't move, no one would see her. I paused a second, making sure she was staying covered, then crept into the stairwell.

It took an eternity to descend. Step down, pause, listen, duck and look, step down again. Coming down a staircase is more dangerous than you'd imagine. If the stairs are enclosed, as these were, then someone standing on the lower level will see you long before you can see them. Hence the stopping, ducking, and looking, which made me feel safer, though I doubt it would have saved me from anyone standing below with a gun.

Actually, I wasn't too worried about guns; supernaturals don't usually use them. If Leah *was* down there, she'd more likely use telekinesis to yank my feet from under me and drag me down the stairs, breaking my spine so I'd still be alive, lying at the bottom paralyzed, when she crushed me with a flying file cabinet. Much better than being shot. Really.

When I finally reached the bottom, I lunged for the door handle. I grabbed it, yanked—and nearly flew face first into the wall when the door didn't move. Once I'd recovered my balance, I looked around, and tugged the handle again. Nothing. The door stood an inch open yet would neither open nor close. A barrier spell? It didn't seem like one, but I cast a barrier-breaking incantation anyway. Nothing happened. I grabbed the door edge. My fingers passed through the crack without resistance, but I couldn't pull it open. I cast an unlock spell. Nothing.

I was keenly aware of time passing, of standing here in plain sight yanking on the door, an easy target, as

Savannah hid in the upper hall, undoubtedly losing patience. After one last round of breaking spells, I flung my back against the wall and caught my breath.

We were trapped. Really trapped. Any moment now, Leah and Sandford and god knows what other kind of supernaturals would arrive and we'd—

For god's sake, Paige, get a grip! The front door's barred. Big deal. How about another door? How about windows?

I glimpsed sunlight through the doorway behind Lacey's reception desk. Staying close to the wall, I eased a few feet left, so I could glance through the doorway. It led into a large meeting room, and at the back of that room was a huge set of patio doors.

I hunkered and bolted across the room. Then I inched along the opposite wall toward the doorway. As I slipped into the other room, a shadow flashed across the sunlit floor. I ducked behind an armchair, barely daring to breathe, knowing that the chair did little to hide me. I cast a cover spell.

The shadow danced across the floor again. Had I already been spotted? I glanced left, being careful to move only my eyes. The shadow returned, skipping over the floor. Realizing it was too small to be a person, I looked up and saw leaves fluttering in the wind just outside the patio doors.

As I was easing from behind the armchair, footsteps pattered across the front hall. I zipped back and cast another cover spell. The steps turned left, receded, returned, went too far right, nearly vanishing into silence, and came back again. Searching the rooms. Were they coming my way now? Yes ... no ... they paused. A squeak of shoes turning sharply. More steps. Growing louder, louder.

I closed my eyes and prepared a fireball spell. When a shape moved through the doorway, I launched the ball. A fiery sphere flew from the ceiling. I tensed, ready to run. As the ball fell, the intruder yelped, raising her arms to ward it off. Catching sight of her face, I flew from my hiding spot and knocked her out of the fireball's path. We hit the floor together.

"You promised to teach me that one," Savannah said, disentangling herself from my grip.

I clapped a hand over her mouth, but she pulled it away.

"There's no one here," she said. "I cast a sensing spell."

"Where'd you learn that?"

"Your mom taught me. It's fourth level—you can't do it." She paused, then offered an ego-consoling, "Yet."

I took a deep breath. "Okay, well, the front door's barred somehow, so I was going to try these." I waved at the patio doors. "They're probably jammed, but maybe we can break the glass."

Again we moved against the wall, in case someone outside was looking in. When I reached the doors, I peeked out. The patio opened into a tiny yard, grass-free, low-maintenance, covered with interlocking brick and raised beds of perennials. As I reached for the door handle, a shadow flickered across the yew hedge at the rear of the yard. Assuming it was another waving tree branch, I stepped forward.

Leah was standing against the bushes. She lifted a hand and waved.

As I whirled toward Savannah, time slowed and I saw everything, not in a blur of movement, but in distinct, slow-motion frames. Leah raised both hands and gestured toward herself, as if beckoning us closer, but her gaze was focused on something over our heads. Then came the crash of glass. And the scream.

I lunged at Savannah, slamming us both to the floor. As we rolled, a dark shape plummeted toward the ground outside. I saw the chair first—Cary's chair—dropping like a rock. No, faster than a rock, it flew so fast I heard it hit the brickwork before my brain had processed the image of it falling. In my mind I still saw the chair in mid-air, tilted backward, Cary sitting in it, arms and legs thrust forward by the force, mouth open, screaming. I could still hear that scream hanging in the air as the chair slammed onto the brick and bright drops of blood sprayed outward.

As I lifted my head, Leah caught my gaze, smiled, waved, and walked away.

I scrambled to my feet and raced out the patio doors, which opened without resistance. Even as I ran to Cary, I knew it was too late. The force of the impact, that horrible shower of blood. Two feet away, I stopped, then doubled over, retching.

Grantham Cary Jr. toppled from the chair, spread-eagled on the ground, his head crushed like an overripe fruit, bursting into a puddle of blood and brains. The force had been so great that a huge shard of glass had impaled his stomach clear through; so great that his arm, striking the corner of a perennial bed, had been severed, his detached hand still gripping the armrest. I saw that, and I remembered Leah, smiling, waving, and I wasn't sure which was worse.

"Paige?" Savannah whispered. Looking up, I saw her face, stark white, staring at Cary as if unable to look away. "We—we should go."

"No," said a voice behind us. "I don't think you should."

Sheriff Fowler stepped through the open patio doors.

❧ Lawyer Roulette

LEAH HAD FRAMED ME for the murder of Grantham Cary Jr.

Take a woman accused of witchcraft and Satanism, a woman known to have engaged in a public feud with the murdered man and who then accused him of intentionally hitting her car and injuring her ward. This woman conspires under false pretenses to meet her former lawyer in his office, on a Sunday, when his wife will be at church early. The police receive a call—a neighbor worried about the angry shouts emanating from the lawyer's office. The police arrive. The lawyer is dead. The house is empty except for the woman and her ward. Whodunit? You don't need Sherlock Holmes to figure that one out.

Again, the East Falls police department wasn't equipped to handle such a case, so they called in the state cops, who took me to their station. The police interrogated me for three hours—the same questions over and over, badgering, bullying, until I could still hear their voices echoing in my head when they left for a cigarette or a coffee.

They'd taken everything I'd done in the last two days and twisted it to fit their theory. My tirade about

Satanism? Proof that I had a wicked temper and was easily provoked. My bakery blowout? Proof that I was paranoid, misconstruing a simple coffee invitation as a sexual proposition. My accusation about the car accident? Proof that I had a vendetta against Cary.

All my arguments about the Black Mass were now seen as protesting too much, denying the very existence of Satanic cults so as to cover up my own participation in such practices. Maybe Cary had learned the truth and refused to represent me further. Or maybe I'd hit on him and thrown a shit-fit when he rebuffed me. Maybe he *had* made a pass at me—but did I really expect them to believe he'd been upset enough over my rejection to slam his new Mercedes SUV into my six-year-old Honda? Grown men didn't do things like that. Not men like Grantham Cary Jr. I was paranoid. Or delusional. Or just plain crazy. Hadn't I stormed off to his house like a madwoman, shrieking wild accusations and vowing revenge? What about Lacey's reports of electrical malfunctioning after my visit? Not that the police were accusing me of witchcraft—rational people didn't believe in such nonsense—but I had done *something*. At the very least I was guilty of murdering Grantham Cary Jr.

After the third hour the two detectives left for a break. Moments later, the door opened and in walked a thirty-something woman who introduced herself as Detective Flynn.

I was pacing the room, my stomach knotted from three hours of worrying about Savannah. Was she here at the station? Or had the police called Margaret? What if this was Leah's plan, to get me locked up while she grabbed Savannah?

"Can I get you something?" Flynn asked as she stepped inside. "Coffee? A cold drink? A sandwich?"

"I'm not answering any more questions until someone tells me where Savannah is. I keep asking and asking and all I get is 'She's safe.' That's not good enough. I need to know—"

"She's here."

"Exactly where? Savannah is the subject of a custody battle. You people don't seem to understand—"

"We understand, Paige. Right now Savannah is in the next room playing cards with two officers. Armed state troopers. Nothing will happen to her. They gave her a burger for lunch and she's fine. You can see her as soon as we're done."

Finally, someone who didn't treat me like a tried-and-convicted murderer. I nodded and took my seat at the table.

"Let's get it over with, then," I said.

"Good. Now, are you sure I can't get you something?"

I shook my head. She settled into the seat across from me and leaned over the table, hands almost touching mine.

"I know you didn't do this alone," she said. "I heard what happened to Grantham Cary. I doubt Mr. Universe could do that to a person, let alone a young woman your size."

So this was the good cop, the one who was supposed to make me spill my guts, an older woman, maternal, understanding. As I sat there looking at her, I realized why such an overused police routine worked. Because, after hours of being yelled at and made to feel like a low-life degenerate, I was desperate for validation, for someone to say, You're not a cold-blooded killer and you don't deserve to be treated this way.

I knew this woman didn't give a damn about me. I knew she only wanted a confession so she could high-five her colleagues who were watching through the one-way glass. Yet I couldn't help wanting to confide in her, to gain a smile, a look of sympathy. But I knew better, so I fixed her with a cold stare and said, "I want a lawyer."

A smirk tainted Flynn's warmth. "Well, that could be difficult, Paige, considering he's just been taken to the county morgue. Maybe you don't understand the seriousness—"

The door opened, cutting her short. "She understands the seriousness perfectly well." Lucas Cortez walked in. "That is why she's asking for her lawyer. I will assume, Detective, that you were just about to honor that request."

Flynn pushed back her chair. "Who are you?"

"Her lawyer, of course."

I tried to open my mouth but couldn't. It was sealed shut, not by desperation or fear, but by a spell. A binding spell.

"And when did Paige hire you?" Flynn asked.

"It's 'Ms. Winterbourne,' and she retained my services at 2:00 P.M. yesterday, shortly after firing Mr. Cary for sexual harassment."

Cortez dropped a file folder onto the table. As Flynn

read the first sheet, frown lines deepening with each word, I managed to strain my eyes far enough left to see Cortez. He pretended to study the poster behind my head, but his eyes were on me, as they had to be during a binding spell.

So spell-boy knew some witch magic. Surprising, but not shocking. I knew better spells, several of which I deeply yearned to cast his way at that moment, but being unable to speak curtailed that impulse. A bit disconcerting, too, that he could cast a binding spell, something even I hadn't fully perfected. Wait—brain flash: if I couldn't cast a perfect binding spell, could Cortez? Hmmm.

"Okay, so you're her lawyer," Flynn said, pushing Cortez's papers aside. "You can sit down and take notes."

"Before I have a few minutes in private to consult with my client? Really, Detective. I didn't pass the bar exam yesterday. Now, if you'll please find us a private room—"

"This one's fine."

Cortez gave a humorless half-smile. "I'm sure it is, complete with one-way glass and video camera. Once more, Detective, I'm requesting a private room and a few minutes alone. . ."

Cortez was still talking, but I didn't hear him. All my mental power went into one final push. *Pop!* My leg jerked. Cortez kept talking, unaware that I'd broken his spell.

I stayed still, saying nothing, waiting. A minute later, Flynn stalked from the room to find us a private chamber.

"Forging my signature on legal documents, sorcerer?" I murmured under my breath.

To my disappointment, he didn't jump. Didn't even flinch. I thought I saw a flicker of consternation in his eyes when he realized I'd broken his spell, but it may have been the lighting. Before Cortez could answer, Flynn came back and escorted us to another room. I waited until she closed the door behind her, then took a seat.

"Very convenient," I said. "How you just happen to be around every time I need a lawyer."

"If you are implying that I am somehow aligned with Gabriel Sandford or the Nast Cabal, let me assure you that I would not debase my reputation with such an association."

I laughed.

"You're too young to be so cynical," he said, returning to his papers.

"Speaking of young, if you are working for Sandford, tell him I'm pretty insulted that he couldn't even bother sending a full-fledged sorcerer. What are you? Twenty-seven? Twenty-eight?"

He sifted through his papers. "Twenty-five."

"What?! You really did only pass the bar exam yesterday. Now I *am* insulted."

He didn't look up from his file or even change expression. Hell, he didn't have an expression to change. "If I was working for the Nasts, then logically they would send someone older and presumably more competent, would they not?"

"Maybe, but there are advantages to sending a guy closer to my age, right?"

"Such as?"

I opened my mouth to answer, then took another look

at Cortez—the cheap suit, the wire-frame glasses, the perpetually funereal expression—and I knew no one was playing the seduction card in this game.

"Well, you know," I said, "I might be able to relate better, be more sympathetic. . ."

"The disadvantages of my youth would far outweigh the advantages of our age similarity. As for how I conveniently show up whenever you need a lawyer, let me assure you, that doesn't require insider information or psychic powers. Murders and Satanic altars are hardly everyday occurrences in East Falls. An enterprising lawyer simply has to cultivate an equally enterprising local contact, and persuade him to keep abreast of any new rumors regarding your situation."

"You're bribing someone in town to inform on me?"

"Sadly, it's easier—and cheaper—than you might think." Cortez pushed his papers aside and met my gaze. "This could be a career-making case for me, Paige. Normally, the competition for such a case would be stiff, but, given that you are a witch, I doubt any other sorcerers will be vying for it."

"But you're willing to make an exception. How . . . big of you."

Cortez adjusted his glasses, taking more than a few seconds, as if using the pause to decide how best to proceed. "It's ambition, not altruism. I won't pretend otherwise. I need your case, and you need a lawyer. It's that simple."

"No, it's not that simple. I haven't run out of options yet. I'm sure I can still find a lawyer."

"If you choose to replace me later, that's fine," he

said. "But for now, I'm the only person here. Your Coven is obviously uninterested in helping or they'd have found a lawyer for you. At the very least they'd be here to offer moral support. But they aren't, are they?"

He'd almost done it, almost gained my confidence, but then, with those last comments, he undid all his efforts. I stood, strode to the door, and tried the handle. Locked from the outside, of course. An unlock spell was out of the question—I was in enough trouble already. As I lifted my fist to pound on the door, Cortez caught my hand from behind. Didn't grab it, just caught and held it.

"Let me work on your release," he said. "Accept my services, free of charge, in this one matter, and afterward, if you aren't satisfied with my performance, you may discharge me."

"Wow—a free trial run. How can I refuse? *Easy*. No deal, counselor. I don't want your help."

I wrenched my hand from his and lifted my fist to bang for the detective. Cortez put his hand against the door, fingers spread, blocking my fist's path.

"I'm offering to get you out of here, Paige." The formality fell from his voice and I thought, just for a second, that I detected a note of anxiety. "Why would I do that if I was working for the Nast Cabal? They want you in here, where you can't protect Savannah."

"I'll get out. They'll set bail and I can make it."

"I'm not talking about setting bail, I'm talking about getting you out. Permanently. No charges. No blemish on your record."

"I'm not—"

"What if they don't set bail? How long are you willing to stay in jail? To leave Savannah in the care of others?" He met my eyes. "Without you to protect her."

The arrow hit its mark. My Achilles heel. For one brief moment my resolve wavered. I glanced at Cortez. He stood there waiting for me to agree. And though there was no smugness in his face, I knew he assumed I would agree.

I whammed my fist against the door, catching Cortez off guard. On the second bang, Flynn yanked it open.

"This man is not my lawyer," I said.

I turned my back on Cortez and walked into the hall.

After Cortez left, they put me back in the private inter-view room. Another hour passed. Flynn didn't return to question me. No one did. They just left me there. Left me to sit and stew, then to pace, then to bang at the door trying to get someone's attention.

Savannah was out there, unprotected, with strangers who had no idea of the danger she faced. Yet again I was constrained by human laws. By law, they could hold me here for any "reasonable length of time" before charging me. What was reasonable? Depended on the person supplying the definition. Right then, for all I cared, they could go ahead and charge me with murder, so long as I could post bail and take Savannah home.

Nearly two hours passed before the door opened again.

"Your new lawyer," said an officer I hadn't met.

For one fleeting moment, one desperate moment of naive hope, I thought the Elders had found someone to represent me. Instead, in walked ... Lucas Cortez.

❧ A Twelve-Step Plan

"GODDAMN IT!" I SAID. "I told you people this man is not my—"

Before I could finish, I found myself once again caught in a binding spell. The officer, having paid no attention, left me alone with Cortez. When the door shut, Cortez undid the spell. I grabbed for the door handle, but he caught my hand.

"You scheming son of a bitch! I don't believe this. I told them—I told that detective—no one's listening to me! Well, they're going to listen now. I didn't sign anything, and if you have papers with my signature, I'll prove it's a forgery. Whatever the penalty is for misrepresenting a client—"

"They aren't going to lay charges."

Pause. "What?"

"They don't have enough evidence to lay charges now, and I doubt they will ever find the evidence they need. The injuries to Mr. Cary make it impossible to argue that you pushed him out the window. Furthermore, I have proven that there is no evidence to indicate you came in physical contact with Mr. Cary at the time of his death. His office was cleaned Saturday night. The only fingerprints found within belong to Mr. Cary and his cleaner, as do the only footprints on the vacuumed carpet near his desk. The scene shows no sign of a struggle. Nor does his body. It would appear that Mr. Cary's chair was lifted from the floor without human intervention and propelled with great force out the window."

"How are they explaining that?"

"They aren't. While they may believe you did it, they cannot prove it."

"How do—" I stopped. "They think I used witchcraft?"

"That is the general consensus, though wisely left unmentioned on all official papers. Since such an accusation would never pass a grand jury, you are free." Cortez checked his watch. "We should leave. I believe Savannah is growing quite restless. We have to complete some paperwork before you can be released. I must insist that you refrain from speaking to any law enforcement officers we encounter during our departure. As your lawyer, I will handle all external communications herein."

"As my lawyer . . . ?"

"I believe I have proven my intentions are—"

"Above reproach?" I met his gaze, keeping my voice soft. "But they aren't, are they?"

"I am not working for—"

"No, you probably aren't. I accept your story, that you're here to offer your services to further your career . . . at my ex- pense."

"I'm not—"

"Do I blame you for it? No. I run a business. I know what someone our age needs to do to get ahead. I need to undercut the competition. You need to take cases the competition won't touch. If you want to bill me for today, go ahead. I'll pay. You earned it. But I can't—won't—work with you. You're a stranger. You're a sorcerer. I can't trust you. It all comes down to that."

I turned and walked away.

Finishing the paperwork proved an ordeal. The grim-faced desk clerk filled out forms so slowly you'd think his wrist was broken. Worse yet, Flynn and the other detectives stood off to the side, watching me with glares that said I wasn't fooling them, I was simply another criminal who'd gotten away with murder.

Cortez, as one might expect, didn't accept defeat so easily. He stuck around to help me with the paperwork, and I let him. Why? Because six hours in captivity was enough for me. If the police knew that my freedom had been arranged by a man misrepresenting himself as my lawyer, could they toss me back inside? Accuse me of fraud? Probably not, but I didn't know the legalities involved and, now that I was free, I wasn't about to start posing any hypothetical questions that might land me in a jail cell. I didn't say that Cortez was my lawyer and I didn't say he wasn't. I ignored him and let the police draw their own conclusions.

When I went to collect Savannah, Cortez took his leave. He said nothing more than a murmured goodbye. To be honest, I felt a bit sorry for him. Sorcerer or not, he had helped me, and it hadn't done him a damn bit of good. I hoped he took me up on my offer of payment. At least then his efforts would have some reward.

I found Savannah in the waiting room—the public waiting room—amidst a half-dozen strangers, none of them the "armed state troopers" Detective Flynn had mentioned. Anyone could have walked into that room, including Leah. On the heels of my anger came another silent thanks to Lucas Cortez for getting me out. If he didn't bill me, I promised myself I'd track him down and pay him anyway.

The waiting room looked like waiting rooms everywhere, with cheap furniture, yellowing posters, and stacks of year-old magazines. Savannah had laid claim to a row of three chairs and was lying across them, sound asleep.

I knelt beside her and gently shook her shoulder. She mumbled something and knocked my hand away.

"Savannah, hon, time to go home."

Her eyes opened. She blinked and struggled to focus. "Home?" She pushed up onto her elbow and smiled. "They let you out?"

I nodded. "I'm free to go. They aren't laying charges."

At my words, an elderly woman turned to stare at me, then mumbled something to the man beside her. I was struck by the overwhelming urge to explain, to turn to these strangers and tell them I hadn't done anything wrong, that my being here was a mistake. I bit it back and tugged Savannah to her feet.

"Have you been out here the whole time?" I asked.

She nodded sleepily.

"I'm so sorry, hon."

"Not your fault," she said, stifling a yawn. "It was

okay. There were cops around. Leah wouldn't try something here." She turned to me. "What happened in there? Did they fingerprint you and everything? Are you going to have a record?"

"God, I hope not. Come on. Let's get out of here and I'll explain what I can."

There was a small crowd at the front door. Well, "small" in comparison to, say, the crowd at Fenway Park on opening day. I saw some media types, some placard-waving types, some rubber-necker ghoul types, and decided I'd seen enough. They were probably there covering a "real" event, something completely unrelated to me, but I opted for the back door anyway, so I wouldn't disturb their vigil.

The police had towed my car to the station, which removed the problem of finding transportation, but it also meant they'd searched it. Though I keep a very tidy car, they'd managed to move everything that wasn't nailed down, and there were traces of powder everywhere. Fingerprint powder, I suspected, though I had no idea why they'd be dusting my car for prints. Given the low homicide rate in this area, they probably used each one as an opportunity to practice every technique they'd learned in police college.

I had a 7:30 Coven meeting in Belham, so Savannah and I grabbed a quick dinner and headed straight there without returning home.

It was 7:27 when we arrived at the Belham community center. Yes, I said *community center*. We had a standing reservation for the third Sunday of each month, when our "book club" would meet in the center's main hall. We even had the local bakery cater the event. When women from town asked to join our club, we told them, with deep regret, that our ranks were full, but took their names for our waiting list.

Our Coven had fourteen initiated witches and five neophytes. Neophytes are girls from ten to fifteen years of age. Witches attain their full powers when they first menstruate, so the neophytes are the girls newly coming into their powers. On their sixteenth birthday, assuming they've reached first menses, witches are initiated, meaning they receive voting rights and begin learning second-level spells. At twenty-one they graduate to third level, and at twenty-five to the fourth and final tier. Exceptions can be made. My mother moved me to third level at nineteen and fourth at twenty-one. And I'd have been really proud of that if Savannah hadn't already surpassed me—and she hadn't even come into her full powers yet.

As Savannah and I crossed the parking lot, a minivan pulled in. I stopped and waited as Abby's older sister, Grace, and her two daughters climbed out. Fourteen-year-old Brittany saw us, waved, and jogged over.

"Hey, Savannah, Paige," she said. "Mom said you guys weren't—"

"I thought you weren't coming," Grace said, frowning as she approached.

"I nearly didn't make it, that's for sure," I replied. "You wouldn't believe the day I've had."

"I heard."

"Oh? Word gets around, I guess."

Grace turned away to yell at seventeen-year-old Kylie, who was still inside the van, chatting on her cellphone.

So the Coven already knew about Cary's death? I'd . . . I'd hoped they hadn't heard. If the news hadn't reached them yet, then that would have explained why no one had come to my aid.

Cortez's words about the Coven still stung. I understood why they hadn't rallied around me at the police station: they couldn't risk associating with me. But they could have discreetly found me a lawyer, couldn't they? Or, at the very least, brought Margaret to check up on Savannah?

Grace walked with me in silence to the doors, then suddenly remembered something she'd left in the van. I offered to walk back with her, but she waved me off. When Brittany tried to follow Savannah inside, her mother called her back. I could hear them whispering as I pushed open the community center doors.

As I walked in, all chatter stopped dead and heads turned. Victoria was at the front of the room talking to Margaret. Therese saw me and motioned to Victoria. Victoria looked up and for a moment seemed stunned. Then she snapped something to Margaret and strode toward me.

"What are you doing here?" she hissed when she'd drawn close enough for no one to overhear. "Did anyone follow you? Did anyone see you come in? I can't believe you—"

"Paige!" called a voice from across the room.

It was Abby, bearing down on me, her arms spread as wide as her grin. She caught me up in a hug.

"You made it," she said. "Thank god. What a horrible day you must have had. How are you feeling, hon?"

I could have sunk into her embrace, I was so grateful.

"They dropped the charges," Savannah said.

I quickly corrected her. "There weren't any charges. The police didn't lay any."

"That's wonderful," Abby said. "We're just so glad to see you're okay." She turned to the others. "Aren't we, everyone?"

A few murmured noises of assent were heard. Not exactly a deafening show of support, but right now it was good enough.

Abby hugged me again, and used the embrace to whisper in my ear. "Just go sit down, Paige. You belong here. Don't let them say otherwise."

Victoria glared at me, then swept to her place at the front of the room. I followed and took my seat in my mother's chair. And the meeting began.

After discussing Tina Moss's pregnancy and eight-year-old Emma Alden's nasty case of chicken pox, Victoria finally deigned to acknowledge my problem. And she made it clear that it was indeed *my* problem. They'd argued against letting me take custody of Savannah from the start, and this only confirmed their fears. Their biggest concern now was not that I'd lose Savannah, but that I'd expose the Coven. It all came back to fear. So, I was to handle this on my own. In handling it, I was not to involve any other Coven witch. I was forbidden even to ask Abby for help babysitting Savannah, because it created a public link between us.

When Victoria finished, I stormed out of the building,

undoing the door lock spell, then crashing through the security perimeter and hoping the mental alarm gave the Elders a collective migraine. How dare they! The Coven existed for two purposes: to regulate witches' business and to help witches. They'd all but abdicated the first role to the interracial council. Now they were denying responsibility for the second. What the hell were we becoming? A social club for witches? Maybe we should become a real book club. At least then we might have some hope of intelligent conversation.

I strode across the empty baseball field, fuming, but knowing I couldn't leave. Savannah was still inside. The Elders wouldn't allow her or anyone else to come after me. Like a child throwing a tantrum, I was expected to walk it off and return.

"May I assume it's not going well?"

I wheeled to see Cortez behind me. Before I could blast him, he continued.

"Yesterday I noted a seven-thirty book club appointment on your calendar, which I feared you might be obstinate enough to attend, despite the danger inherent in pursuing regular activities—"

"Speak English," I snapped.

He continued, unperturbed. "However, I now realize that you were not acting rashly in attending a mere book club, but instead wisely conferring with your Coven and enlisting their help implementing our plan. Now, as you may recall, step three of the initial list requires enlisting the members of your Coven to discreetly support you—"

"Forget it, counselor. They aren't going to be

supporting me, discreetly or otherwise. I am hereby forbidden to impose my problem—*my* problem—on any member of the Coven."

I regretted the words as they left my mouth. Before I could backtrack, though, Cortez murmured, "I'll handle this," and strode off, leaving me trapped in a split second of blind panic as I realized what he was about to do. By the time I tore after him, he was at the community center doors. He gestured sharply, undoing any spells, and marched through.

❧ Fox in the Henhouse

I GOT TO THE MEETING-ROOM DOOR as Cortez started to speak.

"Ladies," he said. "I apologize for interrupting your meeting."

A collective gasp drowned him out as eighteen witches realized they had a sorcerer in their midst. And what did they do? Hex him? Cast repelling spells? To my embarrassment—to my shame—they drew back, chattering like a bunch of chickens seeing a fox in the henhouse. Witches in their prime, witches with fifty years of spellcasting experience, cowering before a twenty-five-year-old sorcerer. Only Savannah stayed where she was, perched on the pastry table.

"You again?" she said. "You don't take a hint, do you?"

"He's—" Therese stammered. "He's a—"

"A sorcerer," Savannah said. "Get over it."

"Lucas Cortez," he said, striding to the front of the room. "As you know, Paige is undergoing a custody challenge and, as a result, has now been implicated in a murder investigation. In order to prevent further legal proceedings and protect Paige's reputation, there are several actions I will require from each of you."

At this point I could have jumped in and explained

that he wasn't my lawyer. But I didn't. I was still smarting from the Coven's rejection. Maybe if they thought I was forced to accept outside help—from a sorcerer, no less—they'd change their minds. And maybe, yes, maybe a small part of me liked watching the Elders squirm.

Cortez hefted his satchel onto the front table. "I don't suppose you have access to an overhead projector?"

No one answered. No one even moved. Savannah jumped off the table, crossed the room, handed him a marker, and pointed to the flip chart. Then she sauntered back to the pastry table, grinning, and winked at me before resuming her perch.

I'd have to speak to Savannah about taking pleasure in the discomfort of others. Still, it was kind of funny, Cortez standing up there, writing down his list, explaining each point, so serious and intent, as the Coven gawked, each one of them hearing nothing but the endless loop of an internal voice repeating, "A sorcerer? Is that really a sorcerer?"

"Are there any questions?" Cortez asked after his presentation.

Silence.

Eleven-year-old Megan, the youngest neophyte, raised her hand. "Are you a bad sorcerer?"

"I lack some proficiency in the higher-order spells, but, at the risk of sounding overconfident, I must say there are worse sorcerers."

I sputtered a laugh, covering it with a cough.

"Mr. Cortez is right," Abby said. "We all need to come together and help Paige in any way we can."

Silence. Dead silence.

"And on that note," I muttered under my breath.

"Cortez," murmured Sophie Moss, who at ninety-three was the oldest witch in the Coven and fast succumbing to Alzheimer's. "I knew a Cortez once. Benicio Cortez. Back in seventy-two, no, seventy-nine. The Miami affair. Horrible—" She stopped, blinked, frowned, then looked at Cortez. "Who are you, boy? This is a private meeting."

On that fitting note of mental acuity, the meeting ended.

After the meeting adjourned, Savannah walked over to Cortez as every other witch practically tripped over her own feet getting as far from him as possible. I was heading to the front of the room to join Savannah and Cortez when the Elders waylaid me.

"Now I have seen everything," Victoria said. "Your mother must be rolling in her grave. Hiring a sorcerer—"

"I haven't hired him," I said. "But I have to admit, I'm considering it. At least someone is offering to help me."

"A sorcerer, Paige?" Margaret said. "Really, I can't help but wonder if you're doing this to spite us. Even speaking to a sorcerer is against Coven policy, and you've obviously been doing that." She glanced toward the front of the room, where Savannah was chatting with Cortez. "And allowing my niece to do the same."

"Only because your niece is getting zero help from her aunt," I said.

Therese motioned for me to lower my voice. I didn't.

"Yes, I've talked to him. Why? Because he is the only person who's offered to help me. He got me out of jail today. You three couldn't even bother sending Margaret to the police station to make sure Savannah was safe. You know I'm not the type who likes to ask for help, but I'm asking now."

"You don't need a sorcerer."

"No, I need my Coven."

"Get rid of the sorcerer," Victoria said.

"And then you'll help me?"

"I'm not making a deal," she said. "I'm giving an order. Get rid of him—now."

With that, she turned and left, the other two trailing in her wake.

Cortez materialized at my shoulder. "Perhaps you'd care to reconsider my offer?" he murmured.

I saw the Elders watching us. Victoria's glare ordered me to get rid of Cortez. The urge to flip her the finger was almost overwhelming. Instead, I did the figurative equivalent.

"You're right," I said to Cortez, voice raised. "We should talk. Savannah, come on, we're going."

I motioned for Cortez to lead the way.

We drove to Starbucks in Belham—taking separate cars, of course. After I'd parked, Cortez took the spot in front of me and still managed to be standing beside my door before I pulled my key from the ignition. He didn't try to open my door for me, but once I pushed it open, he held it steady while I got out of the car.

I ordered Savannah a child-sized hot chocolate. She changed it to a venti caffé mocha. I downsized that to a small decaf caffé mocha. She negotiated a chocolate chip brownie and we settled. Here this stuff was finally getting easier for me and Kristof Nast wanted to spoil it all. Very unfair.

Although the place wasn't exactly booming at nine-thirty on a Sunday night, Cortez opted for a side room where the staff had already put the chairs upside down on the tables. As we headed in, the cashier leaned over the counter, a half-pound of necklaces and amulets clanging against the laminate.

"That section's closed," she said.

"We'll tidy up when we're done," Cortez replied, and nudged us back to the farthest table. Once we were seated, he said to Savannah, "I'm afraid this is going to be another of those very boring conversations. There's a magazine stand over there." He reached for his wallet. "May I buy you something to read?"

"Nice try," she said, and slurped a mouthful of whipped cream.

"All right, then. Let's review that list I gave you."

"Didn't bring it."

"That's quite all right." He hoisted his satchel to the table. "I have extra copies."

"Fine," she said, taking the five dollar bill from his hand. "I don't know why you're bothering, we aren't going to hire you. If we wanted a sorcerer lawyer, I could get someone a whole lot older and more experienced than you."

"I'll remember that."

While I watched Savannah buy her magazine, Cortez shuffled papers. Only when she'd settled at a table across the room did I turn my attention to him.

"Okay," I said. "You want to persuade me that you're on my side? Skip the lists. Tell me everything you know about Cabals. And I mean *everything*."

"Everything?" He checked his watch. "I believe they close in a couple of hours."

"You have thirty minutes," I said. "Fill it."

He did—the full thirty minutes. I figured he'd toss me a few tidbits and hope that would be enough to shut me up. Instead, he laid it all on the table, literally, drawing me diagrams and maps, listing key figures, and so on.

Here's the condensed version. Pretty much everything I'd heard about Cabals was true. Cabals were very old, established groups formed around a central sorcerer family, like a family-run business—but think Mafia, not the neighborhood deli. That's my comparison, not Cortez's; he never mentioned the Mafia, though the parallels were obvious. Both were ultra-secretive, family-oriented organizations. Both insisted on complete employee loyalty, enforced through threats of violence. Both mixed criminal activity with legitimate enterprise. Cortez didn't try to gloss over the uglier parts, simply stated them as fact and moved on.

In structure, though, the Cabal was more Donald Trump than Al Capone. At the top was the CEO, the head of the sorcerer family. Next came the board of directors, composed of the CEO's family, radiating out in power from sons to brothers to nephews to cousins. Within the lower ranks you had unrelated sorcerers, half-demons, necromancers, shamans—whomever the Cabal could hire. No werewolves or vampires, though. According to Cortez, the Cabals had strict policies against employing any supernatural being who might mistake them for lunch.

Everyone in the Cabal, high and low, pursued the same goals: gaining money and power for the Cabal. The more business they brought in, the quicker they rose through the ranks. The more profitable the company was, the more the employees received in year-end bonuses and stock options. Yes, Cabals were listed on the NYSE. Might be a nice investment, too, if you don't mind a little blood on your dividends.

On the surface, Cabals seemed more benign than the Mafia—no car bombs or shootouts. Sorcerers were not common hoodlums. Oh no, these guys were serious businessmen. Double-cross a Cabal and they wouldn't blow up your house and family. Instead, they'd have an incendiary half-demon torch the place, making it look like an electrical accident. Then a necromancer would torture your family's souls until you gave the Cabal what they wanted. Of course, Cortez didn't say this, but he said enough to let me read between the lines.

If all this was true, why didn't the interracial council do something about it? Now I understood Robert Vasic's concern.

"What part is Leah playing in all this?" I asked.

"Only a member of the Nast Cabal could answer that

with any certainty. Whatever information I could impart would be based purely on rumor, and I prefer to deal in fact."

"I'll settle for hearsay. What have you heard?"

"I'm not comfortable—"

"Let me start, then. Last year, Leah and a sorcerer named Isaac Katzen infiltrated a human project to kidnap supernaturals, Katzen as an informant and Leah as a captive. Their plan was for Katzen to point out powerful supernaturals, let the humans take the risks of capturing and containing them, then have Leah win their confidence while imprisoned. A cheap and easy way to recruit supernaturals for the Nast Cabal—"

"They weren't working for any Cabal, that much I know as fact. It is assumed that they were attempting to build their own organization, a scaled-down version of a Cabal."

"Go on."

He hesitated, then said, "They say Leah approached the Nast Cabal after you killed Katzen."

I bit back a denial. I hadn't killed Katzen—I had only brought about the circumstances that led to his death—but if this sorcerer thought I was capable of killing his kind, maybe that wasn't such a bad thing.

Cortez continued, "There have been rumors about Savannah's paternity for years, though Kristof was either unable to locate the girl or unwilling to incur Eve's wrath by interfering in their lives. With Eve gone, Leah offered to help him get Savannah."

"So you think Nast really is her father?"

"I don't know, and I think it has little or no bearing

on the case. The Nasts want Savannah—that's all that matters."

I sipped my chai. "How bad is he? This Kristof? Well, I mean, you may not consider him 'bad,' I guess, but how . . . criminal is he?"

"I understand the concept of good and evil, Paige. Most sorcerers do, they simply choose the wrong side. Among sorcerers, Kristof Nast's reputation is average, meaning you should consider him a dangerous man. As heir to the Nast Cabal, he is backed by immense resources."

I leaned back and shook my head. "At least now I know where the Illuminati myth comes from."

"If it arises from the Cabals, the connections are tenuous at best. The Illuminati were believed to be a secret group of powerful men using supernatural means to overthrow the government. A Cabal's interest in politics is minimal, and far more mundane. Yes, there are Cabal members in government, but only to support fiscal policies that benefit the Cabal. It's all about money. Remember that, Paige: the Cabal does nothing that acts against its own financial interests. It's not the Illuminati or the supernatural Mafia or a Satanic cult. It doesn't ritually murder people. It doesn't abduct, abuse, or kill children—"

"Oh, right. Savannah's thirteen, so technically she's not a child."

He continued in the same calm voice. "What I meant is that they don't follow the classic description of a Satanic cult in that they do not abduct children for ritualistic purposes. To the Cabal, Savannah means profit. Always look at the bottom line and you'll be better prepared to deal with the Cabals."

I checked my watch.

"Yes, I know," Cortez said. "My time is up."

I sipped my nearly cold chai and stared down at the diagrams Cortez had made. Now what? Send Cortez packing again? I didn't see the point, he'd only come back. To be honest, though, it was more than that. The guy had helped me. Really helped me.

It was a sad world when a witch had to rely on a work-starved sorcerer, but I couldn't waste my time whining about how things should be. Cortez was offering assistance when no one else would, and I'd be a fool to refuse. I had seen absolutely no proof that he was anything other than what he claimed to be: a young lawyer willing to take on the shittiest cases to launch his career.

"What would you charge?" I asked.

He took a sheet from his satchel and spent the next few minutes explaining the fee schedule. His terms were reasonable and fair, with a written guarantee that every charge would be explained in advance and he wouldn't do any work that I hadn't pre-approved.

"The moment you feel my services are no longer fulfilling expectations, you may dismiss me," he said. "All that will be clearly outlined in a contract, which I would strongly suggest you have examined by another legal professional before signing."

When I hesitated, he folded the fee schedule in half and passed it to me, then placed his business card on top.

"Take tonight to think about it. If, in the meantime, you have any questions, call me, no matter what the hour."

I reached for the paper, but he laid his fingertips lightly over it, pressing it to the table, and met my gaze.

"Remember, Paige, I can offer you more than normal legal help. No human lawyer you could engage will understand this situation as I do. More than that, should you require additional protection, I will be there. As I've said, I'm not the most proficient sorcerer, but I can help, and I'm quite willing to do so. It may come to that."

"I know."

He nodded. "I'll speak to you in the morning, then."

With that, he gathered his papers and left.

Aloha! ❧

ON THE WAY HOME, Savannah asked what Cortez had said. In the midst of brushing her off, I stopped myself and, instead, told her Cortez's Cabal story.

"I don't get it," she said when I finished. "Okay, maybe Leah wants me for her Cabal. That makes sense. These Cabals, they're always recruiting. Mom told me if someone ever tries to sign me up, I should—" Savannah paused. "Anyway, she said they're bad news. Like joining a street gang. You join, you join for life."

"Did your mom say . . . anything else about the Cabals?"

"Not really. She said they'd come after me, so this makes sense, what Leah's Cabal is doing. But if she wants me, why doesn't she take me? She's a Volo. She could run our car off the road and grab me before we knew what hit us. So why doesn't she?"

Savannah peered at me through the darkness of the car's interior. I glanced into my side mirror, averting my eyes from hers. Okay, this had gone too far. I had to say something.

"Cortez says Leah works for the Nast Cabal."

"Huh."

"You've heard of them?"

She shook her head. "My mom never mentioned names."

"But she said a Cabal might come for you. Did she mention any Cabal in particular? Or why they'd want you?"

"Oh, I know why they'd want me."

I held my breath and waited for her to go on.

"Cabals only hire one witch, see? They'd probably rather not hire any at all, but we've got the best protection and healing spells, so they overlook the whole witch–sorcerer feud just enough to hire one of us. Anyway, they figure if they have to hire a witch, they want a good one. My mom was real good, but she told them where to stick it. She said they'd come for me, and I wasn't to listen to any of their lies."

"Lies?" I looked at her. "Was there any lie in particular?"

Savannah shook her head.

I hesitated, then forced myself to press on. "It might be tempting, to be offered a place in a Cabal. Money, power . . . they probably have a lot to offer."

"Not to a witch. A Cabal witch is strictly an employee. You get a paycheck, but no perks."

"But what if you did get the perks? What if they offered you more than the standard package?"

"I'm not dumb, Paige. Whatever they offered me, I'd know they were lying. No matter how good a witch I might be, to them I'm still only a witch."

Such a chillingly accurate answer, so easily given. What was it like, to be so young and yet so keenly aware of your place in the world?

"It's funny, you know," she continued. "All those times my mom warned me and I barely listened. I thought, why is she telling me this? If they come after me, she'll be here. She'll always be here. You just figure that. You don't think . . . maybe she won't. Did you ever think— with your mom—that something like that could happen? That one day she'd be there, and then she wouldn't?"

I shook my head.

Savannah continued, "Sometimes . . . sometimes I have these dreams. Mom's shaking me and I wake up and I tell her what happened, and she laughs and tells me I was just having a nightmare, and everything's okay, but then I really wake up, and she's not there."

"I've had those."

"Hurts, doesn't it?"

"More than I ever imagined."

We drove a few miles in silence. Then Savannah shifted in her seat and cleared her throat.

"So, are you hiring Lucas?"

I managed a forced laugh. "So it's 'Lucas' now?"

"It suits him. So, are you hiring him or what?"

My natural inclination, as always, was to give her a simple, pat answer, but I felt as if in these past few days we'd cracked open the door between us, and I didn't want to slam it shut now. So I eased it open another inch by telling her Cortez's alleged motivation for taking the case, then went a step further and asked her opinion of it.

"Makes sense," she said. "He's right. With the Cabals, either you're for them or against them. Especially if you're a sorcerer. Those lawyers my mom knew, the ones

I said might help you, they do the same thing Lucas is doing. They take cases against the Cabals."

"Isn't that dangerous?"

"Not really. It's weird that way. If a supernatural goes up against the Cabals, they'll squash him like a bug. But a lawyer with a client who went against the Cabals, or a doctor who fixed up a supernatural attacked by the Cabals—they don't bother him. Mom says the Cabals are pretty fair that way. You don't bother them, they don't bother you."

"Well, I didn't bother them, and they sure are bothering me."

"But you're only a witch. Lucas is a sorcerer. Makes a difference, you know. So, are you hiring him?"

"Maybe. Probably." I glanced over at her. "What do you think?"

"I think you should. He seems all right. For a sorcerer."

There were people outside my house. More than a few. When I neared the house, no one turned. They probably didn't recognize my car—yet. From twenty feet away I hit the garage door opener, and I zoomed inside before anyone could stop me. We went in through the little-used door linking the garage to the front hall, avoiding any potential confrontations.

After sending Savannah to bed, I faced down the dreaded answering machine. The display flashed '34.' Thirty-four messages? My god, how many did the thing hold?

Fortunately, most calls only required an intro. This is

Chris Walters from KZET—delete. Marcia Lu from *World Weekly News*—delete. Jessie Lake from Channel 7—delete. Of the first twelve calls, seven were media, including three from the same radio station, probably trying to land an impromptu interview on their show.

Of the non-media calls, one was an ex-boyfriend and one was a friend I hadn't seen since she moved to Maine in grade seven. Both were calling to see how I was doing. That was nice. Really nice. Better than the other two. The first began (extreme profanity omitted), "You're a lying, murdering *bleep*. Just wait, you *bleep*ing *bleep*. You'll get yours. Maybe the *bleep*ing cops don't—" My finger trembled as I hit the delete button. I cranked down the volume before going on to the next call. Savannah didn't need to hear that crap. *I* didn't need to hear it either, but I told myself I'd have to get used to it, grow a thicker skin.

The next call was more of the same, so I deleted it after the first expletive. Then came a message that I listened to all the way through, one that began, "Ms. Winterbourne, you don't know me, but I'm so sorry to hear what's happening to you out there," and went on to dispense more sympathy and a promise to pray for me. I needed that, I really did.

A scan through the next nine messages revealed seven media persons, one irate woman damning my soul to eternal fire, and one really sweet Wiccan from Salem offering moral support. See? Not so bad. Only 60 percent of strangers were calling for my corpse on a pyre.

I fast-forwarded through four more media calls, then heard one that jolted my spirits.

"Paige? Paige? Come on, pick up!" a familiar voice bellowed over loud rock music and high-decibel chatter. "I know you're there! It's eight o'clock at night. Where else would you be? On a date?" A whoop of laughter, then an ear-piercing whistle to catch my attention from whatever corner of the house I might be lurking in. "It's Adam! Pick up!" Pause. "Okay, fine, maybe you aren't home. I'm still in Maui. I called home and got your message. Dad's in a conference right now. I was just out having a drink, but you sounded pretty upset, so I'll head back to the hotel and give him the message. Aloha!"

What hotel? A name? Maybe a phone number? Typical. I fast-forwarded through the final messages, praying I hadn't missed Robert's call, but sure enough, there it was.

"Paige? It's Robert. I called home and got your messages—one can never rely on Adam for coherent message-taking. As impatient as ever, it seems he only listened to your first one. I won't tell him about the one concerning Leah or he'll be on the next plane to help out, which I'm sure is the last thing you want. I assume you're looking for the information you asked me to gather on Volo half-demons. As luck would have it, that's right here with me. You know how I pack: one carry-on of clothes and two suitcases filled with books and notes I don't need. I'm faxing the Volo notes to you right now. We leave for our flight in an hour, but if you get home before then, call me at (808) 555–3573. Otherwise, I will speak to you tomorrow."

I'd asked Robert for Volo information several months ago, in a spurt of foresight that I'd then forgotten to follow up on. I'd have to wait until tomorrow to find out Robert's thoughts on Cabals. Until then, it wouldn't hurt to know all I could about Leah.

✺ Demonology 101

THE FAX WAS LYING ON THE FLOOR where my machine had spit it. Thank god the police hadn't stopped by for another search. Imagine what they'd have thought if they found this. "No, detective, I'm really not a Satanist. So why am I receiving faxes on Demonology? Well, uh, it's this new Web design idea I'm working on . . ." From now on I'd be a lot more careful about what I left lying around.

To make sense of what Robert told me about Volos requires some background on demons. Demonology 101, so to speak.

Demons exist in both the physical and the spiritual world. They are arranged into hierarchies according to their degree of power. There is probably a ruling demon, someone you *really* don't want to conjure up, but I'd suspect the position changes hands, much like leadership roles in our world.

Among all the various levels, from courtier to archduke, you have your good demons and your bad demons, or to use the correct terminology, eudemons and cacodemons. When I say "good" demons, or eudemons, I don't mean they run around helping people in our world. Most demons couldn't give a damn about us. By eudemons, I'm referring to those who don't actively seek to screw up the human world.

A more accurate description would be chaotic and non-chaotic demons. Chaotic demons, or cacodemons, are almost exclusively the kind who come into contact with the rest of us. A sorcerer or witch could summon a eudemon, but most of us know so little about demonology that we wouldn't be able to distinguish a eudemon from a cacodemon anyway. Even if one said he was a eudemon, he'd probably be lying. A wise spell-caster abjures conjuring altogether.

Move from demons to half-demons. One way cacodemons like to cause trouble in our world is by fathering babies. (They're pretty darned keen on the sex part, too.) To do so, they take human form, having found that any woman with less than a forty-ounce bottle of whiskey coursing through her bloodstream does not respond favorably to seduction by large, scaled, cloven-hoofed beasts.

To be honest, we don't know what a demon's true form is, and it probably bears no resemblance to the cloven-hoofed monster of myth. When they come into the physical world, they take the shape of whatever will accomplish their goal. Want to seduce a young woman? Pull out the old "drop-dead gorgeous twenty-year-old male" disguise. My advice to young women who like to pick up guys in singles bars? Condoms prevent more than venereal disease.

Half-demons inherit the main power of their fathers. Adam's power is fire. Robert is a Tempestras, meaning he was fathered by a storm demon and has some control over weather elements like wind and rain. The degree of power depends on the demon's ranking within the hierarchy. Take the so-called fire demons. An Igneus can induce only first-degree burns. An Aduro can induce burns plus ignite flammable objects. An Exustio, like Adam, can not only burn and ignite but incinerate. The number of demons decreases per level. There are probably a dozen Igneus demons out there making babies. There is one Exustio, meaning Adam probably has only two or three "siblings" in the world.

On to Leah, then. She is a Volo, which is the top telekinetic demon category. Like Adam, she is a rarity, fathered by a singular high-ranking demon. The difference is that Adam, at twenty-four, only recently learned to use his full powers. As with spellcasters, the progression takes time. Although Adam was able to inflict burns by age twelve, it took another dozen years before he could incinerate. Leah, at thirty-one, has likely been in full possession of her power for at least five years now, giving her plenty of practice time.

Cary's death gave a good indication of what Leah could do, and it was the only clear example of her powers that I had. Yes, we'd encountered her last year and, yes, lots of objects had gone flying through the air, but there was a problem. Not only had I not witnessed anything first-hand, but there'd been a sorcerer involved, meaning it was difficult to tell where his contributions to the chaos left off and Leah's began.

Robert's research indicated that a Volo could propel an object as large as a car, though precision, distance, and speed drops as weight increases. A parked car they could probably shift a few feet. They could hurl an object as small as a book across a room with enough force to decapitate a person. Nor do they need to see what they are moving. If they can picture a nearby room from memory, they can displace objects within it.

Why hadn't Leah killed me? I don't know. Maybe the Cabal was holding her back. Cortez said they preferred using legal methods to resolve disputes, thereby minimizing the risk of exposure. So they probably hoped to win Savannah in a court battle, though that didn't mean they wouldn't let Leah off her leash if that failed.

As disturbing as Robert's report was, it was little more than I'd already expected, based on my dealings with Leah to date. Yet he did uncover two tidbits that bolstered my optimism, two possible methods of thwarting Leah. No, not crosses and holy water; such things belong in fairy tales.

First, Robert's research indicated that, unlike Exustio half-demons such as Adam, Volos' powers plummeted as their tempers flared. Piss them off enough and they'd become too flustered to concentrate. Simple psychology, really.

Second, all Volos had a tell, a physical mannerism that preceded an attack. It could be as discreet as an eye-blink or as obvious as a bloody nose, but they all did something before lashing out. Of course, that meant you had to provoke them a bunch of times before you'd discover their tell.

Upon waking, I forced myself to peek through the drawn

front curtains. The street was empty. Whew. I showered and dressed, then roused Savannah for breakfast. After we ate, I called her school and left a message saying she wouldn't be in again today but we'd stop by later for her assignments.

Then I made another call. On the third ring, he answered.

"Lucas Cortez."

"It's me—Paige. I think . . ." I swallowed and tried again. "I'd like to give this a shot. I want to hire you."

"I'm glad to hear that." His cellphone buzzed, as if he was moving. "May I suggest we meet this morning? I'd like to formulate a concrete plan of action as soon as possible."

"Sure. Do you want to come here?"

"If you're comfortable with that, it would doubtless afford the most privacy."

"That's fine."

"Shall we say . . . ten-thirty?"

I agreed and rang off. As I hung up, relief washed over me. It was going to be okay. I'd done the right thing, I was sure of it.

By 9:30, Savannah and I were both at work, me in my office and Savannah at the kitchen table. At 9:45, I gave up any hope of getting something done and turned my attention to my e-mail.

My in-basket had filled up over the weekend, 95 percent of it coming from addresses I didn't recognize. That's what I got for running a business and having my e-mail address, home phone, and fax number listed in the Yellow Pages. I created a folder entitled "Hell: Week One," scanned the list of senders, and, if I didn't recognize the name, dumped the e-mail into the folder unread. I'd have preferred to delete them, but common sense told me I shouldn't. If some maniac broke into my house and knifed this "Satan-worshiping bitch" in her sleep, maybe the police would find my killer's name buried in this heap of electronic trash.

I did the same with my faxes—a quick scan of the first page and, if it contained the words "interview" or "burn in hell," I dumped it into a file folder, then stuck the whole thing under *H*. By the time I finished sorting, I was quite proud of myself for handling things so calmly and efficiently. Over two dozen faxes and e-mails condemning me to eternal damnation, and my hands barely shook at all.

Next I made the incredibly stupid mistake of searching the Internet for references to my story. I told myself that I needed to know what was out there, what was being said. After reading the first headline—*Satanic Witch Cult Surfaces near Salem*—I really should have quit. But I had to keep going. Of the three articles I scanned, two mentioned the "missing Boston baby" rumor, one said I'd been seen skulking around at the local humane society, two accused me of being a member of some Boston "Hellfire Club" and all three said I'd been found at the site of Cary's murder "covered in blood." After that, I decided ignorance really was bliss, and turned off my computer.

It was now 10:15. Time to put on a pot of coffee for

Cortez. As I was measuring coffee into the filter, the phone rang. I checked the display. *Unknown caller*. To answer or not to answer? I chose the latter, but poised my hand over the talk button in case a friendly voice came on.

"Ms. Winterbourne, this is Julie calling from Bay Insurance . . ."

Insurance? Did I have insurance with a place called— oh wait, no, Bay Insurance was a new client. As the voice continued, I hit the talk button, but the machine kept running.

". . . cancel our order. Given the, uh, publicity, we've decided that's for the best. Please bill us for any work you've done to date."

"Hello?" I said. "Hello?"

Too late, she'd hung up. I'd lost a contract. I closed my eyes, breathed deeply, felt the sting. Why hadn't I imagined this, that my business could be hurt by the publicity? But I musn't worry about it. If they didn't want my services, screw 'em. It wasn't like I had trouble finding customers. Once or twice a week I had to turn someone down because my schedule was full. Besides, sure, I might lose a few contracts, but I might also gain some.

While I waited for the coffee to brew, I decided to slog through the rest of my phone messages. As if to prove me right, three calls later I hit this message: "Hi, it's Brock Summers from Boston. I'm with the New England Perception Group, and we'd love to have you do something for our website . . ."

Maybe the old saying is right: there's no such thing as bad publicity.

" . . . already have a website," Mr. Summers continued, "but we're very interested in having you do some enhancements. I've seen your work and I know several people in our field who'd also be interested . . ."

This was good. Really good.

" . . . please check out our current website at www.exor-cismsrus.com. That's e-x-o-r-c-i-s-m-s-r-u-s, all one word. We do seances, poltergeist exterminations, exorcisms, of course—"

I hit delete and sank into a kitchen chair.

"Uh, Paige?"

Savannah stood in the kitchen doorway, binoculars in her hand and a troubled look in her eyes. She glanced over her shoulder, toward the front window.

"Let me guess, we have new lawn ornaments."

She didn't smile. "No, that's not—well, yes, we do, but they've been there for a while. I was peeking out now and then, seeing how many there were. Then, a few minutes ago, I thought I saw a woman with red hair standing down the street, so I grabbed these to check."

I jolted up from the chair. "Leah."

Savannah nodded, and fidgeted with the binoculars. "I was watching her—"

"You don't need to worry, hon. Robert faxed me some notes last night about Volos, and if she's more than twenty yards away, she's too far to hurt us. One good thing about having a crowd out front is that she won't dare get too close."

"It's—it's not that." She glanced at the window again and squinted, as if trying to see Leah in the distance. "I was watching, right? And this car drove up. She walked onto the road, and the driver pulled over and . . ." Savannah passed me the glasses. "I think you need to see this. You can see better from my room."

I went into Savannah's room and looked out the window. There were at least a half-dozen cars lining our street, but my gaze went immediately to one parked five doors down, across the road. As I saw the small white four-door, my breath caught. I told myself I was wrong. It was a common type of car. But even as I lifted the binoculars to my eyes, I knew what I would see.

There were two people in the front of the car. Leah sat in the passenger's seat, and on the driver's side— Lucas Cortez.

"Maybe there's an explanation," Savannah said.

"If there is, I'm getting it now."

I strode into the kitchen, picked up the cordless phone, and hit redial. The line connected to Cortez's cellphone. He answered on the third ring.

"Lucas Cortez."

"Hey, it's me, Paige," I said, forcing lightness into my voice. "Any chance you could pick up some cream on the way into town? There's a corner store right off the highway. Are you there yet?"

"No, not yet. I'm running a few minutes behind."

The lie came smoothly, without a nanosecond of hesitation. You bastard. You lying bastard. I clutched the phone tighter.

"Do you prefer table cream or half-and-half?" he asked.

"Half-and-half," I managed to say.

I lifted the binoculars. He was still there. Beside him, Leah was leaning back against the passenger door.

I continued, "Oh, and be careful when you drive in. I've got people hanging around my place. Don't pick up any hitchhikers."

A pause now. Brief, but a definite hesitation. "Yes, of course."

"Especially red-headed half-demons," I said. "They're the worst kind."

A long pause, as if he was weighing the possibility that this was a joke.

"I can explain," he said finally.

"Oh, I'm sure you can."

I hung up.

❋ Grief on the Run

AFTER HANGING UP ON CORTEZ, I stormed into the kitchen and slammed the phone into the cradle so hard that it bounced out again. I scrambled to grab it before it hit the floor. My hands were shaking so badly I could barely get it back into the cradle.

I stared down at my hands. I felt . . . I felt betrayed, and the depth of that feeling surprised me. What had I expected? It's like the parable of the scorpion and the frog. I knew what Cortez was when I let him into my life. I should have expected betrayal. But I hadn't. At some deep level I'd trusted him, and in some ways his betrayal stung even more than the Coven's. With the Coven, I'd hoped for support, but deep down I knew better than to expect it. They'd told me from the start that they wouldn't help. That was rejection, but not betrayal. Cortez had taken advantage of that rejection to insinuate himself in my life.

"Paige?"

I turned to Savannah.

"I thought he was okay too," she said. "He tricked us both."

The phone rang. I knew who it was without checking caller ID. He'd had just enough time to get Leah out of his car. I let the machine pick up.

"Paige? It's Lucas. Please pick up. I'd like to speak to you."

"Yeah," Savannah muttered. "I'm sure you would."

"I can explain," he continued. "I was driving to your house and Leah hailed me. Naturally, I was curious, so I pulled over and she asked to speak to me. I agreed and—"

I grabbed the receiver. "I don't care why the hell you spoke to her. You lied about it."

"And that was a mistake. I fully admit that, Paige. You caught me off guard when you called and—"

"And you had to stumble and stammer for an excuse, right? Bullshit. You lied without a moment's hesitation. You lied so smoothly I bet a lie detector wouldn't have caught it. I don't care about why you spoke to Leah, I care about how easily you lied, and do you know why? Because now I know you've got a talent for it."

A slight pause. "Yes, that's true, but—"

"Well, at least you're honest about that. You're a skilled liar, Cortez, and that tells me that I can't believe anything you've said to me so far."

"I can see where—"

"What I saw out there today only convinces me that my first instinct was right: you're working for the Nasts. I told myself that doesn't make sense, but now I get it. They made sure it wouldn't make sense."

"How—?"

"I'm a programmer, right? I think logically. Send me a smooth, sophisticated, well-dressed sorcerer, and I'd see through that scam in a minute. But send you and I'll say, This guy can't work for a Cabal. It doesn't make sense. It's not logical. And that was the whole idea."

A pause, so long I wondered if he'd hung up.

"I believe I can clear this up," he said at last.

"Oh, you do, do you?"

"I haven't been entirely forthright with you, Paige."

"*Wow*. Really?"

"I don't mean about being associated with the Nasts—I'm not. Nor was my motivation, as stated, entirely inaccurate, though I am guilty more of omission than deceit."

"Stop right there," I said. "Whatever you tell me next will just be more lies. I don't want to hear them."

"Paige, please, just listen. I told you the version of my story which I believed you would find most palatable and would therefore—"

"Hanging up now," I said.

"*Wait!* You are, I believe, well acquainted with Robert Vasic. You're friends with his stepson, Adam. Would I be correct in assuming you trust him?"

"Adam?"

"Robert."

"What does Robert have—?"

"Ask Robert who I am."

"What?"

"Ask Robert who Lucas Cortez is. He doesn't know me personally, but we do have mutual acquaintances, and if Robert is not inclined to vouch for my integrity, then he will be able to recommend someone who can. Will you do that?"

"What's he going to tell me?"

Cortez paused again. "I think, perhaps, at this stage

it would be better if you heard it from Robert first. If I tell you, and you choose not to believe me, you may decide not to follow up with a call to Robert. Please call him, Paige. Then phone me back. I'll be at my motel."

I hung up.

"What'd he say?" Savannah asked.

I shook my head. "Honestly, I have no idea."

"Yeah, sometimes I can't figure it out either. Too many big words."

I hesitated, then dialed Robert's number, but got the machine again and didn't bother leaving a message. My finger was still on the disconnect button when the phone rang. "Williams & Shaw Legal" and a Boston phone number scrolled across the call display. Had my commercial lawyer found someone willing to represent me? God, I hoped so.

"May I speak to Paige Winterbourne?" a nasally female voice asked.

"Speaking."

"This is Roberta Shaw. I'm an attorney with Williams & Shaw. Our firm works with the Cary Law Office in East Falls. Mr. Cary has asked me to assist with the disposal of his son's current caseload. I've come across your folder among the deceased's files."

"Umm, right. Actually, I am looking for someone to take over the case. If anyone at your firm would be interested—"

"We would not," Shaw said, the chill in her voice bordering on Arctic. "I am simply calling to request that you take possession of your file immediately. It is not in perfect order, but I am not about to ask Mr. Cary or his daughter-in-law to transcribe any of the notes. Under the circumstances, they shouldn't need to look at this file again. Out of consideration to the family, I will ask that you refer all questions to me. The billing will also come from my office."

"Look," I said, "I don't know what you heard, but I had nothing to do with Mr. Cary's—"

"It is not my place to dispute that matter. I have many files to go through today, Ms. Winterbourne. I would like you to collect yours this afternoon."

"Fine. I'll pick it up at the office—"

"That would hardly be appropriate, would it?"

I gritted my teeth. "Where do you suggest—"

"I will be at the Barton Funeral Home all afternoon. They've established an office for me in the funeral parlor, so I may consult with Mr. Cary easily while disturbing him as little as possible. You may meet me there at one o'clock."

"At Grant Cary's visitation? Now that's what I'd call inappropriate."

"You will come to the service door," she said, biting off each word as if it cost her untold effort to speak to me. "There is a parking lot at the side of the building. You turn off—" Papers shuffled. "—off Chestnut. I assume you know where the funeral home is?"

"On Elm," I said. "Beside the county hospital."

"Good. Meet me there at one, in the side parking lot by the service door. Good day, Ms. Winterbourne."

So, with Cortez out of the picture, I was now officially

on my own. If this had all happened a year ago, I'd have said "no problem" and been glad for the chance to prove myself. Last fall, when the rest of the council was reluctant to rescue Savannah, I'd been ready to go in on my own. Had I done so, I'd be dead, no question about it. I'd be dead and I might have got Savannah killed in the process. I learned my lesson then.

Now, faced with another big threat, I knew I needed help and was prepared to ask for it. But who? If I asked someone in the council, I'd put their life at risk for something that was a witch problem and should therefore be handled by witches. But our Coven had abandoned us. Where did that leave us?

I tried instead to concentrate on doing exactly what Cortez had been coming over to do: formulate a plan of action. But here I was stuck. If I went out and tracked down Sandford and Leah, I'd have to take Savannah along, and would probably end up delivering her straight into their hands. For now, the wisest course of action seemed to be to lie low, defend us against their attacks, and hope they simply decided Savannah was more trouble than she was worth. While it irked me to take a defensive position, at this point I refused to take chances with Savannah's life.

At twelve-thirty, I checked the crowd outside. Maybe I was being optimistic, but it seemed to be shrinking. When I went to tell Savannah to get ready, I found her lying on her back in bed. She opened her eyes when I walked in.

"Napping?" I asked.

She shook her head. "Not feeling so good."

"You're sick?" I hurried to the bedside. "You should have told me, hon. Is it your head or your stomach?"

"Both . . . I mean, neither. I don't know." She scrunched her nose. "I just feel . . . weird."

I didn't see any obvious signs of illness. Her temperature was normal, her skin wasn't flushed, and her eyes looked tired but clear. Probably stress. I hadn't been feeling so hot myself lately.

"You could be coming down with something," I said. "I was supposed to go out, but it can wait."

"No," Savannah said, pushing herself up off the covers. "I want to go. I'll probably feel better once I get outside."

"Are you sure?"

She nodded. "Maybe we can rent some videos."

"All right, then. Get ready."

"I bet it's a closed casket," Savannah said as I turned onto Chestnut.

An image of Cary's mangled corpse shot through my brain. I forced it back.

"Well, we aren't finding out," I said. "I'm not setting foot anywhere near that room."

"Too bad it wasn't one of those drive-thru viewings. Then we could see him without anyone knowing."

"Drive-thru viewings?"

"Haven't you heard about those? They had one in Phoenix when my mom and I lived there. We drove by once to see it. It's like a drive-thru bank teller, only you look in the window and there's the dead guy."

"Grief on the run."

"People are real busy these days. You gotta make it easy." She grinned and shifted in her seat. "Isn't that weird? I mean, think about it. You drive up—and then what? Talk into some drive-thru speaker? Tell the guy how much you'll miss him?"

"Just as long as he doesn't sit up and ask if you'd like fries with that."

Savannah laughed. "Humans are so weird." She shifted in her seat again.

"Do you have to go to the bathroom?"

"No. I'm just getting sore from sitting still."

"We've only gone five blocks."

She shrugged. "I dunno. Maybe I've got the flu."

"How's your stomach?"

"Okay, I guess."

I flashed back through everything she'd eaten in the last day. Then my gut knotted. "Did Cortez get near your caffé mocha last night?"

"Huh?" She looked over at me. "You think he poisoned me? Nah. He didn't touch my drink. Besides, potions aren't like that. If someone gives you one, you get sick all at once. This comes and goes. Oh, wait . . . there, it's gone. See?" She twisted to look over her shoulder. "Isn't the funeral home on Elm?"

"Yes—damn!"

I swung the car into the nearest laneway and turned around. As I'd said, the funeral home was next to the local hospital. Actually, the two buildings were attached, maybe for ease of transporting those who didn't respond favorably to treatment. The hospital also afforded an excellent view of the adjacent local cemetery, which the patients must find most heartening.

The lot beside the funeral home was full, so I had to park behind the hospital. With Savannah trailing along behind me, I fairly scampered around to the mortuary, so worried about being seen that I wiggled through a tall hedge rather than walk along the road. Once in the funeral home parking lot, I checked to make sure no one was coming or going, then dashed across to the side door and knocked.

"I think a branch scratched my back," Savannah said. "Who cares if someone sees us? You didn't kill the guy."

"I know, but it would be disrespectful. I don't want to cause any more trouble."

Before she could answer, the door swung open. A woman in her mid-forties peered out, her doughy face fixed in a scowl that seemed more habit than intent.

"Yes?" Before I could answer, she nodded. "Ms. Winterbourne. Good. Come in."

I would rather have stayed outside, but she released the door and vanished into the room before I could protest. I ushered Savannah in, then stepped through into a storeroom. Amidst the piles of boxes was a folding chair and a table covered with files.

Roberta Shaw wore a linen dress, smartly fashionable and tailor-made; my mother ran her own dressmaking business, so I can tell a good piece from a Wal-Mart bargain. Though the dress was top-of-the-line, the expense was wasted. Like too many large women, Shaw made the mistake of choosing oversized clothing, turning an expensive dress into a shapeless piece of sackcloth that fell in folds around her.

As my eyes adjusted to the dimly lit storeroom, Shaw settled into her chair and busied herself with her papers. I waited a few minutes, then cleared my throat.

"I'd—uh—like to get going," I said. "I'm not comfortable being here."

"Wait."

I did. For another two minutes. Then, before I could comment again, Savannah sighed—loudly.

"We don't have all day, you know," Savannah said.

Shaw glared, not at Savannah, but at me, as if Savannah's rudeness could be no one's fault but my own.

"I'm sorry," I said. "She's not feeling well. If you're not ready, we could grab lunch, then come back."

"Here," she said, thrusting a file folder at me. "The bill is on top. We require a certified check, which you can courier to the address shown. Under no circumstances are you to contact the Carys regarding payment or anything else related to your case. If you have questions—"

"Call you. I get the idea."

I walked to the door, yanked on the handle, and stumbled backward when it failed to open. How's that for a gracious exit? Regaining my balance and my dignity, I grasped the handle again, turned, and pushed. Still nothing.

"Is there a lock?" I said, peering down at the handle.

"Just turn and pull, as with any exterior door."

Bitch. I almost said it aloud. Unlike Savannah, though,

my upbringing did not permit me to do any such thing. I tried the door again. Nothing happened.

"It's jammed," I said.

Shaw sighed and heaved herself from the chair. Crossing the room, she waved me out of the way, took hold of the handle, and yanked. The door remained closed. From the other side, I heard voices.

"Someone's out there," I said. "Maybe they can open the door from the outside—"

"No. I will not have you bothering the mourners. I'll call the custodian."

"There's a front door, isn't there?" Savannah said.

Again, Shaw glared at me.

"For obvious reasons, you are not exiting through the front," she said, picking up her cellphone.

I sighed and leaned against the door. As I did, I caught a muffled exchange from outside. I recognized the voices.

"—really too easy," Leah said.

Sandford laughed. "What do you expect? She's a witch."

The voices faded, presumably walking around to the front. I yanked on the door again, this time murmuring an unlock spell. Nothing happened.

"Leah," I mouthed at Savannah, then turned to Shaw. "Forget the custodian. We're leaving. Now."

"You can't—" Shaw began.

Too late. I already had the interior door open and was propelling Savannah through. Shaw grabbed the back of my blouse, but I pulled free and pushed Savannah into the hallway.

A Memorial to Remember ❦

ONCE IN THE HALL, I prodded Savannah forward.

"Take the first door you see," I whispered. "Hurry, I'm right behind you."

To the left, an empty corridor snaked off into unknown territory. Sunlight radiated through a door less than twenty feet away to the right—twenty feet of hallway clogged with somber-suited mourners. I turned left. Following my advice, though, Savannah turned right, toward the front door, through the crowd.

"Sav—!" I whispered loudly, but she was out of reach and moving fast.

I lowered my eyes, prayed no one recognized me, and followed her. I'd gone less than five feet when Shaw's voice boomed from behind me.

"Paige Winterbourne, don't you dare—"

I didn't hear the rest. My name hurtled down the hallway on a blast of whispers.

"Winterbourne?"

"*Paige* Winterbourne?"

"Isn't she—"

"Oh my god—"

"Is that her?"

My first impulse was to hold my head high and march to the door. As Savannah said, I hadn't done anything wrong. But consideration won out over pride and, in deference to the mourners, I ducked my head, murmured my apologies, and hurried after Savannah. The whispers snaked after me, petering out before turning to slander.

I forced more apologies to my lips and pushed through the crowd. Ahead, a huddled quartet swallowed Savannah's thin form. I lifted my head, picking up speed, bobbing on my toes trying to see her.

The crowd around me rustled, whispers swelling into chatter. A brief commotion erupted ahead to my left, inside two large double doors. I paid no attention as I moved forward, gaze scanning hostile faces, struggling to find Savannah while not making eye contact with the mourners. Someone grabbed my arm. I only half turned, catching a glimpse of blonde hair under a black hat.

"I'm sorry," I murmured, eyes still roving the crowd ahead, searching for Savannah.

Without looking, I brushed the hands from my arm, tugging away. Someone gasped. *There!* The back of a dark head appeared near the exit. I lunged forward, but the hands caught me again, nails digging into my arm.

"I'm sorry," I said again, distractedly. "I really have to—"

I turned to brush my assailant off, then saw her face and stopped cold. Lacey Cary stared down at me with eyes rimmed in red grief and black mascara. Around us, the crowd went silent.

"How dare you?" she hissed. "Is this some kind of sick joke?"

"I'm so, so sorry," I said. "I didn't mean—it was a mistake—I needed my file."

"Your file?" Lacey's face twisted. "You—you interrupted my husband's visitation to come and ask me about your file?"

"No, I was told to pick it—" I stopped, realizing this wasn't the time to correct her. I glanced down the hall for Savannah, but didn't see her. "I'm so sorry. I'll just leave—"

Someone pushed through the crowd behind me. The ripples of movement caught my attention and I saw Shaw move into an open gap a dozen feet down the hall.

Shaw took something from the folds of her dress. A doll. The sight was so unexpected that I paused, just long enough to see her lips move . . . and to see that the doll wasn't a doll at all.

"A poppet," I whispered. "Oh god—"

I whirled to run, but not before I saw Leah step up behind Shaw. She lifted a hand and finger-waved at me.

"Savannah!" I shouted, wrenching free from Lacey and throwing myself against the crowd that blocked my path.

Something popped overhead—a small explosion. Then another and another. Glass flew everywhere, tiny razor-sharp shards of glass. Light-bulb glass. Even the sconces on the walls exploded, sinking the hallway into twilight, lit only by the curtained exit at the end. I scrambled for the front door, clawing at everything in my path. An interior door slammed, blocking the way into the front vestibule and plunging the hallway into darkness. Others doors slammed. People screamed.

Someone hit me. No, not just someone, the whole crowd. Everyone around me seemed to fly off their feet, and we shot in a screaming, seething, kicking mass through a doorway. The huge double doors slammed shut behind us, deadening the shouts and cries of those trapped in the hallway.

As I struggled up from the carpet, I looked around. We were in a large room festooned with hanging curtains. Scattered pockets of mourners stared at us. Someone ran to help Lacey to her feet.

"What's going—"

"Has someone called—"

"Goddamn it—"

With the confused shouts my own senses returned, and I leaped to my feet. I heard a small pop, a now familiar sound. I glanced up to see a chandelier over my head. I dove to the ground, covering my head just as the tiny bulbs began to explode.

Only when the shards stopped falling did I peek out, expecting pitch-dark. Instead, I found that I could see a little. Light flickered from a single unbroken chandelier bulb, giving just enough illumination to allow me to make out my surroundings.

Again I sprang to my feet, searching for an exit. People were shouting, screaming, sobbing. They banged at the sealed door and yelled into cellphones. I noticed little of it. My brain was filled with a single refrain. *Savannah*. I had to find Savannah.

I stood, oddly clear-headed amidst the confusion, and

took inventory of my situation. Main door blocked or sealed shut. No windows. No auxiliary doors. The room was roughly twenty feet square, ringed with chairs. Against the far wall was . . . a coffin.

At that moment I realized where I was: the viewing room. Thankfully, as Savannah had guessed, there was no actual viewing. The coffin was closed. Still, my gut twisted at being so close to Cary's body.

I forced myself to be calm. Around me, everyone else seemed to be calming as well, shouts turning to quiet sobbing and whispered reassurances that help was on the way.

I returned to surveying my surroundings. No windows . . . Through the muffling cushion of whispers and sobs came a low moaning. A moaning and a scratching. I hardly dared pinpoint the source. I didn't need to. I knew without looking that the noise came from the far wall. From the coffin.

In my mind I saw Shaw again, holding the poppet and reciting her incantation. I saw her and I knew what she was: a necromancer.

The scratching changed to a thumping. As the noise grew, the room went silent. Every eye turned to the coffin. A man stepped forward, grasping the edge of it.

"No!" I shouted. I dove forward, throwing myself at him. "Don't—"

He undid the latch just as my body struck his, knocking him sideways. I tried to scramble up, but my legs entwined with his and I tripped, falling against the casket. As I fought free, the lid creaked open.

I froze, heart hammering, then closed my eyes,

squeezed them as tight as I could, as tight as I had when I was four years old and mistook the creaking of the pipes for a monster in my closet. The room went quiet, so quiet I could hear the breathing of those closest to me. I opened one eye and saw . . . nothing. From my vantage point on the floor I saw only an open coffin lid.

"Close it," someone whispered. "For god's sake, close it!"

I exhaled in relief. Shaw wasn't a necromancer. Leah had probably simulated the noise in the coffin by moving something within it, hoping to trick a mourner into opening it and displaying Cary's broken remains. Another grotesque prank, designed to slow me down, to stop me from getting to Savannah.

A moan cut short my thoughts. I was still bent over, pushing myself to my feet. Rising, I saw the man who'd hurried over to close the coffin. He stood beside it, hand on the open lid, eyes round and wide. Another moan shuddered through the room, and for one moment, one wildly optimistic moment, I persuaded myself that the sound came from the man. Then a battered hand rose above the satin lining of the casket and grabbed the edge.

No one moved. I am certain that for the next ten seconds not a heart beat in the entire room. The hand grasped the side of the coffin, squeezed, then relaxed and inched down, as if stroking the smooth wood. Another moan—a gurgling, wet moan that raised every hair on my body. The tendons in the hand flexed as it grabbed tighter. Then Cary sat up.

In the dimness of that room, there passed a brief second in which Grantham Cary Jr. looked alive. Alive and whole and well. Maybe it was a trick of the darkness or the deception of a hopeful mind. He sat up and he looked alive. Lacey let out a gasp, not of horror but of exultation. Behind me, Grantham Senior sobbed, a heartbreaking cry of joy, his face fixed in such a look of longing, of hope, that I had to turn away.

Cary lifted himself out of the coffin. How? I don't know. Having seen him after his death, I knew that there shouldn't be an unbroken bone in his body. Yet I understood little of this part of necromancy. I can only say that, as we watched, he struggled from the coffin and stood. And as his form caught the light, that blessed illusion of wholeness evaporated.

The morticians had done their work, cleaning away the blood and gore . . . and it did nothing but unmask the monstrous reality of his injuries. The opposite side of his head was shaved and torn and sewn and crushed—yes, crushed—the eye gone, the cheek sunken and mangled, the nose— No, that's enough.

For a moment, the silence continued as Cary stood there, head swaying on his broken neck, his remaining eye struggling to focus, the wet moan surging from his lips as rhythmic as breathing. Then he saw Lacey. He said her name, or a terrible parody of her name, half spoken, half groaned.

Cary started toward his wife. He seemed not to walk but to drag himself, teetering and jolting, pulling himself forward. His one hand reached out toward her. The other jerked, as if he was trying to lift it but couldn't. It flopped and writhed, the fabric of the sleeve rasping against his side.

"—ac—ee—" he said.

Lacey whimpered. She stepped back. Cary stopped. His head swayed and bobbed, lips contorting into a twisted frown.

"—ac—ee?"

He reached for her. She fainted then, dropping to the ground before anyone could catch her. With her fall, the whole room snapped to life. People ran for the door, pounding and shrieking.

"—ad—" Cary groaned.

His father stopped short. As he stared at his son, his lips moved, but no sound came out. Then his hand went to his chest. Someone pulled him back, shouting for an ambulance. Across the room, a woman began to laugh, a high-pitched laugh that quickly turned to hiccuping sobs. Cary lurched around and stared at the sobbing woman.

"—wha—wha—wha—"

"Peter!" a woman's voice shouted. "Peter, where the fuck are you!"

Everyone who wasn't shocked into immobility watched a woman in a green dress emerge from the curtains behind Cary's casket.

"Peter, you fuck! I'm going to kill you!"

The woman strode into the middle of the room, stopped, and surveyed the crowd.

"Who the hell are you people? Where's Peter? I swear to God, I'm going to kill the fucker this time!"

The woman was young, maybe only a few years older than me. A thick layer of makeup barely concealed a blackened eye. She was thin, rail-thin, the kind of thinness that speaks of drugs and neglect. As she cast a scowl across the room, she swept a fringe of dark-rooted blonde bangs from her face . . . and away from a bullet-sized crater in her temple.

"She's—she's—" someone sputtered.

The woman wheeled on the speaker and lunged at him. The man shrieked and stumbled back as she landed on him, nails ripping at his face.

An elderly woman backpedaled into Cary. Seeing what she'd hit, she screamed and turned sharp, tripping over her feet. Falling, she reached out instinctively, grabbing his useless arm. Cary stumbled. As he collapsed, his arm yanked free, the woman still holding his hand, ripping the stitches the morticians had used to reattach the severed limb.

I turned away then, as Cary saw his arm fly from his body, as his garbled screams joined the cacophony. Only half aware of what I was doing, I ran for the curtained wall from which the dead woman had emerged.

I raced through the curtain-hidden door and found myself in a tiny darkened room. An empty casket sat on something that looked like a hospital gurney. Behind the coffin I could make out the shape of a doorway. I thrust the gurney aside, grabbed the door handle, turned it, and pushed, nearly falling forward when it actually opened. I stumbled through.

❧ Dime Store Magic

I RACED DOWN THE EMPTY HALL. From behind me came the screams of those trapped with the corpses. Other screams hurtled down the hall, seemingly from both directions, different in pitch but no less panicked. I looked both ways, but saw only doors and adjoining halls.

A dim glow emanated far off to my right. I ran toward it. Behind me I heard a distant thumping, like someone climbing stairs. I kept running.

As I passed an adjoining hallway, I glanced down it and saw a mob of people, all pressed against a closed door, banging and shouting. This struck me as odd, made me wonder why my own hallway was empty, but I didn't slow. As I rounded the corner, my salvation came into view: an exit door, sunlight peeping around the edges of the dark curtain.

I raced for the door and was about ten feet from it when a flash of crimson reared up in my path. For a moment the indistinct cloud of red and black writhed and pulsated. Then it exploded into a gaping mouth of fangs and shot for my throat.

I screamed, wheeled around, and collided with a body. As I screamed again, hands grabbed my shoulders. I pummeled and kicked, but my attacker only tightened his grip.

"It's okay, Paige. Shhh. It's nothing."

Recognition penetrated my panic, and I looked up to see Cortez. For one second, relief flooded through me. Then I remembered his betrayal. As I pushed away from him, I saw that his glasses were gone. In fact, the downtrodden-lawyer getup had been replaced by khakis, a leather jacket, and a Ralph Lauren shirt—an outfit far more befitting a young Cabal lawyer. How had I been so easily deceived?

"Oh god—Savannah," I said.

I tore free of his grasp and dove for the door. The demon dog sprang to life, lunging at me. I spun on my heel and shoved Cortez hard, trying to get past him and run the other way. He grabbed me around the waist and yanked me off my feet.

"Savannah is this way, Paige. You have to go through it."

He started pushing me into the jaws of the beast. I clawed at him, scratched, kicked, flailed. My nails connected with something and he gasped, loosening his grip just enough for me to squirm free. I lunged forward, but he grabbed me again, wrapping his arms around my chest.

"Goddamn it, Paige, listen to me! Savannah is that way! There's nothing there—it's a hallucination."

"I'm not halluc—"

He wrenched me around to face the demon beast. It was gone.

"Damn it, watch!" he grunted as I elbowed him in the stomach.

Holding me in one arm, he waved his hand into the air before us. The cloud of red smoke returned, contorting into a massive pair of snarling jaws. I fought with renewed strength, but Cortez managed to keep hold of me and force me to watch. The smoke writhed and pulsed, changing into something that resembled a dragon, with fangs, a forked tongue, and blazing eyes. Then the dragon vanished, becoming the demon dog again, slavering and straining as if on a short lead.

"A vision," he said. "A conjuring. Dime store magic. It acts like a tripwire. Gabriel Sandford set them up by all the exits. Now, Savannah is safe and waiting for us—"

I pushed him away and ran in the opposite direction. Ahead of me, a shape emerged from a doorway. I didn't slow, just put out my hands, ready to push the person aside. Then he turned toward me. It was a man, naked, skin glowing pale in the dim light. The top of his head was missing. His torso was cut open in a Y from shoulders to chest and down to his pelvis. I could see ribs, sawn open. As he stepped forward, something fell from his chest and hit the floor with a splat. He looked at me, lips parting. I screamed.

Cortez's hands closed around my waist. He yanked me into the air and half carried, half dragged me down the hall. When we hit the spot where we'd struggled earlier, the dragon reappeared. I closed my eyes and fought harder.

Seconds later I felt a rush of air and opened my eyes to see Cortez pushing through the exit door. Behind us, the demonic dog slavered and snarled at nothing.

Cortez heaved me off my feet and carried me out the door. Only when we were in the parking lot did he let me down.

"If you'll look over there," he said, panting, "you'll see Savannah in your car."

When my feet touched earth, I shoved him away, looking out over the hospital parking lot. I saw my car—and I saw no one in it.

"Goddamn it!" he said, looking about as he wiped blood from the furrows I'd left in his cheek. "Where the hell is she?"

"I swear, if you've hurt her—"

"There," he said, striding away. "Savannah! I told you to stay in the car."

"And you thought I'd listen?" Savannah replied from behind me. "You cast a lousy lock spell, sorcerer. Hey, Paige, come over here. You've got to see this."

She ran off, leaving me with only a glimpse of her T-shirt. I raced after her, Cortez jogging behind. We rounded the corner to see her at another door. Before I could stop her, she vanished inside. I caught the door before it closed. Savannah stood inside, her back to us.

"Watch," she said.

She waved her hand in front of her. For a second, nothing happened. Then particles of gray floated in from all directions until they formed a loose ball above Savannah's head. I braced myself for another snarling beast. Instead, the gray dust assembled itself into a woman's face, then pieces of it fell away, revealing a grinning skull. The mouth opened in silent laughter and the skull spun three times, then vanished.

"Cool, huh?" Savannah said. "It's sorcerer stuff. Can you do this, Lucas?"

"Dime store magic," he said, wheezing as he caught his breath.

She grinned at him. "You can't, can you? Bet I could." She waved her hand again, triggering the spell. "That is so cool. You get near the door and it goes off. They're at all the doors. You should see all the cops out front." She looked at me for the first time. "You don't look so good, Paige. Are you okay?"

"Leah . . . Sandford," I managed, still winded from panic. "We have to go. Before they—"

"They're long gone," Savannah said. "When I got outside, I saw Leah, and I was just about to run when Lucas grabbed me. I slugged him one and—" She stopped and pointed to the scratches on his face. "Hey, did I do *that*?"

"No, I believe that would be Paige. The bruise from your blow hasn't had time to rise yet. Now, as Savannah is trying to say, Leah and Sandford have left—"

"Oh, right," she continued. "So, Lucas grabs me and I fight, then Leah does her stuff and sends us flying. Before she can get to me, though, this other guy— Sandford, I guess—cuts her off, and he says something to her and they leave."

"They just walk away?" I said to Cortez. "How . . . convenient."

"No, wait," Savannah said. "That's the good part. See, they can't touch Lucas because he's—"

"Not now, Savannah," Cortez said.

"But you have to tell her, or she won't understand."

"Yes," I said, "you have to tell me."

"You didn't call Robert, I presume?"

"He's out of town. And I want to hear it from you. Right now."

Cortez shook his head. "I'm afraid you'll require the extended explanation, for which there isn't time at the moment. However, I will explain as soon as we are safely away from this place."

"Hey, Paige," Savannah said. "Did you see Lucas's bike?"

She raced around the corner before I could stop her. When I caught up, I found her crouching beside, not a bicycle, but a motorcycle.

"It's a Scout," she said. "An Indian Scout. It's, like, an antique. What year did you say again?"

"Nineteen twenty-six. But we need to leave, Savannah."

"It's a collector's item," Savannah said. "Really rare."

"Expensive, huh?" I said, shooting a look at Cortez. "Like the designer shirt. Pretty sharp for a struggling lawyer."

"I restored the bike. As for the clothing, a suit is hardly appropriate for motorcycle riding. My wardrobe contains a limited supply of casual wear, the majority of it gifts from my family, whose budget and taste exceeds my own. Now, we really should—"

"I'm not going anywhere," I said.

Cortez made a noise that sounded remarkably like a growl of frustration. "Paige, this is not the time—"

"I'm not being difficult. I don't think it's a good idea to run. People in there saw me. They'll tell the police, who'll come after me and wonder why I took off."

He hesitated, then nodded. "Quite right. I'd suggest we find an officer to take your statement."

"First, I'm getting those people out, before someone has a heart attack."

Savannah rolled her eyes. "Oh, please. Who cares about them? They wouldn't help *you*. Tell her, Lucas."

"She's right. Paige, I mean. We should get them out."

"Not you too," Savannah said. "Oh god, I'm surrounded."

I waved her to silence and we headed for the back door.

I won't give a play-by-play of what happened next. Between the two of us, Cortez and I managed to undo all of Sandford's spells, unlocking the jammed doors and disengaging the tripwire illusions.

As for Cary and the other walking dead, they simply stopped walking. By the time everyone escaped and the authorities got inside, the necromancer's incantation had worn off. Or so Cortez explained. As I've said, I know nothing about raising the dead. Any necromancer can do it, but I've never met one who dared. The necromancers I know use their power only for communicating with spirits. Returning a soul to a dead body is against every moral code in the supernatural world.

In the chaos outside the funeral home, it took me twenty minutes to find a police officer, who insisted I follow him to the station to give my statement.

Of course, the police thought I'd played a role in what happened. Yet they didn't know *what* had happened. Sure, they heard the stories, witness after witness babbling about dead people walking and talking. But when the police had finally entered the building, they found only corpses strewn across the floor. Horrifying, yes, but hardly proof of the unthinkable.

When I told my story, I repeated only those portions I deemed believable: I'd been lured to the funeral home and tricked into entering the crowded hallway of mourners. Then the lights had gone out. Someone had shoved me into the visitation room and bolted the door. I'd heard people screaming but could see very little in the near-dark. Soon I found my way into a back passage and escaped. I did admit that, while escaping, I encountered a frightening image blocking the hall, but I'd passed through it without incident and figured it must have been some kind of hologram.

Finally, themselves dazed with disbelief and information overload, the police had to let me go. My story made sense and it checked out against that of the witnesses—barring the fact that I hadn't seen the dead rise. With no small reluctance, they released me.

❧ Rebel with a Cause

WE'D TAKEN MY CAR to the police station, Cortez leaving his motorcycle at the funeral parlor. By the time we exited the station, it was nearly five o'clock, and Savannah reminded me that she hadn't yet had lunch. Since Cortez still owed me an explanation, we decided to pick up something to eat at a drive-thru on the highway and find a quiet place to talk.

We stopped at the first fast-food restaurant we hit. The plan was to go through the drive-thru, but then Savannah announced she needed to use the bathroom, and I had to agree I could use one as well, so we went inside. As we walked in, a few people glanced our way. I tried to tell myself it was simply the idle curiosity of bored diners, but then one middle-aged woman leaned over and whispered something to her companions and they all turned to stare. No, not stare. Glare.

"If you'll give me your order, I'll get it while you use the ladies' room," Cortez murmured.

"Thanks."

We told him what we wanted and I gave him some money, then we slipped off to the bathroom. When we came out, Cortez was waiting by the condiment stand, bags in hand.

"I should do the same before we leave," Cortez said, glancing toward the bathrooms. "Shall I walk you to the car first?"

"We're fine."

I took the bags and shepherded Savannah out. Several glares flew our way, but no one said anything. A few minutes later, Cortez joined us in the car.

"Took out your contacts?" Savannah said as he climbed in. "How come?"

"They're well suited for wearing under a helmet, but for all other situations I prefer glasses."

"Weird."

"Thank you."

I sneaked a fry from the bag while they were still warm. "Speaking of helmets, what's with the motorcycle? You had a rental car this morning."

"And I still do, back at my motel. After our . . . altercation this morning, I thought it best to undertake discreet surveillance, should my assistance be required. In my experience, a motorcycle is much more conducive to surveillance work. It operates very well in alleyways and other places where one couldn't hope to fit a car. As well, the full helmet provides an excuse for shielding one's face. Usually it's less conspicuous, though I realize now that may not be the case in East Falls."

"Motorcycle population: zero. Until today."

"Quite right. After this, I shall park the bike and rely on the rental car."

I pulled into a deserted picnic area just off the highway.

As I locked the car, Cortez said a few words to Savannah. She nodded, took her takeout bag and headed to a picnic table on the far side of the lot. Cortez led me to one closer to the car.

"What'd you say to her?" I asked.

"Simply that it might be easier for you and me to speak privately."

"And how many bribery bucks had to go along with that suggestion?"

"None."

I looked over at Savannah unpacking her bag. She saw me watching, smiled and finger-waved, then sat down to eat.

I said to Cortez, "Who are you and what have you done with the real Savannah?"

He shook his head and settled on the bench. "Savannah is a very perceptive young woman. She understands the importance of enlisting aid in this situation. She's willing to give me a second chance, but she realizes it may not be as easy for me to persuade you to do the same."

He unfolded his burger and tore open a ketchup package.

"So that brings us to the first part of my last question," I said. "Who are you?"

"I told you that I am in no way associated with the Nast Cabal, nor do I work for any Cabal. That is entirely accurate. However, I may have intentionally fostered the misconception that I am not associated with any Cabal."

I nibbled the end of a fry while I untangled that last sentence. "So you are 'associated' with a Cabal. Like what, a contract employee?"

"No, I work for myself, as I said." Cortez folded the half-empty ketchup package and laid it aside. "At the Coven meeting, an older woman mentioned a Benicio Cortez."

"Ah, a relative, I presume?"

"My father."

"Let me guess . . . your father works for a Cabal."

"It would be more accurate to say a Cabal works for him. My father is CEO of the Cortez Cabal."

I coughed, nearly sputtering up a half-eaten fry. "Your family runs a Cabal?"

Cortez nodded.

"Are they . . . big?"

"The Cortez Cabal is the most powerful in the world."

"I thought you said the Nast Cabal was the biggest."

"It is. My father's is the most powerful. I say that as a matter of record, not out of any pride in the fact. I, however, play no role in my father's organization."

"You just told me yesterday that Cabals are family-based, led by a sorcerer and his sons."

"In practice, that's true. The son of a Cabal head is introduced to the organization at birth, and in virtually every instance that is where he remains. However, while a son may grow up in the Cabal, he is still required to undergo formal initiation on his eighteenth birthday. Since Cabal membership is, theoretically, voluntary, it is possible for a son to refuse initiation, as I did."

"So you just said, Sorry, Dad, don't want to be part of the family business?"

"Well . . ." He adjusted his glasses. "Technically, of course, since I failed to accept the initiation, I'm not a member of the Cabal. Nor do I consider myself one. Yet because, as I said, such a thing is extremely rare, I find myself in a position where most people still consider me part of my father's organization. It is generally accepted that this rebellion is a temporary situation—a perception that my father, unfortunately, shares and promotes, meaning I am accorded the privileges and protections such a position would provide."

"Uh-huh."

"This position provides me with some stature in the Cabal world, and though I'm loath to take advantage of that association, in some cases it is beneficial, allowing me to initiate activities the Cabals would not permit, were I not who I am."

"Uh-huh." A headache was forming behind my eyes.

"I've simply decided that the best use of my position—a position I neither want nor encourage—is for counteracting some of my race's worst abuses of power. Clearly, taking a young witch away from the Coven and placing her in the hands of a Cabal is such an abuse. Upon learning of Kristof Nast's initiative, I followed Leah and Gabriel and waited for an opportune time to introduce my services."

"Uh-huh. Let me get this straight: having abandoned the family fortunes, you now use your power to help other supernaturals. Like the Caped Crusader . . . in permanent Clark Kent disguise."

I would have sworn he smiled. His lips twitched, at least. "The Caped Crusader is Batman, whose alter ego would be Bruce Wayne. Clark Kent is Superman. Neither analogy, I'm afraid, is quite accurate. I lack the tormented, brooding sexiness of the Dark Knight and, sadly, I've not yet learned to fly—though I did manage to sail a few yards when Leah threw me this afternoon."

I couldn't resist a small laugh. "Okay, but seriously, you know how this whole 'Rebel with a Cause' routine sounds?"

"Unlikely, I know."

"Try crazy. Insane. Preposterous."

"I haven't heard those particular adjectives before, doubtless only because no one dares say them to my face." He pushed aside his untouched burger. "Before you dismiss my story completely, please speak to Robert Vasic. I am confident that he will have sources who can vouch for my sincerity."

"I hope so."

"I can help you, Paige. I know the Cabals, know them more intimately than anyone you could hope—or would want—to meet. I can operate within that world with little fear of reprisals. As Savannah saw today, the Nasts don't dare touch me. That can be very useful."

"But why? Why go through all this to save a stranger?"

He glanced over at Savannah. "Preposterous, as you said. I can't imagine anyone doing such a thing."

I tore a crispy fry tip off, stared at it, and tossed it onto the grass. A crow tottered over for a closer look, then fixed me with a cold, black eye, as if to ask whether it was safe to eat.

"You still lied," I said. "About Leah."

"Yes, and as you've said, I'm very good at it. For a Cortez, it's a skill we learn as other boys learn to swing a baseball bat. For me, lying is a survival reflex. Placed in a situation where truth-telling may be risky, I often lie before I even make a conscious decision to do so. All I can say in my defense now is that I will make every effort not to do so again."

"You do and that's it. I've got serious trust issues with this arrangement already—aligning myself with a sorcerer."

"Perfectly understandable."

"And I am going to speak to Robert first. I need to do that, for my own peace of mind."

"Again, understandable. You expect him back soon, I hope?"

"He's probably already called the house, trying to find me."

"Good. Then I will accompany you home, you can go in and return his call, then we'll come up with a plan of action."

"What about your bike?"

"I'll retrieve it later. Right now, getting this situation straightened out is my first priority."

Feeding Frenzy ❧

AS I ROUNDED THE SECOND-LAST corner to my street, Cortez turned sideways in his seat, so he could see both me and Savannah.

"Now, as I said, it is possible that some members of the media may have established themselves in the vicinity. You must be prepared. Perhaps we should go over the plan again. The most important thing to remember is—"

"No comment, no comment, no comment," I said, with Savannah chiming in.

"You're quick studies."

"Keep the script simple and even we witches can learn it."

"I'm very impressed. Now, when we get out of the car, stick close to me—"

Savannah leaned over the seat. "And you'll protect us with lightning bolts and hail and hellfire."

"I cannot protect you at all if Paige hits the brake and you go flying through the windshield. Put on your seat belt, Savannah."

"It *is* on."

"Then tighten it."

She slipped back into her seat. "God, you're as bad as Paige."

"As I was saying," Cortez said, "our primary objective is to— Oh."

With that one word, my breath caught. A simple word, not even a word really, a mere sound, an exclamation of surprise. But for Cortez to *be* surprised—worse yet, for him to stop in the middle of explaining one of his grand plans to make such an exclamation—well, it boded no good.

I'd just rounded the corner onto my street. A quarter-mile ahead was my house—or so I assumed. I couldn't be sure because both sides of the street were lined with cars, trucks, and vans crammed into every available space, some even double-parked. As for my house, I couldn't see it, not because of the cars, but because of the crowd of people spilling over the lawn, onto the sidewalk, and across the road.

"Pull into the next driveway," Cortez said.

"I can't park here," I said, taking my foot off the accelerator. "I'm sure my neighbors are pissed off enough already."

"You're not parking. You're turning around."

"You want me to run?"

"For now, yes."

I gripped the steering wheel. "I can't do that."

I kept my face forward, but I could sense his gaze on me.

"Getting into your house won't be easy, Paige," he said, his voice softer. "This type of situation . . . it doesn't bring out the best in people. No one would blame you for turning around."

I looked through the rear-view mirror at Savannah.

"Paige is right," she said. "If we back down now, Leah will know we're spooked."

"All right, then," Cortez said. "Pull in wherever you see an opening."

As I scouted for a parking space, nobody spoke. My eyes traveled from group to group: from the national news crews sipping coffee from the Belham Starbucks to the scattered clusters of people with camcorders and curious eyes; from the state police arguing with five bald people in white robes to the men, women, and children pacing the sidewalk, carrying signs condemning my soul to damnation.

Strangers. All strangers. I scanned the crowd and saw no local newsperson, no village cop, not a single familiar face. Up and down the street every door was closed, every curtain drawn. Everyone was willing to shut out the June sun and cool breezes if it meant they could also shut out whatever was happening at 32 Walnut Lane. Shut it out and wait for it to go away. Wait for us to go away.

"When Paige stops the car, get out immediately," Cortez said. "Undo your seatbelt now and be ready. Once you're out, keep moving—don't even pause to look around. Paige, take Savannah's hand and head to the front of the car. I'll meet you there and clear a path."

When we'd turned the corner, a few people looked over—not as many as you might expect, considering they were waiting for a stranger to arrive, but maybe they'd been there so long, seen so many strangers drive by, that they'd stopped jumping every time a new car appeared. When the car slowed, more glanced our way. I saw their faces : bored, impatient, almost angry, as if ready to snap at the next rubbernecker who falsely aroused their expectations. Then they saw me. A shout. Another. A ripple of movement escalating to a stream, then a wave.

I turned the wheel to wedge in sideways behind a news van. For a second I saw nothing but the call letters of a TV station in Providence. Then a rush of people swallowed the van. Strangers jostled against the car, rocking it. A man, knocked flying by the mob, sprawled across the hood. The car bounced. The man scrambled up. I met his eyes, saw the hunger there, the excitement, and for one second I froze.

As the flood of people engulfed the car, I saw the very real possibility that we'd be trapped. I grabbed the handle and flung the door open, putting all my strength behind it and not caring whom I hit. I leaped from the car, wheeled, and grabbed Savannah as she got out.

"Ms. Winterbourne, do you—"

"—have you—"

"—allegations—"

"Paige, what do you—"

The cacophony of questions hit me like a fifty-mile-an-hour wind, almost knocking me back into the car. I heard voices, words, shouts, all blending into one screaming voice. I remembered Cortez saying to meet him at the front of the car. Where *was* the front of the car? The moment I stepped away from the vehicle, people surrounded me, the noise engulfed me. Fingers grabbed my arm. I jerked away, then saw Cortez at my side, his hand around my elbow.

"No comment," he said, and pulled me from the fray.

The crowd released me for a moment, then swallowed me again.

"—do you—"

"—living dead—"

"—Grantham Cary—"

"—dragons and—"

I opened my mouth to say "No comment" but couldn't get the words out. Instead, I shook my head and let Cortez say them for me.

When he managed to free us again, I pulled Savannah closer, my arm going tightly around her waist. She didn't resist. I tried to look over at her, but everything around us moved so fast, I caught only a glimpse of her cheek.

The crowd tried closing in on us again, but Cortez barreled through, pulling us in his wake. We'd gone about ten feet when the mob swelled. Others joined the news-people, and the tone of that single shouting voice went from predatory excitement to vicious rage.

"—killer—"

"—Satanist—"

"—witch—"

A man shoved a newswoman out of our path and stepped in front of Cortez. His eyes were wild and blood-shot. Spittle flew from his lips.

"—Devil's whore! Murdering bitch—"

Cortez lifted his hand chest-high. For a moment I thought he was going to deck the guy. Instead, he simply flicked his fingers. The man stumbled back, tripping over an elderly woman behind him, then screamed depreca-tions at her for pushing him.

Cortez steered us through the gap. If anyone didn't

move fast enough, he shouldered them aside. If they tried to block us, he flicked his fingers at waist level, propelling them back with just enough force to make them think someone had pushed them. After five long minutes we finally reached the porch.

"Get inside," Cortez said.

He turned fast, propelling Savannah and me toward the door as he blocked the porch steps. I fumbled to unlock the door, my mind racing in search of a spell, something that might distract or repel the mob until Cortez could get inside. Mentally thumbing through my repertoire, I realized I had nothing. Yes, I knew some aggressive spells, but my selection was so limited that I had nothing to suit the situation. What was I going to do? Make one person faint? Rain down fireballs? They probably wouldn't even notice the former, and the latter would attract too much notice. The rebel Coven Leader, so proud of her forbidden spells, was useless, completely useless.

While we got inside the house, Cortez staved off the crowd, physically blocking the narrow steps, one hand planted on each side of the railing. It lasted just long enough for us to get through the door. Then someone pushed hard, and a heavy set man pitched against Cortez's shoulder. Cortez backpedaled just in time to avoid being knocked over. His lips moved, and for a moment the crowd held at the steps, stopped by a barrier spell. Cortez shot for the door and undid the spell before it became obvious. The front row of the crowd tumbled forward.

I threw open the screen door. Cortez caught it. As he dashed through, a shadow passed overhead. A young man leaped off the side railing. The spell flew from my lips before I had time to think. The man stopped short, head and limbs jerking back. The binding spell broke then, but he'd lost his momentum and fell onto the porch several feet from the door. Cortez slammed the screen door shut, then the inner door.

"Good choice," he said.

"Thanks," I said, choosing not to mention that it was my only choice and that I was lucky it worked for even those few seconds. I bolted the door, cast a lock and perimeter spell, and collapsed against the wall. "Please tell me we don't have to go out again . . . ever."

"Does that mean we can order pizza for dinner?" Savannah called from the living room.

"You got the fifty bucks for a tip?" I yelled back. "Ain't no pizza boy coming through that mob for less than a Ulysses S. Grant."

Savannah let out a cry, half shriek, half shout. As I raced around the corner, she said something I couldn't make out. A man's body flew across the bedroom hallway. He struck the wall headfirst. There was a sharp crack, then a thud as he collapsed in a heap on the carpet. Cortez hurried past Savannah and dropped to the man's side.

"Out cold," Cortez said. "Do you know him?"

I looked at the man—middle-aged, receding hairline, pinched face—and shook my head. My gaze traveled up the wall to a four-inch hole with cracks radiating outward, like a giant spider.

"Leah," I said. "She's here—"

"I don't believe Leah did this," Cortez replied.

There was a moment of silence, then I looked at Savannah.

"He surprised me," she said.

"*You* knocked him out?"

"She has excellent reflexes," Cortez said, fingers moving to the back of the man's head. "A possible concussion. A definite goose egg. Nothing serious. Shall we see who we have?"

Cortez reached around and pulled the man's wallet from his slacks. When I looked toward Savannah, she retreated into her room. I was about to follow when Cortez lifted a card for my inspection.

As I took the card, the phone rang. I jumped, every frayed nerve springing to life. With an oath, I closed my eyes and waited for the ringing to stop. The machine picked up.

"Ms. Winterbourne? This is Peggy Dare from the Massachusetts Department of Social Services . . ."

My eyes flew open.

"We'd like to speak to you regarding Savannah Levine. We have some concerns . . ."

I ran for the phone. Cortez tried to grab me as I passed, and I dimly heard him say something about preparing and phoning back, but I couldn't listen. I raced into the kitchen, grabbed the receiver, and whacked the stop button on the answering machine.

"This is Paige Winterbourne," I said. "Sorry about that. I've been screening my calls."

"I can well imagine." The voice on the other end was pleasant, sympathetic, like that of a kindly neighbor. "There seems to be a bit of excitement at your place these days."

"You could say that."

A mild chuckle, then she sobered. "I do apologize for adding to what must be a very difficult time for you, Ms. Winterbourne, but we do have some concerns about Savannah's well-being. I understand you're undergoing a custody challenge."

"Yes, but—"

"Normally, we don't interfere in such matters unless there is a serious threat of harm to the child. While no one is alleging Savannah has been mistreated, we are concerned about the current climate in which she is living. It must be very confusing for Savannah, having her mother disappear, then once she's settled in with you, this happens."

"I'm trying to keep her out of it as much as possible."

"Is there anyplace Savannah could go? Temporarily? Perhaps a more . . . stable environment? I believe there is an aunt in town."

"Her great-aunt, Margaret Levine. That's right. I thought of letting Savannah stay there until this is over." Yeah, right.

"Please do. As well, I've been asked to pay you a visit. The board is anxious to assess the situation. A home visit is usually best. Is two o'clock tomorrow afternoon convenient?"

"Absolutely." That gave me less than twenty-four hours to clear the circus outside.

I hung up, then turned to Cortez. "The Department of Social Services is paying a home visit tomorrow afternoon."

"Social Services? That is the last thing—" He stopped,

pushed his glasses up, and pinched the bridge of his nose. "All right. We should expect they'll take an interest. A minor concern. Tomorrow afternoon, you said? What time?"

"Two."

He pulled out his Daytimer and made the note, then handed me the card I'd dropped while running for the phone. I looked at it blankly for a second, then saw the unconscious man lying in the hallway and groaned.

"Back to crisis number twenty-one," I said.

"I believe this is twenty-two—the angry mob was twenty-one. Or, given that they show no signs of leaving, I should say they *are* twenty-one."

I moaned and collapsed onto a kitchen chair, then lifted the card. The unlucky B and E artist's name was Ted Morton. If anyone had told me a week ago that I'd be sitting at my table, collaborating with a sorcerer and contemplating how best to dispose of a stranger whom Savannah had knocked out cold, I'd have . . . well, I don't know what I would have done. It was too ludicrous. Yet, considering all that had happened in the past week, this really wasn't so bad. It certainly ranked a few rungs below watching a man hurtle to his death or seeing his shattered corpse come to life before his family and friends.

Mr. Morton was a so-called paranormal investigator. I have no patience with these guys. I've never met one who wasn't in serious need of a real life. Maybe I'm being intolerant, but these guys are a bigger nuisance than cockroaches in a Florida flophouse. They poke around, inventing stories, attracting con artists, and once in a while stumbling onto a bit of truth.

All through high school I worked at a computer store where my boss was head of the Massachusetts Society for Explaining the Unexplained. Did she ever explain how I vanished every time she came looking for someone to make a fast-food run? She'd walk into the back office, I'd cast a cover spell, she'd murmur, "Gee, I could have sworn I saw Paige come back here," and go in search of another victim.

"Figures," I said, tossing the card back to Cortez. "How do the Cabals handle these people?"

"Cement blocks and deep harbors."

"Sounds like a plan." I glanced over my shoulder at Morton and sighed. "Guess we should do something before he wakes up. Any suggestions?"

"I don't suppose you have a ready supply of quicklime?"

"Tell me you're joking."

"Unfortunately, yes. We require a somewhat more discreet solution. Our best answer would be one that sees Mr. Morton outside the house but does not require taking him far, which would risk calling attention to the endeavor. It would also be preferable if he could be made to forget having been inside the house—which, again, would risk attention when he retells the story. You wouldn't know hypnosis, would you?"

I shook my head.

"Then we'll have to settle—"

Savannah appeared in the doorway. "I have an idea. How about we dump him in the basement, right beneath the hatch? We can break the lock on the hatch, maybe leave it ajar. Then, when he wakes up, he might think he came in through there, fell, and hit his head."

Cortez hesitated, then nodded. "That might work. Paige?"

"If it means we don't have to go outside again, it works for me."

Cortez got to his feet and headed for the back hall.

"Sorry," Savannah said. "I didn't mean to cause more trouble. He surprised me, that's all."

I squeezed her shoulder. "I know. We'd better give Cortez a—"

Someone rapped at the back door. This, unlike the ringing phone and the doorbell, was a first. When I'd looked through the kitchen window earlier, my backyard had been empty, possibly because no one dared be first to climb the fence. Now even that sanctuary had been invaded.

As I listened to the impatient rapping, anger surged through me, and I stomped off to confront my newest "visitor." I glanced out the back-door window to see Victoria and Therese. Worse yet, they saw me.

The Threat 〰

I BACKPEDALED into the living room.

"The Elders," I hissed at Cortez, who was in the back hall returning Morton's wallet to his pocket. "It's the Coven Elders."

"Don't answer the door."

"They saw me."

He swore under his breath.

"I'm sorry," I said.

"It's not you. Hold them off. Count to five, let them in, then stall for a few minutes. Keep them in the hall."

I ran back into the hall, pulled open the sidelight curtain, and motioned that it would take a minute to open the door. Then I undid the lock spell and perimeter spell, and spent so much time turning the dead-bolt that you'd think I had fifty of them. I ushered the Elders inside while blocking their path down the hall.

"You made it through the crowd?" I said. "Geez, it took us—"

"We had to come through the woods," Victoria said. "A most unpleasant experience. Therese has ripped her blouse."

"We had to come," Therese said. "Is it true? What they say? About poor Grantham?"

"We came because you lied to us, Paige. You said there wasn't a sorcerer in town."

"I never said—"

"You implied as much, leaving us all vulnerable to attack. Look what's happened now. This sorcerer brought Mr. Cary back to life."

"No, that was the necromancer. Sorcerers can't raise the dead."

"Which makes us feel so much better," Victoria said, her face contorting into a most unladylike snarl. "We have been invaded, Paige—not only by a half-demon, but by a sorcerer and a necrophiliac—"

"Necromancer," I said. "A necrophiliac is someone who has sex with dead people. Necromancers don't—or at least I hope they don't . . . On second thought, let's not go there."

"Paige Winterbourne! I have had enough of your—"

Thud! Something crashed in the stairwell. Then Savannah's whisper floated up. "Shit! I'm sorry, Lucas. I slipped."

He shushed her, but he was too late. Victoria thrust me aside and strode toward the cellar door. I ran after her and caught up when she was one step from the basement stairs. I lunged to slam the door shut, but I was too late.

"What in god's name—"

"Oh my lord," Therese said, looking over Victoria's shoulder. "They've killed a man."

"We haven't killed anyone," I snapped. "The guy broke into our house and . . . and I—"

"There was a struggle," Cortez said from the bottom

of the steps. "I accidentally knocked him unconscious. We're moving him to the basement, where he can leave through the hatch. Having been struck on the head, he'll be disoriented and will likely believe he fell in that way. As you can see, we have everything under control."

"Under control?" Victoria wheeled on me. "Is this what you call having things under control, Paige? Dead people wandering around mortuaries? Mobs of strangers on your lawn? A sorcerer in your house, dragging a half-dead man into your basement? You took a simple situation and with each passing day—no, with each passing *hour*—you have made it worse."

"Victoria," Therese said, reaching for her friend's arm.

Victoria shook her off. "No, it has to be said. We asked her to leave things alone—"

"I haven't done anything!" I said.

"You disobeyed us. Blatantly disobeyed us, as you have been disobeying us for years. For your mother's sake, Paige, we put up with it. In accordance with her dying wish, we let you take the child, though god knows I wouldn't trust a parakeet to your care."

"That's enough," Cortez said, starting up the stairs.

I waved him back and turned to Victoria. "Tell me what I did. Please. Tell me what I've done wrong. I consulted a lawyer, as you advised. I co-operated with the police when Leah killed that lawyer. I sat in the police station and I answered their questions and I waited for help. For *your* help."

"The Coven doesn't exist to help those who bring trouble on themselves. You took the girl, knowing this demon woman was after her, knowing she was Eve's daughter and therefore didn't belong anywhere near the Coven."

"The Coven exists to help all witches. No one doesn't belong."

"That's where you are mistaken." Victoria looked down the steps at Savannah, then back at me. "You have twenty-four hours to make alternate arrangements for her care. Permanent arrangements. If you do not, you are no longer welcome in the Coven."

I froze. "What did you say?"

"You heard me, Paige. Fix this now or you will be banished."

"You can't banish me—I'm the Coven leader!"

Victoria laughed. "You are not—"

"Victoria," Therese said again. "Please."

"Please what? Please continue this charade? We're too old for these games, Therese. We should have put a stop to them last year. You are not Coven Leader, Paige. Do you really think we'd allow ourselves to be led by a girl so incompetent she manages to turn a simple custody challenge into an all-out witch hunt?"

Cortez appeared at my shoulder. "Please leave. Now."

"Or you'll do what? Knock me out and put me in the basement with that poor man?"

"He's not the one you should be afraid of," said a soft voice. Savannah climbed the steps and smiled at Victoria. "Would you like to see what my mother really taught me?"

I shushed her with a quick shake of my head. Before I could say anything, Victoria strode from the kitchen,

Therese at her heels. Before reaching the back door, she turned and met my eyes.

"This is not an idle threat, Paige. Find a home for the girl and clean this up—or you aren't welcome in the Coven."

What did I do next? Retreat to my bedroom, have a good cry, and wonder where my life had gone so horribly wrong? While the temptation was there, I couldn't afford the luxury of self-pity. I had a feeding frenzy on my front lawn, an unconscious paranormal investigator on my basement stairs, and, somewhere out there, an entire Cabal special projects team devoted to ruining my life. At this point, getting kicked out of the Coven seemed the least of my worries. Deep down I knew it was a threat that could destroy my very purpose in life, my mother's dream that I would lead the Coven into a new age, but I couldn't worry about that now. I just couldn't.

I headed for the kitchen and began listening to messages. I made it through two before Cortez slipped behind me, reached over, and hit the stop button.

"You don't need to listen to that," he said.

"I do. Robert . . . or someone . . ." My voice quavered as badly as my hands. I clenched my hands into fists and tried to steady my voice. "I should listen. It could be important."

"You can check the call display records, Paige."

I shook my head. "I need—I need to do something."

He hesitated, then nodded. "I'll make you a coffee."

"She likes tea," Savannah said from behind us. "Here, I'll show you."

He followed Savannah and I resumed telephone detail.

Caller number six was a familiar and welcome voice.

"Paige? It's Elena. Jeremy read something about you in the paper. Sounds like you're in a bit of trouble. Give me a shout when you get a chance."

"Can I call?" Savannah asked, bouncing down from her perch on the counter, where she'd been supervising Cortez's tea brewing.

"I'd better," I said. "You can talk to her when I'm done."

I went into my room, phoned Elena, and explained everything that had happened. It felt good to get it off my chest, to talk to someone who'd understand. She offered to come and help, and I can't describe how good it felt to hear that. Unfortunately, I had to refuse.

Leah and Elena knew each other from the compound, having both been captives. Leah had befriended then betrayed Elena. Later, when we returned for Savannah, Elena's lover, Clayton, had killed Leah's lover, Isaac Katzen. Undoubtedly, Leah still felt she had a score to settle with the werewolves. If Elena showed up here, Leah might very well decide to take her revenge, and the last thing any of us needed right now was a werewolf-/half-demon grudge match unfolding in downtown East Falls.

Elena understood, but promised to stick close to home for a few days. Should I change my mind, I only needed to call. I don't think she knew how much I appreciated that.

Before I rang off, I put Savannah on and returned to the kitchen.

"Do you take anything in your tea?" he asked.

"No, black's fine." I took the mug from him. "Thank you."

"Perhaps you should call Robert. I'll feel better—"

A moan from the basement cut him off. Morton was awake. At least, I hoped it was Morton, but, considering the events of the last few days, I wouldn't have been surprised to pop open the basement door and find a decomposing zombie tramping up the stairs. Neither of us moved as footsteps sounded. When there was a bang at the basement door, even Cortez hesitated a moment before responding.

Any hopes that Morton would awake and beat a hasty retreat vanished as he continued to pound and shout. He was in the house and, damn it, he wasn't leaving without a fight. And Cortez gave it to him. Not a literal fight, of course. No offense, but I couldn't picture Cortez rolling up his sleeves and cold-cocking anyone. His strength was in words, and after going a few rounds with him, Morton beat that hasty retreat trailing apologies, convinced he really had fallen through the hatch.

❦ The Original Cabal

AFTER MORTON WAS GONE, I heard Savannah say goodbye to Elena. She wasn't even out of the bedroom when the phone rang again. It rang once, then Savannah's animated voice floated down the hallway. Hearing only the lilt in her tone, and none of the conversation, I knew who was calling.

"No way," she said as she walked into the kitchen, phone to her ear. "Yeah, right. Like we'd need you." She snorted. "Oh, sure. You can, like, incinerate them. Dream on."

She paused, listening, then stifled a giggle. There was only one person Savannah giggled for, though she'd sooner die than admit it—and would probably kill anyone who had the nerve to mention it.

"It's for you," she said, holding out the phone. "Adam. He thinks he's going to help us. As if."

"Hello," I said.

"It's about time! Do you know how many times I've called there since this afternoon? Dad gave up hours ago. Either it's busy or we get your machine. Where have you been?"

"You don't want to know."

"I bet I can guess. My mom was watching the satellite news earlier, some show from out there, and guess whose picture she saw?"

"Mine. Lemme guess—it said I was a Satanist, right?"

"Hell, no. It said you were a witch. Now you're a Satanist too? Cool. If you see the big guy, can you ask him to pass along a message for my father? Tell him he's way behind in his child support payments."

"Ha-ha."

"So what's going—" Adam stopped and sighed. "You'll have to tell me later. Dad's here, tapping his foot and making faces. You'd better talk to him. Then get back to me, okay?"

The phone crackled as Adam passed it to Robert.

"Paige." Robert's warm voice rushed down the line. "You should have tracked me down at the conference. This sounds absolutely horrible."

"You don't know the half of it," I said, heading back into my room.

"Tell me, then."

I did.

"How can I help?" he asked when I finished.

I could have cried. I feel foolish admitting it, but those four words meant so much.

"The stuff on Leah is great," I said. "But I also need some information on Cabals." I hesitated, almost afraid to go on. "Have you heard of the Cortez Cabal?"

"Certainly." He paused. "Is that who's after Savannah?"

"No."

"I'm glad to hear that. The Cortezes are the most dangerous of a dangerous lot—the original Cabal."

"The first one, you mean?"

"Yes. Hold on. I'm in my study. Let me pull up the

file." A stream of keystroke clicks followed, then, "Here it is. The Cortez Cabal was founded during the Spanish Inquisition. They precipitated the Break."

My breath caught. "The break between witches and sorcerers. They were the ones who handed us over."

"Exactly. After doing so, the Cortez family formed a group originally based on the witch concept of a Coven, though it quickly took on an entirely different focus. The name 'Cabal' came later, after they relocated to the New World. It's a play on words, a mingling of truth and irony. You know what the word means, I assume."

"A secret society formed to conspire against something, usually the government."

"That's the joke, of course. A joke at the expense of the Illuminati myth. The only thing a sorcerer Cabal conspires to do is make money. The name also derives from 'cabala,' linking it to sorcery and mysticism. Finally, there's the allusion to 'caballero,' meaning a Spanish gentleman, which, of course, they were."

"About the Cortez Cabal . . ."

"Oh, yes. I'm sorry." He chuckled. "I suppose etymology doesn't help you much, does it? Was there anything in particular you wanted to know about them? If they aren't behind the attack on Savannah—"

"It's related. I need to know about the family. The main family."

"The Cortez Cabal is headed by Benicio Cortez and his sons. I believe there's a brother or two, plus assorted nephews and cousins."

"The sons . . . Do you know their names?"

"Let me see. There's Hector, then . . . I'm not certain

of the middle two brothers, but the youngest, of course, is Lucas."

"'Of course'?"

"Outside the Cabals, Lucas Cortez is the best known of the four brothers. He has quite a reputation—" Robert stopped, then laughed. "I think I see where this is leading. Dare I presume you've met young Cortez?"

"You could say that."

"Let me guess: he wants to help you protect Savannah from this other Cabal."

"I'm guessing he does this kind of thing a lot, huh? What's your take on this . . . crusade of his?"

"Well, let's see. The most unflattering view of the situation is that it is nothing more than youthful hell-raising—a spoiled delinquent protected by a blindly doting father. The middle ground, and the view most widely subscribed to, is that this is simply a developmental stage—the prodigal son rebelling against his family, a moral revolt that will last only until he realizes poverty isn't much fun, whereupon he'll return to the fold. The most optimistic view, of course, is that he truly is committed to what he's doing."

"Saving the world from the evil Cabals."

"He's around your age, isn't he? The age of idealism. The time to join protests and causes. To enlist in the Peace Corps. To fight evil Cabals. To put your life on hold to raise a thirteen-year-old stranger."

"Hmmm."

"If Lucas Cortez is offering to help, don't turn him away. No matter what people in the Cabal world say about him, no one denies the honesty of his intentions.

For your situation with Savannah, I'd say the boy is perfectly suited to help. No one knows more about the Cabal world, and he can operate in it with impunity."

"About the Cabals," I said. "They seem much more . . . important than I thought. Than my mother thought."

Silence hummed down the line. "Your mother and I had different views on some subjects concerning the council and its mandate."

"She chose to ignore the Cabals."

"She . . ." He paused, as if choosing his words with care. "She thought our efforts were better directed elsewhere. I wanted to investigate Cabals more, if only to further our understanding of them. Your mother disagreed."

"So you left the council."

"I—I felt I was no longer the right person for the job. My interests lay elsewhere. Your mother and I were getting older, getting tired and discouraged. I thought we should pass on the torch to the younger generation, to you and Adam. She wasn't ready for that."

Maybe because she thought *I* wasn't ready. "I . . . I should go. Can I call you back? If I have more questions?"

"Even if you don't, I'd appreciate an update when you get time, and I'm sure Adam would like to speak to you. I'll stave off his questions for now, but call him when you have a chance."

I promised I would, then signed off.

I found Cortez alone at the kitchen table, reading a week-old copy of *The Boston Globe*.

"Where's Savannah?" I asked.

He folded the paper and laid it aside. "In her room, if the music is any indication. You were speaking to Robert?"

I nodded. "He confirmed everything you said. I'm sorry I gave you a hard time."

"Perfectly understandable. If I'd expected you to trust me, I'd have told you the truth from the start. You have every reason to be wary, both of sorcerers and of anyone connected to Cabals—a wariness I would suggest you maintain. In nearly all cases your mistrust will be well founded."

I stood in the middle of the kitchen and looked around, not sure what I was seeking.

"Is there something else?" he asked.

I shook my head. "I'm just feeling . . ." I shrugged. "Out of sorts, as my mother would say."

As I mentioned my mother, I thought of what Robert had said about my mother's reluctance to give me a bigger role in the council. She'd always made me feel as if there was nothing I couldn't do, no challenge I wasn't strong enough to meet. Had that just been motherly support?

Victoria's words replayed in my head: *god knows I wouldn't trust a parakeet to your care . . . a girl so incompetent she manages to turn a simple custody challenge into an all-out witch hunt.*

"Paige?"

I realized Cortez was watching me.

"It's going to get rougher, isn't it?" I said. "This is only the beginning."

"You're doing fine."

Suddenly uncomfortable, I put my teacup in the microwave. I reheated it, keeping my face to the microwave until it was done. When I turned around, I forced a smile.

"I'm the world's lousiest hostess, aren't I? Letting my guest make me tea. What can I get you? Coffee? Soda? Beer? Something stronger?"

"Tempting, but I'd better forgo anything harder than coffee tonight. I don't want to sleep too soundly with that crowd out there. You, on the other hand, have more than earned a few shots of anything you can dredge up."

"If you're keeping sober for guard duty, so am I." I sipped my tea, made a face, and dumped it. "I'll make that coffee for two."

Savannah burst into the kitchen, startling us both. "Good, you're off the phone finally. Lucas and I wanted to talk to you."

"No, we didn't," Cortez said, shooting a look at Savannah. "Tomorrow, I said. Tonight we all need our rest."

"Tomorrow? I can't wait until tomorrow! They're driving me crazy *now*."

"Who's driving you crazy?" I asked.

"Them!" She waved her arm toward the living room. When I didn't respond, she glared at Cortez. "See? I told you she's in denial."

"She means the crowd outside," Cortez said. "We are not in denial, Savannah. We are ignoring them, which, as I explained, is the best course of action under the circumstances. Now, perhaps tomorrow—"

"They're bugging me *now!*"

"Have they done something?" I asked, looking from Savannah to Cortez.

"They're there! Isn't that bad enough? We need to do something."

"Like what?"

Cortez shot Savannah a warning look, but she ignored him.

"You know," she said. "*Magic.* I was thinking hail."

"Hail? Are you serious, Savannah? Do you have any idea how much trouble I'm in already?"

"We've already discussed this," Cortez said. "I've explained to Savannah that, as useful as magic might be, in some cases, such as this, it would be far more detrimental than beneficial."

"What's wrong with hail?" she asked. "It's normal weather stuff."

"Not when the temperature hasn't dropped below sixty in a week," I replied. I turned to Cortez. "Don't worry about it. She doesn't know how to make hail."

"No, but you do," Savannah said.

Cortez looked at me. "Really? I've heard of such spells, but I've never encountered one."

"That's 'cause it's witch magic," Savannah said. "Special witch magic. Paige has these really cool grimoires she's working on, and—"

"And we're not conjuring up a hailstorm," I cut in. "Or using any other kind of magic to get rid of those people. They'll leave on their own."

"Denial," Savannah whispered loudly to Cortez.

"Bedtime," I said. "It's nearly eleven."

"So? It's not like I'm going to school ever again."

"You're going as soon as this mess calms down. Until then, you should keep to your normal routine. It's already past your bedtime. Now *go*."

She stomped off.

Bar Games

I PULLED THE COFFEE-BEAN bag from the cupboard.

"I don't suppose you'd let me see that hailstorm spell," Cortez said.

"Hailstorm is an exaggeration. I can conjure up a handful of nearly frozen ice pellets. More like a slush shower. How bad is it out there, anyway?"

"Let's just say, if the temperature plummets tonight, I'd recommend testing out that hail spell."

I walked into the living room and parted the curtains to see a solid mass of people, even more than had been there when we arrived. Though it was eleven at night, all the flashlights and camping lanterns lit up the yard bright enough for a ball game. Camera vans lined the road, their windows rolled down, crews waiting inside, sipping coffee and talking, like cops on a stakeout. While the media stuck to the road, strangers covered nearly every square inch of my yard. Strangers on lawn chairs drinking soda. Strangers with camcorders filming everything in sight. Strangers huddled in circles clutching bibles. Strangers carrying placards reading *Satan Lives Here* and *Thou Shalt Not Suffer a Witch to Live*.

Cortez walked up behind me.

Still holding the curtain, I half turned and looked up

at him. "This afternoon, when we got here, you thought we should go to a hotel. Do you think . . . that is. . . ." I shook my head and smiled wryly. "I'm not good at this—asking for advice."

"You want to know if I still think we should leave?"

"Yes. Thank you."

"I don't. My initial concern pertained to the dangers and difficulties of getting past the crowd. Having done that, I believe, as I told Savannah, that we are best to stay here and ignore them." He gently plucked the curtain from my hand, and let it fall closed. "The mob mentality is, naturally, a concern. However, the presence of media should counteract any urge to violence, and the size of the crowd itself makes it unlikely that any rogue element could take control."

"But I know what Savannah means." I glanced at the closed curtain and shivered. "I feel . . . under siege."

"True, but think of it instead as an insulating buffer. No Cabal would act with such a crowd of witnesses. You are much safer here than you would be in an isolated motel."

"But if they won't act in front of witnesses . . . what was that at the funeral parlor? Not exactly a private demonstration."

"No, and I can promise you whoever came up with that scheme is in line for a serious reprimand. Someone acted without proper authorization, and will be duly punished. I've already reported the incident. It will be handled by an intra-Cabal judiciary review."

"Uh-huh. And that, I'd guess, is a bad thing."

His lips curved in the barest smile. "I won't bore you

with an explanation, but yes, it's a bad thing. From here on you can expect Gabriel Sandford's team to act in accordance with standard Cabal rules of engagement."

"They have rules for ... ?" I shook my head. "Let me get that coffee going before I do need something stronger."

I walked into the kitchen, then turned around. "How about a snack? I don't think either of us ate our burgers this afternoon."

"If you're having something, then I'll join you, but don't—"

"How about cookies? Do you like chocolate chip?"

He nodded. After turning on the oven, I took a cookie sheet from underneath the stove and grabbed a Tupperware container from the freezer. I pulled off the lid and tipped the box to show Cortez the tiny balls of cookie dough within.

"Instant fresh cookies," I said.

"Good idea."

"My mom's, not mine. Mothers know all the tricks, don't they?"

"Cooking was never my mother's forte. We tried cookies once. The dog wouldn't touch them."

I paused in transferring the cookie dough to the sheet. Had he lived with his mother, then? Obviously. Mother *and* father? Did sorcerers leave their sons with their mothers? Or did they marry? I wanted to ask, to compare stories. I was always curious to see how other races did things. It was like learning baking tricks from my mother; other races were bound to have learned tactics for living in the human world, tactics that I might be able to apply to the Coven to make our lives easier, less furtive. I thought of asking, but it seemed too much like prying.

Once the cookies were in the oven, I loaded up the coffee maker, then excused myself to use the bathroom. When I returned, Cortez was pouring brewed coffee into mugs.

"Black?" he asked.

"Black for tea, cream for coffee," I said, opening the fridge. "Strange, I know, but black coffee's just too strong. That's how you take yours, right?"

He nodded. "A taste acquired in college. Spend enough nights poring over law texts and one learns to take caffeine hits strong and black."

"So you really are a lawyer. I'll admit, when you said you misrepresented yourself in the beginning, I was hoping you didn't mean that part wasn't true."

"No need to worry. I passed the bar last year."

"Pretty young, isn't it? You must have fast-tracked your way through school." I turned on the oven light and crouched to check the cookies.

"I condensed my studies," he said. "As, I believe, you did."

I smiled up at him as I stood. "Did your homework, huh, counselor?"

"A degree in computer science, completed nearly three years ago. From Harvard, no less."

"Not nearly as impressive as it sounds. There are far better schools for computer science, but I wanted to stick close to home. My mother was getting older. I was worried." I laughed. "Wow, I've gotten so used to saying that, I can almost convince myself. Truth is, my mom was fine. I wasn't ready to leave the nest. Mom ran a successful business, and we always lived simply, so she'd put aside enough for me to have my pick of schools. I got a partial scholarship, and we decided Harvard made sense. And, of course, it looks great on a résumé." I took two small plates from the cupboard. "So where'd you go to school? No, wait, I bet I can guess."

He lifted his brows quizzically.

"It's a theory," I explained. "Well, more of a bar game, actually, but I like to give it the veneer of scientific respectability. My friends and I have this hypothesis that you can always tell where someone went to school by the way they say the name of their alma mater."

Another brow arch.

"I'm serious. Take Harvard, for example. Doesn't matter where you came from originally, after three years at Harvard, it's *Hah-vahd*."

"So before you went to Harvard, you pronounced the *r*?"

"No, I'm a Bostonian, it's always been *Hah-vahd*. Wait, the cookies are almost done." I turned off the timer with five seconds to go, then pulled out the tray and moved the steaming cookies onto a rack.

"Let me understand this theory," Cortez said. "If someone was from the Boston area and went to college elsewhere, they would cease to pronounce *Harvard* as *Hah-vahd*."

"Of course not. I didn't say it was a perfect theory."

He leaned back against the counter, lips curving slightly. "All right, then. Test this hypothesis. Where did I go to school?"

"Have a cookie first, before they harden."

We each peeled a cookie from the rack. After a few bites I cleared my throat with a swig of coffee.

"Okay," I said. "I'm going to list some colleges. You repeat each one in a sentence, like 'I went to *blank*.' First, Yale."

"I went to Yale."

"Nope. Try Stanford."

I listed all the major law schools. One by one, he repeated them.

"Damn," I said, "it's not working. Say *Columbia* again."

He did.

"Yes . . . no. Oh, I give up. That sounded close. Is it Columbia?"

He shook his head and reached for another cookie. "May I suggest that your logic is flawed?"

"Never . . . Oh, okay. Like I said, it's not a perfect theory."

"I'm referring not to the theory but to the assumption that I attended a top-tier law school."

"Of course you did. You're obviously bright enough to get in, and your father could afford to send you anywhere, *ergo* you'd pick from the best."

Savannah appeared in the doorway, dressed in a lily-print flannel nightgown. Someone from the Coven had given her the gown for Christmas, but she'd never worn it until tonight. The plastic tag still hung from the sleeve. She must have dug it up from the depths of her closet, a concession to having a man in the house.

"I can't sleep," she said. She glanced at the rack on

the counter. "I knew I smelled cookies. Why didn't you come get me?"

"Because you're supposed to be sleeping. Take one, then get back to bed."

She took two cookies from the rack. "I told you, I can't sleep. They're making too much noise."

"Who?"

"The people! Remember? Mobs of people outside our house?"

"I don't hear anything."

"Because you're in denial!"

Cortez laid his empty mug on the counter. "All I hear is a murmur of voices, Savannah. Less than you'd hear if we had the television on."

"Go sleep in my room," I suggested. "You shouldn't hear the noise from there."

"There are people out back now too."

"To bed, Savannah," Cortez said. "We'll re-evaluate the situation in the morning and discuss taking action then."

"You guys don't understand anything."

She grabbed the last cookie and stomped off. I waited until her door slammed, then sighed.

"This is tough on her, I know," I said. "Do you think they're really keeping her awake?"

"What's keeping her awake is the knowledge that they're there."

"It would take a lot more than an angry mob to scare Savannah."

"She isn't frightened. She simply finds the idea of being trapped by humans quite intolerable. She believes, as a supernatural, she shouldn't stand for such an intrusion. It's an affront, an insult. Hearing them is a constant reminder of their presence."

"Sure, I suppose surrounding our house could be seen as an indirect threat. But no one's throwing rocks through the windows or trying to break in."

"That doesn't matter to Savannah. You have to see it from her point of view, in the context of her background and her upbringing. She's been raised—"

"Wait. Sorry, I don't mean—do you hear that?"

"What?"

"Savannah's voice. She was talking to someone. Oh god, I hope she's not trying to provoke—"

Leaving the sentence unfinished, I hurried to Savannah's room. When I got there, all was silent. I knocked, then opened the door without waiting for an invitation. Savannah was glaring out the window.

"Did you say something to them?" I asked.

"As if."

She retreated to her bed and thumped onto the mattress. I glanced at the phone. It was across the room, untouched.

"I thought I heard you talking," I said.

Cortez appeared at my shoulder. "What spell did you cast, Savannah?"

"Spell?" I said. "Oh, shit! *Savannah!*"

She collapsed onto her back. "Well, you guys weren't going to do anything about it."

"What spell?" I demanded.

"Relax. It was only a confusion spell."

"A sorcerer confusion spell?" Cortez asked.

"Of course. What else?"

Cortez spun and disappeared down the hall, sprinting for the front door. I raced after him.

❧ The Riot

SAVANNAH HAD CAST a confusion spell once before. Though I hadn't witnessed the results, Elena told me what happened. During their escape attempt at the compound, Elena had been heading down a darkened hall to disarm a pair of guards. An elevator filled with guards responding to the alarm came to rest behind her. The doors opened. Savannah cast a confusion spell. The guards started firing—at each other, at Elena, at everything in sight. She hadn't told Savannah that she'd nearly been killed, and I hadn't seen the sense in bringing it up later. Now I saw the sense.

Cortez started for the front door, then stopped and headed toward the rear. "Wait here," he said, pulling open the back door. "I'm going to countercast."

"Can't you do that from inside?"

"I need to be at the locus of her cast, the presumed target area."

"I'll go to her window and direct you."

"No—" He stopped, then nodded. "Just be careful. If anything happens, get away from the glass."

He checked to make sure no one was looking, then ducked out. The crowd in the back was less than a third of that out front, no more than a dozen people. With the patio lights off and the additional shadow cast by the roof overhang, the back door was in darkness, so Cortez was able to slip through without being seen.

I hurried to Savannah's bedroom. She was still lying on her bed, arms crossed. I moved to the window.

Cortez appeared a moment later. There must have been people out there who'd seen him escort me into the house earlier, but no one gave any sign of recognizing him now. As Cortez slipped through the crowd, I looked over the sea of faces, searching for a sign of panic or confusion. Nothing. Cortez moved behind a couple selling cans of soda, then glanced toward the window. I shifted left, positioning myself where Savannah had been. Standing on tiptoes brought me to her height.

"You're both as bad as the Elders," Savannah said. "Making a big fuss out of nothing."

I waved Cortez to the right a few steps, then motioned for him to stop. His lips moved as he countercast. When he finished, he glanced around, as if trying to determine whether the spell was broken. Yet there was still no sign that Savannah's spell had worked at all.

I motioned for him to come inside. He shook his head, waved me away from the window, and headed into the crowd. I released the curtain but didn't step away, only shifted out of his direct view. He traversed the crowd, pausing here and there before moving on.

"I don't think it worked," I said.

"Of course it did. *My* spells always work."

I bit my tongue and kept my attention on Cortez. When someone shouted, I jumped. A man laughed, and

I followed the sound to see a couple of young men jostling one another and laughing between gulps from a paper-bag-covered bottle. Guess my lawn had replaced the Belham Raceway as the leading source of community entertainment.

As I shifted my gaze away to search for Cortez, one of the men's shouts turned angry. The other slammed his fist into his companion's jaw. The bottle flew from the first man's hand and struck the shoulder of a woman in a lawn chair. As the woman cried out, her husband leaped to his feet, fists raised.

Cortez came running from the other side of the crowd. I waved my arms, gesturing for him to stop, trying to communicate that the fight had nothing to do with the spell. Then someone saw me. A cry went up.

I stumbled back from the window. A clod of dirt struck the glass. Someone screamed. The shouts lost their edge of excitement and turned angry, then seemed to drift away from the window.

"Go into my room," I said.

Savannah set her jaw and stared at the ceiling.

"I said get to my room!"

She didn't move. The shouting became frenzied. Someone howled like a dog. I grabbed Savannah by the arm and hauled her into my bedroom, away from the front of the house. Then I raced to the living room.

I cracked open the curtains, hoping to see Cortez and make sure he was okay. The moment I moved the drapes, something hit the glass. I fell back, curtain still in my hand. When I looked up, a man was plastered against the window. Two matronly women held him by the hair while a third pummeled his stomach. I let the curtain fall and ran to the front door.

I once dated a soccer buff. One afternoon, as we watched a European game on television, a riot broke out. I'd stared at the screen in horror, unable to believe that such an outpouring of violence could occur over something as trivial as a sporting event. The scene outside now reminded me of that soccer riot. I had to help, to do something. If this was anything like the riot I'd seen, people would be hurt—and one of them might be the innocent guy who'd gone outside trying to stop it.

I hurried onto the front porch. No one noticed me. The loosely gathered crowd had become a seething mass of bodies, hitting, kicking, biting, scratching. Stranger attacked stranger while others huddled on the ground, protecting themselves from the onslaught. A half-dozen people had escaped the crush and stood at a distance, gaping as if unable to tear themselves away.

From a car window, a video-camera lens panned across the scene. I had to stifle the urge to march over, grab the camera, and smash it against the pavement. I don't know why, but even with all that was happening, that bothered me the most. After a glare at the driver, I diverted my attention to the crowd, searching for Cortez.

Finding one person in that mob would be like spotting a friend at a Columbus Day sale. I climbed onto the porch swing for a better look. Bracing myself against the house, I stepped onto the railing. As I did, it occurred to me that I was making myself much more visible than was safe. It also occurred to me that this might be the best thing I could do, to divert the crowd's attention by revealing the long-hidden object of their vigil.

"Hey!" I shouted. "Anybody want an interview?"

Nobody even turned. No, strike that, someone did turn. Cortez. He was restraining a huge man intent on attacking an elderly woman. Cortez had the guy in a headlock, but the man must have outweighed him by a hundred pounds, and every time the man swung his arm, Cortez flew off his feet. I jumped from the railing and dashed into the fray.

I moved through the crowd with surprising ease. Sure, a few fists flew my way, but when I kept moving, my would-be attackers found less active targets. With a confusion spell, no one cares whom they attack, so long as they attack someone.

When I reached Cortez, I grabbed the elderly woman to lead her to safety.

"You fucking bitch!" she screeched. "Get your filthy hands off me!"

She clawed my face and punched me in the stomach, then knocked me down as I doubled over. A man tripped over my prone form, righted himself, and kept running. As I struggled to my feet, Cortez lost his grip on the other man, who scrambled up and barreled into the crowd after the elderly woman. I lunged for him, but Cortez caught my arm.

"We can't," he panted, wiping blood from his mouth. "It doesn't help. We need to break the spell. Do you know the countercast?"

"No." I saw a woman crawling through the crowd, ducking blows. "It doesn't seem to be affecting everyone."

"It is. They're all confused. Some don't react violently to it."

"I'll get those people to safety, then. You keep working on the spell."

I hurried to the crawling woman, helped her to her feet, and ushered her through the throng. At the road, we crossed, and I left her sitting on the far curb before heading back. It took several minutes to find someone else trying to escape, and several more to get him out of the mob.

As I went back for a third time, I realized my mission was like saving single seal cubs from the slaughter. While I rescued one person, at least two more were beaten unconscious. Either Cortez's countercast wasn't working or the violence had picked up enough momentum to continue on its own.

"Thought you could get away, did you?" a voice said at my ear. It was one of the Salvationists. He slammed a bible into my face. "Get thee hence, Satan!"

A hand caught my arm. I looked into the rolling eyes of a young woman.

"Bitch!" she shouted. "Look what you did to my shirt!" She grabbed it, pulling the front forward with a seam-ripping wrench. It was covered in dirt and blood. More blood smeared her hand. In the opposite fist she held a Swiss Army knife, bloodied blade exposed.

Without thinking, I grabbed for the knife. The blade sliced across my palm. I yelped and fell back. Cortez appeared, seizing the woman from behind. She spun and struck. The short blade plunged into Cortez's side. She yanked it out and pulled back for a second stab.

I cast a binding spell, stopping the woman in mid-strike. I threw myself on her, knocked her down, and grabbed the knife. The spell broke then, and she fought, kicking and screaming. Cortez dropped to his knees and tried to help me restrain her, but adrenalin seemed to triple her strength and it was like restraining a wild animal. We both cast binding spells, but neither worked. If only we could calm people. Yes, of course: a calming spell. I cast one, then another, reciting the spell in an endless loop until I felt her limbs go slack beneath me.

"Hey," she said, "what are you— Get off me. Help! Fire!"

Around us, people had stopped fighting and were milling about, wiping bloodied noses and muttering in confusion.

"Perfect," Cortez said. "Keep casting."

I did. We got to our feet and, with Cortez shielding me, moved through the crowd as I repeated the calming spell. It didn't work on everyone. As I'd feared, the aggression had taken on a life of its own, and some people didn't want to stop, yet enough people did stop that they were able to restrain those who kept going.

"Now, to the house," Cortez said. "Quickly."

"But there's more—"

"It's good enough. Any longer and people will start recognizing you."

We ran for the front door.

Once inside, Cortez called the police. Then I led him to the bathroom, where we could assess injuries. Savannah stayed in my room, door closed. I didn't tell her it was over. Right then I was afraid of what else I might be tempted to say.

The slice across my hand was the worst of my injuries—hardly fatal. I slapped on a bandage and turned my attention to Cortez, starting with a cold compress for his bloodied lip. Next, the knife wound. The blade had passed through his right side. I pulled up his shirt, cleaned the wound, and took a better look.

"It looks okay," I said. "But it could use a couple of stitches. Maybe when the police get here, we can take you to the hospital."

"No need. I've had worse."

I could see that. Though I'd pulled his shirt up only a few inches, I could see a thick scar crossing his abdomen. He was reed-thin, but more muscled than one might expect from his build. I guess there's more to fighting Cabals than courtrooms and paperwork.

"I'll make a poultice," I said. "It usually pulls the wound together better than stitches anyway. Less chance of scarring, too."

"Handy. I'll have to ask for a copy of the recipe."

I opened the bathroom cupboard and took out the poultice ingredients. "This is my fault. She's cast that spell once before, with even worse results. I should have told her to wipe it from her repertoire."

"I wouldn't go that far. The confusion spell can be very useful, under the right circumstances, or as a spell of last resort. The caster has to understand it, though—which Savannah obviously doesn't."

"Does it always work like that?"

"No. Her casting is surprisingly strong. I've never seen a confusion spell affect so many people in such a clearly negative fashion. The spell always exacerbates any underlying tendency toward violence. Perhaps under these circumstances I should have expected such a reaction, assuming the sort of people who congregate around such a story are not the most mentally balanced of individuals."

"That's an understatement."

The doorbell rang.

"The police," I said. "Or so I hope."

It was the police. They didn't stay long. Outside, people had either left or resumed their vigil as if nothing had happened. The police took some statements, helped people to the paramedics, and secured the area. Afterwards, they left behind a cruiser and two officers to keep watch.

Savannah finally appeared as I was putting the poultice on Cortez.

"Don't expect me to say I'm sorry," she said, standing in the bathroom doorway. "I'm not sorry."

"You—do you know what you've done?" I stalked across the bathroom and pushed open the window. "Do you see that? The ambulances? The paramedics? People got hurt, Savannah. Innocent people."

"They shouldn't have been there. Stupid humans. Who cares about them?"

"*I* care about them!" I ripped the bandage off my hand. "I suppose you don't care about this either. Well, there is something you should care about—"

I grabbed her shoulders and turned her to face Cortez, then pointed out his swollen lip and wounded side.

"Do you care about that? This man is here to help you, Savannah. To help *you*. He could have been killed out there trying to undo the spell you cast."

"I didn't ask him to undo it. If you two got hurt, it's your own fault for going out there."

"You—" I flung her arm down. "Get to your room, Savannah. Now."

Her eyes glistened with tears, but she only stomped her foot and glared at us. "I'm not sorry! I'm not!"

She ran for her room.

❧ **All About Eve**

"I AM SO SORRY," I said as we walked into the living room. "I know I should be able to handle her, I really should. I keep telling myself I'm making progress, teaching her control, but then something like this happens and it's—it's pretty obvious I haven't taught her anything at all."

I dropped onto the sofa. Cortez took the armchair and moved it around to face me before sitting.

"She doesn't like humans," I continued. "She hates the Coven. She probably hates me. Sometimes I wonder why she sticks around."

"Because her mother told her to. Before Eve died, she told Savannah that if anything happened to her, she was to find the Coven and take refuge there."

"Who told you that?"

"Savannah. We talked earlier this evening. She has some concerns and hoped I might be able to mediate on her behalf."

"What'd she say? No, let me guess: I'm a wonderful guardian, I understand her, and I always know exactly the right thing to do and say."

A slight smile. "She admitted you two don't always get along. Naturally, she says you don't understand her, you don't give her enough responsibility, you're over-protective—all the things every teenager says to every adult. Do you know what else she says? That you have potential."

"I have . . ." I couldn't stifle a small laugh. "*I* have potential."

"Don't take it too hard—she says I have potential too. Neither of us is measuring up to her standards quite yet, but at least there appears to be hope for us."

I stared at the front curtains. "Still, potential or not, I don't think I'm what Eve had in mind when she told Savannah to take refuge with the Coven. The problem is—" I stopped. "God, I'm blathering. What time is it, anyway?"

"Not that late. You were saying?"

I hesitated. I wanted to keep talking. Maybe exhaustion had worn down my defenses. Or maybe Cortez just seemed like someone I could talk to.

"Sometimes I . . . I wonder if the Elders aren't right, if I'm not endangering the Coven by keeping Savannah here."

"Do you mean you want to find someone else to take her?"

"God, no. What I mean is that maybe we're both endangering the Coven by staying. That I should leave and take her with me. Only I can't. This . . . this is my life—the Coven, being Coven Leader. I want . . . I want to . . ." I heard the passion in my voice, the near-desperation. My cheek heated. "I want to do a lot. I can't leave." I looked away, embarrassed by my outburst. I wanted to stop but, having started, couldn't until I'd said everything I wanted to say.

"About Savannah," I said. "I want to show her how to take her power and use it for good. Only sometimes, like tonight, that seems completely delusional. I can't— I can't seem to make her understand the difference between right and wrong. I can't make her *care*."

He glanced toward Savannah's room. "Should we use a privacy spell?"

I nodded. A privacy spell is witch magic. It allows two people to converse without being overheard. Both speakers have to cast it, which we did. Cortez fumbled the first time, but recast and got it to work.

"How much do you know about Eve?" Cortez asked.

"She was kicked out of the Coven for using dark magic. But after that . . . I don't know. It couldn't have been too bad or the council would have got involved." I shook my head. "Okay, that's a cop-out. We knew she was into bad stuff—not bad enough to warrant attention, but she was definitely practicing dark magic. It's just that, well, we can't chase after everyone, we have to choose—"

"Which cases warrant your attention. You don't need to explain that to me, Paige. As difficult as it is, sometimes we have to forgo chasing down the worst offenses and pick the battles we can win. Yes, Eve practiced dark magic. Not just dark—the darkest of the dark. Her focus, however, was not on using it but on teaching it to other spellcasters, witches, sorcerers, whoever could pay her fees."

"Teaching? Why?"

He shrugged. "It was a very lucrative business. Such information is very difficult to obtain through standard sources."

"So she didn't use dark magic for her own gain, she just taught it to dozens of others. That's no better, maybe even worse."

"Exactly as I see it, yet in most supernatural circles Eve's choice gave her the veneer of respectability. She was highly regarded as a teacher."

A car door slammed outside. I jumped and reached for the curtain, then heard an engine start.

"Another departing guest," I said. "Do you think Savannah's spell scared them off? Or is it just past their bedtime?"

Cortez opened his mouth, then snapped it shut.

I managed a small smile. "You were going to lie, weren't you? Tell me what I want to hear, that they're running for their lives, never to darken my doorstep again."

"I caught myself."

"Thanks," I said, my smile turning genuine. "I appreciate the sentiment, but I appreciate the honesty more."

We looked at each other for a moment, then I reached down and picked up a pillow that had been knocked off earlier. I plumped it and returned it to its spot.

"So," I said. "Back to Eve. She was a teacher. Any Cabal connection? Did they ever hire her?"

"No. All of the Cabals had censured her, meaning that its members were forbidden to seek her teachings."

"Because she was a witch?"

"No, because she imparted dangerous spells without teaching the requisite methods of control for using them. I'm not defending the Cabals. If they set limits on the type of magic they allow, they are limits of practicality, not morality. As the degree of darkness increases, so does the risk of danger. Eve's magic was the worst sort. I can say that based not on rumor but on experience."

"You met Eve?"

"'Met' would be an exaggeration. I encountered her. Several years ago I investigated a sorcerer who'd been casting spells far too advanced for his abilities and was responsible for several rather gruesome deaths. After handling the situation, I traced the source of his spells, and it led me to Eve Levine. I managed to confiscate several of her grimoires, but not before getting a taste of her power."

"She bested you?"

Cortez rubbed a hand across his mouth. "Ah, one could . . . say that." When he lowered his hand, a tiny smile played at his lips. "In the interests of being honest, I must admit it was a bit . . . more humiliating than that, and certainly not a story I'd wish to hear repeated."

"My lips are sealed."

"Eve used sorcerer magic against me, and I consider myself lucky to have escaped. Her proficiency far outstripped that of most sorcerers. That's why Isaac Katzen targeted her for recruitment."

"You mean by having her kidnapped last year."

"Exactly. An unwise move. Again we move into the realm of gossip, but given my first-hand knowledge of Eve's power, I'm inclined to believe the story. They say that Eve survived only one day in captivity before her captors killed her. Katzen had assumed that his powers would be greater than those of even the strongest witch, and therefore led the humans to believe Eve would be easily handled. They were unprepared for her level of expertise and, given the very real possibility of losing both her and Savannah, chose to kill her and keep the more manageable child. Their biggest mistake, though, was taking Savannah in the first place. You don't corner a lioness with her cub."

"Do you think— I mean, when you met Eve, did you get any sense of her as a mother? Was she good to Savannah?"

"I never saw Savannah. From what I've heard, that was typical. No one outside Eve's immediate circle of friends was permitted contact with the child. Certainly I'm not qualified to make such a judgment, but from what I've seen of Savannah, I would assume Eve was a decent mother, perhaps better than decent. In some ways it might have been better if Eve had been negligent. Savannah has a very strong bond with her mother— you have to remember that. When you speak against dark magic, you speak against Eve."

"I need to understand Eve better, I know that." I paused. "But I can't—it's not—this wasn't how I was raised. I know . . ."

I looked over at Cortez. His eyes were on mine, waiting with a mixture of quiet interest and understanding that made me want to go on.

"I should have talked to her about the confusion spell," I said. "I should have told her what happened the last time. We should have discussed when, and when not, to use it. I *know* all this, I see it—but I can't do it. Dark magic. . . ."

I looked down and picked at the bandage on my hand.

Cortez was still watching me, that same look of patient waiting on his face.

"It's not—my mother taught me—I was raised to see dark magic as bad. Always. No exceptions. And now I see exceptions, but—" I pressed my hands to my eyes. "God, I am so tired. I can't believe I'm babbling like this."

"You're not—"

I interrupted him by undoing the privacy spell, then scrambled to my feet. "You're staying the night, I assume?"

"Yes, I thought that would be best. But—"

"Here, I'll show you where I keep the guest supplies." I headed for the back hall. "I've got extra toothbrushes . . . there should be some unisex deodorant."

"That's not necessary, Paige. I brought the saddlebags from my bike, and they're fully equipped with overnight provisions."

"Are they out in the car?"

"Yes, I can retrieve them later. I know this is difficult for you, Paige. If you'd like to talk—"

"Talked your ear off already, haven't I?" I forced a laugh as I walked into the front hall and took my keys from the rack. "Here are my car keys. You go grab those saddlebags and I'll put bedding on the sofa bed. You'll find fresh towels in the bathroom closet, along with shampoo, soap, and whatever else you might need."

I headed into the living room. By the time he returned with his saddlebags, I was in my room.

The Arrival

"you're up!"

I bolted awake as Savannah sailed across the room and thudded onto my bed.

"Thank god, 'cause Lucas is cooking breakfast and I'm getting kinda worried. When's the last time you tested the fire extinguisher?"

I pulled myself upright, looked around, looked at Savannah. Was I dreaming? The last time we'd spoken, she'd stormed off to her room; now she was rifling through my closet, chattering away as if nothing had happened.

"He says he's making an omelet, but I'm not so sure. Doesn't look like any omelet I've ever seen. Are you getting up today? It's nearly eight-thirty." She held my green cashmere sweater up to her chest, and grinned. "Whaddaya think? This winter, maybe?"

"Who else are you going to fit in there with you?"

"You know, you're not supposed to talk like that in front of me. Young women are very susceptible to negative body-image perceptions. I read that last month in *Seventeen*. You're not fat, not by a long shot. At least you've got boobs." She turned to the mirror, pulled her T-shirt tight against her nearly flat chest, and frowned.

"You think maybe I'm a late bloomer? Or is this it?"

Was this the same girl who caused a riot on my front lawn? Who then vowed that she didn't care who'd been hurt? I'd told Cortez that I needed to understand her. How? One minute she was making strangers attack one another, the next she was a normal thirteen-year-old girl, worried about clothes and breast size.

"—time we go shopping, I want new bras and panties. Stuff like yours—lace and satin and colors. Real lingerie, not that white cotton stuff. I'm starting high school next year, don't forget. I'll have to change for gym with other girls. Even if I don't have boobs, I can't be looking like a little kid."

"Savannah," Cortez said from the hall, "I asked you not—" He stopped, seeing me sitting up in bed in my chemise. He quickly stepped back, out of view. "My apologies. Savannah, I asked you not to bother Paige. She needs her sleep. You were supposed to be doing homework, remember?"

"Oh, please. I'm in danger of being handed over to a psycho half-demon and brainwashed into slavery for supernatural mobsters. You think anyone cares whether I know how to conjugate verbs?"

"Go conjugate, Savannah," I said. "Please."

"And close Paige's door so she can rest, please."

Savannah sighed and flounced out of my room, swinging the door half closed behind her. I collapsed back onto my bed and considered staying a while, but I knew, if I did, I might never get up again. Time to face the day . . . whatever it might bring.

When I walked into the kitchen, Cortez was at the stove, his back to me.

"Savannah has vetoed my omelet, but I assure you it's quite edible. If you prefer, I can probably manage toast."

"The omelet will be fine. Better than fine. Tomorrow I'll set my alarm. Guests shouldn't need to fend for themselves."

"You don't need to play hostess for me, Paige. You have quite enough to worry about."

I grabbed two glasses and filled them with orange juice. "Look, about last night—I didn't mean to unload on you."

"You didn't unload. You have justifiable concerns, and I think we should discuss them. If you'd like to talk—"

"I'd like to talk about coming up with a plan. Yesterday was crazy, and I know I was running around like a chicken with my head cut off, but I'm not usually that disorganized. After breakfast I'd like to sit down and discuss a plan of action."

"Excellent idea."

Contrary to what Savannah had implied, the omelet looked good, and tasted just fine. Once we were both sitting down eating, I noticed the ringer light on the phone flashing. Cortez followed my gaze.

"I turned the ringer off to let you sleep," he said. "Shall I—"

"No, leave it off. You were right yesterday, I should just start reviewing call display records. I don't need to hear a constantly ringing phone, and I really don't need to hear those messages. Is the machine off?"

He shook his head. "I just turned the volume down. That seemed safest."

"Good idea." At a loud bass thump from Savannah's room, I glanced toward the back hall. "Did she even apologize to you?"

"I believe her mood is intended as an apology."

"Making nice."

"Exactly."

I lowered my voice. "Do you think she regrets it? At all?"

"That's difficult to say."

"Hey," Savannah said, swinging through the kitchen doorway, "anyone notice how quiet it is this morning? I just looked out my window, and guess what? They're gone. Poof." She grinned. "Like magic."

"Yes, I'd noticed that," Cortez said, taking another bite of his omelet.

"Are you going to say anything?"

"Such as?"

She sighed. "Oh, come on, Lucas. You aren't still mad at me, are you? Don't be like that. Admit it—it wasn't such a bad idea after all."

"What wasn't?" I said. "The confusion spell? I hope you're kidding, Savannah."

Her eyes clouded. "No, I'm not. Look outside. *Look*. They're gone. I made them leave."

"First, they are not all gone," Cortez replied. "There is still a small contingent remaining. Most, however, have left, due perhaps in part to your actions, but quite probably owing more to this—" He walked to the counter and picked up several sheets of paper. "It appears

East Falls has grown weary of its recent influx of tourists."

He laid the sheets on the table for Savannah and me. They were printouts from a website covering local news.

"I hope you don't mind, Paige, but I took the liberty of using your computer this morning. After last night's problem, I feared the number of onlookers might increase. When I saw that the reverse had occurred, I was curious."

I scanned the articles. The headline on the top one read: *Old Fashioned Shunning Shuts Down Media Onslaught.* In colonial New England, one of the most severe punishments a Puritan community could inflict on its members was shunning. Instead of exiling you, they banished you socially, pretended you didn't exist. Parents have always known how infuriating such a punishment is; the worst thing you can do to a child is to ignore her. That's what East Falls had done to the crowds of strangers drawn to my story.

After a half-day of being beset by the plague of locusts, the people of East Falls had withdrawn into their homes, locked their doors, and taken their phones off the hook. That left the media searching in vain for quotes and sound bites. Then, when dinnertime came, no one could find an open restaurant within twenty miles of East Falls. Even the grocery and variety stores had closed early. When they tried to find lodgings, every motel, hotel, and bed and breakfast in the county was suddenly full.

Sure, people could drive to Boston for food and shelter—if they had enough gas; all the local stations had closed at nine. This didn't stop the most intrepid reporters and ghouls from hanging around, but more than enough had decided it simply wasn't worth their while. No one was giving interviews. I wasn't coming out of my house. The dead weren't rising in the local cemetery. There was really nothing much worth seeing in East Falls. For now, at least.

"This is bullshit," Savannah said, swiping the papers to the floor. "People didn't leave because of this. They left because of me, because of my spell."

"Your spell may have frightened off a few," Cortez said. "But under normal circumstances it would have only increased the level of public interest. Yes, some would have left—those who were merely victimized by the spell and who played no active role in the violence. A confusion spell exacerbates violent tendencies. Those who enjoyed the emotional release would stay. And more would come—the sort of people who hope for a replay. Without this shunning, the situation would have only worsened. I know that you didn't understand the full ramifications of the spell you cast."

Her eyes hardened. "I knew exactly what I was doing, sorcerer."

"Don't you talk to him like that," I said.

Cortez lifted his hand. "You didn't understand it, Savannah. I know that. No one holds you responsible—"

"I *am* responsible! I got rid of them. Me! You—you two—you have no idea—" She grabbed the tablecloth, wrenching it and spilling dishes onto the floor. Then she turned and stalked away.

When I stood to go after her, the doorbell rang.

"Goddamn it!" I said. "Does it never end?"

"Let me get the door. Ignore Savannah for now."

He headed for the door. I followed.

Cortez persuaded me to wait around the corner while he opened the door. Though I hated any perception of hiding, he had a point. There were still nine or ten people on my lawn waiting for me to make an appearance. After last night's riot, I couldn't risk another scene.

"Good morning, officer," Cortez said.

I slumped against the wall. Now what? I'd seen more cops in the last few days than on a weekend *Law & Order* marathon.

"Department of Social Services," the officer said. "Come to see Miss Winterbourne. I thought I'd better escort them to the door."

What could be worse than a police visit right now? A child welfare visit.

"I believe your appointment was for this afternoon," Cortez said. "While we appreciate your interest in Savannah's well-being, I really must ask you to return then. We had an incident here last night, a very upsetting incident, and as you might imagine, my client had a difficult night and is not yet prepared for visitors."

"That 'incident' is the reason we're early," a woman's voice replied. "We're very concerned for the child."

The child? Oh, right . . . my loving ward, currently barricaded in her room. Oh god. Would they want to see Savannah? Of course they would. That's what they were here for, to evaluate my parenting skills. I would have laughed if I hadn't been so close to crying.

Cortez argued for several minutes, but it soon became apparent that he was wavering. I didn't blame him. If we refused to admit Social Services, they'd think we had something to hide. Well, we *did* have something to hide. Plenty, in fact. But god knows, if we didn't let them in now, things might be even worse when they returned.

"It's okay," I said, walking into the hall. "Come in, please."

A fiftyish woman with an auburn bob introduced herself as Peggy Dare. I didn't catch the name of the timid blonde with her. It didn't matter; the woman whispered hello and never said another word. I escorted them to the living room and offered coffee or tea, which they refused.

"May we see Savannah?" Dare asked.

"She's resting," Cortez answered. "As I said, last night was very hard on all of us. Naturally, Savannah, given her youth, was particularly affected by the violence."

"She's very upset," I managed.

"I understand," Dare said. "That, of course, is why we're here. If you would let us speak to her, perhaps we can verify the extent of the damage."

"Damage?" Cortez said. "That seems rather judgmental."

"It wasn't intended that way. We've come with an open mind, Mr. Cortez. We only want what's best for the child. May we see her, please?"

"Yes, but unless I'm mistaken, part of your mandate

is to assess the physical environment. Perhaps we can begin with that."

"I'd like to begin by speaking to Savannah."

"As I've said, she's sleeping, but—"

"I am not, Lucas!" Savannah shouted from her room. "You are such a liar!"

"She's very upset," I repeated.

Cortez turned toward the hall. "Savannah? Could you please come out for a moment? There are some people here from Social Services who would like to speak to you."

"Tell them to go piss up a rope!"

Silence.

"Haven't heard that one in a while," I said, struggling to smile. "Sorry about that. I've been working on her language. She's very upset."

"More than upset," Cortez added. "The events of last night were extremely traumatic. Paige has been trying to soothe her all morning. Professional help may be necessary."

"I'm not the one who needs professional help!" Savannah shouted. "You don't see me running around trying to save the world. Wonder what a therapist would say about that?"

"What is she talking about?" Dare asked.

"She's confused," I said.

"I'm not the one who's confused! And I didn't mean just Lucas. I meant you too, Paige. You're both crazy. Fucking looped."

"Excuse me," I said, hurrying for the back hall.

When I got to Savannah's room, the door opened. She

glared at me, then marched into the bathroom and locked the door. I grabbed the handle and rattled it.

"Open this door, Savannah."

"Can I take a pee first? Or are you controlling that now too?"

I hesitated, then walked back to the living room. Dare and her partner sat on the sofa like dumbfounded bookends.

"You—you seem to be having some discipline issues," Dare said.

Savannah screamed. I raced for the bathroom door, casting an unlock spell under my breath as I ran. Before I could grab the handle, the door flew open and Savannah burst into the hall.

"It's here!" she said. "Finally! I was starting to think it was never going to come."

"What's here?" I asked, hurrying to her. "What's wrong?"

"Nothing's wrong." She grinned. "I'm bleeding."

"Bleeding? Where? What happened?"

"You know. My period. My first period. It's here."

She lunged into my arms, hugged me, and kissed my cheek. The first spontaneous display of affection she'd ever shown, and I could only stand there like an idiot, thinking, Well, that explains a lot.

"Your . . . you got your period?"

"Yes! Isn't that great?" She whirled around and punched the air. "Watch out, Leah. I'm—" She stopped when she noticed Dare and her partner standing in the hallway. "Who the hell are you?"

At Last, a Plan ❧

GETTING RID OF THE SOCIAL WORKERS proved remarkably easy. After that display they couldn't wait to run back to their office and file their report. I tried to get them to stay and conduct the complete interview—now that Savannah was soaring high and eager to please—but they were having none of it.

Within minutes, they were gone. Cortez had done nothing to help me persuade them to stay. The moment they'd left, he ushered us into the living room, waved us onto the sofa, and began to pace. Cortez pacing—not a good sign.

"You're quite certain?" he asked Savannah.

"About Paige being a good guardian? Sure. That's why I said so, but I don't think they were listening. I told the blonde girl that I wanted to keep living here, but she jumped back like I had mono or something."

"I'm not referring to your statement," Cortez said. "Your menses—you're certain it's arrived?"

"Duh, yes. Girls don't start bleeding down there for no reason."

"It makes sense," I said. "She hasn't been feeling well, probably cramps. Plus the mood swings."

"What mood swings?" Savannah said.

"Never mind, hon. You're fine. I'm very happy for you. We both are."

Cortez didn't look happy. He seemed agitated—not a powerful description when applied to most people, but in Cortez it was the equivalent of a breakdown.

"Do you know about the ceremony?" he asked.

"I was going to talk to Paige about it," she replied. "And how do you know about the ceremony, sorcerer?"

She said it with a smile, but he waved the question away and turned to me.

"Yes," I said. "I know about the first menses ceremony."

"Do you know about the variations?" he asked.

"Variations?"

"I take that as a no." He paced to the window and back. Then he stopped, ran his hand through his hair, adjusted his glasses, and collected himself. Before continuing, he settled into the armchair across from us. "I mentioned before that the Nast Cabal's interest in Savannah is largely contingent upon capturing her at such a young age. That is not without reason—good reason. If a witch is taken before she begins to menstruate, she's much easier to turn."

"Brainwash," I said.

"Recruit, persuade, brainwash—call it what you will. A witch who has not reached puberty is the ideal candidate. That in itself is not surprising, as anyone with any knowledge of youth psychology can tell you that it's a very vulnerable age."

Savannah snorted.

Cortez continued. "However, in the case of a witch,

it's more than that. By varying the menses ceremony, it's possible to secure the loyalty of a witch."

"You mean enslave her."

"No, no. Altering the ceremony can impose certain limitations on a witch's powers, which can then be used to persuade her to remain with the Cabal. It's difficult to explain. There are nuances and implications I don't fully comprehend. The crux of it is this: Alter the ceremony and you have the ideal recruit. Allow the ceremony to proceed unchanged and you might as well forget the whole thing."

"So if we can get through the ceremony, they won't want Savannah? Nothin' wrong with that, counselor."

"Except for two small considerations. First, if they discover Savannah has reached her menses, they'll do everything in their power to get her before the eighth night."

"How would they know that?" Savannah asked.

"Shamans," I said. "They have shamans, don't they?"

Cortez nodded. "The Cabals have everything."

"A shaman can diagnose illness. A shaman would know whether you'd matured to the point of first menses yet. All a shaman has to do is touch you. Jostling you in a crowd would be enough. They must have had one check you out before they started all this."

"Are you saying I need to stay indoors for a week? You're kidding, right? I have graduation next week, you know. If they still let me graduate after all this."

"They will," Cortez said. "I'll make certain of it. Our most pressing concern, however, is preventing the Nast Cabal from learning of your good news. Paige, is the house protected against astral-projection?"

"Always."

"Then there's the second consideration. Once Savannah has completed the unaltered ceremony, they won't want her. However, given the reputation of her mother and the problems she caused the Cabals, the Nasts won't simply walk away. If they can't have Savannah, they'll make sure no one else can."

"You mean they'll kill me," she said.

"She doesn't need to hear this," I said.

"I think she does, Paige."

"Well, I disagree. Savannah, go to your room, please."

"He's right, Paige," she said quietly. "I need to hear this."

"She needs to know exactly what danger she faces," Cortez said. "We need to protect her until after the ceremony, then tell them their opportunity has passed."

"What?" I said. "But if they know that, they'll kill her. You said so yourself."

"No, I said they might kill her if they believe she's completed the unaltered ceremony. However, if the eighth night was to pass *without* a ceremony, Savannah's powers would be irrevocably weakened. Hence, she'd pose no threat."

"I'm not skipping the ceremony," she said.

"You won't," I said. "We just need to convince them that you did."

We worked on "the plan" for three hours, sharing information, floating ideas, drawing up lists—Cortez's lists, of course. Savannah stuck around for the first hour before deciding that verb conjugation sounded like more fun.

We had a week to wait—a long time to spend locked in the house. We debated the wisdom of staying here versus finding a safe place to hole up for the week. After considering the options, we agreed that we'd stick around until we figured out the Nast Cabal's next move. They'd gone to a lot of trouble to make my life hell, and Cortez suspected they might now simply sit back and wait for me to cave. If we ran, they'd surely follow. For now it seemed best to play wait-and-see for a day or two.

Although Savannah's ceremony wouldn't take place for eight days, there were a few things that had to be done the first night, such as gathering the juniper. That meant we had to go out. As well, the ceremony book was kept at Margaret's house, and Cortez agreed that I needed to look through it as soon as possible, so we added that to our list of chores for the evening. Until then, we'd just sit tight.

After lunch, while Cortez made some legal-type calls related to the DSS visit, I decided to clear my mind with some spell practice. I took the grimoires from my knapsack and put them into another bag that I hid in the second compartment under my bedroom floor. I got as far as the hall when someone banged at the front door.

I winced and returned my knapsack to its hiding place. By the time I got to the front hall, Cortez was undoing his lock spells. When he reached for the deadbolt, I waved him back.

"I've got it."

He hesitated, then stepped behind me as I opened the door. There stood two state cops. I'd probably seen them before—the county detachment wasn't large—but I'd moved past the point of bothering to attach names to faces.

"Yes?" I said through the open screen.

The older officer stepped forward but made no attempt to open the door or demand admittance. Maybe he enjoyed having a wider audience. Unfortunately for him, most of the crowd and all the TV crews were gone, though the kids with the camcorder had returned.

"We were asked by town council to escort these good people to your door."

He stepped back. A man and a woman, both of whom I knew only vaguely, stepped forward.

"Councilor Bennett and Councilor Phillips," the man said without indicating who was who. "We'd like to bring to your attention—" He paused, cleared his throat, then raised his voice for the benefit of the smattering of people below. "We'd like to bring to your attention a request by the East Falls town council." He paused, as if for effect. "The council has agreed, most magnani-mously, to divest you of this property for a fair market value."

"Div—did you say *divest*—"

"Fair market value," he said, voice rising another notch. He glanced around, making sure he had his audience's full attention. "Plus moving expenses. Furthermore, we will assess the value of your home as it stood before any damage occurred."

"Why not just tar and feather me?"

"We have a petition. A petition signed by over 50 percent of the voting population of East Falls. They are asking you, in light of recent events, to consider relocating, and with their signatures they are endorsing the town's generous offer."

The woman held out a roll of paper, letting the end fall to the ground like some kind of medieval proclamation. On it I saw dozens of names, names of people I knew—neighbors, shopkeepers, people I'd worked with on the Christmas charity dinner, parents of children at Savannah's school, even teachers who'd taught her—all asking me to move out. To leave.

I grabbed the list, tore it up the middle, and thrust half into each of the councilors' hands. "Take this back to the council and tell them where they can stuff their generous offer. Better yet, tell everyone on this damned list that they'd better get used to me, because I'm not leaving."

I slammed the door.

I stood in the doorway between the living room and front hall, held there as if by a binding spell. I kept seeing that list, mentally repeating the names. People I knew. People I thought knew me. Granted, they didn't know me well. But I wasn't a stranger. I'd helped with every school and charity event. I'd bought cookies from every Girl Scout, apples from every Boy Scout. I'd donated time, money, effort, whatever was needed, wherever it was needed, all because I knew how crucial it was to Savannah's future that I fit in. And now they overlooked all that and turned their backs on me. Not just turned away but thrust me away.

Yes, what had happened in East Falls was terrible: the appalling discovery of the Satanic altar and its mutilated cats, the unspeakable horror of Cary's death and funeral. I didn't blame the town for not rushing to my aid with casseroles and condolences. They were confused, afraid. But to judge so blatantly, to say "we don't want you here"—such a rejection burned worse than any epithet hurled by a stranger.

When I finally broke from my trance, I crossed the room and dropped onto the sofa. Savannah sat beside me and put her hand on my knee.

"We don't need them, Paige. If they don't want us here, screw 'em, we can take their money and get a better place. You like Boston, right? You always said that was where you wanted us to live, not this backwater dump. We'll move there. The Elders can't complain. It's the town's fault, not ours."

"I won't go."

"But Paige—"

"She's right, Savannah," Cortez said. "At this point it would appear an admittance of guilt. When this is over, Paige may well decide to reconsider the offer. Until then, we can't dwell on it." His voice softened. "They're wrong, Paige. You know they're wrong, and you know you don't deserve this. Don't give them the satisfaction of upsetting you."

I closed my eyes and pressed my fingers to the lids, cutting off impending tears. "You're right. We have work to do."

"There's nothing we need to do right now," Cortez said. "I'd suggest you rest."

"I'll go practice my spells."

Cortez nodded. "I understand. Perhaps I could—" He stopped short. "Yes, that's a good idea. Spell practice should help take your mind off things."

"What were you going to say?"

He took his Daytimer from the end table. "There were a couple of spells . . . I thought . . . Well, perhaps later, after I've made some more calls, and you've had some time to yourself . . . if you wouldn't mind, there are a few witch spells I'd like to ask you about."

He flipped through his Daytimer, eyes on the page, as if he wasn't awaiting an answer. I couldn't help smiling. The guy could handle homicide cops, bloodthirsty reporters, and the walking dead with implacable confidence, but turn the conversation to something as remotely personal as asking to discuss spells with me and suddenly he seemed as flustered as a schoolboy.

"I'll show you mine if you show me yours," I said. "Spell for spell, even trade. Deal?"

He looked up from his book with a crooked smile. "Deal."

"Make your calls, then, and give me an hour to clear my head, then we'll talk."

He agreed and I headed downstairs.

An hour passed. An hour of practice, an hour of failure. Was there not some benevolent force in the world that rewarded perseverance and good intentions? If such a being existed, couldn't it look down on me now, take pity, and say, "Let's toss the poor kid a bone"?

One good killing spell to protect Savannah—that's all I asked for. Well, okay, if there was such a benevolent force out there, it probably wasn't about to give anyone the power to kill. But I needed to know how to do it. Couldn't whatever supreme being governed witchcraft realize that? Yeah, right. If such an entity existed, it was probably looking down and laughing, shouting, "Those spells don't work, you little fool!"

"Those spells don't work," said a voice at my ear.

I jumped about a foot, nearly toppling from my kneeling position. Savannah peered down at my grimoire.

"Well, they don't, do they?" she said. "Other than those few you got working, the rest just fail, right?"

"You've tried them?"

She dropped down beside me. "Nah. I can never find where you hide the grimoires. But I know what you're practicing from your journal, remember? I wondered if I should tell you they don't work, but I figured you wouldn't listen. Lucas thinks I should tell you, so you stop wasting your time."

That stung, the thought that she'd been talking to a near stranger about things she didn't feel comfortable discussing with me. Yet I had to admit she was right. I wouldn't have listened. I didn't want to hear anything that might relate to her background, to her mother. That had to change.

"Why don't you think they'll work?"

"Know, not think."

"Okay, then, why do you *know* they won't work?"

"Because they're witch magic."

"And what's wrong with witch magic? There's nothing—"

"See, I told Lucas you'd do this."

I settled back onto the floor. "I'm sorry, Savannah. Please continue."

She grinned. "Wow. I like that."

"Don't get too used to it. Now talk."

"None of the strong witch spells work because the middle spells are missing. That's why my mom and other witches—non-Coven witches—use sorcerer magic for all their strong spells."

"They use sorcerer magic?"

"You didn't know that?"

"Ummm, well, I—" I forced the words out. "No, I didn't know that."

"Oh, sure, all the really powerful spells are sorcerer magic. We can all do the simple witch stuff, like the Coven spells, plus a bunch of others, but for the strong spells we need to use sorcerer magic. That's the problem, see? My mom used to get all worked up about it. She blamed the Coven for losing the middle spells. At least, they *said* they lost them, but she always figured they threw them away. It was wrong, she said, because it denied witches—"

Savannah stopped as Cortez appeared in the doorway.

"Sorry to interrupt." His lips twitched as if suppressing a smile. "We appear to have a situation out back. I don't mean to intrude on your practice, but I thought perhaps you could use a break."

"Just a sec," I said. "Savannah was telling me something important."

"It can wait," she said, jumping to her feet. "What's outside?"

"I don't believe I could do it justice with a verbal description," he replied. And smiled.

With that, Savannah was off and up the stairs.

They Aren't Naked, They're Skyclad ❧

WHEN I GOT UPSTAIRS, I shooed a near-hysterical Savannah away from the kitchen window, lifted the blind, and looked out to see five women kneeling in a circle on my lawn. Five naked women: not just topless or scantily dressed, but absolutely without clothing.

I jumped back so fast I collided with Cortez.

"What the hell is that?" I asked.

"I believe the commonly accepted term is *Wiccan*."

"Wiccans?"

"Or I should say, that is how they introduced themselves when I ventured out to request that they dress themselves and vacate the premises. They indicated that they are members of a small sect of Wiccan from a Coven somewhere in Vermont. No relation to your Coven, I presume?"

"Ha-ha."

"They seem quite harmless. They're performing a cleansing ceremony for your benefit."

"How . . . nice."

"I thought so." He grinned then, an action I'd never have thought his face capable of performing. "One other thing it behooves me to mention. On their behalf. A request. One that I really would advise you to honor."

"What is it?"

"They've asked you to join them."

Had I not been a firm believer in non-violence, I swear I would have slugged him. Instead, I collapsed against the counter, laughing. Laughing far harder than the situation warranted. After one week of hell, I must admit that naked Wiccans on my back lawn was a welcome diversion.

"I take it that's a no?" Cortez said, still grinning.

"'Fraid so."

"I'll convey my regrets, then. And I'll ask them to leave."

"No," I said. "I'll do it."

"Are you sure?"

"Hey, these are the first supporters I've seen. The least I can do is tell them to get lost myself."

"Can I come?" Savannah asked.

"No," Cortez and I said in unison.

I peered out the back door before exiting.

Except for the Wiccans, my yard was empty. When I stepped outside, the Wiccans stopped their ceremony, turning as one body and bestowing beatific smiles on me. I approached slowly. Cortez followed at my heels.

"Sister Winterbourne," the leader said.

She threw open her arms, embraced me, planted a kiss on my lips, then another on my left breast. I yelped. Cortez made a choking noise that sounded suspiciously like a stifled whoop of laughter.

"My poor, poor child," she said, clasping both my hands to her chest. "They've frightened you so. Not to worry. We're here to offer the support of the Goddess."

"Praise be to the Goddess," the others intoned.

The leader squeezed my hands. "We've begun the cleansing ceremony. Please, unburden yourself of your earthly vestments and join us."

Cortez choked again, then leaned down to my ear and murmured, "I should check on Savannah. If you decide to comply with their request, let me know. Please."

He retreated to the house, racked by a sudden fit of coughing. I grabbed the nearest discarded robe.

"Could you please put this—could you all put these— could you get dressed, please?"

The woman only bestowed a serene smile on me. "We are as the Goddess requires."

"The Goddess requires you to be naked on my lawn?"

"We aren't naked, child. We're skyclad. Clothing impedes mental vibrations."

"Uh, right. Look, I know this is all very natural, the human form and all that, but you just can't do this. Not here. It's illegal."

Another beatific smile. "We care not for the laws of men. If they come for us, we will not go without a fight."

"Oh god."

"God*dess*, dear. And take not her name in vain."

"Blessed be the Goddess," the others intoned.

"That's—uh—very—I mean—" Be polite, I reminded myself. Witches should respect Wiccans, even if we don't quite get the whole Goddess-worship thing. I knew some Wiccans and they were very nice people, though I must admit they'd never arrived in my backyard naked and kissed my tits. "You're—uh—from Vermont, I hear," I managed. That was polite enough, wasn't it?

"We're from everywhere," the leader said. "We're roving missionaries, free spirits not enslaved by any traditional system of belief. The Goddess speaks to us directly and sends us where she will."

"Praise be to the Goddess," her companions chanted.

"Oh, well, that's very nice," I said. "While I do appreciate your support"—Oh god, please get out of my yard before someone sees you!—"this really isn't a good time to talk."

"We could come back," the leader said.

"Gosh, could you? That'd be great. How about next Monday? Say, eight o'clock?"

I grabbed the robes and passed them out, nearly tripping in my haste. Soon the Wiccans were dressed and heading for the side gate.

"Um, actually, you know, you should go out the back," I said. "Through the woods. It's a great walk. There's a lot of, uh . . . nature."

The leader nodded and smiled. "Sounds lovely. We'll do that. Oh, wait." She reached into the folds of her robe and passed me a card. "My cellphone number and e-mail address, should you care to contact me before Monday."

"Uh, right. Thanks."

I unlatched the gate leading into the woods and held it as they filed through. Just as the last one was leaving, a figure brushed past them and caught the gate before it closed. Leah stepped through, twisting her head over her shoulder to watch the Wiccans go.

"Nice friends," she said. "Witches, I presume?"

"Piss off."

"Oww, getting testy, I see. Rough week?"

"What do you want?"

"I came to"—she snatched a twig from the ground and brandished it.—"challenge you to a duel. No, wait, that's not it. I came to talk, though a duel would be kind of fun, don't you think?"

"Get off my property."

"Or you'll—" She glanced over my shoulder and stopped. "Oh, look who's still here—the baby Cortez."

Cortez stepped up beside me. "This is inappropriate, Leah."

She laughed. "Oh, I like that. *Inappropriate.* Not surprising, rude, foolhardy. No, it's *inappropriate.* He has such a way with words, don't you think?"

"You understand me perfectly well," Cortez said.

"Yes, I do, but perhaps we should explain for the benefit of our non-Cabal friend. What Lucas means is that my presence here, unaccompanied by Gabriel Sandford, the sorcerer and therefore the project leader, is a direct violation of Cabal rules of engagement." She grinned. "There, I almost sound like him, don't I? Between you and me, Paige, these guys have way too many rules. So, Lucas, does your daddy know you're here?"

"If he doesn't, I'm quite certain he'll learn of it, though as you're well aware, that will hardly impact the situation."

Leah turned to me. "In English, that means Daddy Cortez doesn't give a damn . . . so long as his darling baby boy doesn't get hurt. If you think I'm nuts, you should meet his family." She twirled a finger beside her head. "Certifiable. This one runs around acting like he's the last of the Knights Templar. And what does Daddy do about it? Brags about him. The kid ruins profitable business ventures, even for his own family, and Daddy couldn't be prouder. Then there's his stepmother ... Can you call someone your stepmother when they were married to your father both *before* and *after* you were conceived?" Leah leaned toward me and said in a stage whisper, "Born on the wrong side of the sheets, this one."

"I believe the technical term is 'bastard,'" Cortez said. "Now, if you're quite done—"

"What's the bounty up to now, Lucas?"

"I'm asking you to leave."

"Humor me. What is it? One million? Two? I could really use that kind of cash."

"I'm sure you could. Now—"

"Does Paige know about the bounty? I bet she doesn't. I bet you neglected to mention that tidbit, like you probably neglected to mention the reason for it. Here's a tip, Paige. If you ever want to make a fortune, have a talk with Delores Cortez. Or one of Lucas's brothers. They're all willing to pay very well to get rid of him. Can you guess why?"

"Because my father has named me as his heir," Cortez said. "A political ploy, as you well know, Leah, so please stop trying to make trouble. I'm sure Paige couldn't care less about my personal situation."

"You don't think she'd have a problem being indebted to a future Cabal leader?"

"I'm sure she's aware that such a coronation will never take place. Even if my father insists on pursuing his course, I have no interest in the position."

"Oh, come on. We've all seen *The Godfather*. We all know how this turns out."

"Take your gossip and go," I said. "I'm not interested."

"No? What if I make you an offer you can't refuse?" She grinned and winked at me. "Gotta talk to these Cabal guys in language they understand."

There was something so disarming, so childlike, about Leah that it was hard to stand before her and remember how dangerous she was. As she mugged and teased, I had to keep repeating to myself, This is the woman who killed my mother.

"I'm going inside now," I said.

"We both are," Cortez added, putting his hand on my elbow.

She rolled her eyes. "Geez, you guys are no fun at all. Fine. I'll get serious, then. I want to talk."

I walked away. Cortez followed. When we were inside, I made the mistake of looking out the kitchen window. Leah stood there waving a cellphone. I saw the ringer light flickering on my phone and picked up the receiver.

"Is this better?" she asked. "A Volo's range is about fifty feet, which I'm sure you already know, being the genius you are. How about I just start walking backward and you tell me when you feel safe?"

I slammed down the phone and struggled for composure. "I can't do this," I whispered. "She—she killed my mother."

"I know." Cortez laid his hand against my back. "Let me handle it."

A shout rang out from the front lawn. Steeling myself, I walked into the living room and peeked out the curtain. A video camera rolled across the lawn like a tumbleweed, the teenage owner stumbling after it. The dozen or so onlookers watched and laughed. Then a woman's hat flew off.

"That bi—" I bit off the epithet, wheeled around, and strode into the kitchen. "She wants to talk? Fine, we'll talk. I'll go out there and show her that she doesn't frighten me."

"No," said Savannah's quiet voice behind us. "Let her come in. Show her that she really doesn't frighten us."

We let Leah in. As Cortez said, she could do no worse damage in here than she could out there. Sad but true. If Leah wanted to kill us, she had a fifty-foot radius from which to act. No walls could stop her. All we could do was be on alert.

"She has a tell," I said to Cortez. "Whenever she's about to move something, she'll give herself away. Watch for tics, jerks, sudden movements—anything."

He nodded, then went out back to escort Leah inside. A minute later, the back door opened. Leah walked in and looked around. Then her eyes lit on Savannah and she smiled.

"Savannah," she said. "My god, you've gotten big, kiddo. You're almost as tall as me."

Savannah looked at her for ten long seconds, then

turned on her heel and marched off to her room. Leah stared after her, frowning as if perplexed by her welcome.

"What have you done to her?" she asked.

"Me? You're the one who—"

Cortez lifted his hands. "As Leah pointed out, we sorcerers are very fond of rules. The cardinal rule of mediation, as I'm sure Leah is well aware, is that neither party is permitted to mention past wrongs or disparage the other. Is that understood?"

"Why are you looking at me?" Leah asked. "She started it."

"No, I believe you did. Paige is, without question, the injured party in this matter. Upset her and the mediation is over."

"What makes you think I'm here to negotiate?"

"If you aren't, you may leave now."

She rolled her eyes. "God, he's so much fun, isn't he?" She walked into the living room and plunked herself down on my sofa. "Nice little place you have here, Paige. Must have been a tidy inheritance."

"Out," Cortez said. "Get out now, Leah."

"What did I do? I was only complimenting Paige on her house and commenting that—whoops—" She grinned. "Guess I can see how that last remark might be, uh, 'inappropriate.'"

"Let her talk," I said, clenching my fists so tight I felt blood well up where my nails dug into my palms. "What did you come here for?"

"I don't like the way this is going," she said, lounging back against the cushions. "These Cabals, they're as bad as Isaac said. All their rules and codes of conduct. And the paperwork! Honest to god, you would not believe it, Paige. Kill some dumb-ass human and they make you fill out a zillion forms in triplicate. Once, I accidentally shot a perp, and even Internal Affairs didn't make me fill out so many forms. Would you believe Kristof reprimanded us for that great gag in the funeral home? We 'exceeded authority' and 'exercised questionable judgment,' and now he's fuming because there's going to be some kind of joint-Cabal disciplinary hearing over it. God, I'm telling you, those Cabal watchdogs have about as much of a sense of humor as baby Cortez here."

"What do you want, Leah?" I asked.

"First, immunity. If I back out of this deal, the Nast Cabal will be all over my ass. I want Lucas here to promise me his daddy's protection."

"I play no role in the Cortez Cabal—"

"Oh, stuff it. You're a Cortez. If you say I'm protected, I am. For my second demand, I want joint custody of Savannah."

"Is that all?" I said. "Whew, I thought you wanted something big. How about weekends?"

Leah wagged a finger at Cortez. "I don't think she's taking this seriously."

"Imagine that," Cortez murmured.

"Dare I ask why you want joint custody of Savannah?"

"Because I like the kid. Because I think you'll ruin her. And because she could prove useful."

"So, in return for granting these two demands, you'll do what? Take on the whole Nast Cabal for us?"

She laughed. "I'm not suicidal, Paige. If you give me what I want, I'll back out of the fight."

"That's it?"

"It should be enough. I'm the best damned weapon they have. You'd do well to get on my good side now, Paige. Something even you should consider, Lucas."

"Truly an offer we can't refuse," he said. "I believe I speak for Paige in saying get the hell out, Leah. You're wasting our time."

She sat upright and leaned forward. All humor drained from her eyes. "I'm making you a serious offer, sorcerer. You don't want me in this fight."

"No? If your position is so strong, surely you wouldn't be here right now. The Cabals always reward talent. Shall I hazard a guess as to why you've had this sudden change of heart?"

"Wait," I said. "Let me give it a shot. I'm a newbie at this Cabal stuff, so I want to be sure I'm getting it right. You say you're here because you don't like the choice you made, teaming up with the Cabal. I think you're telling the truth. But not because they have too many rules. Because, suddenly, you're not in charge any more. Sure, you have one incredible power, but that's it. A one-trick pony. Put you in a room full of magical races and you're a nobody, a grunt worker. Am I getting close?"

Her eyes blazed hate.

I continued. "This all started because you went to the Nast Cabal and offered them a deal. Maybe you found out about Savannah's father, or maybe you just picked them out of a hat and they invented the paternity story. They took you up on the offer, and then took over. All you'll probably get are a nice year-end bonus and an office with a window. Worst of all, you lose Savannah. You sold out for an office with a view."

A brass urn flew from the bookshelf, sailed across the room, and smashed into the wall. Leah flung herself from the sofa, skewering me with a glare before turning that glare on the urn.

"Whoops," I said. "Did you miss? Maybe you aren't as good as you think you are."

This time the whole bookshelf jerked free from its moorings. It shuddered, rocked once, and came to rest, still upright. I cast a binding spell before she could try again.

"When I let go, you leave," I said. "Don't think I've forgotten what you did to my mother. And don't think for one second that I can't kill you where you stand, or that I'm not considering it at this very moment."

When I released the binding spell, Leah glared at me once, then stormed from the house, slamming the door in her wake.

"So her power decreases as her emotions escalate," Cortez observed. "Very interesting."

"And handy. Did you figure out her tell?"

Cortez shook his head.

"Damn. Well, I can't worry about that now. I need to discuss something with Savannah." I started to leave, then stopped. "Should I be worried? About retaliation?"

"From Leah? No. The Cabals have clipped her claws. She knows the penalty for acting without their assent, particularly if those actions jeopardize a current project. It's considered treason, punishable by death. A very unpleasant death."

"Good."

Cortez adjusted his glasses. "I have, uh, finished my work. Once you've spoken with Savannah, perhaps we could . . . that is, if you feel up to it—"

"The spell swap," I said with a smile. "Don't worry, I haven't forgotten. It's next on my list. Just let me finish with Savannah."

❧❦ The Key

"TELL ME ABOUT THE SORCERER SPELLS AGAIN."

We were sitting cross-legged on Savannah's bed.

"Almost any strong spell a witch casts is sorcerer magic," Savannah said. "Like the knock-back spell I used on that paranormal guy? Same thing Lucas used on those people out front. You know some sorcerer spells, right?"

"A few."

"I can teach you more. Or Lucas can. They're pretty good, but witch magic would be better—you know, that whole thing about us each being better at our own spells. Except witches don't have a choice. I mean, we have all the primary spells, and some of those are good, like the binding spell. Sorcerers can't beat us at the protection and healing stuff. That's why the Cabals recruit witches. If we had our own spells, though, we'd be way stronger."

"But the grimoires I have *are* witch magic. Strong witch magic."

"Right. That's what my mom said too. Those were her books, you know."

"My grimoires?"

"Yep." Savannah picked up her stuffed bear and smoothed its fur, keeping her gaze on the toy as she continued. "She used to talk about them. The lost books. Only they weren't lost, I guess, the Coven just hid them. She kinda figured that. Anyway, she talked about them all the time, how much she wanted them back, even though they didn't work."

I struggled to keep up with her, to piece the fragments together. A million questions ran through my mind, but I decided to start at the end.

"She couldn't get any of them to work?"

"None. But you could, which is weird. You're an okay spellcaster and all, but my mom was amazing. But then, she was probably only your age when she tried them, so maybe—" Savannah stopped. "That's weird, huh? I hadn't thought of that—you guys both trying them, both being around the same age. That means . . ." Her lips moved as if calculating. "You were around when my mom left, weren't you?"

I nodded. "I must have been four or five, but I don't remember her. You know, I never thought of this, but I bet we've got photos of your mom around here somewhere, in one of my mother's old albums. She was always snapping pictures at Coven picnics and parties. There must be photos."

"You think so?" Savannah laid down her stuffed bear. "That'd be cool. I don't have any pictures."

"You don't—oh god, of course you don't. I never thought . . ."

"That's okay. When we moved . . . I noticed you didn't put the pictures of your mom back up. I kinda wondered why not, but then I kinda understood too. It's tough enough sometimes without being reminded."

Our eyes met. I felt mine well up and rubbed my hand over them. "I'll look for the photos as soon as I can," I said.

Savannah nodded. "Okay, Lucas is waiting for you, so let's talk about the grimoires."

"Right. Now, why did your mother say they didn't work?"

"'Cause they're tri—uh, tre—tertiary spells, that's it. That means you need to know the middle spells first. Only we don't have them—the witches, I mean. We've only got the primary ones. The Coven got rid of the middle ones."

"Got rid of them?"

"That's what my mom figured. The Coven decided the spells were too strong, so they burned them or something."

"Who told her that? My mother?"

"No, no. My mom never had any problems with your mom. It wasn't her fault, what happened. It was the Elders'."

"So the Elders claimed they destroyed the books."

"No, I meant it was the Elders' fault my mom left the Coven. They didn't know anything about the secondary books. Another witch told my mom about those."

I rubbed my temples. This wasn't making any sense. I longed to tell her to stop, to go back and proceed logically from the beginning, but I was almost afraid that if I did, I'd lose everything, like a wisp of smoke I had to catch before it vanished.

"So a non-Coven witch told your mom that these intermediate spells were missing."

"Right. Mom found this witch who had a copy of one of those grimoires."

"The grimoires I have now?"

"Right. Mom stole the grimoires from Aunt Margaret's library. She was the keeper of the books or whatever they called it. Aunt Margaret, I mean."

"She still is. So your mother took the books and found out they didn't work."

"Right. So she went back to Aunt Margaret and asked why. Aunt Margaret figured out that my mom stole them, so she told Ruth and the Elders. Your mom said it didn't matter, since the spells didn't work, but Victoria flipped out and caused a big stink about it, and my mom got fed up and left the Coven."

"Uh-huh." My head was starting to hurt.

"So how'd you get them?"

"Hmmm?"

"Where'd you find the grimoires?"

I had to pause and clear my mind even to remember. "I found them in the Coven library. In Margaret's collection."

"Wow. So she didn't throw them out after all? Weird."

"Very weird. When we go there later, to get the ceremony book, I'll have some questions for her."

Savannah nodded. We finished talking, then I went to find Cortez.

When I heard Cortez rustling around in the kitchen, I smiled and quickened my pace, suddenly eager to—to what? I stopped in the hallway, and it took a moment to realize that I'd been hurrying to tell him the news about the grimoires.

Naturally, I was excited. If I could unlock the secret of these spells, it would mean not only that I'd have stronger spells to protect Savannah but that I'd have stronger spells to offer all witches. This could truly be the key to everything I'd dreamed of. With these spells I could help witches regain their rightful place in the supernatural world.

The implications were mind-boggling, and of course I wanted to share them with someone—but there was more to it than that. I didn't want to tell just anyone; I wanted to tell Cortez. Logically, as a sorcerer, he probably couldn't care less about newly discovered witch spells, or if he did, he'd want to suppress them to ensure his race's supremacy. Yet I couldn't imagine Cortez doing that. Somehow, as foolish as it might sound, I felt he'd be happy for me or, perhaps even more importantly, that he'd understand. I could take this news to every witch in the Coven, and some might congratulate me, might even be pleased for me, but they wouldn't really understand. With Cortez, I felt it would be . . . different.

I paused in the hall and considered telling him. Seriously considered it. But I decided to speak to Margaret first, and then, if I really had what I thought I had here, I'd talk to Cortez about it.

I walked through the kitchen door to see Cortez eyeing two canisters of tea.

"You don't want the one on the left," I said. "It's a sleeping brew."

"That's what I was trying to figure out. Savannah

told me the sleeping brew was on the right, but I believe she returned the canisters to the wrong places."

"I don't doubt it. Sometimes I think she puts things back in the wrong places on purpose, so I won't ask her to tidy up. I remember trying that with my mom, only she decided it just meant I needed more practice tidying up." I took the canisters. "Both these, however, are caffeine-free, so for today I think I'll stick with coffee."

"I just brewed a pot."

"Damn, you're good. Let's grab some, then, and start the spell swap."

❦ Spellcasting Monopoly

BEFORE WE STARTED, I popped a frozen lasagna into the oven for dinner. Then I brought out my Coven grimoire and spellcasting journals and ushered Cortez into the living room. With his help I moved the coffee table aside. Then I settled onto the carpet, cross-legged.

"This okay?" I asked.

He nodded and sat across from me.

"This is all I've got," I said, laying out my grimoire and journals. "Well, all that works, anyway. These are the Coven-approved spells, and in my journals I've written down a few others that I picked up. I may not have what you're looking for."

"No, you probably do. I believe they'd all be Coven-sanctioned, probably level three or four. I'm still struggling through third level, but there are a couple of fourth-level spells I'd like to discuss, in the expectation—or hope—that I progress that far."

"You know your levels, then," I said. "Good. But how come—no offense, but you are a Cabal CEO's son, so you must have access to the best spells available, even witch spells."

"Obtaining witch spells is not as simple a matter as you might expect, largely due to the ongoing animosity between the races. Most sorcerers won't avail themselves of witch magic, no matter how practical it might be. For those, such as myself, who wish the knowledge, it can be very difficult to obtain. Witches, quite understandably, are loath to give us access to their power. The lower-level spells are commonplace, but the higher ones are well guarded by the few witches who can cast them."

"Any decent witch can cast them. Even fourth-level isn't tough, if you have the experience." I hesitated, remembering what Savannah had said. "Unless, of course, you're a witch who prefers sorcerer magic, in which case, I suppose, you might never gain that level of experience."

"Precisely. Even Cabal witches who can cast the more difficult witch spells don't like to part with the information. Given my Cabal standing, they don't dare refuse my requests, but I suspect they leave out a critical word or two of the incantation, so it will appear that I simply lack the skill to cast it properly."

"Passive-aggressive witches. Got a few of them around here too." I took a cookie from the plate Cortez had laid between us. "Okay, so what do you want to know?"

"First, the cover spell."

I pretended to choke on my cookie. "Let's just start at the top, shall we? Next to the binding spell, that's probably the best defensive weapon we've got. No wonder the Cabal witches are giving you phony spells."

"Is that a no?"

"It's yes, but it's gonna cost ya, and I don't mean dollars, either—though that might be a good way to knock down my bill."

Cortez picked up a cookie. "Speaking of my bill, I should point out that such payment was only part of my initial money-hungry lawyer guise. My services are offered pro bono, so to speak. If you are inclined to pay me, though, given the choice between monetary and magical remuneration, I would far prefer the latter."

"You'd rather have new spells than cash?" I grinned. "My kinda guy. I'll warn you, though, being of the same bent myself, I'd rather pay your bill with a check and trade on the spells."

A crooked smile. "Quite acceptable. For the cover spell, then . . . ?"

"Well, here you have the advantage, because I don't know of many sorcerer spells. There's the one you did the other day—I think Savannah called it the knock-back spell—but she knows that, so I'll get it from her. There's that anti-confusion spell, which, granted, didn't seem to work, but with Savannah around I may need to know it."

"And you had the calming spell, which *did* work. I'd certainly like that."

I sipped my coffee as I racked my brain for more sorcerer spells. "Barrier spell—I definitely want that."

"Barrier spell?" His brows arched. "That one, as you say, is 'gonna cost ya.' I'm still working on that one myself."

"Cover spell for barrier spell?"

He nodded and took another cookie.

"And calming for anti-confusion." I laughed. "I feel like I'm trading baseball cards here. Or playing

Monopoly. I'll give you Broadway for Atlantic and one railroad."

"Is that how you play Monopoly? I always suspected my father was doing it wrong."

"How did your father play it? Or dare I ask?"

He bit into his cookie and chewed before answering. "He took the title rather seriously. Global domination was the goal, at any cost. To win, one had to control all the property and drive one's competitors to bankruptcy. Bribery, usurious interest rates, housing development kickbacks—it was a very complicated, cutthroat game."

"Sounds like . . . fun."

"It was not without challenge, but it left one with the feeling of having accomplished relatively little of consequence at an overwhelming moral price. And it was, as you might imagine, ultimately not much fun. I eventually started arguing the case for a more equitable division of assets, with needs-driven interest rates and financial aid for those experiencing a temporary downturn in fortunes. My father, of course, disagreed but was ultimately unable to sway my beliefs, and I soon stopped playing with him. An early sign of things to come, I fear."

I laughed and shook my head. "So, you don't play Monopoly any more, I'm guessing."

"It wasn't my game."

"What is your game? What do you like to do when you're not saving the world?"

He finished off his cookie. "Games have never been my forte. Sports even less so. I am, however, reasonably proficient at poker. I bluff quite well, a skill that has made me a few dollars when the need arose."

I grinned. "I can imagine that."

"How about you?"

"Not big on the sports either. I do like games, though. Anything that's fun. Pool's a favorite."

His brows went up. "*Pool?*"

"What? I don't strike you as the pool shark type? Pool's great. Helps me build up concentration and precision for spellcasting. If you can sink a shot in a noisy pool hall, with friends trying to spoil your shot and a few bottles of beer swimming through your system, then you can cast a spell under the worst circumstances."

"That makes sense. I'll admit, I could use more practice spellcasting under adverse conditions. Do you find—"

A shrill whistle cut him short. He frowned and looked in the direction of the sound, through the kitchen doorway and toward the answering machine on the counter.

"It appears your overloaded machine has finally surrendered," he said.

I pushed myself to my feet as the machine whistled again. "That's not it."

I walked into the kitchen and turned up the volume.

"Paige! Pick up!" Adam's shout reverberated through the kitchen. "You don't answer, I'm going to assume the worst and catch the next plane—"

I lifted the receiver. "Good excuse. I'm sure you can very well guess why I'm not answering the phone."

"Because you're overwhelmed and understaffed . . . or under-friended."

"Under-friended?"

"Lacking the support of friends—there should be a word for that. Point is, you could obviously use my help."

"To do what, answer the phone? Hold on." I covered the mouthpiece and turned to Cortez, who was still in the living room. "I'm sorry, I really should take this. I'll be back in a few minutes."

I took the phone to my room and told Adam what was going on. I didn't tell him about the grimoires. If I had, I can imagine his response. I'd tell him that I might finally have unlocked the secrets of true witch magic, and he'd have said something like, "Whoa, that's great, way to go, Paige . . . Oh, and that reminds me, I finally got my Jeep to stop making that knocking noise." Adam is a great guy, and a wonderful friend, but there are things in my life he just doesn't get.

We chatted until I heard the distant ding of the oven timer.

"Whoops," I said. "Lost track of time. Dinner's ready. I have to go."

"You sure you don't need me?"

"Positive. And don't bother trying to call here, I'll phone you with an update as soon as I can."

I ended the conversation and headed into the hall.

Savannah's voice floated from the kitchen. "—just friends. Good friends, but that's it."

The oven door clanged shut. I walked in to see Cortez taking the lasagna from the oven as Savannah watched from her perch on the counter.

"Supervising?" I asked.

"Someone has to," she said.

"While you're up there, grab the plates." I leaned over to turn off the oven. "I'll take it from here. Thanks."

Cortez nodded. "I'll wash up."

Savannah watched him leave, then jumped from the counter and scurried to my side. "He was asking about Adam," she announced in a stage whisper.

I took the foil off the lasagna. "Hmmm?"

"Lucas. He was asking about Adam. You and Adam. I came in, you were gone, he said you were on the phone, so I checked call display on my phone and told him it was Adam. Then I said you'd be a while because you guys, like, talk forever, and he said, 'Oh, so they're pretty good friends,' or something like that."

"Uh-huh." I sliced into the middle of the lasagna, making sure it was cooked through. "I think the lettuce is wilted, but could you check it for me?"

"Paige, I'm talking to you."

"And I heard you. Lucas asked if Adam was a friend."

"No, he didn't ask if he was a friend. Well, yes, he did, but he meant, you know, is Adam a *friend*. He wasn't just asking, he was *asking*. Get it?"

I frowned over my shoulder at her. Cortez walked into the kitchen. Savannah looked at me, threw up her hands, and stomped off to the bathroom.

"Mood swings?" Cortez asked.

"Communication breakdown. I swear, thirteen-year-old girls speak a language no linguist has ever deciphered. I remember some of it, but never enough to decode entire conversations. Is wine with dinner okay? Or too risky?"

"Wine would be wonderful."

"If you can grab the glasses from over the stove here, I'll run downstairs and grab a bottle."

After dinner, while Cortez and Savannah cleared the table, I changed my clothing. Retrieving the juniper might require some backwoods searching, so I exchanged my skirt for my sole pair of jeans. With a mother who was a dressmaker, I'd grown up loving fabrics—the luxurious swish of silk, the snug warmth of wool, the crisp snap of linen—and I'd never understood the allure of stiff jeans and limp cotton T-shirts. Unless, of course, you plan to go tramping through the forest for spell ingredients. I considered changing into a sweatshirt, but opted instead to leave on my short-sleeved silk blouse and throw a jacket over it; some sacrifices are just too great.

Once dressed, I went into the living room and pulled back the curtain to see whether the crowd was still small enough for us to make an easy escape. But I couldn't see anything: the window was blacked out, covered with paper.

"Well, I don't want to see you people, either," I muttered.

I was about to let the curtain fall back into place when I noticed writing on the sheets. No, not writing, print.

They were newspapers. Someone had cut out newspaper articles about me and plastered them over my front window.

There were dozens of articles, taken not just from tabloids but from webzines and regular newspapers. The tabloids screamed the loudest: *Lawyer Murdered in Gruesome Satanic Rite; Mangled Corpses Return to Life.* The webzines were quieter but nastier, less constrained by the threat of slander: *Kidnapped Baby Brutally Murdered in Black Mass; Zombie Cult Raises Hell in Funeral Homes Across Massachusetts.*

The most disturbing voices, though, were the quietest—the somber, almost clinical headlines from the regular press: *Murder Linked to Allegations of Witchcraft; Mourners Claim Corpses Reanimated.* I scanned the headers atop the articles: *The Boston Globe, The New York Times,* even *The Washington Post.* Not front page news, but still there, tucked farther back. My story, my name—splashed across the most prominent papers in the nation.

"They're still out there." Cortez tugged the curtain from my hand and let it fall, hiding the papers from view. "Not many, but I wouldn't advise we take the car. The Nasts have undoubtedly assigned someone to watch the house, and we don't want them following us."

"Definitely not."

"Since we have to stop at Margaret Levine's, I would suggest we walk there, going through the woods, and borrow her car."

"If she'll let us. What about your rental— Oh, geez,

your bike! We left it at the funeral home. I should call a tow truck—"

"I've done that."

"Good. Did they tow it someplace safe?"

He hesitated, then said, "It wasn't there when they arrived. Could you get Savannah? I knocked at her door, but she has her music too loud to hear, and I didn't dare intrude."

"What do you mean, your bike wasn't there? Someone stole it?"

"So it would appear. No matter. The police have been informed and, failing that, I had an excellent insurance policy."

"Oh god, I'm sorry. I should have thought—I completely forgot about it yesterday."

"Given everything that happened, the bike was the last of my concerns. You suggested we return for it before we came here, and I decided against that, so it's entirely my own fault. Now, if you'll get Savannah—"

"I'm so sorry. You should have mentioned it. God, I feel awful."

"Which is precisely why I didn't mention it. Compared to what you've lost these last few days, and what you stand to lose, a motorcycle is quite inconsequential. As I said, I had insurance and I can replace it." He glanced at his watch. "We really have to go. Collect Savannah and meet me at the back door."

He gently moved me out of the way and went into the kitchen to gather his papers. I was about to follow when the clock struck six, reminding me that we did indeed need to hurry: the Salem shop that carried some of the material for Savannah's ceremony closed at nine.

I banged on Savannah's door.

"Just a sec," she called. The music clicked off, followed by the slam of the closet and various drawers. Finally, she opened the door and handed me a plastic grocery bag.

"Hold this," she said, then grabbed her brush and ran it through her hair. "I figured out how we can get around without being seen. I should have thought about that earlier, but I forgot about it."

"Forgot about what?"

She pointed at the bag. "That."

I opened it and screamed.

Tools of the Trade ❦

OKAY, I DIDN'T SCREAM. More of a yelp, really. Maybe a shriek.

What was in the bag? The long-lost Hand of Glory. Just what I wanted to see.

At my cry, Cortez came flying down the hall. Once we assured him that no one was mortally wounded, I explained how Savannah came to be in possession of the hand.

"... and then I forgot about it," I finished.

"So did I," Savannah said. "Until now, when I was putting away my homework and saw my bag."

"You put that thing in your schoolbag?"

"Wrapped up, of course. The cops would never look in there. Now we can use it to sneak out of the house. We just light the fingers on fire and carry it outside. It'll make us invisible. Well, maybe not invisible, but it'll stop people from seeing us."

Cortez shook his head. "I'm afraid that's a myth, Savannah. The Hand of Glory only prevents sleeping people from waking, and it does that very poorly."

"You've tried it?" she asked.

"Several times, until I learned a spell that worked better." He lifted the hand from the bag. "And smelled better. This hand is very crudely done. Quite fresh, too. That weakens its power. Whoever made this didn't even follow the proper methods of anointing and preserving. I'd be surprised if it worked at all. I'd say its purpose is more fright than sleight."

"Dime store magic?" Savannah said.

"Definitely. See here? Where the bone comes through? Now, if this was done correctly—"

I shivered. "Am I the only one totally grossed out by that thing?"

They both looked at me blankly.

"Apparently so," I muttered. "Can I skip this lesson? I'll start walking to Margaret's and you two can catch up."

"Paige is right," Cortez said, returning the hand to the bag. "We haven't time for this. I would suggest, though, that we take the hand along, so we can dispose of it away from the house."

I nodded and we headed for the back door. Cortez grabbed his leather jacket, then wrapped the bag as small as it would go and shoved it into a pocket. I couldn't suppress a shudder. Yes, I know I'd resolved to better accept the darker side of Savannah's nature, but I couldn't imagine ever toting around body parts as if they were tools like chalices and grimoires.

When we stepped outside, the evening was already growing cool, and Savannah, dressed in a midriff-bearing T-shirt, decided to run back in for a sweater.

Once she was gone, I pointed at the pocket containing the bag. "You really use stuff like that?"

"I use whatever works."

"Sorry. I didn't mean to sound . . ."

"A lot of magical objects aren't things I would otherwise choose to handle. It's like magic. You can refuse to learn the stronger, more distasteful spells, or you can acknowledge that they may, under some circumstances, be necessary."

"I know that. With the spells, I mean. But I'm . . ." I hesitated, then pushed on. "I'm having trouble with it. Getting my head around the idea that I might have to . . ."

"Do bad to do good?"

I managed a small smile. "Exactly. I've been thinking about that a lot—killing someone to protect Savannah. I know it might come to that, but I've never . . . And what if I had to do more than disable an enemy? What if protecting her meant hurting an innocent bystander? I'm really . . ." I took a deep breath. "I really have trouble with it."

"So do I."

I looked up at him, but before I could say anything, Savannah burst through the door.

"All set?" I asked.

She nodded and off we went.

I spent the ten-minute walk to Margaret's thinking about the grimoires. What bothered me most was the realization that if only Savannah had felt comfortable talking to me about her mother, we could have cleared this up months ago. Now that I finally was ready to listen, it might be too late.

I was still working through Savannah's story. She said that the Coven-sanctioned spells were primary spells, which you had to master before you could progress to secondary spells. Only once you knew the secondary spells could you hope to cast a tertiary spell successfully, like the ones in my secret grimoires. I'd never heard of such a thing before.

Although Coven spells are divided into four levels, hypothetically a witch could start at fourth level. It would be excruciatingly difficult, but not impossible. It's like programming languages. They start you out with something easy, like C. You learn that, then move on to the higher languages. That's not to say you can't jump straight into a higher-level language; people do it all the time. But if you've mastered something like C, the learning curve on other languages decreases significantly. You understand concepts like data structures and functions, which can be ported into any language.

What Savannah said implied something altogether different. If I understood her correctly, every Coven spell was a primary spell, the bottom building block for witch magic. Yet that didn't explain why I'd mastered four spells from the tertiary grimoires. Savannah said Eve hadn't been able to make any of them work. Now, I'd love to believe that I'd mastered them due to my superior spellcasting abilities, but even I am not that smug.

Eve had stolen the grimoires from Margaret. I'd . . . well, I'd pretty much done the same thing. The Coven maintains a library. The tomes are kept in a fortified closet in Margaret Levine's house. With advance notice, witches may visit the collection. Some books may not leave the house; others may be borrowed. To borrow one, you have to fill out a card and return the book within a week. I think the only reason the Elders haven't instituted late fines is because I'm the only one who ever borrows anything. Coven witches aren't even permitted to step into the closet and peruse the collection. Margaret keeps a list posted inside the door, from which they must choose their books. Only Elders and the Coven leader can go inside.

Three years ago, as I was pestering Margaret for a better reference book on herbs, someone knocked at the front door and she took off to answer it, leaving the library. It was like leaving a kid with an open closet full of candy. The moment she was gone, I was in that closet. I knew exactly what I wanted: the prohibited spellbooks.

Now I wanted answers. More than that, I had a hope, a slim hope, that Savannah was both right and wrong: that she was right about the existence of a grimoire that would unlock the spells I now possessed, and that she was wrong in thinking the Coven had destroyed it.

We arrived at Margaret's place, a two-story house on Beech. I opted for the rear door, both as a courtesy and so she couldn't freak out about me showing up on her front doorstep for all of East Falls to see. Being the village pariah does make social calls most trying.

I persuaded Savannah to wait outside with Cortez. Savannah understood her great-aunt well enough to know that Margaret would speak more freely to me alone.

I rang the doorbell. A minute later, Margaret peeped

through the curtain. It took another minute for her to decide to answer it. Even then, she only opened the inside door, keeping one hand on the knob of the screen door.

"You shouldn't be here," she whispered.

"I know."

I wrenched the screen door open and stepped inside. Rude, I know, but I didn't have time for courtesy.

"Where's Savannah?" she asked.

"She's safe. I need to talk to you about some grimoires."

She paused, then peered over my shoulder, scanning the yard, as if I'd brought an entourage of reporters with me. When she didn't see anyone, she closed the door and ushered me farther into the living room, which was filled with boxes of books.

"Please ignore the mess," she said. "I've been organizing the donations for the library book sale. A nerve-wracking task. Absolutely horrible."

I thought of offering to switch places, let her handle the Black Masses and walking dead for a while, but wisely clamped my mouth shut and settled for a quasi-sympathetic nod.

Margaret was the volunteer head librarian at the East Falls library (open two evenings per week plus Saturday afternoons). She'd taken the position after retiring as librarian at the East Falls High School. If this gives the impression that Margaret Levine was a timid little old lady with a steel-gray bun and wire-rimmed glasss, let me correct that. Margaret was five foot ten and had, in her youth, been pursued by every modeling firm in

Boston. At sixty-eight she was still beautiful, with the kind of long-limbed, graceful beauty that her gangly great-niece showed every sign of inheriting. Margaret's one physical flaw was a blind insistence on dyeing her hair jet black, a color that must have been gorgeous on her at thirty but looked almost clownish now.

The one stereotypical librarian characteristic Margaret did possess was timidity. Not the studious timidity of the intellectual, but the vacuous timidity of the, well, . . . intellectually challenged. I've always thought Margaret decided to become a librarian not because she loved books but because it gave her a chance to look intelligent while hiding from the real world.

"Victoria is very angry with you, Paige," Margaret said as she cleared books from a chair. "You shouldn't upset her so. Her health isn't good."

"Look, I need to talk to you about a couple of grimoires I borrowed from the library." I tugged the knapsack from my shoulder, opened it, and removed the books. "These."

She frowned at them. Then her eyes went wide. "Where did you get those?"

"From the library upstairs."

"You aren't supposed to have those, Paige."

"Why? I heard they don't work."

"They don't. We shouldn't have them, but your mother insisted we keep them around as historical relics. I forgot all about them. Here, give them to me and I'll see what Victoria wants done with them."

I shoved the books back into my knapsack.

"You can't take those," she said. "They're library property."

"Then fine me. I'm in enough trouble with Victoria already—keeping these books isn't going to matter."

"If she finds out—"

"We won't tell her. Now, what do you know about these grimoires?"

"They don't work."

"Where did they come from?"

She frowned. "From the library, of course."

Okay, this wasn't getting me anywhere. One look at Margaret's face and I knew she wasn't holding anything back. She wouldn't know how. So I explained what Eve had told Savannah about the books.

"Oh, that's nonsense," Margaret said, fluttering her long fingers. "Absolute nonsense. That girl wasn't right, you know. Eve, I mean. Not right at all. Always looking for trouble, trying to learn new spells, accusing us of holding her back. Just like . . ."

"Like me," I said.

"I didn't mean it like that, dear. I've always liked you. A bit impetuous, but certainly nothing like that niece of mine—"

"It's okay," I said. And to my surprise, it was. I knew I wasn't "just like Eve," and didn't want to be, but the comparison didn't rankle as it once would have. I continued, "You said these spells don't work, right? So how come I can cast four of them?"

"That's not possible, Paige. Don't be telling stories—"

"Shall I demonstrate?" I grabbed the first grimoire from my bag, opened it to a marked page, and thrust it at her. "Here, follow along. It's a fireball spell."

Margaret clamped the book shut. "Don't you dare—"

"Why? You said the spells don't work. I say they do. And I think you know why."

"Be sensible, Paige. If they worked, why would we keep them?"

And that, I believe, was the smartest thing Margaret Levine ever said. No one was covering up anything. The Coven really didn't think these spells worked; otherwise they wouldn't have kept them. What a horrible thing to admit, that the very group designed to support and aid witches would have destroyed their strongest source of magic.

"I want to see the grimoires," I said. "All of them."

"We aren't trying to hide anything from you, Paige. You have to stop accusing us—"

"I'm not accusing you of anything. I just want to see the library."

"I don't think—"

"Listen to me. Please, just listen. Why do you think I'm here? Some sudden whim to learn new spells? I'm here because I need to know that I've done everything I can to protect Savannah—to protect your niece. That's all I want. Let me see the library and I swear, when this is over, you can tell Victoria what I've done. Tell her I stole the grimoires, I don't care. Just let me see what's up there."

Margaret threw up her hands and headed for the stairs. "Fine. If you don't believe me, come up and see. But you're wasting your time."

❧ Stopping by for a Spell

THE FIRST THING I DID was inspect the library closet for hidden compartments. You know, sliding panels, loose floorboards, massive books with incredibly boring titles that really contained forbidden grimoires—that sort of thing.

While I looked, Margaret paced behind me making noises of exasperation. I ignored her. Finally, though, I had to concede that there was no secret niche or hidden books, so I scanned the rows of titles, looking for the ceremony tome. When Margaret paced out of sight, I slid the thin volume into my knapsack. She probably would have let me have it anyway, but I wasn't taking the chance.

With the ceremony book in my bag, I turned my attention to looking for potential secondary-spell grimoires. That didn't take long. Of the forty-three books in the library, there were only four that I hadn't read. A flip through each assured me they were just as dull and useless as their titles implied.

"The grimoires are all right here," Margaret said, waving at a half-shelf near chest level. "All of them."

"All of them" comprised exactly six books. One contained the current collection of Coven-sanctioned spells. Another held spells that had been removed in the past few decades, which my mother had let me copy from her grimoire into my journals. The other four were books of spells long forbidden to Coven witches. There were two reasons why these hadn't been destroyed: first, my mother would never have permitted it; second, the damn things were practically useless.

For years I'd known that these "forbidden" spellbooks existed. For years I'd pestered my mother to let me see them. She finally capitulated by sneaking them out for me as an eighteenth-birthday gift. Inside I found useless spells, like ones to evaporate a puddle of water or extinguish a candle. I hadn't bothered to master more than two dozen of the hundred-odd spells in these books. Most of them were so bad I almost didn't blame the Elders for removing them from the Coven grimoire, if only to conserve space.

As a last resort I flipped through one of these grimoires. I paused at one spell I'd learned, an incantation for producing a small flickering light, like a candle. The Coven-sanctioned light-ball spell was far more useful. I'd learned this one only because it involved fire, and I was always trying to overcome my fear of flames.

When I glanced at the spell, something in it snagged in my brain, made me pause. Under the title "Minor Illumination Spell" the writer had added "elemental, fire, class 3." I'd seen that notation before, recently. I yanked one of the two secret grimoires from my bag and flipped to the dog-eared page with the fireball spell. There it was, under the title: "elemental, fire, class 3."

Oh god, could that be it? My hands trembled as I

flipped to another spell I'd mastered in the third-level grimoire, a wind-summoning spell. Beneath the title: "elemental, wind, class 1." I racked my brain for the names of the two dozen spells I'd learned in the forbidden manuals. What was that one . . . ? Yes, that was it! A spell for extinguishing fire. A silly little spell that summoned a mere puff of wind, barely enough to blow out a candle. I'd tried it a few times, got it to work, then moved on. Grabbing another grimoire from the shelf, I flipped through until I found it. "Minor Wind Summoning Spell: elemental, wind, class 1."

These were the secondary grimoires. I knew now why I'd been able to master four tertiary spells: because I'd learned the secondary spells from these books.

The doorbell rang. Margaret jumped like a spooked cat.

"It's Savannah," I said.

I scooped all four grimoires from the shelf, shoved them into my bag with the other two, and headed for the stairs.

"You can't take those," Margaret called after me.

I bounded down the stairs and opened the back door.

"Lucas says we have to go," Savannah said. "It's getting late."

"I'm done. Just let me grab my shoes." I remembered our other purpose and turned to Margaret. "Could I borrow your car? Just for tonight. Please?"

"I don't think—"

"I'll be careful. I'll fill it up, wash it, whatever. Please, Margaret."

"Savannah?" She noticed her niece for the first time.

"Did you leave her outside alone, Paige? What are you thinking?"

"I didn't leave her alone. Now, I really need to borrow your car."

"Who—" She peered outside, her eyes picking out Cortez's form in the yard. She slammed the door. "That's—you—you left my niece with a sorcerer?"

"Oddly enough, I'm having trouble finding babysitters."

"Lucas is fine, Aunt Margaret," Savannah said. "Can we borrow your car? I need the stuff for my first menses—"

"Savannah just got her period," I cut in. "I'm out of supplies for menstrual tea, and she's having very bad cramps."

Savannah pulled a face of sheer agony.

"Oh, yes. I see." Margaret's voice softened. "This is your first time, isn't it, dear?"

Savannah nodded, lifting wounded puppy eyes to her great-aunt. "It really hurts."

"Yes, well . . . I suppose, if you need to use my car . . ."

"Please," I said.

Margaret retrieved the keys and handed them to me. "Be careful in parking lots, I had someone dent the door just last week."

I thanked her and prodded Savannah toward the door before Margaret could change her mind.

Next stop: Salem, Massachusetts, world-renowned epicenter of the American witch-hunt craze.

One can argue about the causes of the witch craze that visited Salem in 1692. Theories abound. I even read something recently that attributed the madness to some kind of blight on the rye crops, a mold or something that drives people crazy. What we do know, without question, is that life wasn't a whole lotta fun for teenage girls in Puritan America. In the harsh New England winters it was even worse. At least the boys could go out hunting and trapping. Girls were confined to their homes and household tasks, forbidden by Puritan law to dance, sing, play cards, or engage in basically any form of entertainment.

As we drove into Salem, I imagined Savannah plunked into that world. Regimented, repressed, and restricted. Bored as hell. Is it any wonder they'd be eager for diversion? Maybe a little mischief? In the winter of 1692 the girls of Salem found exactly that, in the form of an old woman, a slave named Tituba.

Tituba belonged to Reverend Samuel Parris and was nursemaid to his daughter, Betty, whom, by all accounts, she doted on. To amuse herself during those long winter months, Tituba showed Betty and her friends some magic tricks, probably mere sleights of hand learned in Barbados. As the winter passed, word of this new entertainment swept through the community of teenage girls, and one by one they found reasons to visit the parsonage.

In January, Betty, the youngest of the group, fell ill, her Puritan conscience perhaps made uneasy by all this talk of magic and sorcery. Soon other girls caught the "fever." Reverend Parris and others insisted that the girls name their tormentors. Betty named Tituba, and at the end of February the old slave was arrested on a charge of witchcraft.

And so it started. The girls soon grew addicted to the attention. No longer relegated to house and hearth, they became celebrities. The only way to prolong their fifteen minutes of fame was to up the ante, act wilder, more possessed. To name more witches. So they did. Soon, any woman that the girls might have reason to dislike fell victim.

Four Coven witches died. Why? The witch hunts often targeted social or gender deviants, particularly women who didn't comply with accepted female roles. This described many Coven witches. Outspoken and independent, they often lived without a husband—though that didn't mean they were celibate—a lifestyle choice that wouldn't have been too popular in Puritan New England. It was that lifestyle, not practicing witchcraft, that put those witches on the gallows.

I tried telling that to the Coven once. How did they react? They agreed with me completely, and declared that if those women had had the sense to keep their heads down and conform, they wouldn't have died. I could have beat my head against the wall.

Today, the Salem witch hunts are a tourist attraction. Makes my skin crawl, but the upside is that there are plenty of practicing Wiccans in the area, and several new-age shops in Salem that sell ingredients I'd have a hard time finding elsewhere.

Most of "tourist" Salem had shut down around the dinner hour, but the shop we wanted was open until nine. The roads were quiet and we found parking easily, then headed to the tourism core, several tree-lined streets restricted to pedestrian traffic. It took less than twenty minutes to gather what I needed, then we were back in Margaret's car and heading for the highway.

"We have two hours to kill," I said as I turned back onto 1A. "Any ideas? We can't collect the juniper until after midnight."

"What do we need juniper for?" Savannah asked.

"It'll protect us against interference by evil spirits."

"Oh, right. So when are we getting the grave dirt? That needs to be gathered right at midnight."

"Perhaps we can find a juniper tree at the cemetery," Cortez said.

"What cemetery?" I said. "There's nothing about grave dirt in the ceremony, Savannah. We have everything we need except the juniper."

"Uh-uh. We need grave dirt."

"Savannah, I know the ceremony. I went through it myself, and I double-checked my mother's notes last night."

"Yeah? Well, *my* mother told me everything about the ceremony, and I know I need grave dirt."

"You need earth. Regular dirt collected any time, anywhere."

"No, I need—"

"May I make a suggestion?" Cortez cut in. "In the

interest of avoiding later trouble, I would advise that you clarify your respective understandings of the ceremony."

"Huh?" Savannah said.

"Compare notes," he said. "There's a sign for a park ahead. Pull off, Paige. As you've said, we have time."

"That's not part of the ceremony," I said, pacing between two trees as I listened to Savannah. "Absolutely not. It couldn't be."

"Why? Because the Coven says so? This is what my mother told me to do, Paige."

"But it's not the right ceremony."

Cortez cleared his throat. "Another suggestion? Perhaps we should consider the possibility that this is a variation on the Coven ceremony."

"It's not," I insisted. "It can't be. Listen to the words. They say—No, never mind."

"My Latin is perfectly serviceable, Paige," Cortez said. "I understand the additional passage."

"You might understand the words, but you don't understand the meaning."

"Yes, I do. I have some knowledge of witch mythology. The additional passage is an invocation to Hecate, the Greek goddess of witchcraft, a deity the Coven and most modern witches no longer recognize. The invocation asks Hecate to grant the witch the power to wreak vengeance on her enemies and to free her from all restrictions on her powers. Now, as to the ability of Hecate to grant such a wish, I admit I place little credence in the existence of such deities."

"Same here. So what you're saying is that the passage doesn't do anything, so there's no harm in doing it?"

He paused, giving the question full consideration. "No. While I doubt the existence of Hecate per se, we must both admit that there is some force that gives us our power. Hecate is simply an archaic reference to that force." He glanced at Savannah, who was sitting on a picnic table. "Could you excuse us, Savannah? I'd like to speak to Paige."

Savannah nodded and, without protest, headed off to the empty swing across the park. I really had to learn how he did that.

"I told you about the Cabal's variation on your ceremony," Cortez said when she was gone. "Isn't it possible that other permutations exist?"

"I guess so. But this . . . this is . . ." I shook my head. "Maybe the extra passage doesn't mean anything, maybe it doesn't make any difference, but I can't take that chance. I'd be asking that Savannah be granted something I don't think any witch should have."

"You'd be asking to grant Savannah her full powers, without restriction—an ability you don't think any witch should have?"

"Don't twist my words around. I went through my mother's ceremony and I'm fine."

"Yes, you are. I'm not saying—"

"And I'm not asking for reassurances. Savannah's already a stronger spellcaster than I am. Can you imagine how dangerous she could be with more power?"

"I can't argue this for you. You're the witch, you're

the only one who can perform the ceremony for her."
He stepped closer, putting his fingertips on my arm.
"Go talk to her, Paige. We have to settle this before
midnight."

❧ A Grave Dilemma

"I WON'T!" Savannah shouted, her voice echoing across the vacant park. "I won't do your stupid Coven ceremony! I'd rather have no ceremony at all than be a useless Coven witch."

"Like me."

"I didn't mean that, Paige. You aren't like them. I don't know why you waste your time with them. You can do so much better."

"I don't want to do better. I want to *make* things better. For all of us."

She shook her head. "I won't do your ceremony, Paige. I won't. It's mine or nothing. Don't you understand? This is what my mother told me to do. It's what she wanted for me."

When I didn't respond fast enough, Savannah's face contorted with rage.

"That's it, isn't it? You won't do it because it comes from my mother, because you don't trust her."

"It's not that I don't trust—"

"No, you're right, it isn't. It's because you hate her. You think she was some kind of monster."

I stepped toward Savannah, but she flung me off with such force that I tripped and fell against the picnic table.

"My mother looked after me. *She* wouldn't have let Leah come near me again."

I flinched. "Savannah, I—"

"No, shut up. I'm sick of listening to you. You think my mother was evil because she practiced dark magic? That didn't make her evil, it made her smart. At least she had the guts to get out of the Coven, not hang around learning stupid little baby spells and thinking she's queen of the witches."

I stepped back, bumping the table again and falling hard onto the bench. Cortez hurried from the woods, where he'd been burying the Hand of Glory. I shook my head to warn him off, but Savannah stepped into my line of vision and towered over me.

"You know what?" she said. "I know why you won't do that ceremony for me. Because you're jealous. Because your mother made you go through that useless Coven ceremony and now it's too late, you're stuck. You can't go back and do it over again. You can't get more powerful. So you're going to hold me back because your mother didn't—"

"Enough," Cortez said, pushing Savannah away from me. "That is enough, Savannah."

"Back off, sorcerer," she said, turning on him.

"You back off, Savannah," he replied. "Now."

Savannah's face fell, as if all that anger suddenly gave way.

"Go back to the swings and cool down, Savannah," he ordered.

She obeyed, giving only a tiny nod.

"Let her go," Cortez whispered when I made a motion

to stand. "She'll be fine. You have a decision to make."

With that, he sat beside me and didn't say another word while I made that decision.

Would I force Savannah to settle for less than her full potential? Once the choice was made, there was no reversing it. A witch has exactly one night to turn the tide of her destiny. Melodramatic, but true.

Was I jealous of Savannah for still having the opportunity to become a more powerful witch? No. The thought hadn't occurred to me until she mentioned it. Now that she had, though, it did give me something to think about. The chance had passed for me. If, as Eve claimed, this other ceremony would make a witch stronger, then yes, it stung to think I'd missed out. Given the choice, I'd have picked the stronger ceremony without question. Even without knowing whether it worked, even without knowing how much more power it could give me, I would have taken the chance.

Did I trust Savannah with this power? Give me the ability to kill and you'd never need to worry about me suffocating some jerk who cut me off on the freeway; knowing I possessed the power would be enough. But Savannah was different. She already used her power at the slightest provocation. Yesterday, when we found that investigator in our house, Savannah had thrown him into the wall. Would she have settled for that if she could have killed him? Yet I couldn't wait around to see whether she'd outgrow her recklessness; either I performed that

ceremony tomorrow or I never did it at all. And with
that came another responsibility: if I gave Savannah those
powers, I would need to teach her to control them. Could
I do that?

Savannah's mother may have passed along some atti-
tudes with which I strongly disagreed, but Eve had loved
her daughter and wanted the best for her. She'd believed
that the "best" was this ceremony. Did I dare dispute
that?

How could I make a decision like this so quickly? I
needed days, maybe weeks. I had only minutes.

I walked up behind Savannah as she swung, her sneakers
scuffing the dirt into clouds.

"I'll do the ceremony," I said. "Your ceremony."

"Really?" Seeing my expression, her grin collapsed.
"I didn't mean it, Paige—what I said."

"What's said is said."

I walked back to the car.

I drove in silence, answering only questions directed at
me.

"Can I see the grimoires, Paige?" Savannah asked,
bobbing from the back seat. I nodded. "Maybe I can help
you learn these. Or we can learn them together."

I had to say something. I'm no good at holding
grudges; it feels too much like sulking.

"Sure," I said. "That . . . sounds good."

Cortez glanced back at the grimoire in Savannah's

hands, then looked at me. He didn't say anything, but his look oozed curiosity.

"Later," I mouthed.

He nodded, and silence prevailed until we reached the outskirts of East Falls.

"Okay," I said as we drove into town, "we've got a decision to make. We need this grave dirt, but I'm not going near the East Falls cemetery. The last thing I need is for someone to look down from the hospital and see me darting amongst tombstones. So, we have two choices. One, we can go to the county cemetery. Two, we can go to the one here in town and you can get the dirt, Cortez."

He sighed.

"Okay, I guess that answers my question—we head to the county cemetery."

"It wasn't the proposition to which I was registering my objection."

"So what's wrong?"

"Nothing."

Savannah leaned over the seat. "He's pissed because you're still calling—"

Cortez cut her off. "I'm not 'pissed' about anything. The town cemetery is closer. I'll get the dirt."

"You don't mind?"

"Not at all. I should be able to retrieve dirt through the fence without having to enter the cemetery proper, and therefore without risk of being seen."

"Is that where they buried Cary?" Savannah asked. "By the fence?"

"I think he was cremated."

Cortez nodded. "A course of action which, had it not been determined prior to the visitation, I'm quite certain would have been considered afterward."

"No kidding," I said with a shudder. "After that, I'm a cremation convert."

"Wait a sec," Savannah said. "If they cremated Cary, how are we going to take dirt from his grave?"

"We aren't."

"Lucas can't take it from just anyone," Savannah said. "It has to be from the grave of someone who was murdered."

"What?"

"Uh, didn't I mention that?"

"No."

"Ummm, sorry, guys."

"We have"—I checked the clock—"forty-five minutes to find the grave of someone who was murdered. Great. Just great."

"Pull over again," Cortez said. "We're going to need to give this some thought."

We'd been sitting at the side of the road for nearly ten minutes. Finally, I sighed and shook my head.

"I can't even think of the last person who was murdered in East Falls. The Willard girl was killed by a drunk driver before Christmas, but I'm not sure that counts."

"We ought not to take the chance."

I thudded back against the headrest. "Okay, let me

think." I bolted upright. "I've got it! The woman in the funeral home. The one behind the curtain. Someone shot her. I don't know the story—probably because I've been avoiding the papers—but that's murder, isn't it? Or could it be manslaughter?"

"Premeditated or not, it appears a clear case of homicide, and that will be sufficient. Is she buried in town?"

"Oh god, I don't know. I didn't recognize her. She probably wasn't from East Falls, but I can't be sure. Shit! Oh, wait. It would say in the local paper, right? If we could get last week's paper—"

"How are we going to do that?" Savannah asked.

"Hold on, let me think." I paused, then smiled. "Got it. Elena. She's a journalist. She should have resources, right?"

"She'll have access to online news-wire services." He passed me his cellphone. "Tell her to search for anything on Katrina Mott."

"Where'd you get the name?" Savannah asked.

"From the notice board outside the funeral home yesterday. There were only two services listed."

"Good memory," I said.

He nodded and turned on the phone for me.

As I'd hoped, Elena hadn't gone to bed yet, though it was past eleven on a weeknight. Not that her social calendar was any busier than mine—she stuck pretty close to home, which was several hours from any late-night city clubs—but she had the advantage of housemates over the age of thirteen, neither of whom had to get up early for work or school. Plus there was the whole werewolf thing, which often necessitated late nights. When I called, she was outside playing touch football with visiting Pack mates. Rough life, huh?

She took the information and called back within five minutes.

"Katrina Mott," she said. "Died Friday, June 15. Shot to death by her common-law husband during an argument because he—and I quote—'wanted to shut her (obscenity deleted) mouth for good.' Sounds like murder to me. Hope the bastard gets life."

"Life in prison and a lifetime of haunting, if there's any justice in the world. Does it say where she was being buried?"

"Uh ... oh, here. Memorial at East Falls Funeral Parlor followed by interment Tuesday morning at Pleasant View Cemetery."

"The county cemetery. Perfect. Thanks."

"No problem. You sure you don't need help? Nick's here for the weekend. The three of us could come—Clay, Nick, and I. Or is that exactly what you *don't* need?"

"Something like that. No offense, but—"

"None taken. If you need more subtle muscle, I can sneak down without Clay. For a while at least. Until he finds me. Sounds like you have everything under control, though."

I made a noncommittal noise.

"Call me if you need me, okay?" she continued. "Even if you just want a bodyguard for Savannah. She's still coming up here next month, right?"

"Absolutely."

She laughed. "Do I hear relief in your voice? We're looking forward to having her."

"Uh-huh. Let me guess, 'we' as in you and Jeremy."

Another laugh. "Clay's fine with it. Not counting down the days, but not complaining either. With Clay, that's a sign of near approval."

"Approval of Savannah, not me."

"Give it time. You're still staying for the weekend, right? And we're driving down to New York? The two of us?"

"Absolutely."

Savannah was waving for the phone.

"I·have to go," I said. "Savannah wants to talk."

"Pass her over and I'll talk to you soon."

As I passed Savannah the phone and started the car, I couldn't help smiling. For two minutes there, I'd forgotten everything else. Two minutes in which I could again see the future progressing exactly as I'd planned it before all this started. I'd get through this. Then I'd go on to enjoy my summer. I'd have a Savannah-free week to squeeze in some social time with my Boston-area friends, plus a New York weekend to develop my friendship with Elena.

For the first time since Leah arrived in East Falls, I could envision a day when all this would be a memory, something to talk about with Elena over drinks at an overpriced New York nightclub. With that came a renewed burst of optimism. I would get past this.

Now I just had to gather dirt from a murdered woman's grave before the stroke of twelve. I could handle that.

A Good Walk Spoiled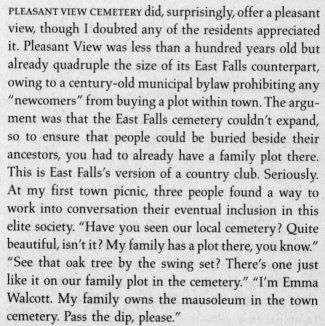

PLEASANT VIEW CEMETERY did, surprisingly, offer a pleasant view, though I doubted any of the residents appreciated it. Pleasant View was less than a hundred years old but already quadruple the size of its East Falls counterpart, owing to a century-old municipal bylaw prohibiting any "newcomers" from buying a plot within town. The argument was that the East Falls cemetery couldn't expand, so to ensure that people could be buried beside their ancestors, you had to already have a family plot there. This is East Falls's version of a country club. Seriously. At my first town picnic, three people found a way to work into conversation their eventual inclusion in this elite society. "Have you seen our local cemetery? Quite beautiful, isn't it? My family has a plot there, you know." "See that oak tree by the swing set? There's one just like it on our family plot in the cemetery." "I'm Emma Walcott. My family owns the mausoleum in the town cemetery. Pass the dip, please."

Though it already holds many more graves than East Falls, the Pleasant View site is so large that the burials are spaced out, some tucked in valleys, some nestled in wooded groves, some amidst meadows of wildflowers. Legend has it that an unnamed philanthropist donated the land and decreed that nature be left as unspoiled as possible. Members of the East Falls elite say the old guy gave away the property to save on taxes and the county was too cheap to clear it, but they're just jealous because they're gonna spend eternity surrounded by a hospital, a funeral home, and a 7–Eleven.

The parking lot for Pleasant View was empty, as one might expect at eleven-thirty on a Tuesday night. Eschewing the lot, I pulled over along the side road.

"How are we going to find her?" Savannah asked, squinting into the darkness beyond the car.

"At the front gates there's a map showing where everyone's buried."

"That's handy."

"Handy and necessary," I said. "Some of these graves are almost hidden in the trees. The only problem is that they may not have added Ms. Mott yet, in which case we'll have to do some searching."

As we neared the map, a horrible thought struck me. What if Mott hadn't been buried today? Her death notice listed the funeral for this morning, but that was before her corpse got up and started slugging people.

To my relief, Katrina Mott's grave had been penciled in on the map.

"Would you like me to collect the dirt?" Cortez asked.

I shook my head. "There's no risk of being seen here, so I'll do it. You two can wait back at the car."

"Uh-uh," Savannah said. "It's my dirt. I'm helping you get it."

"I'll stand watch within the cemetery," Cortez said.

"You don't have to," I said. "It's dark, secluded. No one can see us."

"Humor me."

Katrina Mott's grave was near the middle, nestled in a U-shaped cluster of cedars. Sounded easy enough to find, and it probably was—during the day. At night, though, all trees look alike, and my ability to judge distances was severely compromised by the fact that I could see only five feet in either direction. If there was a moon overhead, it went into hiding the moment we entered the cemetery.

After stumbling over two graves, I cast a light-ball spell. A glowing ball appeared in my palm. I tossed it and it hovered before me, lighting my way.

"Now *that* is definitely handy," Cortez observed.

"You don't know this one?" I asked.

He shook his head. "You'll have to teach me."

"She's teaching it to me first," Savannah said. "After all, *I'm* the witch."

Cortez was about to answer, then stopped and looked around. "There—Ms. Mott is buried over that hill."

"How do you know that?" Savannah asked.

His lips twitched in a tiny smile. "Magic."

"He memorized the map," I said. "It went gully, hill, three oaks, then another hill. There's the oaks. Now let's get moving. We've only got ten minutes."

"It doesn't need to be precisely on the stroke of twelve," Cortez said. "That, I fear, is a romantic yet illogical embellishment. Illogical because—"

"Because the 'stroke of twelve,' according to someone's watch, probably won't be dead-on." I glanced at the graves near my feet. "Sorry, folks. No pun intended."

"So what does it mean, then?" Savannah asked.

"Simply that you must gather the dirt in the dead of ni—" He looked around. "That is to say, roughly at midnight, give or take an hour or so."

"Well, I'm not hanging around," I said. "If I can grab it now, I'm doing that and getting out of here."

"Go ahead," Cortez said. "I see some juniper over there. I'll gather that, then stand watch partway up the hill."

"Don't you think it's spooky out here?" Savannah asked as we tramped up the hill, having left Cortez behind.

"Peaceful, actually. Very peaceful."

"Do you think that's what it's like when you die? Peaceful?"

"Maybe."

"Kinda boring, don't you think?"

I smiled over at her. "Yes, I suppose so. Maybe just a little peace, then. A break."

"Before what?"

I shrugged.

"Come on, Paige. What do you think happens? After all this."

"I'll tell you what I'd like to happen. I'd like to come back."

"Reincarnation?"

"Sure. Come back and do it all over again. All the

good and all the bad. That's what I'd want for my eternity."

"Do you believe what they say? That you keep coming back with the same people? All the people you cared about?"

"It would be nice, don't you think?"

She nodded. "Yeah, that would be nice."

We climbed in silence the rest of the way. When we got to the top of the hill, Savannah paused.

"Do you hear that?"

I stopped. "What?"

"Voices. Like whispers."

"I hear the wind."

I started forward again, but she grabbed my arm.

"No, really, Paige. Listen. I hear whispering."

The wind rustled through the trees. I shivered.

"Okay," I said, "now you're scaring me. So much for a peaceful walk."

She grinned. "Sorry. I guess it is just the wind. Hey, what if Leah's necromancer buddy followed us here? This place would be even worse than the funeral parlor, wouldn't it?"

"Thanks for bringing that up."

"Oh, I'm kidding. There's no one here. Look." She gestured at the vista below the hill. "You can see all the way to the entrance. Nobody's there. Anyway, Lucas is guarding the path. He's an okay sorcerer. Not great, but at least he could shout and warn us."

"Sure, but Leah would probably knock him unconscious before he finished whatever he was trying to shout."

Cortez's voice floated up on the still night air. "I can hear you perfectly well. This is a cemetery—there isn't much in the way of noise interference."

"Sorry," I called down.

"Did you hear me too?" Savannah asked.

"The part about me being an 'okay sorcerer'? 'Not great'? No, I believe I missed that."

"Sorry."

A sound floated up, something suspiciously like a chuckle. "Quiet down and get moving before we learn whether it really is possible to make enough noise to wake the dead."

"What are we putting the dirt in?" Savannah asked as we approached the trees surrounding Mott's grave.

I took a sandwich bag from my pocket.

"A Baggie?"

"A Ziploc Baggie."

"You're putting grave dirt in a Ziploc? Shouldn't we have a fancy bottle or something?"

"I thought of bringing a jam jar, but it could break."

"*A jam jar?* What kind of witch are you?"

"A very practical one."

"What if the Baggie breaks?"

I reached into my pocket and pulled out another one. "Backup Baggie."

Savannah shook her head.

I pushed through the cedars. Three graves lay in the

cup formed by the *U*. I didn't need to check the head-stones to find Mott's; the fresh dirt had not yet been covered with sod. Perfect.

I took a small trowel from my coat pocket, bent over, and was blinded by a sudden glare of light. As I stumbled backward into Savannah, I dowsed my light-ball—yet the light was still there. Someone was shining a flashlight into our faces.

Savannah started an incantation, but I clapped my hand over her mouth before she could finish.

"See?" a woman's voice said. "It *is* her. I told you so."

The flashlight dropped and I found myself standing before four people, ranging in age from college-bound to mid-retirement.

"Wow," whispered the youngest, a woman with rings through her lower lip. "It's the witch from the news-papers."

"I'm not— What are you doing here?"

"Seems we should ask you the same thing," a twenty-something man in a ball cap said.

A middle-aged woman, the one who'd spoken first, shushed him. "She's here for the same reason we are."

"To find the treasure?"

She glared at him. "To communicate with the spirit world."

"Is it true you saw her rise from the dead?" the younger woman asked, pointing at Mott's grave. "That is so cool. What was it like? Did she say anything?"

"Yeah," Savannah replied. "She said, 'Bother me again and I'll rip your—'"

I prodded her to silence. "Do you people know what

you're doing? It's called disturbing a gravesite. A—uh—" I slipped my trowel behind my back. "A very serious offense."

"Nice try," the young man said. "My brother's a cop. We can't get in trouble unless we dig her up. We aren't stupid."

"No," Savannah said, "you're just hanging around a cemetery looking for buried treasure. 'Hey, wait, I think I found something! Nope, just another rotting corpse.'"

"Mind your tongue, child," the older woman snapped. "While I disagree with the concept of using the spirits for material gain, necromancers in the ancient world often did exactly that. They believed that the dead could see all—the past, the present, and the future—thus allowing them to locate hidden treasures."

The elderly man beside her made a noise.

"Quite right," she said. "Bob wishes me to clarify that the dead are believed to be able to find *any* treasure, not just that which they themselves may have buried."

"He said all that with a grunt?" Savannah asked.

"Mental telepathy, dear. Bob has moved beyond the realm of verbal communication."

"Maybe so, but he hasn't moved beyond the realm of human justice," I said, bending to pick up a saucer of dried mushrooms, which I doubted were shiitake. "Bet these help with the mental telepathy. Maybe you can explain this to the police."

"There's no need to threaten us, dear. We're no danger to you or anyone else. We simply want to communicate with poor Miss Mott. A spirit who has been raised once remains very close to the surface, as I'm sure you're aware. If we can contact her, perhaps she can relay a message from the other side."

"Or tell us where to find treasure," the young man said.

The young woman rolled her eyes. "You and Joe, always on about your treasure." She looked at me. "Joe's another member of our group. Joe and Sylvia. Only Joe had bowling tonight and Sylvia doesn't like to drive after dark."

"Uh-huh."

"We don't need to worry about these guys raising the dead, Paige," Savannah said. "They're so dumb they couldn't raise—"

I elbowed her to silence. "I'm going to ask you, once more, to leave."

The young man stepped forward, towering over me. "Or what?"

"Better be careful, or she'll show you," Savannah said.

"Is that a threat?"

"That's enough," I said. "Now, we're all leaving—"

"Who's leaving?" the young man said. "I'm not leaving."

The older woman's mouth was set. "We aren't leaving until we've communicated with the spirit world."

"Fine," Savannah said. "Here, let me help you."

Her voice rose, words echoing through the silence as she recited an incantation in Hebrew. I whirled to stop her. Before I could, she finished. All went silent.

"Damn," she muttered, leaning in so only I could hear her. "It's supposed to—"

Her body went rigid, head jerking back, arms flying out. A deafening crack ripped through the silence, like the thunder of a hundred guns fired at once. A flare of light lit up the sky. Savannah stood on tiptoe, barely touching the ground, body shaking. I dove for her. As my fingers grazed her arm, something hit me in the gut, throwing me into a tombstone.

Kinda Cool . . .
in a Bad Way ❦

WHEN I RECOVERED from my fall, I saw that Savannah had collapsed. The four would-be necromancers stood ringed around her prone body. I pushed myself up and ran to Savannah. She was unconscious, her face white.

"Call an ambulance," I said.

Nobody moved. I checked Savannah's pulse: weak but steady.

"Wow," the young woman said. "That was, like, so cool."

"Call a goddamned ambulance!" I snarled.

Again no one moved. Around us, the air had gone still, but I could feel the crackle of energy. At a sound near the trees, I looked up and saw a shape moving toward us. Someone was coming.

Cortez. Perfect. He had a cellphone.

I raised my head to tell him to hurry and saw the figure emerge from the trees. But it wasn't a figure at all. It was a writhing mass of reddish light that twisted on itself, turning blue, then green, then yellow. To my left, wisps of light wafted from the ground, congealing into masses that hovered over the earth then shot into the air. We all stared, transfixed, as one after another, these airy phantasms of color rose from the soil around us.

"Oooh," the young woman said. "They're so pretty."

Lights shot up all around us, gaining in speed, hurling into the air. One soared up right beside me, then swerved and dove at my head. The breath flew from me, was literally sucked from my lungs. I gasped. The light darted off into the trees.

Suddenly the ground began to shake. Light streamed from the earth. Something knocked me hard, pushing me away from Savannah. A deafening howl rent the air. I dove toward Savannah, but a geyser of light erupted between us, pushing me back. The ground quaked, knocking me to my knees. Howl after howl tore through the night.

"Savannah!" I shouted.

The moment my mouth opened, the air was ripped from my throat. A globe of light surrounded my head, sucking the air from me. Pain cleaved through my chest. I couldn't breathe. As I fought, the light seemed to take form. I clawed at my attacker, but my fingers passed through it.

"Stop fighting!" a voice said at my ear.

I struggled harder, legs and arms flailing against the thing.

"Goddamn it, Paige, don't fight! You're making it worse!"

Cortez? As my brain registered his voice, my body went still for a brief second. The light evaporated and I fell back, hitting the ground and gulping air. Cortez bent over me.

"They're koyut," he explained. "They feed off energy. If you fight, you only produce more."

I pushed him away and sat up, wildly looking about for Savannah.

"She's right here," Cortez said, pointing at a prone form behind him. "She's fine. I'll carry her. We need to move past the trees."

He grabbed her up and we ran. When we reached the meadow beyond the trees, Cortez stopped me.

"We need to wake her," he said. "What did she cast?"

"I—I don't know."

I looked back toward the grove. Light trumpeted up from treetops. The howls were muted, as if soundproofed within the grove. A man screamed.

"I need to help the others," I said, starting to run.

Cortez lunged and grabbed me. "Koyut don't kill. As soon as people lose consciousness, the koyut leave them alone. We need to concentrate on Savannah. What did she say?"

"It was Hebrew. I'm not good at Hebrew. I think—" I closed my eyes and willed my thumping heart to slow so I could concentrate. "She said something about summoning forces. Forces or energies, I'm not sure which."

"Summoning the energies of the earth. It's a sorcerer spell."

"You know it?"

"I know *of* it. I haven't learned it because it's not something I can ever imagine needing to use. It calls on the spirits of the earth, not to perform any particular task, but simply to respond and do as they wish. It's considered a chaos spell."

"No kidding," I said. "What was Savannah thinking?"

"It—it's never worked before," Savannah's thin voice said beside us. "All it ever does is make some noise and flashing lights. Like a prank. Dime store magic. Only this time—"

"Only this time it behaved precisely as intended," Cortez said. "Owing, no doubt, to your increasing strength. Plus the fact that you chose to cast it in a cemetery, a place rich in energy."

I knelt beside Savannah. "Are you okay?"

She pushed herself up onto her elbows. "Yeah. Sorry about that, guys." She gave a tiny smile. "Only it was kinda cool, wasn't it?"

We both glared at her.

"I mean, kinda cool in a bad way."

"I would suggest that is one spell you can safely remove from your repertoire," Cortez said. "I would also suggest that we return to the car before the lights attract—"

"I still need the dirt," I said.

"I'm fast," Savannah said. "I can get it."

"No!" we said in unison.

Cortez insisted on following me to the edge of the trees, so he could jump in if anything went wrong. It didn't. By now the lights had dimmed to a soft glow, illuminating the glade and the four figures lying blissfully unconscious within. I scooped dirt into both bags, shoved them into my pocket, and headed back to Cortez and Savannah.

"So that's what spirits look like?" Savannah asked, watching the swirling, multicolored glow.

"Not human spirits," I said. "Nature spirits and their energy. Let's go."

Savannah stepped away from the trees, then stopped and stared, transfixed.

"Yes, very pretty," I said, reaching for her arm. "Now move!"

Her body went rigid. A wave of physical energy shot from her, knocking both Cortez and me off our feet. The ground shivered. A low, nearly inaudible moan seemed to emanate from the earth itself. Geysers of dirt erupted, borne up on rocketing streams of light. Then the wind began to scream—not wail, but scream a high-pitched, endless shriek that made me double over, hands clamped to my ears.

Cortez grabbed my shoulder and shook me, mouthing "To the car" once he had my attention. He hoisted Savannah's limp form over his shoulder and began to run. I followed.

As we crested the hill, I saw lights in the distance— not the glow of spirits, but the very human illumination of flashlights and headlights. I looked at Cortez, but he had his head down, struggling to get Savannah to the top of the steep hill. I shouted to him, but the wail of the wind sucked the words from my mouth. Lunging, I snagged the back of his shirt. He twisted, nearly tumbling onto me. I steadied him and gestured toward the road.

The flashing lights of police cars now cut through the night, joining a mob of flashlight beams spilling through the cemetery gates. Cortez's lips moved in a soundless curse and he wheeled around. I pointed at the woods to our left and he nodded.

As we raced for the woods, the shrieks and lights pursued us. No, that's a poor choice of words, implying that the spirits were trying to attack us; they weren't. They simply followed, arising from the ground in our tracks. Elsewhere, the commotion appeared to be dying down. Or maybe it just seemed that way in comparison with the chaos erupting around us. I wasn't about to stop for a scientific survey of the situation.

Once we reached the woods, Cortez lowered Savannah's body to the ground. Then he raised his hands, and said a few words. As he swept his right hand across the air, the spirits vanished.

"I thought you couldn't do that kind of magic," I said, wheezing as I struggled for breath.

"I said I saw no need to learn how to conjure such spirits. I did, however, see a distinct need to learn how to un-conjure them. Unfortunately, it's a geographically limited spell."

"Meaning if we leave the woods, they'll return. Fine by me. I haven't run that fast since grade school. No, strike that, I've *never* run that fast."

I lowered myself to the ground beside Savannah and checked her vital signs. She was unconscious but breathing fine.

"How come they keep following her?" I asked.

"To be honest, I have no idea. Perhaps they're feeding off her energy. I would assume, from my knowledge of witch folklore, that the sudden surge in a witch's powers during first menses renders those powers unpredictable."

"That's an understatement."

I leaned against a tree. At my feet, a wisp of light

floated from the earth. I jumped up so fast I banged my head against an overhanging limb.

"I thought you—"

Cortez waved me to silence. As I watched, the light drifted upward. Unlike the earlier spirits, this light was pure white and it floated up as lazily as smoke from a dying fire. When it reached a height of about five feet, it stopped and shimmered, growing denser.

At a motion to my left, I turned and saw four more towers of light, each a different height. I looked inquiringly at Cortez, but he lifted a hand as if telling me to watch and wait. The cones of light took on form. Particles of light flowed from all sides, adding to the shapes and giving them definition.

Before me stood five people dressed in colonial-era clothing: a man and a boy in doublets and breeches, a woman and a teenage girl in fitted jackets, skirts, and white caps, and a toddler, its gender indeterminate in its long white gown. Though the light remained white, the forms were so solid I could see the wrinkles around the man's eyes. Those eyes stared directly into mine. The man turned to the woman and spoke, lips moving soundlessly. She nodded and replied.

"Ghosts," I said.

The girl tilted her head and frowned at me, saying something to her mother. Then the boy reached out toward Cortez. His father leaped forward and caught his arm, lips moving in a silent scolding. Even the toddler stared up at us, wide-eyed. When I stepped toward the child, the mother swept up the little one in her arms, glaring at me. The father moved toward his wife, motioning the other two children closer. The boy's hands made the sign of the evil eye.

"Only they don't know who the ghosts are," I said.

Cortez gave a tiny smile. "Do you?"

The family, now clustered together, turned and began to walk away. The toddler grinned and waved at us over his mother's shoulder. I waved back. Cortez extended his left hand. I thought he was going to wave, but he said a few words in Latin. As he balled his hand into a fist, the family began to fade. Just before they vanished, the daughter glanced over her shoulder and shot us an accusing glare.

"Rest in peace," I whispered. I turned to Cortez. "I thought you said Savannah's spell was for summoning nature spirits, not ghosts."

"It is, but it seems to be doing a lot it was never intended to do."

"How do we stop it?"

"By getting her out of this graveyard."

"That'll end it?"

"I hope so. Now, when we leave these woods, the spirits will return, but, as you saw, they intend no harm. You simply have to move through them, as you moved through that sorcerer illusion in the funeral home."

"Got it. If we head south, we'll hit the road. There's no fence, so we can—"

A howling cut me off. This wasn't the howls of the spirits but the distinct howl of a dog on a scent.

"The hounds of hell, I presume," Cortez said.

"I wouldn't bet against it. But I think those are tracking dogs, probably with the police."

"Ah, I forgot about the police. Problem number sixty-three, I believe."

"Sixty-four—the unconscious bodies scattered around Katrina Mott's grave are sixty-three. Or they will be, when they wake up." I took a deep breath. "Okay, let's think. There's a stream to the west. Dogs can't follow a trail through water. Plus, it's in the opposite direction, so we'll get a head start."

"West it is, then." He hauled Savannah's limp form over his shoulder. "Lead the way."

So we ran—away from the gun-toting state troopers, through a swirling mass of spirits, pursued by baying hounds, surrounded by the screams of the damned. You know, I think the mind has a saturation point beyond which it just doesn't give a damn. Spirits? Hounds? Cops? Who cares? Just keep running and it'll all go away.

This whole running-away business is getting tedious, so here's the condensed version: Run to water. Tramp through water. Fail to evade hounds. Throw fireballs at hounds. Make mental note to send sizable donation to SPCA. Reach road. Jog to car. Collapse, wheezing, beside car. Get dragged into car by Cortez. Mutter excuse about childhood asthma. Make mental note to join a gym.

"Do you have the dirt?" Cortez asked.

"Dirt?"

I cannot describe the look on his face. The shock. The disbelief. The horror.

"Oh, *that* dirt." I pulled both bags from my pocket. "Got it."

I relinquished the driving to Cortez so I could stay in the back seat with Savannah, who was still unconscious.

Good thing I did, too, because while I consider myself an excellent driver, I have little experience at it, having always preferred to walk or ride my bike. The upshot being that, had I been behind the wheel, I would have been ill prepared to handle what happened next.

Cortez pulled onto the road, not turning us back toward the highway but heading farther down the dirt road, away from the cemetery front gates. Before we reached the first crossroad, however, sirens sounded behind us. I twisted to look out the rear-view mirror and saw a state police car bearing down on us, lights flashing.

"Shit!" I said. "Don't pull over!"

"I wasn't about to. Are you both buckled in?"

"Yes."

"Hold on, then."

With that, he turned off the headlights and hit the gas.

The Conscientious
Car Thief ❧

MARGARET'S CAR WAS an Oldsmobile. An old Olds, probably from the mid-eighties. This meant that it went like a bat out of hell but didn't corner so well, as Cortez discovered the first time he sailed around a bend and nearly into the ditch. On the plus side, the Olds, being a wide-bodied car, was also good at off-roading.

Yes, I said "off-roading," as in leaving the road and cutting through a farmer's field. Imagine it, please: it's past midnight, with no discernible moon or stars, the headlights are off, and you're rocketing across a rutted field at forty miles an hour. Let me assure you, for sheer terror, it ranks right up there with getting your breath sucked out by a koyut.

How we managed to get to the other side without flipping over is beyond me. The car never even slid. Before we'd gone fifty feet into the field, the police cruiser backed off.

We shot out the other side onto empty country roads.

"Are you okay?" Cortez asked as he slowed the car.

"Jostled, but fine. That was some driving."

"Where are we?" Savannah asked, sitting up.

"Heading home," I replied.

Cortez glanced in the rear-view mirror. "Unfortunately, we have something of a predicament. I would presume those officers made a note of our license plate."

"You're right. I didn't think of that."

"Not to worry. It simply means we have to abandon the car outside town and walk in through the woods. When we get to your house, you'll need to call Miss Levine and apprise her of the situation. If the police arrive before morning, she can claim the car was stolen while she slept. If they don't contact her by nine, I would advise that she call and report the car missing."

"Police?" Savannah said, blinking sleepily. "What police?"

"Don't ask," I said. "And don't ever cast that spell again. Please."

"I conjured cops?"

"In a manner of speaking," Cortez said. "I'm going to pull over up here. I believe that leaves us with about a twenty-minute walk."

He parked the car with the nose pulled into a stretch of forest, leaving the tail end out, so it could be found, but not easily.

"Should we leave the keys in the ignition?" I said as I hoisted my knapsack onto my shoulder.

"No, that would raise too many questions as to how the thieves obtained the keys. Better to make this look like a typical car-theft." He opened his jacket and pulled out a tiny tool case.

"You're going to hot-wire it?" Savannah said, leaning

over the seat. "Cool. Did you boost cars when you were a kid?"

"Certainly not."

"Let me guess," I said. "Another of those questionable but necessary skills. Like knowing how to un-conjure ghosts and drive a getaway car."

"Precisely."

"How many cars have you boosted?" Savannah asked as we got out of the car and headed down the road on foot.

"Two. Both times, I assure you, it was an absolute last resort. I found myself without transportation and in urgent need of it. Fortunately, neither vehicle was damaged, and I was able to leave them in safe places, after washing them and filling the tanks."

I grinned. "Bet that had the cops scratching their heads—a conscientious car-thief."

Savannah rolled her eyes. "Don't you guys ever do anything bad?"

"I lifted a tube of lipstick when I was twelve."

"Yeah, you told me about that one." She looked at Cortez. "Know what she did? Stole it, then felt so bad she mailed the money to the store. Tax included. You guys are really setting a bad example, you know."

"A *bad* example?"

"Sure. How do you expect me to live up to it? I'm going to need serious therapy someday."

"Don't worry," I said. "I've budgeted for that."

"She probably has," Savannah muttered. "What about—"

"Car coming," I said. "Off the road."

We tramped into a field.

"Do you do this a lot, Lucas?" Savannah asked. "Car chases and evading the cops and stuff?"

"On occasion, though I would hesitate to say it qualified as often."

"The real question is: how often do you have to do it this often?" I said.

He smiled. "Not often."

"So, we're special?" Savannah said.

"Very special."

"I don't think that's good," I said.

I transferred the knapsack to my other shoulder. Cortez reached to take it from me, but I waved him back.

Savannah tripped in a groundhog hole, then jogged up beside Cortez. "So what kind of case is this? Compared to your other ones?"

"Frenetic."

She glanced at me for clarification.

"He means we're keeping him busy. Mainly because we're causing half the trouble ourselves."

Cortez smiled. "I must admit, you two do have a unique predilection for creating new challenges."

"Unique," Savannah said. "He means we're special."

"Uh-huh," I said.

We re-entered the house the same way we'd left, coming through the woods then darting across the yard and in the back door. A quick peek out the front confirmed that such caution was warranted. There were still three or four people camped out on my lawn. One of them had even erected a pup tent. I considered charging site rental fees.

After sending Savannah off to bed, I called Margaret. The conversation went something like this:

Me: Ummm, we had a problem with your car . . .

Her: An accident! Oh dear, no. My insurance rates—

Me: Not an accident. We're all fine, including the car. We just had to ditch it.

Her: You drove it into the ditch?

Me: Sorry, I meant "abandon." The police saw the license number and—

Her: Police?

Me: Everything's fine, but when the police find it, say it was stolen.

Her: Stolen?

Me: Right. Say it was in the driveway when you went to bed and you never saw it again. Don't mention the keys. And if the police say anything about the cemetery—

Her: Cemetery?

Me: Tell them you don't know anything about it.

Her: But I don't!

Me: Good. Whatever they say, you know nothing. You haven't seen me in days. If they find my prints in your car, it's because I borrowed it last month, okay?

Her: Prints? Do you mean fingerprints? What on earth have you—

Me: Gotta go. Thanks for letting us borrow the car. I'll make it up to you. Bye.

When I walked into the living room, Cortez was standing in front of the television, flipping channels.

"TV," I said as I collapsed onto the sofa. "Great invention. The perfect mindless antidote for a hellish day. So what's on?"

"*Night of the Living Dead.*"

"Ha-ha."

"I'm quite serious." He turned back a few channels and stopped on a black-and-white image of the moaning undead lurching around a farmhouse.

"Kinda looks familiar," I said. "Haven't I seen this before?"

"Yesterday. In the funeral home."

"No, that's not it. Those undead were much scarier. And they didn't lurch. Well, Cary did, but only 'cause he was kind of squashed. Hmmm ... where have I seen this? Ghouls surrounding a house, trapping the inhabitants within, refusing to leave. Wait! That's my front lawn. Look, there's a naked woman! Bet she's a Wiccan."

Cortez chuckled. "I'm glad you can laugh about it."

I hesitated, then glanced over at him. "You know, if this gets to be too much ... I mean, this isn't quite the nice, easy court case you probably imagined. I'd understand if you wanted to back out."

"And miss all the fun?" He shot a crooked grin my way. "Never."

We looked at each other a moment, then he quickly turned to the TV and started channel surfing.

"No, wait," I said. "Go back to the movie. I could use some light entertainment. Flesh-eating zombies might be just the ticket."

He returned to the old movie, then glanced from the recliner to the couch, as if trying to decide where to sit. I gestured at the other end of the sofa. He nodded and sat beside me.

"What're we watching?" Savannah asked, bouncing into the room wearing her nightgown.

"Paige and I are watching *Night of the Living Dead.* You are going to bed."

"I just conjured a cemetery full of spirits. I think I'm old enough to watch a horror movie." She plopped into the recliner. "Do we have chips or anything?"

"You think I've been shopping lately?" I said. "Pretty soon we'll be down to pickles and preserves."

"Are those the zombies?" she sniffed. "Talk about lame."

"It's an old film," I said. "The special effects aren't very advanced."

"What special effects? That's a guy with mascara smeared under his eyes. I've seen scarier people at the mall."

"Did Paige tell you to go to bed, Savannah?" Cortez said.

"Oh, fine. It's a dumb movie anyway." She flounced from the room.

A few minutes later, I sighed.

"It *is* a pretty dumb movie. But I'm too wired to sleep."

"I, uh, believe you mentioned something about new grimoires?"

I sat up. "Geez, that's right. I almost forgot. I wanted to try them out tonight."

"You were, I believe, going to tell me . . ." He let the sentence fade out.

I grinned. "I was going to tell you about them, wasn't I?"

So I did.

Pressure Valve

"IT'S POSSIBLE," he said when I finished telling him about the grimoires.

"Possible? Are you saying my logic is flawed?"

"I wouldn't dare. I'm simply saying that it makes sense and therefore it's possible. Non-Coven witches have been using sorcerer magic for generations. It would be good to see them get their own back."

I smiled. "Would it? You know what it would mean, don't you? These spells could level the playing field."

"As it should be."

I leaned back into the sofa cushions. "Is this the same guy who made a crack about the 'hereditary limitations' of witch powers?"

"I affected the persona with which I thought you'd be most comfortable. I've dealt with enough witches not to underestimate their abilities. Not every sorcerer hates or even dislikes witches. Many do, though, even those who'd be considered decent, moral men."

"Decent, moral sorcerers?"

"No, that's not an oxymoron. Not every sorcerer is evil. To say that would be akin to saying that every witch is weak and fearful, which I'm sure you wouldn't appreciate. A stereotype becomes a stereotype when a significant percentage of a population appears to conform to it. Unlike some stereotypes, that of the morally corrupt sorcerer is, unfortunately, valid."

"Absolute power corrupts absolutely."

"Exactly. Those who chase the dream of absolute power, as many sorcerers do, find themselves obsessed by it."

"So you don't crave stronger powers?"

He met my gaze. "What I crave, as I believe you do, is stronger knowledge—the best possible repertoire of spells and the power to do my best with them. When I say I'm pleased that you found these grimoires, I must admit, I can't help but see it as an opportunity to acquire new spells."

"Can't blame you for that. Don't you think maybe we're being naive? Believing that we'll never be corrupted by our own quest for power?"

"Perhaps."

"There's a definitive answer."

"Wouldn't it be naive of me to think I couldn't possibly be naive?"

"Enough," I said. "You're making my head spin. Time to try out a new spell."

He shifted forward. "Would you . . . object to an audience?"

I grinned. "Not at all."

I gathered my books and we went down to the basement.

When I said I hoped to learn a new spell, I meant exactly that: one new spell. As much as I longed to test-drive the whole book, hoping to learn even one spell might be pushing it. To cast a spell from the tertiary-level grimoires, I first had to master a new one from the secondary spellbook, which would take time.

I further dampened my own enthusiasm by insisting on proceeding in a logical fashion. Tonight I wanted not only to learn something new but to try out my theory. Was it necessary to learn the corresponding secondary spell before one could cast the tertiary?

To test this, I selected the suffocation spell. Since I'd practiced it already for hours without success, it was the perfect choice. If I could perform it after learning the secondary spell, it would support my hypothesis. The suffocation spell was classified as an air elemental, class five. A search through the secondary book showed that I hadn't learned any air spells. Perfect.

The corresponding secondary air spell was one that caused hiccups. Maybe in grade school that would have been fun, but for anyone over the age of ten it was a pretty silly spell. Logically, though, it made sense; both hiccups and suffocation are interruptions to breathing. When I'd run through these grimoires the first time, I'd tried this spell, just for fun, but stopped before mastering it. If my theory was right, that might explain why the suffocation spell had shown some signs that it might eventually work—because I'd partially learned the secondary spell.

Struck by a thought, I dug out my Coven-sanctioned grimoire and flipped to a page near the end: a spell to cure hiccups, which I'd learned years ago. That one was an air elemental spell, class five. The primary spell. First you learn to cure hiccups, then you learn to cause them, then you learn to cut off breathing altogether.

"Mind if I give you hiccups?" I asked Cortez.

"What?"

"Hiccups. I need to give you a case of hiccups. Is that okay?"

"I can't say I've ever had a girl offer to give me that."

"It's a spell," I said. "Don't worry, I know one to cure them too."

"You'll have to teach me that one. The curing, not the giving. I've never had much luck with holding my breath."

"No? Then just wait until you see the spell I'm going to try next."

Before I could hope for a successful cast on the hiccup spell, I needed to practice it. Having Cortez there wasn't a distraction, probably because he was considerate enough to sit behind me, so I wouldn't feel like I was performing.

After twenty minutes of tinkering with the spell, the rhythm felt right, so I asked Cortez to move in front of me. When he did, he faced the wall rather than look straight at me. That made it easier. So easy, in fact, that the spell worked on the second try. Then, of course, I had to do another half-dozen trial runs, to be sure I had it right. When I debated yet another try, Cortez proclaimed me fully proficient in the hiccup spell and begged leave to regain his breath.

Next, I moved to the suffocation spell. I'd start by casting it on myself. Lucas had been through enough that night. It took twenty minutes before I could recite the incantation. It wasn't a difficult incantation. It was in Latin, the spellcasting language with which I was most familiar. The delay resulted from one simple factor: nerves. So many of my hopes rode on this spell that I stumbled over the words. I tried to tell myself that it didn't matter that much, that if I failed, I'd find another way, but to no avail. I knew how important this was and couldn't persuade myself otherwise. I scarcely dared utter the words for fear I'd fail, as if, in fumbling just this once, the magic would somehow vanish, never to be recovered.

After tripping over the incantation a few times, I changed tack and began with the second line. By leaving off the opening, I guaranteed that the spell would fail, so I could concentrate on the recitation. Having tried this spell many times before, I quickly picked up the rhythm.

The words flowed, the inflections and tones rolling off my tongue. A well-cast spell is true music. Not a chant or a song, it is the music of pure language, the music of Shakespeare or Byron. Put emotion and conviction behind those words and it has the power of opera; without even understanding the words, you can feel their meaning.

I closed my eyes and poured my heart into it, poured in every ounce of longing and frustration and ambition. My voice rose until I couldn't feel the words coming from my throat, could only hear them echoing around me. Again and again I repeated the incantation. Then I heard the first line flow, unbidden. The words rose to a crescendo, and with the final line the breath flew from my lips. I gasped, almost choked.

The moment my breath returned, the words started again, as if of their own accord. The window above my head rattled as I recited the incantation. Rose-bush branches lashed and scratched against the pane. When the words finished, I sputtered, breathless.

Again I started anew. The hatch doors buckled and groaned. As the spell neared the end, the doors suddenly blew open. A gust of wind whooshed in, knocking over the baskets of clean laundry. With the last word, my breath was sucked out with such force that I fell forward and blacked out.

The next thing I knew, Cortez was grabbing my shoulders. "Are you all right?" he asked as my eyes opened.

My lips curved in a slow grin. "I think it worked."

"I should say so," he replied, surveying the windswept piles of laundry surrounding us. "Now, having proven that the spell works and that you can cast it successfully, I don't suppose you'd mind if I had a try."

I yanked the grimoire away. "No. Mine."

With a laugh, I waved the spellbook just out of reach. He grinned and grabbed for it, but I whisked it away, nearly falling backward. He lunged. As his face came close to mine, he paused and blinked. I knew what he was thinking. And I knew he wouldn't do it. So I did.

I lifted my mouth to his and kissed him.

Cortez's eyes widened. I laughed, nearly breaking the lip-lock, but before I could fall back, he pulled me to him, surprising me with the force of his kiss. Whatever Cortez lacked in technique, he more than made up for in zeal, and in that kiss I tasted something that made my head spin and set my insides afire and brought to life every other romantic cliché I'd ever laughed at. The intoxication of the spellcasting still lingered, infused now with a fresh passion and the sheer elation of feeling that passion returned. I felt giddy, electrified, invincible. For the first time in days, I felt that I was everything I'd once believed myself to be.

We tumbled into a pile of clean laundry. Cortez rolled over, pulling me on top of him. His hands moved to the back of my head and fumbled with my hair clip. I reached back and released it. As my hair fell free, Cortez entwined his fingers in it and kissed me even harder. Then he slipped one hand from my hair and snapped his fingers over our heads. The light went out. He murmured a few words against my mouth and the unlit candles from my spellcasting practice ignited.

My laugh vibrated between our lips. "Show-off."

He pulled back and arched his brows. "It's called being romantic." His lips curved in a grin. "And maybe showing off. A little."

"Well, don't. This is *my* seduction."

"Is it?"

"I started it, didn't I?"

"Quite right. I'll leave you to it, then."

I cast the witch spell to extinguish the candles, then the one to relight them. Cortez chuckled and pulled me onto him again. We kissed for a few minutes. When he tugged my blouse from my jeans, I shook my head and backed up, breaking the kiss.

"My lead, remember?" I said.

I wrapped my fingers in his shirt front and pulled him up until he was sitting. Then I straddled his hips, kneeling, and wriggled until I felt his erection exactly where I wanted it. His breath caught. I smiled and tugged off his glasses.

"Do you need these?" I asked.

He shook his head.

I laid them aside and began unbuttoning his shirt. After three buttons I pressed my lips to his throat, tickling my tongue along it, feeling him swallow. I moved my fingers down to the next button and undid it, then slid my tongue down, tracing circles down his chest. Between each unfastening I ran my fingers across the bared skin.

When I got to the final button, I shimmied back so I was sitting by his knees. Then I bent forward and teased his belly button with my lips, my tongue dipping lower until I undid the button on his pants and, slowly, tugged down the zipper. I could hear his breathing above me, raspy and uneven, and my own hunger ignited.

I ran my tongue along the top of his underwear, letting it slide just underneath. Then I shifted my body forward, lips moving back up his chest, until I was straddling him again. When I was back at eye level, he wrapped his hands in my hair and pulled my mouth to his. His hands slid under my shirt, but I backed off again and grinned.

"Not yet," I said.

He opened his mouth, but I put my finger to his lips and scuttled backward, pushing myself up. Then I stepped back, grinned down at him, and pulled off my shirt. My socks followed, then my jeans, falling in a puddle at my feet. I stepped out and kicked them aside. I unbuttoned my shirt and let it slide away. Then I took my time with the rest, the bra and panties.

When I let the panties fall, for a few seconds Cortez only stared. Then he grinned, scrambled to his feet, and covered the ground between us in one stride.

I arched onto my tiptoes to kiss him and we nearly tumbled down. As my balance faltered, he caught me and redirected our fall onto the pile of clean clothes. I tugged his shirt off his shoulders, running my fingers across and down his back. His pants were still undone. I wriggled my hands under the waistband and pushed them down, leaving his briefs in place.

He kicked off his pants and moved his hands under my rear, pulling me against him. Then his right hand shifted and, from the corner of my eye, I saw him reach out. He murmured something against my lips and Savannah's stereo turned on.

"Ahem," I said, pulling back. "My seduction."

"Consider me seduced."

As he lowered his mouth to mine, the crooning of a boy band filled the room. Cortez's eyes widened and his hand flicked again, moving the tuner. I laughed. He flipped past a jazz station, then returned and, with another flick, adjusted the volume to a whisper.

"Not bad," I said.

I cast the wind incantation, softening the emphasis in the right places so a cool breeze tickled across our skin. Cortez kissed me, then moved his lips over my chin and down my neck. As he kissed my throat, he murmured something and flicked his fingers. The candle flames refracted into a hundred shards of light. I chuckled and arched my back as his lips went to my breast. I let myself enjoy that for a minute, then tugged away and pulled myself up until I was sitting, straddling his chest.

I whispered a spell and a small fireball appeared in my hand. Cortez looked from it to me and tilted his head, eyes questioning. I grinned and cast a dampening spell, putting out the ball and leaving only my fingers glowing.

"Interesting," he said. "But I don't see—"

I pressed my hot fingers against his chest. He gasped. I traced the heat down his chest, then slid my hand under his briefs and stroked him. He moaned, closing his eyes and leaning back.

"See now?" I asked.

"Teach me that," he said hoarsely.

I grinned. "Maybe."

I peeled off his briefs and slid one hot hand under his balls, caressing them, as I stroked his shaft with the other. He arched back, moaning. I continued, measuring his breathing until I heard just the right tempo, then stopped, still holding him tight.

"Do I win?" I asked.

"Yes. God, yes." He paused, then pulled free of my grasp, eyes flying open. "No."

"Changed your mind?" I said with a grin. "That's okay. You're right, maybe it isn't such a good idea." I started backing off him. "We should keep this professional. After all—"

He lunged for me, knocking me onto my back and stretching over me.

"I meant 'No' as in 'I don't concede defeat.' Not yet."

He kicked off his briefs, then grabbed me by the hips. We rolled, entangling ourselves in the linen. The soft sheets and clean scent of lemon engulfed us. As we kissed, I felt Cortez's lips move and opened my eyes to see his hand arc above us. A low thrumming drowned out the radio, then a fog of purple and blue light rose from the floor.

"Tell me that isn't the koyut," I murmured against his mouth.

He chuckled and slid his fingers between my thighs, teasing. I arched back and closed my eyes. When I opened them, the fog was wafting toward us. It touched my arm first, sending a tingle of energy through it. I gasped. Cortez chuckled again and pushed his fingers into me. The fog wrapped around us. Every hair on my body rose and I pressed my head into the sheets, luxuriating in the sensation.

"That is—" I gasped after a few minutes. "You have to teach me that."

He smiled, pulled out his fingers, and slid on top of me. "I'll teach you anything you want."

❧ Good Morning

AFTERWARDS, I DISENTANGLED MYSELF from the sheets and his arms, and got to my feet. He lifted his head and frowned.

"Wait," I said.

I went to the cold cellar and grabbed a bottle of wine. When I returned, Cortez was still wrapped in the clean sheets, watching me.

"Good?" I said, holding out the bottle.

"Hmmm?" He blinked, then looked at the bottle. "Oh, yes. Wine. Good. Great."

I laughed. "I suppose I'd be insulted if it *was* the wine you were staring at."

He grinned then, a slow, lazy grin that did something to my insides. "Guess I'm still in shock."

"Don't tell me I'm the first damsel in distress who's ever seduced you."

"I can say, with absolute certainty, that you are the first woman who has ever even *tried* to seduce me, on or off a case." He reached for the bottle. "Do you need a corkscrew for that?"

"Of course not, I'm a witch." I said a few words and the cork flew out. "I don't suppose you know how to conjure glasses."

"Sorry."

"The kitchen's so far away. Do we need glasses?"

"Absolutely not."

He hooked his arm around my waist and pulled me down onto his lap. We each took a drink from the bottle.

"I'm sorry about your bike," I said.

"My . . . ? Oh, right. It's nothing. I had insurance."

"Still, I am sorry. I know replacing it won't be the same thing, if you restored it and all."

"*If* I restored it?"

"I didn't mean—"

He chuckled. "You don't need to explain. I'm well aware that I hardly seem the type to be tinkering with transmissions and carburetors. To be honest, short of that particular hobby, my mechanical skills approach nil."

"You can hot-wire cars."

Another chuckle. "Yes, I suppose there's that. As for the motorcycles, one of my mother's boyfriends got me started restoring them when I was Savannah's age. At first I took it up in hopes it would add a certain cachet to my social life."

"You hoped it would help you pick up chicks? Did it?"

"Hardly. I quickly outgrew that notion. Or so I thought, though I must admit that part of my motivation in choosing to take the motorcycle to the funeral home was a semi-conscious desire to present myself in a more attractive light."

"I was very impressed."

He fell back onto the sheets and laughed, startling me. "Oh, I could tell. You were *very* impressed. About as impressed as you were when you discovered I was the son of an infamous Cabal CEO."

"The heir of an infamous Cabal CEO."

I said it teasingly, but the humor drained from his eyes. He nodded and reached for the wine bottle.

"I'm sorry," I said. "New topic. So, where do you live?"

"Back to the heir question first. It's true, and it's not a subject I want to avoid. I want to be honest with you, Paige. I want—" He hesitated. "My father has very good reasons for naming me heir, reasons that have nothing to do with me and everything to do with the politics of succession and keeping my older brothers in line."

"A purely strategic decision? I can't believe that."

"My father harbors some delusions regarding the nature of my rebellion. He's wrong. I will never be the employee—or leader—of any Cabal. Nor am I naive enough to take the reins of leadership in hopes of reforming it into a legitimate business."

"Is it true—?" I shook my head. "Sorry, I don't mean to pry—"

"It's not prying, Paige. I'd be far more concerned if you didn't care. Ask away. Please."

"About the bounty. Is it true? I mean, if you're in danger—"

"I'm not. Or if I am, it's a permanent situation and nothing that impacts the present circumstances. No one in Nast's organization would dare collect such a reward. Let me say, first, that Leah has a tendency to get her facts confused. My father's wife and my three half-brothers do not all have contracts out on me. Last I heard, only Delores and my eldest brother were offering bounties. Carlos, the youngest of Delores's sons did at one time, but recent debts have forced him to withdraw the offer. As for William, he's never tried to hire anyone to kill me—probably because he hasn't the wits to think of it."

"Are you serious?"

"About William? Unfortunately. He's intelligent enough, but lacks initiative."

I bumped his shoulder. "Ha-ha. You know what I meant. Are you serious about your brothers putting bounties on your head?"

"Quite, though I wouldn't suggest you mention it to my father. He's quite convinced he cleared this matter up years ago. Killing the bastard heir is absolutely forbidden. Any family member caught attempting it will be severely punished. He tried threatening them with death, but that didn't work, so he revised it to the worst possible fate: disinheritance."

"You guys raise the dysfunctional family to a whole new level, don't you?"

"The Cortezes have always been overachievers."

We passed the bottle again.

"You asked where I lived," he said.

"Right."

"I believe the standard expression for my situation is 'no fixed address.' Since graduating, I haven't been in one place long enough even to sublet an apartment. My work—legal and otherwise—keeps me on the move. With my extracurricular activities, I'm obviously ill-suited for a steady job at a law firm. Instead, I do piecemeal legal work for supernaturals."

"Lawyer to the paranormal."

"Almost as bad as 'superhero,' isn't it? It provides me enough to live on, no more and no less. More importantly, it gives me the opportunity to do what I really want."

"Save the world?"

"Something which I'm sure you know nothing about."

"Hey, I don't want to save the *whole* world, just my corner of it."

He laughed and tightened his arms around me. We kissed for a few minutes, then I reluctantly pulled back.

"I want to know more," I said. "About you, about what you do. But I suppose we should get some sleep."

"Probably. If these last two days have been any indication, we'll need our rest." He reached over and retrieved his glasses, then looked at me. "Any chance we can avoid separate sleeping quarters tonight? I know Savannah's presence is a concern—"

"One easily handled by a locking spell or two."

In the morning, I awoke to find myself alone. At first I thought Cortez had slipped out in the night and returned to the sofa, which would be a bad sign. But as I stretched, I noticed that his side of the bed was still warm.

I glanced at the clock. Eleven A.M.? I hadn't slept this late since college. No wonder Cortez was up.

I tumbled from bed, still groggy, pulled on my kimono, and headed for the bathroom. The door was ajar, so I gave it a shove—and whacked it against Cortez, who was bent over the sink, shaving.

"Sorry," he said.

"For what? Standing near a door?"

A small smile. "For leaving the door open, thereby causing you to believe the room was vacant." He waved to the mirror, which was fogged from his shower. "I opened it for some air. I couldn't find the—"

I flicked a switch outside the door and a whoosh filled the room.

"Ah, the fan," he said.

"Lousy setup. I'll be in my room. Just knock when you're done."

Before I could leave, he grabbed my arm, tugged me inside, and closed the door. Then he pulled me against him and lowered his mouth to mine. Well, that certainly alleviated any "morning after" awkwardness.

I kissed him back, wrapping my hands around his neck. Tendrils of damp hair tickled my fingers and the clean tang of soap filled my nose. When my tongue slipped into his mouth, I tasted mint. Toothpaste.

I jerked back and slapped my hand over my mouth. "I have to brush my teeth." In the mirror, I saw that my hair frizzed out in a way that could only be called witchy. "Shit! My hair!"

Cortez wrapped a handful around his fist and bent to kiss my neck. "I love your hair."

"Which is more than you can say for my breath."

As I reached for the toothpaste, he turned me around. "Your breath is fine."

As if to prove it, he kissed me again, deeper this time,

lifting me up onto the counter and pressing against me. I slid my fingers under his open shirt to push it off his shoulders, but he caught my hands.

"This, I believe, is my seduction," he said. "Not, of course, that I wish to discourage you from taking the initiative in future. Nor to discourage you from disrobing me or from disrobing yourself, particularly in the . . . enchanting fashion you employed last night, but—"

"Are you seducing me or talking about it?"

He grinned. "I could talk about it, if you like. In terms perhaps more amenable to the situation."

"Tempting," I said. "Very tempting. If I wasn't worried about Savannah waking up—"

"Quite right. There will be plenty of time for talk later."

His mouth came down to mine as he undid my sash. He slipped his hands inside my kimono and traced his fingers up my sides, slowly, then moved to cup my breasts. As his thumbs found my nipples, I arched my back and moaned.

Something hit the door, hard enough that we both jumped, me falling into his arms.

"Is someone in there?" Savannah demanded between pounds.

Cortez looked at me. I motioned for him to answer.

"I am," he said.

"Are you almost done?"

"Umm, no, I'm afraid not, Savannah. I'm just starting."

"Oh, geez," she groaned.

The door creaked, followed by a rasp and a thump as

she dropped to the floor. We waited another minute. Not only did Savannah not leave, but her noises of impatience escalated in frequency and volume.

Cortez leaned down to my ear. "Are you sure you *want* to keep her?"

I smiled, shook my head, and waved him toward the door.

"What about you?" he mouthed.

I slid off the counter, backed into the corner by the toilet, and cast a cover spell. Cortez nodded, then opened the door.

"Finally!" Savannah said. "There's only one bathroom here, you know."

He brushed past her without a word, footsteps echoing down the hall.

"Grouchy this morning, aren't we," she called after him.

Savannah closed the door and proceeded to her urgent business. That business, contrary to what one might expect, had nothing to do with the toilet. First she brushed her hair—with my brush. Then she sampled some new lipstick—mine. Then she rooted around under the cupboard and pulled out my hidden stash of high-priced shampoo and conditioner—hair products that, may I point out, were intended for curly hair. Finally, she grabbed my perfume and sprayed it around as if it was air freshener. I had to bite my lip to keep from yelping.

Next, a shower. As Savannah began to undress, I averted my eyes, shifting my gaze as far to the side as possible. After several minutes in that position my eyes began to water. When I finally had to glance back, she was standing in front of the mirror, just standing there, looking at herself and frowning. I looked away again.

"Well, I'm a woman now," she muttered to her reflection. "Hurry up and do something." She snorted. "What a ripoff."

With that, she stamped to the shower and got in. When the water began, I eased from my hiding spot and darted to the door, stopped, stepped back, did a quick swish with mouthwash, and left.

After dressing, I walked into the kitchen to find Cortez surveying the contents of the fridge. He looked up when I entered, glanced behind me for Savannah, then pulled me in for a kiss.

"Last one for today, I presume," he said, then sniffed. "You smell nice."

"Not intentionally," I muttered. "My mom always said never to use the cover spell to spy on someone or you might see something you don't want to. Well, I just learned why my shampoo and perfume disappear so fast. And now I know why my friends always complained about their siblings using their stuff." I grabbed the fridge door. "Did you get that growing up?"

"No," he said as I peered into the nearly empty fridge. "I grew up an only child, like you."

I paused, confused. I knew he had three older brothers— Oh, wait. I recalled what Leah said about his parentage, that he was . . . Words failed me. Oh, I knew a few: illegitimate, conceived out of wedlock, plus the "b" word, which I wouldn't mention even if Cortez used it himself. Everything sounded so negative, so archaic. Maybe the terms were archaic because there was no need for such a designation at all. If a child is conceived during an extramarital affair, the burden for any questionable judgment rests with the parents, not the child. In the twenty-first century we should be enlightened enough to realize that. Yet by the way Leah had brought it up, such a casually tossed barb, I knew it wasn't something the rest of the Cabal world let Cortez forget.

"Not much in there," he said, looking over my shoulder. "If the eggs are still good, I could make an omelet. Yes, I know I made that yesterday, but my repertoire is exceedingly limited. It's that or, possibly, a hard-boiled egg, though I have been known to boil them into golf balls."

"You've done enough. I'll get breakfast. Eggs, pancakes, or French toast?" I glanced at the bread, the edges blooming a lovely shade of periwinkle. "Forget the French toast."

"Whatever is easiest."

"Pancakes," Savannah said as she swung into the kitchen.

"You set the table, then, and I'll cook."

❧ The Vote

BY THE TIME BREAKFAST—or should I say brunch?—ended, it was past noon. Cortez insisted on cleaning up and also insisted on Savannah's help. I took my mug of coffee and was heading into the living room when the phone rang. Cortez checked the call display.

"Victoria Alden. Shall we let the machine pick up?"

"No, I'll get it. After the last few days, Victoria is one problem I can handle . . . Hello, Victoria," I said as I picked up the phone.

Silence.

"Call display, remember?" I said. "Great invention."

"You sound very cheerful this morning, Paige."

"I am. The crowd's gone. The media has stopped calling. Things are definitely looking up."

"So, stealing Margaret's car and leading the police through a cemetery last night are things you would consider to be an improvement in your current situation?"

"Oh, that was nothing. We were very careful, Victoria. The police won't know it was me. They haven't even called."

"I phoned concerning the future of one of our Coven members."

I paused, then winced, my euphoria fading. "Oh, geez.

It's Kylie, isn't it? She's decided not to stay with the Coven. Look, I've been talking to her, and I'll speak to her again when all this is over."

"This isn't about Kylie. It's about you."

"Me?"

"After hearing of your latest escapade, we called an emergency Coven meeting this morning. You've been banished from the Coven, Paige."

"What—you—" Words dried up in my throat.

"The vote was eight to three, with two abstaining. The Coven has decided."

"N—no. Eight to three? That can't be. You rigged it. You must have—"

"Call Abigail, if you wish. I'm sure she is one of the three who voted to allow you to stay. She'll tell you it was a fair and open count. You know the rules of banishment, Paige. You have thirty days to leave East Falls, and you are prohibited from taking any of your mother's—"

"No!" I shouted. "No!"

I slammed the phone down. Without turning, I sensed Cortez behind me.

"They banished me," I whispered. "They voted to kick me out of the Coven."

If he replied, I didn't hear it. Blood crashed in my ears. Somehow I managed to stagger the three steps to the recliner and drop into it. Cortez sat on the armrest, but I turned away from him. No one could understand what this meant to me, and I didn't want anyone to try. As he bent over me, his lips moved and I braced myself against the inevitable "I'm sorry."

He said, "They're wrong."

I looked up at him. He leaned down and brushed the hair from my face, using the movement to stroke my cheek with his thumb.

"They're wrong, Paige."

I buried my face against his side and began to sob.

I knew the Elders were beyond help; all the older witches were. They were set in their ways and their beliefs, and I could do little to change that. I wouldn't waste my time trying. Instead, I wanted to focus on the younger generation, the ones like Kylie, who was heading off to college this fall and seriously contemplating breaking with the Coven.

Save the younger generation and let the older one wither away. From there, I could reform the Coven, make it a place witches came to, not escaped from. Once the Coven had regained its strength and vitality, we could reach out to other witches, offer training and fellowship and a powerful alternative to those, like Eve, who saw power only in dark magic. I'd make the Coven more flexible, more adaptable, more attractive, better suited to fulfilling the needs of all witches. A grand plan, to be sure, and maybe not one I could even realize in my lifetime. But I could start it. I could try.

This was more than a vision, it was the embodiment of every hope I'd had since I'd been old enough to form hopes. I couldn't imagine leaving the Coven, literally could not envision it. Never at any time in my life had I wondered what life would be like outside the Coven. I'd never dreamed of living anywhere but in Massachusetts. I'd never dreamed of falling in love and marrying. I'd never even dreamed of children. The Coven was my dream, and I'd never considered anything that would interfere with that mission.

So what was I to do now? Roll over and cry? Let the Elders drive me away? Never. When the initial pain of being banished subsided, I stepped back for a logical assessment of the situation. So the Coven had kicked me out. They were scared, reacting to an age-old fear instilled in them by Victoria and her cronies. Terrified of exposure, they took the easiest route—ridding themselves of the cause of that threat. The people of East Falls had done the same thing with their petition. Once the danger passed, however, both would welcome me back. Well, maybe "welcome" was optimistic, but they'd allow me to stay, in the town and in the Coven. With the right amount of will and determination, anything can be fixed.

"Wh—where's Savannah?" I asked, drying my eyes.

"In the kitchen. Making tea, I believe."

I pulled myself upright. "Seems everyone's been doing a lot of that lately—taking care of Paige."

"Hardly. You—"

"I appreciate it, but I'm okay," I said, squeezing his hand as I got to my feet. "We've got things to do today. For starters, I should go through Savannah's ceremony with her. I know it's still a week away, but I want to make sure she remembers everything and that we have all the ingredients."

He nodded. "Good idea. While you do that, if you don't mind, I'll toss my change of clothing in the laundry."

"Oh, that's right, you've only got the two sets. Here, give me your dirty clothes—"

"I've got it, Paige. You go on with Savannah."

"Later, we should get your bags from the motel and bring them back here." I paused. "That is, if we're staying here. We should discuss that, too."

He nodded and I walked to the kitchen doorway. Savannah looked up from measuring tea.

"Leave that, hon," I said. "Thanks for thinking of me, but I'm fine. How about we run through that ceremony of your mom's, make sure I get it right?"

"Sure."

"Let me get my stuff, then, and we'll head downstairs."

Savannah followed me into my room. As I pulled my knapsack from its hiding place, the window smashed behind me. Savannah screamed and I wheeled around just as a football-sized rock crashed into the far wall. It hit the throw rug, rolling once and leaving a trail of red. Thinking it was blood, I spun to face Savannah, but she was running to the window, unharmed.

"Get away from there!" I yelled.

"I want to see who—"

"No!"

I grabbed her arm and wrenched her back. As I turned toward the room, I saw a word smeared in red paint on the rock: *BURN*.

I dragged Savannah from the bedroom as Cortez came sprinting from the kitchen.

"I was in the basement," he said. "What happened?"

I grabbed the phone and dialed 911 as Savannah explained about the rock. Cortez's face went grim and he marched to the kitchen window to look out back. As I was telling the 911 dispatcher what had happened, he took the phone from me.

"Get the fire department here now," he demanded. "Police and fire. Immediately."

While he gave details, I ran to the window. My shed was engulfed in flames, fueled by the gasoline for the lawn mower and god knows what other flammable liquids.

Suddenly the shed exploded. The boom resounded through the house. When the next crash came, I thought it was still the shed—until shards of glass hit my face and something struck my shoulder.

Cortez yelled and dove at me, grabbing the back of my shirt and yanking me backward so hard I flew off my feet. As he pulled me from the kitchen, I saw what had hit me: a bottle stuffed with a flaming rag. I was barely out of the room when whatever filled the bottle ignited. A ball of fire flared, filling my kitchen with flame and smoke.

"Savannah, get down!" Cortez shouted. "Crawl to the door!"

At the back of the house I heard another window break. My office! Oh god, all my work was in there. As I wrenched free of Cortez's grasp, I remembered what other room was at the back of the house, and what even more precious contents it held.

"My bedroom! The ceremony material and the grimoires."

Cortez tried to grab me, but I lunged out of his reach. Sirens and shouts sounded, nearly drowned out by the crackle of fire. Two steps from my room, a cloud of smoke hit me. I reeled back, gagging. Instinctively, I breathed deeper, gasping for air and filling my lungs with smoke. After a split second of animal panic, sense returned and I dropped onto all fours and crawled into my room.

My bed looked like a demonic fire-beast, a four-legged mass of flame devouring everything within reach. A gust of wind billowed through the window, blowing smoke into my face and blinding me. I continued forward, moving from memory, fingers outstretched. I found the knapsack first, and wrapped the straps around one hand as the other continued to search. When I touched the edge of the trap door, I stopped and began feeling around it. My fingers connected with the white-hot metal of the clasp and I jerked away, backing into the flaming throw rug.

For one moment it was too much. The ancient fear of fire gnawed away reason, filling my brain with the smell, sound, taste, and feel of the flames. I froze, unable to move, certain I would die here, condemned to a witch's death. The horror of that thought—the very idea of curling up and surrendering to fear—restored my senses.

Ignoring the pain, I flipped the clasp and opened the trap door. A moment later I had the second backpack. I seized the straps, yanked it from the cubbyhole, and started to creep backward, crablike, toward the door. I'd gone barely two feet when Cortez grabbed my ankle and dragged me out.

"That way," he said, pushing me forward. "To the door. Don't stand up. Shit!"

He tackled me, knocking me to the floor just as I felt flames lick my calves. As he beat at flames on my back, I twisted to see that the hem of my skirt had also ignited. I kicked against the wall, but the sharp movement only made the flames burn brighter. Stopping me, Cortez backed up and slapped the fire out with his hands. Then he grabbed the knapsacks from my hand.

"I have them," he said. "Don't look back. Just keep moving."

I started forward. The rear of the house was ablaze. Tongues of fire licked across the house toward the front, and when I passed the living room, I saw the drapes ignite. Breathing through my mouth, I pushed forward, willing myself to crawl over small pockets of fire in my path. In the front hall I paused to glance over my shoulder for Cortez. He waved me forward. I crawled to the open back door and toppled outside.

A man in a uniform caught me and shoved a cloth over my nose and mouth. I inhaled a deep breath of something cold and metallic. I grabbed the man's arm, gesturing that I could breathe without medical help. Above me, his face wobbled out of focus. I wrenched around, looking behind me for Cortez. I saw the open doorway and empty hall. Then my limbs gave way and everything went black.

✦ Package Deal

I AWOKE WITH A HEADACHE that felt like a chisel striking behind my eyes. When I lifted my head, bile rushed to my mouth and I hunched over, gagging and spitting. Every time I tried to rise, nausea forced me down. Finally, I gave up and collapsed.

Where was I? When I opened my eyes, I saw only darkness. The last thing I remembered was drifting off to sleep with Cortez beside me. Flashes of nightmare illuminated the darkness. The taste of smoke made me retch again. As I did, my fingers clenched the sheets and I ran my thumb over the cloth. These weren't my sheets.

"Cortez?" I shifted onto my side. "Lucas?"

As I squinted into the darkness, my eyes adjusted enough to make out shapes. Another twin bed to my left. A nightstand beside me. I reached for the light and flicked the switch, but nothing happened. My fingers crept to the bulb and found an empty socket. I jumped up, stomach lurching with the sudden movement.

Across the room, Savannah muttered in her sleep.

"Savannah?"

She made a noise, half stirring.

The door swung open. A woman stood in the entrance,

illuminated by the hall light. I blinked twice, but my eyes wouldn't focus.

"Finally! We thought you girls were going to sleep all day."

With that voice, my heart stopped. *Leah*. I flung myself from the bed and tried to locate Savannah. My legs buckled under me and I fell to the carpet.

"Stay in bed," a man's voice warned. "You won't be ready to walk yet."

I tried to push myself up from the floor but couldn't. Leah and her partner stood outside the door, neither making any move to help me. A staccato series of beeps filled the silence, then the man murmured something.

"A cellphone?" Leah said when he finished the call. "Jesus, Friesen, he's in the next room."

"Standard communication procedure. Mr. Nast wants to see them immediately."

The man moved into the light and I recognized him as the "paramedic" who'd helped me out of the burning house. Early thirties, dirty blond brush cut, with the oversized build of a quarterback and the misshapen face of a boxer.

But who was Nast? I should have known, but my brain wouldn't focus any better than my eyes. I repeated the name in my head, my stomach clenching with each iteration. Nast was . . . wrong. Someone I didn't want to meet. My gut told me that. But . . .

"My throat hurts," Savannah moaned.

"We'll get you a cold drink in a sec, kiddo," Leah replied. "You just lie there and relax."

Savannah. Nast. The connection fired. Savannah's
father, Kristof Nast. Oh god.

"Sa—Savannah?" I managed, struggling to my feet.
"I have to ta—talk to you, hon."

"No talking," Friesen said. "Mr. Nast will want her
to save her energy."

I made it to Savannah's bed and sat down on the edge.
I had to swallow several times before my throat would
open. "Nast is—" I stopped, realizing I couldn't just blurt
it out. She needed to know more. "Kristof Nast. He's a
sorcerer. He's the head—no, the son of the head of the
Nast Cabal."

She blinked. "Like Lucas?"

"No, not like Lucas." At the mention of Cortez's name,
I remembered the last time I'd seen him, crawling behind
me in the burning house. I hadn't seen him get out. Had
they—? Oh god. I swallowed hard and tried not to think
of that. "The Nast Cabal—"

"Enough," Leah interrupted. "If you haven't told her
by now, we should leave it for a surprise. Do you like
surprises, Savannah?"

Savannah glared at her. "Don't talk to me."

"Savannah, there's something else—" I began.

"Nope," Leah said, grabbing my shoulders and
propelling me off the bed. "It's gonna be a surprise. Trust
me, kiddo, you're gonna love this one. You've hit the
genetic jackpot."

Before I could argue, Friesen lifted Savannah up,
ignoring her protests, and took her from the room. Leah
followed. I stood there staring at the partly open door,

waiting for it to close. A moment later Leah popped her head back in.

"Those drugs make you stupid, girl?" she said. "Come on."

I only looked at her.

"I told them they OD'd on the stuff," she said. "What are you waiting for? Shackles and chains? You aren't a prisoner here. Nast wanted to talk to Savannah, and this was the only way he figured he could do it."

"So . . . so I can leave here? I'm free to go?"

"Oh, sure." She grinned. "If you don't mind leaving Savannah behind."

She disappeared. I followed.

Nast may have been "in the next room" as Leah said, but he must have decided to hold the meeting elsewhere, because we headed downstairs, taking a circuitous route to the living room.

During the walk, my mind cleared. My head and throat still felt like they were stuffed with cotton, but at least I could think and take in my surroundings. We were in a house—a farmhouse, judging by the vista outside the windows. The windows were unbarred, some even propped open. We passed a front and a side door, and neither Leah nor her partner so much as glanced back to see if I'd make a break for it. They didn't need to. As long as they had Savannah, I wasn't going anywhere.

Any hope that I could still tell Savannah about Nast vanished when we walked into the living room. Sandford stood by the fireplace. Seated next to him was a tall man with thinning blond hair and broad shoulders. As we entered, he turned and I found myself looking into an exact replica of Savannah's big blue eyes. My heart dropped. I knew then that Kristof Nast was indeed Savannah's father.

"Savannah," Nast smiled. "You have no idea how long I've waited for this."

"Tell this guy to let me go!" She wriggled, trying to get free. "Put me down. *Now!*"

Nast waved for Friesen to release Savannah. "My apologies, princess." He chuckled and glanced at Sandford. "Still any doubt she's mine?"

"I'm not yours," Savannah said, pulling her shirt into place. "Not yours, not hers"—she jabbed a finger at Leah—"not anyone's. Now take me home or there's going to be trouble."

"Savannah, hon," I said, "I need to tell you something. Remember I was telling you about Kristof Nast—"

"This is him?" Her gaze raked over Nast, and she dismissed him with a snort. "He's the CEO's son? He's what, fifty? By the time he takes over, he'll be ready to retire."

"I'm forty-seven, actually," Nast said with an indulgent smile. "But I take your point. All the better for you, then, isn't it?"

"Isn't what?"

"If I'm so old. All the quicker to get your inheritance."

"Why? What are you, sorcerer? My mom's lawyer?"

Nast looked at me. "You haven't told her?"

"Savannah," I said, "this is—"

"I'm your father," Nast said.

He smiled and reached for Savannah. She jumped back, arms flying up to ward him off. She looked from me to Nast, then back to me.

"That's not funny," she said.

"Savannah, I—" I began.

"No one's joking, Savannah," Nast said. "I know this must come as a shock, but you are my daughter. Your mother—"

"No," she said, voice quiet. She turned to me. "You would have told me, right?"

"I—" I shook my head. "I'm so sorry, hon. We don't know for sure. Mr. Nast claims he's your father. I couldn't believe that. I wanted proof before I told you."

Nast laid a hand on Savannah's arm. When she flung him off, he bent to her height.

"I know you're angry, princess. This wasn't how I planned this. I thought you knew."

"I . . . I don't believe it."

"You don't have to. Now that we've moved beyond human courts, we can clear this up with a simple blood test. I've arranged for our doctors to conduct the test as soon as we get back to California."

"California?" Savannah said. "I can't—I'm not—I won't go. I won't."

"My apologies, I'm getting ahead of myself. I'm not taking you anywhere against your will, Savannah. This isn't a kidnapping. I'm sorry if I had to resort to such drastic measures to get you here, but I feared it was the only way Paige would allow me to present my case."

"Case?"

"For custody."

She looked from me to him. "We're going to court?"

He laughed. "No, thank god. I've decided to circumvent the horrors of the legal system. No human judge can decide where you belong, Savannah. No person can decide that. It's your life, and it should be your decision."

"Good. Then I'm staying with Paige."

"Don't I get to argue my side? Paige has had nearly a year to make her case, surely you can grant me thirty minutes to make mine. That's all I ask, princess—thirty minutes to explain why you should stay with me."

"And if I don't want to?"

"Then you're free to go back to East Falls with Paige."

"Bullshit," I said.

Nast looked up, startled, as if the walls had spoken. When he turned to me, his gaze focused somewhere above my head, as if I was literally beneath his notice.

"You doubt my word, Paige?" All indulgent humor drained from his voice. "I'm a Nast. My word is inviolable."

I felt the weight of Savannah's gaze on me. In that moment I realized what I had to do: I had to shut my mouth. Nast was right, this was her choice. Coven or Cabal. White magic or dark. If I swayed her decision, I'd always feel the pull of the other side working against me. Let her hear what Nast was offering and she'd see that Eve had made the right decision in sending her to the Coven. Though I doubted Nast would let her leave that easily, I'd jump that hurdle when it came. If I dragged her out kicking and screaming, I'd lose her forever.

Before stating his case, Nast insisted on feeding us. He'd ordered pizza. He even had a delivery guy bring it, further underscoring the point that we weren't being held captive at some top secret location.

Though Leah and Friesen shared in our meal, Nast looked at the pizza as if expecting the mushrooms to start crawling. He assured us, as if we cared, that he'd be eating lunch later, at a business meeting in Boston.

So we were still in Massachusetts? As I thought this, I realized he'd said lunch, not dinner or supper. With that came the shock that we'd slept through Wednesday and had been gone now nearly twenty-four hours. Again I thought of Cortez, but I knew there was no sense asking; they'd only tell us what we wanted to hear.

"Can we get started?" Savannah said. "The pizza's great and all that, but I want to get this over with."

Nast nodded. "First, let me say that your mother was a remarkable woman and I loved her very much. It just . . . it didn't work out for us. After you were born, she asked me to stay away, so I did, but I always planned to be part of your life someday. With your mother's death, that's happened earlier than I expected."

"How come she never mentioned you to me?"

"I have no idea, Savannah."

"Get on with your case, then, so I can go home."

Nast reclined without putting a single rumple in his suit. "Well, I hardly know where to start. Do you understand how a Cabal is organized?"

"Sort of."

Nast gave her a quick rundown, concentrating on the importance of the head sorcerer family. "As my daughter, you would be an important part of that family, with all the rights and privileges that entails."

"May I ask a question?" I said.

"I don't think—"

"It's a reasonable question. I'm not challenging or disagreeing with anything. I just want to clarify a point. As I understand it, sorcerers typically have only sons, meaning Savannah would be the only girl—or woman— in the family. How would that impact her position?"

"It wouldn't." Nast paused, then said, "Let me expand on that. I want to be completely forthcoming with you, Savannah. Within our Cabal, the Nast family's power is absolute. If we say you are to be accepted, you will be. Now, as regards matters of succession, there would likely be some dispute over whether you could inherit leadership. However, that point is moot. I have two very capable sons, and the oldest has already been named as my heir."

"So what do I get?" she asked.

"Everything else." He shifted forward, leaning toward her. "I'm a very wealthy, very powerful man, Savannah. One who can give you everything you've ever wanted. I'm sure Paige has done her best, but she can't offer you the advantages I can. More than money, Savannah, I'm talking about opportunity—access to the best tutors, the best spellbooks, the best materials."

"Sure—in return for my immortal soul. I'm not a dumb little kid, sorcerer. I know why you grabbed me. Because of the ceremony."

My heart shot into my throat and I motioned her to silence.

"It's quite all right, Paige. We've been aware of Savannah's menses since yesterday morning."

"Before you grabbed us?" I said. "Who told you?"

"We can discuss that later. The point is—"

"The point is," Savannah said, "that you grabbed me so you can change the ceremony and make me a Cabal slave."

"Cabal slave?" Nast laughed. "Is that what Paige told you?"

"It wasn't Paige."

"Ah, Lucas, I presume. Well, as much as I respect the Cortezes, I must say that Lucas Cortez is a very confused young man. He's had some . . . unfortunate experiences with Cabal life and has formed some rather wild opinions. As for the ceremony—"

"Wait," Savannah said. "I want to know about Lucas first. Is he okay?"

"He's fine, Savannah. Now—"

"What happened to him?"

"That's not—"

"I want to know."

"We delayed his escape, but not unduly. Last time we saw Lucas, he was in the hands of the paramedics. Unconscious from smoke inhalation, but otherwise uninjured."

As he spoke, Savannah kept darting concerned glances at me, taking in my reaction. Gabriel Sandford followed those glances with interest.

"So you didn't hurt him?" she pressed.

"Harming Lucas Cortez would cause a diplomatic incident of epic proportions. Killing him would start a blood feud the likes of which the Cabals haven't seen in over a century. A Cabal son has absolute immunity. That's what I'm offering you, Savannah. You'll never need to hide again."

He paused, checking to see if he had her full attention now. He did.

"About the ceremony," he continued. "Yes, there is a version that enhances a witch's employability in a Cabal, though it's a far cry from enslavement. You won't undergo that, though. There are several other ceremonies you can choose from—"

"I want the one Paige was going to do. The one my mother wanted."

"Done."

She blinked, then recovered and sat straighter. "And I want Paige to do it. No one else."

"Done." Nast stood and crossed the room to sit beside her. "I'm your father, Savannah. I want what's best for you, and in matters of witchcraft I trust your mother's judgment. If you wish to have a more experienced witch perform the ceremony, I'll provide that. But if you want Paige, that's fine. She can stay with you until next Wednesday, and she'll perform the ceremony your mother chose for you."

"Then what will happen to Paige? After the ceremony?"

"She'll be free to go."

Savannah slanted me a look. "What if I don't want her to go?"

Nast hesitated. "I'm sure Paige has her own responsibilities with the Coven—"

"They kicked her out. They're all stupid and useless. She's too good for them, anyway. If I stay, Paige stays. She can be my tutor."

"No offense to Paige, but we have far superior teachers of witchcraft."

"Then she'll be my companion or my nanny or something. That's what rich kids have, isn't it? Servants? I want Paige. She stays with me and she gets to learn everything I learn."

"I don't think—"

"Package deal," Savannah said. "Take it or leave it."

He took it.

❧ Mr. Nast's Witch

"I DIDN'T MEAN IT," Savannah said after we'd returned to our bedroom, which had now been equipped with a working light. "About the servant part. I was just saying that."

I barely heard her. I couldn't remember the walk back to the room, couldn't remember who'd brought us or what they'd said. All I could hear was Savannah's voice accepting Nast's proposition.

"You're mad at me, aren't you?"

"No, I'm not mad. Just . . . confused. It's a lot to take in. I'm sorry I didn't tell you earlier, about him claiming to be your father."

"Things got pretty crazy. You wanted proof first. I guess I understand that."

The truth was, I'd held back out of fear that something like this would happen, that Nast would breeze in and offer Savannah the world. In failing to tell her, I'd lost my chance to warn her. Anything I said now would seem churlish, disgruntled lies woven to sway her to my side. Even as she bounced around the room, chattering, I could feel her slipping away. As Nast said, I'd had nearly a year to make my case. Why hadn't I done a better job? She'd called the Coven stupid and useless.

That's the alternative I'd shown her—a world where witches were stupid and useless.

I knew I should stay silent, let her see things for herself, but it took every bit of restraint to keep from shaking her and shouting "What are you doing?!" Instead, I settled onto the bed before saying, "I'm glad you want me around, Savannah, but you know I can't do this. I'm Coven leader. I can't just leave—"

"They kicked you out!"

"Yes, they're angry, but—"

"You said you'd stay with me. You promised."

"I know and I will, but—"

"Well, this is my decision. I want to be here, and if you want to help me, you have to stay."

She plopped onto the opposite bed, turned her back to me, and crossed her arms. We sat like that for a few minutes. A few times she half turned, as if waiting for me to argue. When I didn't, she twisted to face me.

"Don't be mad, Paige," she said. "Did you hear what he said? The best tutors, the best books, the best materials. I'll get all that, and I'll share it with you. Isn't that what you wanted?'

I didn't answer.

"You're worried because it's a Cabal, right? I know what Lucas said, but, well, maybe he—my—Nast is right. Not that Lucas is lying—I don't mean that. But he could be confused. Maybe he saw some really bad stuff, stuff that doesn't normally happen."

Again I said nothing.

"Fine, be that way. Go back to stupid little East Falls,

to your burned-down house. I won't go. They don't want us there. Every time you walk down the street, people are going to be pointing and saying stuff. Well, they won't say stuff about me. I'll be in California. I bet Adam will come visit me. He won't be like this."

"I'll stay with you, Savannah. You know I will."

She hesitated, then smiled and leaned across the bed to hug me. "It's going to be okay, Paige. You just watch. This will be the best thing that's ever happened to us."

Still drowsy from the drugs, we dozed for an hour or so. Then a knock at the door woke us both. A woman peeked through.

"May we come in?" she asked.

Without waiting for a response, she pushed the door open and walked in. She was in her early forties, more handsome than pretty, with an angular jaw and a salt-and-pepper brush cut. Behind her was another woman, about twenty years older, with the same jawline and silver hair cut in a stylish bob.

"I'm Greta Enwright," the younger woman said. "This is my mother, Olivia."

"Livy, please," the older woman said. "We're so pleased to meet you. Both of you." She bustled in behind her daughter and laid a silver tray on the nightstand. "I know your mother liked her tea, Paige. I took a chance on guessing you'd developed the same tastes."

I blinked. "You knew my mother?"

"From years back. More years than I care to count."

A tinkling, girlish laugh. "I grew up in the Coven. My mother left when I was a teenager."

"You're—you're a witch?"

"Oh, I'm so sorry. An incomplete introduction, Greta. I've always thought that strange, that we should be able to recognize sorcerers but not our own sisters. Greta is Mr. Nast's witch." Another laugh. "That sounds perfectly horrible, doesn't it? And much too familiar. Cabals, as you may know, only employ one witch. A very prestigious and exclusive position, which I was fortunate enough to be able to pass on to Greta when I retired. And now"—she turned a broad smile on Savannah— "we meet our official successor. I can't tell you how pleased we are."

Savannah hesitated, looking from mother to daughter. "You're not mad? I mean, I'll be replacing you, won't I?"

Greta laughed, a throaty chuckle that was the very opposite of her mother's. "It'll be some years before you're ready for that, Savannah. By then I'll be ready to retire myself. An early retirement, most likely, but Mr. Nast has promised me a full pension. If anything, I should be thanking you."

Olivia nodded. "And Mr. Nast has brought me out of retirement to help you get adjusted, for which he is more than adequately compensating me, so I should be thanking you as well."

"You guys'll be teaching us?"

"Us?" Greta repeated.

"Her," I said. "So you'll be her tutors?"

"In witch magic only," Olivia replied. "For the rest,

you'll have proper tutors. Sorcerers, I mean. They have the true magic."

"Maybe not for long," Savannah said, jumping from the bed. "Paige has these grimoires—"

I tried to stop her, but only half-heartedly. As much as I wanted to keep the grimoires secret, I was curious to hear the opinion of these women. I'd never met a Cabal witch. I'd expected—let's be honest, I'd expected them to be a lot different, more intimidating, more dangerous, more, well, evil.

Savannah told them about the grimoires and our theory. "Of course, Paige still has to test it. We could be wrong."

I refrained from telling the other witches that I *had* tested the theory, successfully. For now, better to keep that to myself.

"It sounds promising," Greta said. "But I wouldn't get my hopes up, ladies. Sorcerer magic is the magic of power. With all respect to women and equal rights, witch magic just doesn't measure up."

"I wouldn't waste my time on it," Olivia said. "Your tutors will teach you everything you need to know. As for those grimoires, I doubt they survived the fire."

"No, Paige went back for them." Savannah turned to me. "Where are they?"

"Cor—Lucas had them. I gave them to him."

"Lucas Cortez?" Olivia said. "Oh my, that's right, I heard young Lucas was involved. He has quite the reputation, but we've never had the chance to meet him, have we, Greta? That must have been quite an experience.

You'll have to tell us all about him. Let me pour the tea first."

Once the tea was poured, we sat on the edges of the beds. Olivia asked about Cortez. I let Savannah reply, discreetly cutting her short after a few sentences.

"Oh, he is an odd one," Olivia said, clucking. "I feel so sorry for his father. Mr. Cortez is handling the situation remarkably well, though I must say, he lets the boy get away with far too much. But all parents do, don't they? A Cabal leader is no different from any father. You'll see that, Savannah. Mr. Nast dotes on his boys, and I'm sure he'll treat you just the same."

"As for Lucas Cortez," Greta said, "young men are always looking for dragons to slay. And pretty damsels to rescue." She slid a smile my way. "It's only a stage. Soon he'll come to see that Cabals aren't the monsters he thinks they are."

"What are they?" Savannah asked. "I mean, what are they really like?"

"Excellent employers," Greta said. "Everything an employee could ask for. They offer comprehensive benefits, stock options, a solid pension plan, and excellent remuneration."

Olivia laughed. "None of which interests you in the least, does it, Savannah? And with good reason. You won't ever need to worry about those things. Your biggest concern now will be whether you want to spend your summer vacation in France or Italy."

"And what kind of sports car you want for your sixteenth birthday," Greta added.

"I want a Porsche," Savannah said, grinning at me.

"A Porsche convertible, like Clay's. Only red. I want it in red."

"You'll get it," Greta said. "This will be a whole new life for you, Savannah. A life any girl, and any witch, would envy."

Good and Evil

BEFORE DINNER, GRETA AND OLIVIA decided to squeeze in Savannah's first lesson. They took us outdoors to a grove beyond an unused barn. Leah and Friesen came along, presumably to guard Savannah from any external threat but more likely to guard her from any joint escape plan I might hatch. They needn't have bothered. As long as Savannah wanted to stay, I was staying right beside her.

Greta started with witch magic, but it was clear her heart wasn't in it, and as soon as she'd ascertained that Savannah already knew the basics, she moved on.

"Now we're going to show you some sorcery," Greta said. "Of course, you'll have a better tutor for this later, but I thought you might like to see a sampling of what you'll learn. When we get back to Los Angeles, we can work more on your witch skills."

Olivia grinned. "For now we'll have some fun."

Over the next hour Greta and Olivia demonstrated a half-dozen spells. One was a variation on Cortez's fog spell. Another shot a bolt of electrical energy from the caster's hand. A third conjured colored lights. Obviously they were showing off, selecting spells that were little more than the magical equivalent of Fourth of July fireworks. Dime store magic, as Cortez would say. I wanted to turn up my nose at it, but the truth was, I was impressed.

As they cast, I couldn't help thinking of all the possible uses for their spells. The fog spell would be handy for escapes, particularly in conjunction with the cover spell. The electrical bolt seemed an excellent variation on the fireball spell, something else to add to my repertoire of non-lethal defense. I wanted to find fault, to find evil, but I couldn't. There was nothing wrong with this magic. Although it wasn't any better than the magic in the tertiary witch grimoires, it wasn't any worse, either—at least, not in the sense of being any less moral.

"Could you cast that fog spell again?" I asked.

Greta smiled. "You like that one?"

"It's interesting. It contains components of wind and fire elemental witch spells, but the construction is much different. The invocation to Boreas is particularly unique. I suppose that's leftover vestiges of its origin."

Greta and Olivia stared at me as if I was speaking Greek, which in a way I was, since the spell itself was in Greek. After a moment of silence, Olivia laughed.

"To tell the truth, Paige, we have no idea what it says. We've never translated it."

"You don't know Greek?" Savannah said. "I thought all witches had to know Greek. And Latin and Hebrew. Enough to understand the spells, at least."

"We don't bother with that," Olivia said. "I know some Latin from my school days, but it's not important. The grimoires tell you what the spells do, and your tutors will explain the pronunciation."

"Would you like to try a casting?" Greta asked Savannah.

"Sure."

"Which one?"

Savannah grinned at me. "All of them. Teach us all of them."

That evening, Nast hosted a formal dinner party for his daughter. Savannah received her first little black dress, which was about two sizes too small in length and two sizes too big in width, but she was too excited to notice. She also received her first pair of heels and her first makeover, as Greta and Olivia fussed over and primped her into a "little princess." Only Nast and Sandford joined us for dinner, both in tuxes. I didn't recognize half of what I ate.

Afterwards, Nast presented Savannah with a family crest ring. Then he gave me an amulet, a gesture that clearly pleased Savannah—which was, I'm sure, the intent. It was a pretty piece, but non-magical, probably something he'd grabbed at an antique jewelry store that afternoon in Boston.

Next, everyone else in the house, from Sandford to the witches to the half-demon guards to the shaman cook, filed through with gifts. Once, in a museum, I saw a mural depicting an ancient Pharaoh sitting on his throne as a parade of foreign dignitaries presented him with exotic offerings. That's what this looked like. And like any normal thirteen-year-old girl, Savannah lapped it up.

❧

After dinner, we retired to our room. It was only eight-thirty, but we couldn't keep our eyes open.

"Did you see what Greta gave me?" Savannah pulled an amethyst-encrusted silver dagger from the pile of gifts by her bed. "A new athame. Isn't it great? I bet it was expensive."

"Very."

"Can I see the amulet Kristof gave you?"

Nast had asked Savannah to call him by his given name until she felt ready for something more indicative of their relationship. A wise move, I had to admit.

I passed Savannah the necklace.

"Cool. Bet it's an antique."

"I'm sure it is."

"It was nice of him, don't you think? To get you something?"

I nodded.

Savannah yawned and stretched back on the bed. "I'm so tired." She lifted her head to look at me. "Do you think they put something in our cocoa?"

I wanted to shout, "Yes! Don't you see? Don't you see everything? The gifts, the party—it's all a sham." Yet the truth was that I wasn't so sure of that myself. Yes, it was over the top. And patently unfair, since I could never compete. But was it a sham? I didn't know, so I settled for answering Savannah's question as honestly as I could.

"I think they probably gave us something to help us sleep. It doesn't feel any stronger than a sleeping potion. Probably valerian root, judging by the aftertaste."

"Well, I don't know about you, but I'm going to bed. Greta said she has a surprise for me tomorrow. A really good surprise."

"I'm sure she does," I said.

Someone knocked at the door. When I called a welcome, Olivia popped her head in.

"Paige? Mr. Nast would like to speak to you."

Savannah moaned. "Can't it wait until morning? I'm so tired."

"He only wants to speak to Paige, dear. I'll stay and keep you company while she's gone."

Savannah sat up. "I want to go with Paige."

Olivia shook her head. "Your father was very clear: Paige only."

"But—"

"I'll be fine," I said.

"Of course she will," Olivia said. "Nothing's going to happen to her, Savannah. Your father understands how much you've come to rely on her." She turned to me. "Mr. Nast is in the living room."

I nodded and left.

No one escorted me downstairs. I passed Friesen and another half-demon guard, whom I'd only heard called Anton. Both cast subtle glances my way but gave no sign that they were watching me. I knew they were, though.

Despite my intent to stay with Savannah, I'll admit to an inkling of temptation as I passed the front door. Earlier I hadn't thought of running. Now, however, as I neared the living room, I had to ask myself what Nast wanted.

I knew Nast had no intention of taking me back to Los Angeles. So long as I was alive, I'd be a threat. A minor one, but a threat nonetheless. Once I'd served my purpose, he'd have me killed. The only question was: when?

As I passed the door, I wondered whether I'd already outlived my usefulness. I hesitated, but only for a second. Nast's hold on Savannah wasn't strong enough to risk incurring her wrath. I had a few more days at least—enough time to come up with a plan.

When I pushed open the living-room door, Nast was inside, laughing as Sandford relayed an anecdote about a shaman.

"Paige, come in," Nast said. "Have a seat."

I did.

"Would you like a drink? Port? Claret? Brandy?"

"Claret would be fine. Thank you."

Sandford's brows arched, as if surprised I'd accept a drink. I had to trust in my conviction that they wouldn't kill me yet, and behave as if I trusted them.

Once Sandford passed around glasses of claret, Nast settled back in his chair.

"You asked earlier how we knew about Savannah's menses. I thought you should know the truth, though dinner hardly seemed an appropriate time to discuss it." He sipped his drink, taking his time before continuing. "I'll be blunt, Paige. Victoria Alden told us."

The glass almost fell from my hand.

"I realize you won't believe me," he continued. "Let

me offer proof that I've been speaking to Miss Alden. As for the ceremony, the Coven disapproved of it, but your mother did it for you. Miss Alden believes you borrowed Margaret Levine's car Tuesday night, not to get the tea ingredients as you told Margaret, but to get the required ceremonial materials."

I leaped to my feet. "What did you do to Victoria?"

"I beg your pardon?"

"You said Victoria told you. You forced her to talk, didn't you? What—"

Sandford's laugh cut me short.

Nast smiled. "Touching, isn't it? How she jumps to the defense of her Coven sister, even after that very person has exiled her from the Coven? We didn't hurt Victoria, Paige. We never even contacted her. She called us."

"No, she wouldn't do that."

"Oh, but she did. She got Gabe's number from Mr. Cary's office, then called and offered us a deal: information for protection. She'd tell us crucial details about Savannah if we'd promise to take my daughter and leave town."

"No! She'd never—!"

"You don't believe me?" Nast lifted a cellphone from the table by his arm. "Call her yourself."

I made no move to take the phone.

"No? Allow me, then."

He dialed the number, lifted the phone to his ear, and said a few words, then passed it to me. I snatched the phone from his hand.

"Tell me he's lying," I said.

"He isn't," Victoria replied. "I have the Coven's interests to consider, Paige. I will not—"

"You—do you have any idea what you've done?"

"I've given Savannah to her father."

"No, you've given her to a—"

"A Cabal. Yes, I realize that. I know all about them, despite what I said the other day. Savannah is the daughter of a sorcerer and a black witch. She deserves to be where she's going. Evil begets evil."

"No!" I shouted, flinging the phone against the fireplace.

"Hear that crash, Gabe?" Nast said. "It's the sound of illusions shattering." He looked at me. "I thought you should know, so you're fully aware of the situation. You may leave now."

Without even waiting for me to go, he turned back to Sandford and resumed their conversation. I stormed from the room.

Comprehensive Insurance Policy ❧

SAVANNAH WAS ASLEEP when I returned to our bedroom. Olivia left with only a murmured goodbye, perhaps realizing I was too stunned to hear her, much less respond.

How could the Elders have betrayed us? Banishing me from the Coven I could understand—barely—but this ... this was beyond fathoming. They'd sold Savannah for their own peace of mind. How could their own security be worth so great a price?

No matter how much I railed against the Elders, I had always believed them to be good women. They'd spent their lives fighting the temptation of evil and rooting it out of their Coven. Yes, they went too far, placed too many restrictions on us, robbed us of our potential. Yet I never doubted that their intentions were good.

Here, though, I was faced with something I could not deny—that they had acted in a way that made them no better than the Cabals, perhaps even worse. In chasing so relentlessly after morality, the Elders had become the very thing they'd fought so hard against: evil. I blanched at the word, instinctively feeling the need to justify, to moderate. Yet there it was. What else could you call their betrayal but an act of unforgivable evil?

Perhaps now more than ever, I wanted to save the Coven. If I did, though, I'd never forget this lesson.

We had a late breakfast with Nast, who was heading back into Boston for business that day but promised to return before dinner. After breakfast, we spent an hour in our room—Nast not yet having given us free run of the house. At eleven, Greta and her mother came to give Savannah her surprise.

"What is it?" Savannah asked as we trooped downstairs.

"If I told you, it wouldn't be a surprise, would it?" Greta replied.

"We'll tell you this much," Olivia said. "It's for your ceremony. Only five more days."

"But I thought—" Savannah glanced at me. "Kristof said Paige could do the ceremony."

"Oh yes, Paige will be conducting it. We'll have to use our own material, though. All Paige's things were lost in the fire. A shame, really. I warned—mentioned to Mr. Nast that he might want to rescue the magical items first, but he didn't see the need."

"You'll get all new tools anyway, Savannah," Greta said. "Better, too. Also, better materials for your ceremony. Do you know whose grave we got the dirt from? Abby Borden, Lizzie Borden's stepmother. She was killed near here, you know."

"Really?"

"Really. Now *there's* someone who was definitely murdered."

"When did you gather it?" I asked. "It has to be on the first night of her menses."

"Oh, that's an old wives'—or old witches'—tale," Olivia said. "That's one thing you'll learn, Savannah: a lot of what you've heard is nonsense. Gathering items on certain days, performing rituals at specific times—"

"You mean I don't need to wait until the eighth day?"

"No, that one's true. Or so we believe, though no witch I know has ever been willing to test the theory and risk hampering her daughter's powers."

When we arrived at the back door, Roberta Shaw and Anton were waiting to escort us outside. I hadn't seen the necromancer since Monday, at the funeral home. Shaw hadn't been among the staff who'd presented Savannah with gifts, so I'd assumed she'd been sent packing. Seeing her still here made me wonder whether Nast's condemnation of the funeral home debacle had been more show than substance.

"What's she doing here?" Savannah said, shooting a glare at Shaw.

"I asked Mr. Nast if Roberta could accompany us instead of Leah," Greta explained. She lowered her voice, "I don't know about you, but I don't trust that Volo."

"Well, I don't trust that necro, either," Savannah said.

Olivia hushed her. "She was only doing her job, Savannah. Now come along."

We passed the barn and entered the forest.

"So are we practicing the ceremony?" Savannah asked.

"No, we're performing a rite—a special protection rite."

"Cool."

"Very cool," Greta agreed. "Not many young witches get this. It requires very unique ingredients. When we mentioned it to Mr. Nast, though, he gave us carte blanche. Anything to help his little girl on her special day."

I resisted the urge to make retching noises. "What kind of protection does it give?"

"The best. Think of it as a comprehensive insurance policy. It'll prevent everything from demonic interference to having Savannah wake up with the flu next Wednesday."

"Huh," I said. "Sounds good."

"It's sorcerer magic."

"Of course."

They led us into the woods. We passed the spot where we'd practiced the afternoon before. As we walked, Savannah glanced back at Shaw and Anton.

"Who's carrying the material?" she asked.

"What material is that, dear?" Olivia said.

"For the ritual."

"Everything we need is at the site."

"I should have brought my new athame."

Both Greta and Olivia frowned, then Olivia laughed.

"Oh, that's right, Coven witches still use their tools. You'll find we've moved beyond that. We all still have an athame as a keepsake—a reminder of our past. As I'm sure you know, the tools aren't actually required for casting."

"My mom used them," Savannah said.

"That's because she was raised Coven. It takes a while to shake the old ways. I clung to my tools for years, like a security blanket. You'll find we only use tools that are imperative for casting."

"The same goes for materials," Greta said. "We've done away with all the non-essentials: gemstones with symbolic meanings, incense for mood, candles for atmospheric lighting. All they do is complicate and prolong a ceremony."

"Maybe," Savannah said. "But don't you think they make it kinda . . . fun?"

Greta laughed. "Cabals don't have a budget for fun."

"Modern witches have made witchcraft modern," Olivia said. "You'll come to appreciate that, Savannah. It makes things much easier if we discard the baggage, both literal and figurative."

"And here we are," Greta said. She stepped off the path, pulled back a bush, and waved us through.

Savannah stepped into the clearing first. Through the bushes, I saw her walk forward, eyes on the towering trees. Then she stopped short and yelped. I dove through the bushes to find her standing over a prone figure. It was a boy, maybe fifteen or sixteen. I hurried forward, then saw the steady rise and fall of his chest.

"He's sleeping," Savannah said. "Weird. He must live around here, huh? Guess we should find someplace else—"

"He's supposed to be here," Greta said. Savannah stared at the young man. He wore a faded denim jacket and jeans. He had light brown hair tied at the nape and the kind of soft, pretty face that markets so well to preteen girls.

"Who is he?" Savannah asked.

"Prince Charming," Greta said. "You've heard of Sleeping Beauty? Well, this is the girl-power version."

Savannah gave a half-laugh, turning away as her cheeks went scarlet. "No, really, who is he? A sorcerer?"

"He's nobody. Just a human boy." Greta grabbed a small bag from the side of the clearing. "Now, as I've said, we skip all the ritual preliminaries, so you can just go right ahead and kneel beside him."

"What? Why?"

My gut went cold. "What's going on here?"

"The protection ritual, as we said. Savannah, kneel beside the young man and put your hand on his chest."

Savannah hesitated, then started to kneel.

"No," I said. "Get up, Savannah." I looked at Greta and Olivia. "We aren't doing anything until you tell us exactly what this ritual entails."

Greta turned her back on me.

"Hey—!" I said.

I was cut off, frozen in a binding spell. Savannah started scrambling to her feet, but Anton put his hands on her shoulders and pressed her down.

"Hey! Don't you—! Paige!" Savannah swung her gaze up to Olivia, who stood behind me and was undoubtedly casting the binding spell. "Let her go! *Now!*"

"Paige is a Coven witch," Greta said. "She doesn't understand." She pulled a thin-bladed knife from her bag and knelt on the other side of the boy.

"Wh—what are you doing?" Savannah asked.

"A top-level protection spell requires an exchange— a life protected for a life lost. You should know this, Savannah. Your mother did."

"No! My mother never—she wouldn't—" Savannah looked at the boy, then wrenched her gaze away and struggled against Anton's grip. "You can't do this! I forbid it."

"You *forbid* it?" Greta's lips twisted. "Did you hear that, Mother? She's giving orders already. Well, 'princess,' it's your father who gives orders around here, and he told us to do whatever was necessary to keep his little girl safe. Anton, put her highness's hand on the boy's chest. Over the heart, please."

Anton forced Savannah's hand to the boy's left breast. Greta moved the blade to the boy's throat.

"No!" Savannah cried. "You can't do this! You can't! He didn't—he didn't do anything."

"He's a nobody, Savannah," Olivia said from behind me. "A runaway. The only meaning his life has is in protecting yours."

"Don't bother, Mother," Greta said. "It's obvious Eve coddled the girl. What do you think dark magic is, Savannah?"

"It's not this. I know it isn't. My mother never did this."

"Of course she did. She just never let you see it."

Greta pressed the blade against the boy's throat.

"No!" Savannah struggled harder, forcing Anton to put all of his weight into holding her down.

"He's a pretty boy, isn't he?" Greta said. She put her left hand behind the boy's head and lifted it. "Would you like to give him a kiss, Savannah? A last kiss? No? All right, then."

She slashed the knife over the boy's neck so fast that it seemed not to have left a mark. Then his throat split open. Anton shoved Savannah's head forward. Blood jetted into her face and she started to scream.

Brotherly Love ❧

I WON'T DETAIL THE NEXT few minutes. I can't. It broke my heart the first time, and even thinking about it now is enough to bring me to tears. Savannah's terror and rage were indescribable. All I could do was stand there and watch, trapped in a binding spell.

Twenty minutes later I was in the bedroom, tucking Savannah into bed. Ringed around us were Nast, Sandford, and Leah.

On hearing the screams, Leah and Friesen had come running. In the chaos that ensued, no one had escaped Savannah's blind fury. Leah had a bloodied nose, and even I had a scratch across my upper arm. Eventually Shaw managed to sedate Savannah, and she'd collapsed where she stood. Then Anton had carried her back to the house.

Once I'd finished getting Savannah into bed, Nast waved for everyone to leave the room. When I tried to stay, he motioned for Leah to remove me. I brushed her off and followed Nast and Sandford into the hall.

"I can't believe they did that," Nast said.

"They say you gave them carte blanche," Sandford replied.

"Not for this."

"It's a common spell, Kris. Not too common, given the risk that comes with kidnapping and killing humans, but it's common enough."

"But to take her, unprepared, without a word of explanation . . ."

"I did warn you, Kris," Sandford said, lowering his voice so Leah couldn't hear. "They expected Greta's daughter to succeed her."

"You think they did this intentionally?"

"Duh, no, really?" I said, stepping forward. "Of course it was intentional! I can't believe you placed Savannah in the hands of women who had every reason to want her gone. I'm surprised they didn't kill her instead of the boy." I looked from Sandford to Nast. "Oh, I see. You figured they'd toe the party line because they're witches—too stupid, or too cowed, to plot against you."

"Are we done with her yet?" Sandford asked, jerking his chin at me.

Nast looked at me, but his gaze was unfocused, distracted. "Just get her out of here. I'll decide what to do with her later. I haven't time for this right now."

The moment Sandford asked his question, I'd started whispering the fog spell. I flicked my hand now and a cloud of smoke burst from my fingertips, swirling up like a smokescreen. I raced into the bedroom, slammed the door, and cast a lock spell. I tugged once on the windowsill, found it had been painted shut, then grabbed a chair and threw it through the glass.

"Savannah!" I said, shaking her shoulder.

She gave only a low groan. I grasped her around the waist and pulled her off the bed. Then I looked out the window. We were on the second story. Maybe I could jump, but I could hardly throw Savannah out.

Leah pounded at the door. Sandford shouted orders, calling the others. I thought fast. Did I know any spells for getting Savannah down? No. Either I could find a way to lower her to the ground or I'd have to carry her. The first would take too long. I tried lifting her, but could barely get her off the floor.

The door flew open. Friesen burst through and grabbed Savannah from me. Leah followed at his heels.

"See, guys?" she said. "No rush, like I said. She wasn't going anywhere."

"Take her to the secured room," Nast said.

Leah leaned over me and said in a mock whisper. "Just a tip: next time, run for the front door."

Friesen and Sandford laughed.

They put me in a secured basement room, and bound and gagged me, leaving me incapable of spellcasting. Then Shaw shot a dose of sedative into my arm. I was unconscious before they left the room.

I don't know how much time passed, but when I awoke, I found myself staring into Cortez's eyes. I struggled to sit upright, smiling behind my gag. Then the eyes blinked, and I saw within them something so cold I skittered backward.

Somewhere in the room, Gabriel Sandford laughed. "Scared of her own shadow. Just like a witch."

The man bending over me blinked again. He had Cortez's eyes, but older. Older and soulless. When he moved back, I saw that the resemblance ended at the eyes. This man was in his early forties, shorter than Cortez, with a severe patrician look that might have been handsome if he smiled, but his frown lines suggested he never did.

"You're certain?" he asked. "About the relationship?"

"Certain?" Sandford said. "What do you want? A videotape of your brother banging her?"

The man turned a cold stare on Sandford, who straightened and cleared his throat.

"I can't be absolutely sure, as she's not likely to admit to it," Sandford said, his tone formal. "Yet all evidence points to that conclusion. Your brother is searching frantically."

"Frantically?"

"Very."

The other man's brows lifted. "I don't think I've ever seen Lucas frantic about anything. That seals the matter, then. Kill her."

"And put her head in his bed?"

The man's lip curled ever so slightly. He only shook his head, as if Sandford's quip wasn't worthy of an answer.

Sandford stiffened and dropped his gaze. "Would you prefer I send him a videotape, then? Of her death?"

"That should do."

"Degree of suffering?"

"Average. Enough to hurt him, not enough to convince him it was overtly personal."

"I'll send my best."

"No, you'll send your most expendable. An independent contractor. That will be more cost-effective, and will make it more difficult for Lucas to trace it back to you. You'll involve no one else from the Nast organization in this matter, and you'll eliminate the contractor once he's finished the job. Once I leave, you'll move her to a second location. From there, you'll arrange for the contractor to kidnap and kill her. You'll then include this note with the videotape."

He handed an envelope to Sandford. When Sandford looked down at it, the man continued, "The note simply makes it clear that her death is Lucas's fault, that had she not become involved with him and his 'crusade,' she'd still be alive."

Sandford smiled. "A little guilt's always good for the conscience."

"Now make sure this cannot be linked to you or the Nast Cabal. As for me, I was never here."

"That goes without saying. We have a deal, then?"

The man nodded.

"Just to, uh, be clear . . ." Sandford continued. "If I do this, I'm guaranteed a position in the Cortez Cabal, at a 20 percent salary increase."

"That's what I said, isn't it?"

"I just wanted to be sure. I'm taking a big risk here. It would have been easier if I could have persuaded Kristof to get rid of her, but he's still stalling, worried about that witch-brat of his. When he finds out this one disappeared on my watch, I'll probably be out of a job, friend or not. So, of course, I want to be sure—"

The man's gaze hardened. "Did I give you my word?"

"Y—yes, sir. Forgive me."

"I appreciate your having brought this . . . unique opportunity to my attention, Gabriel. You will be very well compensated for it." The man turned toward me, lips curving in a humorless smile. "I must say, it's almost a shame she has to die. My father's been worrying that Lucas will never provide him with grandsons. It's hard to perpetuate a dynasty when the current heir shows no inclination to father future heirs. He'd be so pleased to hear that Lucas has finally found someone. Then he'd meet her . . . and probably drop dead of shock." He shook his head. "A witch? Unbelievable, even for Lucas."

"Not *just* a witch," Sandford said. "The head of the American Coven."

"Oh, *there's* a dynastic alliance guaranteed to make the Cortez Cabal the laughingstock of the supernatural world. I'm doing my father such a favor, it's a shame I can't tell him about it."

The man turned to leave. As he walked out, a fireball flew from the ceiling and struck the side of his head. He wheeled on Sandford.

"Don't look at me," Sandford said quickly, stepping back. "That wasn't one of our spells."

The man glanced at me. I glared back, pouring every bit of hate and fury into that glare. He opened his mouth as if to say something, then shut it and settled for returning my glare before stalking out the door.

"I want her dead by sundown. FedEx the tape to Lucas's motel room. Overnight express."

Send-off ❧

DESPITE CORTEZ'S BROTHER'S WARNING about involving others, Sandford had at least one ally, the half-demon Friesen. Less than thirty minutes after Sandford left me alone again, Friesen walked in. Without a word, he tossed me over his shoulder. He carried me from the room and across the basement to a hatch much like the one in my house, opened it, and pushed me through.

I tumbled out the hatch door into a weed-choked garden. After being in the near-dark so long, the blast of sunlight made my eyes water. I struggled to wiggle free of my bonds, but they were tied tight. Friesen hefted himself through the hatch, picked me up, oblivious to my struggles, and slipped across the backyard to the barn. Inside, a panel van was waiting. So was Gabriel Sandford. As Friesen carried me toward the van, Sandford snapped his cellphone shut.

"Done," Sandford said. "He'll be at the cabin in two hours."

Friesen nodded. With me still over his shoulder, he flipped open the van's rear gate, laid me inside, face up, then stepped back. His gaze traveled slowly over me, pausing at my chest and bared legs.

"Shut the door and get moving," Sandford said, "before someone notices she's gone."

Friesen gave me another slow once-over, then slid his gaze toward Sandford. "I was just thinking . . . you're sending Lucas Cortez a video, right? Of her death? Why not . . . you know . . . bump it up a little?" His gaze shot back to me, a gleam of hunger alight in his eyes. "I'll do it for you."

"You'll do what?" Sandford caught the look Friesen was giving me and his lip curled. "Rape wasn't part of the deal, and it's not going to be. Just take her to the cabin and let the professional do his work."

"Seems like a waste, don't you think?"

"No, I'd prefer not to think about it at all, thank you very much." Sandford started to turn away, then frowned at Friesen, who was still staring as if I was a free buffet dinner. He shook his head and threw up his hands. "Oh hell, do what you like—but do it away from the house and before you get to the cabin, okay? You've got two hours. Now move."

Friesen smiled and slammed the gate.

As we pulled away from the house, I started to count. I had to get out of here before Friesen got far enough to pull over, and by the looks he'd been giving me, he wasn't going to wait any longer than necessary.

When I reached a hundred, I decided we were out of sight of the house, so I closed my eyes and concentrated on mentally casting the suffocation spell, aiming it at Friesen. Nothing happened, which was not surprising since I couldn't speak. Yet back at the house, someone had lobbed a fireball. The spell came from my secret grimoires, so it had to have been me, though I wasn't sure how I'd done it. Had my fury somehow manifested itself in an unintentional spell? I hoped so, as I hoped I could do it again, this time choosing my spell.

The van slowed, then pulled to the side of the road. Already?! We couldn't be more than half a mile from the house. Friesen put the van in park. Then he swiveled, undid his seat belt, and squeezed through the front seats. I fought the urge to struggle and instead put everything I had into a mental cast. Nothing happened.

Friesen loomed over me. I inched backward across the floor.

"Not yet, honey," he said, crouching over me. "Nothing to worry about yet. I'm just going to take a better look."

As he unbuttoned my blouse, I rocked and twisted but couldn't move enough even to hamper him. He spread my shirt apart and grinned.

"Red," he said, gaze glued to my bra. "Black's okay, and white's kinda nice, but there's nothing like a girl who wears red." He stroked a finger across the bra cup. "Silk, I bet. A girl who really knows how to dress."

While he fiddled with the front clasp, I squeezed my eyes shut and concentrated on casting something, anything. My bra popped open. Friesen inhaled sharply.

I opened my eyes and tried to wriggle away. He reached down for my breast but stopped before his fingers touched me. He held his hand there a moment, then squeezed it into a fist and pulled back.

"Not yet," he murmured. "Prolong the fun."

He grabbed my hips. I kicked at him, but all he did was tug me sideways so I was facing the front of the van. Then he reached down and hiked my skirt up around my waist. I writhed and bucked, trying to get away, but he only grinned broader.

"Red silk," he said, chuckling as he touched my panties. "A matching set, of course. Very nice. Poor Lucas. The boy probably didn't know what hit him. You sure knew what you were doing, honey, I gotta give you credit for that. A first-class ticket to the good life . . . even if it did mean screwing that geek." He smiled and ran a finger up the inside of my thigh. "If you gotta go, I figure the least I can do is give you a better send-off."

He took another look at me, then straightened and went back to the driver's seat. As the van pulled onto the road, he readjusted the rearview mirror so he could see me.

"There now, that's better. Couldn't ask for a better view."

My fear crystallized to rage, blind rage.

The van swerved onto the shoulder. Friesen swore. My head bounced up, then slammed down on the metal floor. Something jabbed into my scalp as Friesen yanked the van back onto the road.

"Damn," he said, glancing in the mirror and chuckling. "More of a distraction than I thought."

The cut on my scalp throbbed. I twisted to see the corner of a metal strip of edging protruding from the van's side. I wriggled upward until I'd aligned the jutting metal with my gag. Then I lifted my head, trying to snag the top edge of the cloth. The van hit a washboard of ruts and the metal sliced my cheek.

Friesen's gaze went back to the mirror. I stopped and waited until he'd looked his fill and returned his attention to driving. I brushed my cheek against the metal strip. This time the gag caught.

I wriggled the cloth down over my top lip. Then the van hit a bump and the snag came loose. I worked my jaw until enough of my mouth was free that I could mumble. I cast the suffocation spell. Friesen coughed. I froze.

He glanced in the mirror again and smiled. "Seem to be getting a bit short of breath. Must be those red panties. Let's see if I can't find a place to pull over."

When he looked away, I cast again. Nothing. Quickly, I recast. He coughed, then wheezed. The van swerved. Friesen fought to keep it on the road, gasping for what seemed like an eternity. Finally, the van went off the road, thudding over grass.

The right side dipped. For a moment the van continued thumping along, slowly sliding into the ditch. Then the world spun. I flew from the floor, hit the side, then struck the roof, knocking around in the van until I didn't know which end was up. Then everything stopped.

When I lifted my head, the seats were above me. The van had come to rest on its roof. I shifted, trying to flip onto my back. The van groaned and trembled, settled, and went still.

I looked around, searching for something that had broken off sharp. The window nearest to me had broken, but it was safety glass—useless. I looked overhead. One of the seats had broken, exposing a metal rod that looked suitably sharp. It took about twenty minutes and plenty of cursing, but I finally cut through the bindings on my hands. I undid my legs and crawled out through the broken window.

Friesen was still in his seat belt, hanging upside down. He had a gash on his head and his eyes were closed. I crept forward and saw that he was unconscious but alive. Though I was tempted to do something more painful to the bastard, I let him be. Unconscious was good enough.

I spent the next few minutes searching Friesen and the van for a cellphone. Of course I couldn't find one. That would be too easy. Finally, I gave up and sealed the doors with the strongest lock spells I had.

As I fastened my bra and buttoned my blouse, I looked around. The van had landed in a field. When I reached the road, I paused to get my bearings. I had a decision to make: return to the house or go for help? It seems an obvious choice, doesn't it? I'm not stupid. Surely I should realize that the wisest course of action would be to get to safety, bring in some muscle, then go back for Savannah. But I couldn't do that. Right now, I knew where to find her. If I went for help, she might not be there when I returned. Yes, it was insane, but I had to go back.

I headed deeper into the fields, out of sight from the road, and began the long walk back to the house. What would I do when I got there? I didn't know. If I could rescue Savannah, I would. It seemed unlikely I could do it alone, I admit that. If it wasn't possible, maybe I could get a message to her, telling her I'd return. At the very least I could assess the situation, go for help, then hurry back to keep watch over her from a distance.

We must have driven at least three miles. Fortunately, Friesen had only turned once and the roads were spaced so far apart that I could easily guess where to turn.

After about a mile of tramping through the fields, I heard a distant motor and froze. Though I was too far from the road to be spotted, I crouched and waited for the vehicle to pass. A farm pickup drove by, moving well below the speed limit. Once it was out of sight, I straightened and resumed walking.

I'd gone about another mile when the faintest notes of a scream blasted through the silence. I dropped to the ground. The fields were silent. I waited another minute, but when all remained quiet, I rose and began moving forward, slower now.

I'd gone about another hundred yards when I saw a stretch of trees surrounding what looked like a two-story white house. Yes, there had been huge evergreens along each side, as a windbreak. Before I could break into a run, I picked up the sound of voices. I dove for the ground again and lay flat on my stomach in the long grass.

"I'm not going back in there!" Sandford, his voice shrill.

"If I tell you to, you will." Nast, cool and calm.

"No, I will not. As of now, I'm no longer a member of your fucking organization. I quit, you got that? Quit!"

"You have a contract."

"You want me to tell you where you can shove that contract? I am not going in that house. She's your daughter. *You* get her out."

A yelp and a thud in quick succession. Then silence. I inched forward until I could see the two men through the trees. They were in the side yard. Sandford crouched on the ground, nose and mouth streaming blood. Nast stood a few feet away, arms crossed, waiting.

"Please, Kris, be reasonable," Sandford said, pulling himself to a sitting position but making no effort to stand. "You're asking me to risk my life for a witch."

"I'm asking you to help my *daughter*."

"How long have we known each other? You asked me to take this assignment as a special favor, and I did. Now it's all gone to hell, but I'm still with you, aren't I?"

"You'll be well-rewarded for that loyalty, Gabriel. Bring Savannah out of that house and you can expect a six-figure bonus."

Sandford wiped a bloodied hand across his shirt. Then he looked up at Nast. "A bonus plus a vice-presidency. With a twelfth-floor office."

"A tenth-floor office . . . and I'll forget who was supposed to be looking after the witch when she vanished."

Sandford hauled himself to his feet and nodded. "Done."

"I want her unharmed. Not a scratch. Understood?"

Sandford nodded again and headed toward the front door. I waited until he was out of sight, then scurried to the woods and circled around to the other side of the house.

A Lesson in Respect

THE SIDE DOOR STOOD OPEN. I scampered across the yard and into the house.

When I stepped inside, the first thing I saw was the necromancer Shaw's body. She lay crumpled at the foot of a narrow set of stairs. I checked each way before moving further. Overhead I heard one, maybe two sets of footsteps. I crept to Shaw's body. From the angle of her head I guessed she'd fallen down the stairs and broken her neck.

What had happened here? I'd only been gone an hour or so. Now Shaw was dead, Nast was standing around outside, and Sandford was searching, with great reluctance, for Savannah. From what Sandford said, I gathered Savannah was at the root of all this. But how? Whatever the explanation, I needed to find her before anyone else did.

As I moved past Shaw, the look on her face stopped me in my tracks. Her eyes were open so wide the whites showed all around the irises. Her lips were curled back over her teeth. And the expression—stark terror. Perhaps at the moment of her dying, an image flashed through her mind, that of some other necromancer sucking her soul from eternity and plunking it back into her broken corpse. Fitting, really.

I stepped over her and began ascending the stairs. They were enclosed on both sides, and the passage was so narrow it was a wonder Shaw had fallen down them at all and not become wedged halfway. These must be back steps, probably a secondary set leading from the kitchen.

The stairs exited through an open door on the second floor. When I'd climbed high enough to see past the door, I paused for a better look. The door was at the end of the upstairs hallway. At the opposite end were the main stairs, the ones I'd been using when I was here. Of the six bedroom doors, one was wide open, two were partially open, and the other three were closed.

"Savannah?" someone called.

I jumped, then recognized the voice. Sandford.

"Savannah . . . come on, sweetie. No one's going to hurt you. You can come on out now. Your dad's not mad."

Oh yeah, like *that* was a big concern. How old did he think Savannah was? Five? Hiding in a corner, cowering in fear of a spanking?

I listened for any return noise, but none came. Except for Sandford's voice and the creak of his shoes, the house was silent.

As I eased into the hall, something rustled overhead. Sandford's shoes squeaked as he stopped, pausing to listen. Footsteps sounded above me. I closed my eyes as I followed them, then shook my head. They were too heavy to be Savannah's. I guessed Anton or one of the witches was searching the attic for Savannah.

Sandford's shadow advanced out of an open doorway

near the end of the hall. I ducked into another open room and slid behind the door while he passed. Another door opened, then shut. Footsteps receded.

I glanced around, finding myself in Greta and Olivia's room. The dresser top was bare, the closet open and empty except for a sweater that had fallen on the floor and been forgotten. It looked as if the two witches had left in a hurry. Had they fled when they realized Nast suspected their motives in killing the boy? Or had something else scared them off?

I looked around again, then returned to the hall and pulled the bedroom door half shut behind me, as it had been when I found it. As I turned, there was a click and the hall light went on.

I started to run, but hands grabbed me, one going over my mouth. Then an exclamation of disgust and the hand shoved me aside.

"What are you doing here?" Sandford said. "Where's—"

"What happened? What's Savannah done?"

Sandford only snorted. He turned away from the room he'd just checked and headed for the next closed door.

"Hey," I said, jogging after him, "tell me what's going on. I can help."

"I don't need a witch's help. Just stay out of my way."

To underline the point he flicked his fingers, sending me flying into the far wall. As his hand closed on the door handle, I cast a lock spell.

"Either I help you or I hinder you," I said, getting to my feet. "Now which—"

The door flew open. For a second I thought he'd broken

the lock spell. Then a man walked through, stepping off the bottom of the attic stairs.

"Anton," Sandford exclaimed. "You're okay. Good."

Anton fixed Sandford with bright green eyes, a brighter green than I remembered.

"Did you call me?" he asked. His voice was nothing short of beautiful, a melodious tenor that reverberated through the hall.

Sandford frowned, as if confused by the voice, and shook his head sharply. "I'm guessing you haven't found the girl, have you? Come on, then. We'll head downstairs."

"I asked you a question, sorcerer," Anton said, eye to eye with Sandford. "Did you call me?"

"No, but I can use you now. We'll—"

Anton turned to face me. In the dim light his skin seemed to give off a glow of its own.

"Ignore her," Sandford said. "We need—"

"Did you call me, witch?"

As Anton stepped toward me, I instinctively backed up, hitting the wall. His hand reached out as if for my throat, but instead cupped my chin and tilted my face up to his. At the touch of his hand, I jumped. The skin was hot.

"Did you summon me?"

Even if I had known how to answer, his hand held my jaw too tightly to speak. His grip was iron hard, strong but not painful. His eyes searched mine, as if looking for his answer there.

"The girl?" he murmured. "A mistake. Yes, clearly a mistake. A forgivable one, I suppose. This time."

I knew then, what had taken control of Anton's body.

A demon, a high-ranking one, the kind that should never—and usually *could* never—be summoned.

I dropped my gaze. The demon loosened his grip on my chin and stroked my cheek with his forefinger.

"Smart witch," he murmured. "Don't worry, it was a mistake."

Behind him, Sandford's lips moved in an incantation. Though no sound reached my ears, the demon swung around, letting me go and turning on Sandford.

"What are you doing?" the demon demanded.

Sandford's lips kept moving, but he shrank back as the demon bore down on him.

"What do you think I am?!" the demon thundered, pushing his face into Sandford's. "You dare try to send me back? With a spell to dispel some mewling spirit?"

Sandford's voice rose, words spilling from his mouth.

"Show some respect, sorcerer!"

The demon grabbed Sandford by the shoulders. Sandford squeezed his eyes tight and kept casting.

"Fool! Disrespectful fool!"

With a roar, the demon pulled back his hand and slammed it into Sandford's chest—slammed it *through* his chest, rather, fingers disappearing inside Sandford's torso. The muscles on the demon's arm tightened, as if squeezing. Sandford's mouth opened in a silent scream. The demon withdrew his hand, bloodless, and let Sandford's body fall to the floor. Then he turned to me.

A protective spell flew to my lips, but I swallowed it and forced myself to stand up straight, meeting his gaze, firm but not defiant.

He strode back to me and his hand cupped my chin

again, lifting my face to his. His eyes searched mine. I fought the urge to look away. For a long minute he just stared at me . . . into me. Then his lips curved in a smile and he released my chin.

He stood there watching me for a moment, then headed down the hall. After a few steps, he lifted his hands and Anton's body dropped to the floor. A sharp wind, as hot as a furnace blast, encircled me and was gone.

I wrapped my arms around myself, shaking despite the heat. Looking down at Sandford, I saw that his shirt was neither torn nor bloodied, as if I'd only imagined what I'd seen. Shivering, I stepped over his lifeless body.

Anton's corpse lay several feet away, also blocking the hall. He was on his stomach, face turned toward the wall, eyes closed. As I lifted my foot to step over him, his body convulsed. I jerked back, stumbling into Sandford. Anton's body shook and twisted, bucking off the floor. Finally, it went still.

I fought to control my racing heart. I lifted my foot slowly. Dime store magic, I told myself. Yet that mantra no longer worked, no longer held true. There were things here that could hurt me, things my brain could barely fathom.

As my foot passed over Anton's head, his eyes opened and I fell back with a shriek. Anton's head rose and jerked from side to side. Then it revolved nearly full circle, bones snapping. His eyes met mine. The bright green irises were gone, replaced by dull yellowish disks with huge pupils. Those reptilian eyes fixed on mine, wide and unblinking. The mouth opened and a stream of high-pitched gibberish flew out. Then the thing that had been Anton rose up onto its fingertips and toes, lifting itself just inches above the floor, and skittered into the next open room. From within came more gibbering, then the scratching of nails moving fast against the wooden floor.

I dove past the open door and ran for the front stairs, taking them two at a time. Halfway down, the step beneath me split in two. I stumbled and grabbed the railing. The next step cracked, then the next and the next, pieces dropping into the empty hole below. I raced back up the stairs, hearing the steps crackle and splinter in my wake.

I dashed for the back stairs, gaze trained on the doorway ahead. Something hissed in my path and I stopped short. Anton—or what had been Anton—was crouched over Sandford's corpse. The creature hissed and snuffled at my approach, but kept its face against Sandford's torso, as if sniffing it.

I looked back at the front steps, now a twelve-foot sheer drop. Then I glanced at the creature. It still hadn't lifted its head, didn't even seem to know I was there. If I could just step over—oh god, you must be kidding! I bit back my horror and steeled myself. A short run, a jump, and I'd be at the back stairs. I just couldn't think about what I was jumping over.

As I prepared to sprint, I changed my mind. I'd flunked track and field in elementary school, being unable to clear even the lowest hurdle. If I ran and jumped, I risked kicking the creature and pissing it off. Instead, I tiptoed across the hall, pressed myself against the wall, and began slowly sidestepping toward Sandford's body. His arm was stretched over his head.

Carefully I stepped over it, then continued inching sideways, past his head and along his upper chest. The creature was still crouched over Sandford's stomach, its feet braced against the wall.

I lifted my foot to step over it. Its head shot up and twisted around, reptilian eyes meeting mine. Strings of Sandford's flesh hung from its mouth and teeth. It hissed, spraying me with gore. I screamed then, screamed as loud as I could, and wheeled, instinctively heading back to the front steps. I only got as far as Sandford's outstretched arm, tripped over it, and sailed to the floor. Something moved across my legs and I reared up, kicking and screaming. I couldn't stop screaming. Even knowing I was wasting energy—and possibly attracting more horrors—I couldn't stop.

The thing that had been Anton squirmed over me, pinning me to the floor. As hard as I punched, I couldn't even make it flinch. It moved up my chest until its face was over mine, dribbling bits of bloodied flesh onto my mouth and cheeks.

I shut my mouth then, shut it fast. In my head, though, I was still screaming, unable to focus or think, seeing only those yellow eyes boring into mine. The thing opened its mouth and gibbered, a high-pitched stream of noise that stabbed through my skull.

It lowered its face to mine. I squeezed my hands between its shoulders and mine and pushed with everything I had. It bared its teeth and hissed louder, spraying me with saliva and blood, but I kept pushing and finally managed to wriggle from under it.

I scrambled to my feet and kicked it in the head. It

shrieked and gibbered. I turned to run, but a woman blocked my path. I recognized her as the shaman cook.

"Look out!" I shouted. "Run!"

She only bent and waved her hands at the creature, as if shooing a cat. It hissed and snarled. As I glanced back at the thing, it lifted itself onto its fingers and toes and skittered through another open door.

"Oh god, thank you," I said. "Now let's get—"

The woman grabbed my arm. "He was here."

"Yes, a lot of things are here! Now let's—"

The woman stepped in front of me, blocking my path again. I looked her full in the face for the first time. Her eyes were white—pure white, devoid of irises and pupils. Before I could run the other way, she pulled me to her.

"He was here," she repeated, her voice a breathless whisper. "I can smell him. Can you smell him?"

I struggled to get free. She didn't even seem to notice my efforts. She licked her lips.

"Yes, yes, I smell him. One of the masters. Here. Here!" She moved her face down to mine, nostrils flaring. "I smell him on you." Her voice and body quivered with excitement. "He spoke to you. He touched you. Oh, you have been blessed! Blessed!"

Her tongue shot out and licked my cheek. I yelped and dove past her. She grabbed for me, but I kept running.

I tore down the hall and back steps, vaulting over Sandford then Shaw without so much as a stumble. At the bottom of the stairs I didn't pause to look around. I dove through the first open door, slammed it behind me, and leaned against it, gulping air. I was shaking so badly the door itself quavered under me.

After a moment I realized it wasn't me making the door shake. The whole house was quaking.

Beneath my feet, the floor rattled and groaned. I looked around wildly. The floorboards buckled, then gave way, splinters spraying upward as a wave of spirits flew through, formless rays of light like in the cemetery. The force of them hurled me into the air. As I rocketed across the room, a huge gaping maw appeared in front of me. Before I had time to scream, I sailed through the apparition and hit the floor.

All around me, spirits jetted into the air, moving so fast that I could feel their passing. The very fabric of the house moaned and shifted, threatening to blow apart. I fought to move, but the pressure of the passing spirits was like a gale-force wind, holding me still and snatching the breath from my lungs.

It stopped as suddenly as it had begun. The spirits had broken through the ceiling and were gone.

I took a minute to breathe, just breathe, then looked around. Between me and the door, the floor was gone, leaving a gaping hole into the basement. I glanced at the window, but it was barely eighteen inches square. No part of me was eighteen inches, round or square.

After a few more deep breaths I approached the hole in the floor. From below, I caught a sound that made my heart leap. Savannah's voice. She was in the basement, chanting an incantation.

I dropped to my knees, grabbed the edge of the floor, and leaned into the hole.

"Savannah? It's me, hon. It's Paige."

She continued chanting, her voice a distant whisper. I cleared my throat.

"Savannah? Can you—"

The house rocked suddenly, like a boat cut from its moorings. I flew face first into the hole and somersaulted, landing hard on the dirt floor beneath. For a moment I couldn't move; the commands wouldn't travel from my brain to my muscles. Panic washed through me. Then, as if in a delayed reaction, all my limbs convulsed, throwing me awkwardly into a sprawl. I scrambled to my feet, ignoring the pain that slammed through me.

From somewhere beyond came Savannah's faint voice. Looking around, I saw I was in an empty coal cellar. I moved to the only door and opened it. Savannah's voice became clear. I caught a few words of Greek, enough to tell me, if I hadn't already guessed, that she was conjuring. Conjuring what, though, I couldn't tell. I hurried toward her before I found out.

Show and Tell

AS I FOLLOWED SAVANNAH'S VOICE, I heard another. Nast.

"You have to stop, sweetheart," he said. "You can't do this. It isn't possible."

Savannah kept chanting.

"I know you're angry. I don't know what happened—"

Savannah stopped in mid-incantation and howled, "You killed her!"

"I didn't kill anyone, princess. If you mean that boy—"

"I mean Paige! You killed her. You told them to kill her."

"I never—"

"I saw her body! Leah showed me! I saw them carry her to the van. You promised she'd be safe and you killed her!"

I stepped into a room with a mammoth wood-burning furnace and walked around it to see her on the other side, kneeling, facing the far wall.

"I'm right here, Savannah," I announced. "Nobody killed me."

"Oh, thank god," Nast said. "See, sweetheart? Paige is fine."

"You killed her! You killed her!"

"No, hon, I'm right—"

"You killed her!" Savannah screamed. "You killed her! You promised! You promised and you lied!"

Tears streamed down Savannah's face. Nast stepped forward, arms wide to embrace her. I lunged to grab him but missed.

"Don't—!" I shouted.

Savannah's hands flew up and Nast shot backward. His head slammed against the concrete wall. His eyes widened then closed as his body slumped to the ground, head falling forward.

I ran to him and felt for a pulse, but there was none. Blood trickled from the crushed back of his head, wending down his neck and over my fingers.

"Oh god. Oh god." I gulped air, forcing calm into my voice. "It's okay, Savannah. It'll be okay. You didn't mean it, I know that."

She'd started chanting again. Her hands were clenched and raised, her head down, eyes squeezed shut. I tried to decipher the spell, but the words flowed so fast they were almost unintelligible. I could tell she was summoning, but what . . . ?

Then I caught a word, a single word that told me everything. *Mother*. Savannah was trying to raise her mother's spirit.

"Savannah," I said, keeping my voice soft. "Savannah, hon? It's me. It's Paige."

She kept casting, repeating the words over and over in an endless loop. My gaze moved to her hands, caught by a flash of something red. Blood streamed down her wrists as her fingers bit into her palms.

"Oh, Savannah," I whispered.

I moved toward her, hands outstretched. When I was only inches from touching her, her eyes flew open. They were blank, as if seeing only a shape or a stranger. She shouted something and banged her hands against her sides. My feet flew from under me and I sailed into the far wall.

I stayed on the floor until she returned to her incantation. Then I pushed myself to my knees.

From my new angle, the light from the basement hall caught Savannah's face, glistening off the tears that streamed down, soaking the front of her shirt. The words flew from her lips, more expelled than spoken, moving seamlessly from spell to spell, language to language, in a desperate bid to find the right way to call forth her mother's spirit.

"Oh, baby," I whispered, feeling my own eyes fill with tears. "You poor baby."

She'd tried so hard, moving from one life to another, making every effort to fit into a new world populated by strangers who couldn't, wouldn't, understand her. Now even that world had fallen apart. Everyone had deserted her, failed her, and so she was desperately attempting to summon the one person who'd never failed her. And it was the one thing she could never do.

Savannah could call forth every demon in the universe and never reach her own mother. She might accidentally have raised the spirits of that family in the cemetery, but she could not call on her mother, buried in an unknown grave hundreds of miles away. If such a thing were possible, I would have contacted my own mother, despite every moral qualm against such a thing. How many times in this past year would I have called her, to ask for advice, for guidance, for anything—just to speak to her?

My own grief washed through me then, my own tears flowing in a sobbing gush, breaking past the dam I'd so carefully erected. How different everything would have been if my mother had been here. She could have told me how to deal with the Coven, could have interceded on my behalf. She could have rescued me from jail, comforted me after that hellish afternoon in the funeral parlor. With her there, it would never have been this way. I would never have *fucked up so badly!*

I hadn't been ready—not for Savannah, not for Coven leadership, not for anything that had befallen me since her death. Now I was here, in this strange basement, listening to the howling chant of Savannah's grief and knowing that if I did not stop her, she would summon something we couldn't control, something that would destroy us both.

I knew this yet could do nothing. I didn't have any idea what to do. Hearing Savannah shout her mother's name, voice rising in a crazed crescendo, I did the only thing I could think of: I asked my own mother for help. I closed my eyes and called to her, summoning her from the depths of my memory and pleading for help. When Savannah paused to gulp air, I heard someone calling my name. For one second my heart leaped, thinking I had somehow succeeded. Then the voice came clear.

"Paige?! Savannah?! Paige?!"

It was Cortez, upstairs. I whispered a word of thanks

to my mother, or providence, or whatever had sent him, then raced past the furnace and up the stairs. When I reached the top, I saw Cortez run past the end of the hall.

"Here!" I called. "I'm here!"

The house shook. I braced myself in the doorway, tensing for the next outbreak, but nothing came. As the house shuddered and went still, I flew down the hall, meeting Cortez halfway. He grabbed me in a fierce hug.

"Thank god," he said. "Where's Savannah? We have to get out. Something's happening."

"It's Savannah. She's—"

"Well, look at that," Leah's voice said behind us. "The white knight arrives just in time. You're such a lucky girl, Paige. All my knights die and leave me to finish their battles."

We pulled apart and faced her.

"You have your deal, Leah," Cortez said. "We don't have time for you. I'll speak to my father. You'll be immune from any repercussions."

"Repercussions?" She laughed. "What repercussions? I'm about to save Thomas Nast's son and granddaughter, risking my life for theirs. I'll be made VP for this."

"No, you won't," I said. "There is no son to save. Kristof Nast is dead."

Cortez blinked but recovered in a heartbeat. "You understand what that means, Leah. If you walk out of here alive, you'll be the sole survivor of a Cabal disaster— a disaster that killed the Nast heir. Thomas Nast won't reward you. You'll be lucky if he doesn't kill you."

"He will when he finds out that you initiated this

tragedy," I added. "You told Savannah that I was dead, that her father killed me. You set her off. Whatever plan you had, it backfired. Take the offer and go before we change our minds."

A clay pot flew from beside the front staircase. Cortez pushed me out of its path and tried to twist away, but it hit him in the gut so hard he was slammed against the wall. He slid to the floor and doubled over, gasping. I ran to him, but Leah shoved me back.

"If there's one thing I know," she said, stepping over Cortez as he retched and coughed, "it's how to turn a sow's ear into a silk purse. A Cabal project gone horribly wrong—one Cabal heir dead—why not make it two? And collect a very nice bounty in the process. With a houseful of bodies, no one's going to question two more."

I cast the suffocation spell, but it failed. As she bent over, I launched a fireball, my one foolproof offensive spell. It hit her in the back of the head. As she whirled, a knick-knack table flew up and smashed against my side, knocking the next spell from my lips.

Leah advanced on me. Behind her, Cortez struggled to sit, coughing up gobs of crimson phlegm. His eyes widened and his right hand shot up, fingers flicking. The spell knocked me sideways. As I stumbled, a splintered table leg slammed into the wall right where I'd been standing.

She strode over to Cortez, who'd managed to sit up. She grabbed his face, and shoved him backward to the floor. Cortez struggled, but his eyes blazed with pain.

Again I tried the suffocation spell. This time it took hold. Leah gasped, released Cortez, and turned on me.

Something hit me in the side of the head and I went down, breaking the spell. When Cortez moved, she sent the clay pot crashing into his stomach again. He fell back, eyes wide, face contorting.

I cast the suffocation spell. Again it caught. Again Leah broke it, this time by hitting me in the back of the head with a ceramic knick-knack and knocking me to my knees. She stepped forward, towering over me.

"Seems you've learned a new trick since you got Isaac killed," she said. "It doesn't really work any better than the fireballs, though, does it? Another useless witch spell. Or is it just another useless witch?"

I dropped and rolled out of her reach. When I came up, Leah bore down on me. Behind her, Cortez lifted his left hand, squeezed it into a fist, opened it, and then repeated the motion in rapid succession, lips moving soundlessly. A spell?

I saw Leah copy the motion, balling her left hand into a fist. Cortez slammed his hand to the floor, motioning me down. I dove as another knick-knack flew past, shattering against the wall. The tell! That was it. The hand motion was Leah's tell.

I leaped to my feet and cast the suffocation spell. With the first gasp, her left hand clenched. I hit the floor and rolled without breaking my concentration. The clay pot flew past. Her hand balled again and I scampered to the side, narrowly avoiding an ottoman that sailed in from the living room.

"Running out of things to throw?" I said. "Maybe we should move to the kitchen. Plenty of pots and pans there. Maybe even a knife or two."

Her face contorted with rage as she gasped for air. Her hand clenched, but this time nothing happened.

"Oooh, impotence!" I exclaimed. "Never good."

Another fist. Again nothing happened. Leah's face was purpling now, as she struggled in vain to breathe. She leaped at me and hit me in the chest, sending us both down. Her fist hit my cheek and the spell broke. I recast it, nearly tripping over the words in my haste, but it worked, and she only got a sniff of air before I cut off her oxygen again.

Leah began to choke. I grabbed her by the shoulders and threw her off me, pinning her to the floor. Her eyes widened and bulged. She was suffocating now, dying.

Indecision flitted through me. Could I do this? I had to. Around us, the house groaned; pieces of plaster fell from the walls. It was starting again, and I had to get Cortez and Savannah out. We'd given Leah the chance to leave and she'd refused. She'd never let us walk out alive. I had to kill her. Yet I couldn't look into her eyes and watch her die—I couldn't. So I shut my eyes, concentrated as hard as I could, and waited for her body to go still. Once it did, I waited another thirty seconds, then scrambled off her, not looking back, and stumbled to Cortez's side.

He'd pushed himself onto all fours. I opened my mouth, but the house shook again and an ear-splitting howl drowned me out. Cortez jabbed a finger toward the front door. I shook my head, but he pushed himself to his feet, grabbed my arm, and started to drag me. When we made it to the porch, the house rumbled. A beam supporting the porch snapped, and we dove onto the grass just as the porch collapsed on itself. Then the house went still and the howling fell to a drone.

Summoning Eve

"IT'S SAVANNAH," I said, words tumbling out. "She's trying to raise her mother's spirit."

"She can't."

"I know, but she won't stop. She doesn't even seem to know I'm there. I can't get near her."

The house groaned and shuddered. When I made a move to run back inside Cortez grabbed my arm, then started coughing uncontrollably, splattering blood-soaked sputum.

"I need to stop her," I said. "Before she summons something else or brings the house down."

"I know a spell—" Coughing obliterated his next words. "—look like Eve."

"What?"

"A spell that'll make you look like Eve. It's not perfect. The success depends on whether the viewer is inclined to believe the deception. Savannah obviously is."

"Impersonate her mother?" I shook my head hard. "That's . . . that's . . . I can't do it. I won't betray her that way. It isn't right."

"You have to. Any minute now, that house is coming down. Would Eve rather you let her daughter die in there? Yes, it's wrong, but it's justified. We'll never tell

Savannah the truth. You're giving her one last moment with her mother, Paige. I know you understand how much that means to her."

"Oh god." I rubbed my hands over my face. "O— okay. Do it. Hurry, please."

Cortez cast the spell. It seemed to take forever. Twice he fell into a coughing fit, and my heart seized. How badly was he hurt? What if he—No, I couldn't think of that. Not now.

Finally, he finished. When I opened my eyes and looked down, I saw my own short fingers, my own silver rings.

"Did it—" I glanced up at him. "Did it work?"

"If you need to ask, then you won't see it. The illusion depends on the viewer's willingness to believe."

I closed my eyes and forced past my own doubt. I needed this to work. I needed to become Eve.

When I looked again, my fingers shimmered then lengthened, nails growing long and manicured, rings disappearing. I got to my feet, expecting disorientation but finding none. My body moved as it always had. As Cortez said, the illusion was in the eye of the beholder.

Since the front door was now inaccessible, I jogged around to the side entrance. As I swung through, I saw Cortez limping along, using the side of the house for support.

"Go on," he said. "I'll meet you downstairs."

"No. You need to stay here."

"I won't let Savannah see me, Paige. The illusion will be complete. I'm only coming along as backup, in case of an emergency."

I hurried to him and put my hand against his chest, halting his progress. "Please. Stay out here. You're hurt."

"I can still cast—"

"No, please." I met his eyes. "If something goes wrong, you'll never get away in time. I need to know you're okay. I'll be fine."

The house creaked. Shingles slid off, one striking me on the shoulder. Cortez nudged me toward the house. I didn't need a second hint. With one backward glance I was gone.

I raced down to the basement. From inside the furnace room Savannah continued her pleas, voice rising and falling. I pressed my hands to my face and inhaled deeply, fighting to control my hammering heart. I had to believe. *She* had to believe.

When I rounded the corner into the room, Savannah stopped. She went still, completely still, as if sensing me there but fearing to turn and face disappointment.

"Savannah?" I said.

To my ears my voice still sounded like my own, and as she turned, I nearly broke and ran. Instead, I held my breath and waited. Her eyes met mine. She blinked, then rubbed her palms over her eyes.

"Mom?"

"I heard you calling."

"Mom!" She leaped from her knees and ran to me, arms flinging around my chest. Burying her head against my shoulder, she started to sob. "Oh, Mom, it's such a mess. I . . . I did everything wrong."

Instinctively I reached to stroke her hair, forgetting who I was supposed to be and speaking as myself. "You didn't do anything wrong. Nothing at all."

"Yes, I did. I made Paige stay here with me, and now she's gone." Her voice broke in a sob. "I—I think she's dead, Mom. It's my fault. I made her stay and they killed her."

"No," I said sharply, putting my hand under her chin. "Paige is fine. You need to get out of this house, Savannah, before it collapses."

As if to emphasize the point, the house began to shake. Splinters popped from the beams overhead.

"I—I didn't mean to do this. I just kept casting and casting and things kept coming, but they weren't you. I only wanted you."

"I'm here now." I kissed her forehead. "But you have to go, Savannah. I love you very much, but I can't stay. You know that."

"Oh, Mom. I miss you so much."

My voice caught. "I know. I miss you, too. So much."

A beam broke over the furnace, then another. Chunks of the ceiling fell through.

"You have to go, Savannah," I said. "Please."

I hugged her tight, so tight her ribs crackled in protest. She gave a hiccuping laugh, then reached up to kiss my cheek.

"Can I see you again?" she asked.

I shook my head. "I'm sorry, sweetheart, but it only works once. I'll be with you, though. Even if you can't see me. You know that." I hugged her again and whispered in her ear, the words flowing unbidden, as if someone else was speaking. "You were my whole world, Savannah. The best thing I ever did."

She gave me a crushing hug, then stepped back. The ceiling groaned.

"Go," I said. "I'll be right here watching. Go on."

She walked backward, eyes never leaving mine. Overhead, the beams began to pop like matchsticks.

"Hurry!" I called. "Up the stairs now. Run!"

"I love you, Mom."

"I love you too, baby."

She threw me a kiss, then turned and ran. I waited, listening to her footsteps, needing to make sure she was gone before I bolted. I heard Cortez shout. Heard Savannah answer.

Then the ceiling caved in.

The Eighth Day

I'M STILL NOT QUITE SURE how I made it out. Sheer luck, I suppose. Guess I was entitled to one miracle. I managed to duck inside a crawl-space when the house collapsed around me. After that, well, after that is a bit of a blur, but I made it out with only cuts and bruises.

Savannah never realized I'd impersonated her mother. She assumed I'd been trapped in the house while searching for her. As Cortez said, we'll never tell her. She deserves that fantasy, one I envied her—a few last minutes with the person who meant more to her than anyone in the world.

We still had to do Savannah's ceremony in a few days, but with Leah and Nast dead, no one would impede that now. So it was all over. *All over.* I should have felt relief at those words, yet I couldn't, because it truly *was* over. My life as I'd always known it was over.

I didn't get my happy ending. Maybe I've seen too many Hollywood movies, but I honestly believed everything would turn out okay. If I survived, if I saved Savannah, then I would get my karmic reward. My tattered life would miraculously mend. The media would forget about me overnight. The town would forgive me, welcome me back. The Coven would overthrow Victoria and reinstate me as Coven Leader. I'd return to find that my house hadn't been burned to the ground, only barely scorched, all my belongings still intact.

But my house was a hollow shell. Anything that hadn't burned had been scavenged by human vultures. When we returned to survey the damage, we were beset by reporters. The tabloids screamed *Mob Justice: Vigilantes Try to Burn Massachusetts Witch*. Some claimed I'd caused the fire accidentally while conducting a Satanic ritual, using body parts dug up from the cemetery the night before. Hordes of screaming strangers banged against the taxi windows, chasing us up the street. The front page of every Boston paper carried the story of the burning, augmented with news of "renewed efforts" by townspeople to cleanse East Falls of my presence. Within a day the more enterprising reporters began drawing links between me and the "unholy" destruction of a farmhouse thirty miles away.

I called every Coven member, assuring them that Nast was out of our lives for good. I told them what Victoria had done. It didn't matter. I'd tainted the Coven. Only a handful would even consider having me back.

We stayed in Massachusetts only long enough to file an insurance claim. Between the money from the claim and money I still had from my mother's estate, I had enough to move anywhere I wanted and start over. For most women my age, this would be a dream come true. It wasn't my dream, but I'd make it mine. I swore I would.

When we pulled out of Boston three days later, I watched the city lights fade behind me, perhaps for the last time, and a wave of sadness washed over me. But no tears came. Surprisingly few tears had come in the last few days. Even as I'd surveyed the ruins of my life, I realized that I still had exactly what I'd fought for.

I had Savannah.

I remembered what Cortez had said, warning me that I might lose everything I had in my quest to protect her. I'd said that it didn't matter. Well, I guess that's what happens when you make a deal with the Fates; they take you at your word. Still, they did leave me with two consolation prizes, which I valued more than I could have imagined.

First, I had the grimoires. When the firefighters rescued Cortez from my burning house, he'd still been carrying the two bags, the one with the grimoires and the one with my tools and the material for Savannah's ceremony.

My second bonus reward? Cortez was fine, and still with us. Through his network of contacts, he'd found a doctor in Boston willing to examine him, no questions asked. He had three cracked ribs, internal bruising, and a possible concussion. The doctor had advised a hospital stay, but Cortez settled for a chest binding and some painkillers, and then we'd set out on the road.

I hadn't told him of his brother's plan to have me killed. What would be the use? He already knew his brothers hated him. If I told him, he might decide he was putting my life in danger and leave, and I wasn't risking that.

We'd been driving for two days now. I still didn't

know where we were going. For now, it was a cross-country summer tour. Savannah thought that was pretty cool. But she'd tire of it soon. Hopefully, I'd find a place to settle before she did.

We'd stopped this morning—some town in Virginia. At least I think we were still in Virginia, though we may have crossed into Kentucky. Today was the big day. The eighth day.

Since dawn we'd been preparing for the ceremony. Now that it was dark, we'd driven to a state park, slipped past the locked gates, and headed into the forest. I'd found a site almost immediately, a good-sized clearing ringed with trees, as the ceremony prescribed. We were still early, though, so Savannah had grabbed a flashlight and taken off to see if she couldn't find something better. My choice was fine, but I suspected she was simply too excited to sit still.

I'd found a fallen log and sat down to pore over my notes. I was reading them through for the third time when a hand pressed between my shoulder blades, fingers rubbing the knot of tension there.

"How are you doing?" Cortez said, taking a seat beside me.

I managed a shaky smile. "It feels like I'm about to do my SATs, driver's test and thesis presentation all rolled into one."

He squeezed my hand. "You'll do fine."

I leaned against him and he put his arm around my shoulders.

"What would you think about heading out to the coast?" he asked. "Washington or Oregon. You might like it there. Lots of open space, and the ocean. It's not the East Coast, but . . ."

"I visited Portland once. I liked it."

"We'll go there, then."

"So you're going to . . . I mean, we haven't discussed . . ." I took a deep breath and plowed on. "Are you coming with us? For now, I mean?"

"For now . . . and for as long as I'm welcome." He slid a quarter-smile my way. "The problem, as you undoubtedly have already discerned, will not be keeping me around but getting rid of me."

"I can live with that."

I leaned over and kissed him. When we pulled apart, he adjusted his glasses and looked at me.

"When I, uh, mentioned the Pacific Northwest, it wasn't a random suggestion. With Kristof dead, on a case in which I was involved, I may need to lie low for a while."

"What will happen?"

"I don't know. I can say with certainty that my presence won't place you or Savannah in danger. I'd never do that. The matter of Kristof's death will be handled through proper Cabal channels. If I'm in danger, I'll hear of it long before anyone comes for me. My father should be able to handle it." He shook his head. "It seems no matter how far and how fast I run, I always end up relying on my father to—" He stopped. "I'm sorry."

"Tell me."

He entwined his fingers with mine and smiled. "Later. I only wanted you to know that I'm not placing you in danger, but that it would be wise for me to keep out of sight for a while. My father may—will summon me home to Miami. I'd prefer to be as far away as possible when that happens."

Savannah burst from the forest. "Is it time?"

I nodded. "Wait here. I'll cast a perimeter spell around the site."

"We'll have everything set up when you return," Cortez said, dropping the knapsack from his shoulder.

"No, I'll do—" I bit my lip. "Sure. Thanks."

I walked until I could no longer hear the murmur of their voices, then continued another ten feet before casting the perimeter spell. Fighting my way through the thick woods, I circled the site, casting as I went. Then I looped around again, just to be sure. When I returned to the clearing, Cortez and Savannah were kneeling on the ground, laying out the final objects.

Cortez shifted to a crouch. "Is this correct?"

I took the notes from him and walked around the tableau, scrutinizing it from every angle. Along both the north and south sides of the cloth they'd laid a quartet of tools: a small pot, an athame, a candle, and a chalice. The north candle was purple, for power; the south one blue, for wisdom and truth. Off the cloth they'd left the Baggies of dirt, the juniper, and a bottle of water.

Savannah handed me a necklace, a lodestone on a strip of rawhide, like the one now around her own neck. I put it on, surveyed the tableau once again, and bent to move the blue candle an inch to the left and rotate the northern athame about twenty degrees east. They'd probably been fine to begin with, but I felt better making the adjustments. Control isn't a habit you can break overnight.

"Okay, we're almost ready. Savannah, have you buried the cloth?"

She nodded.

"Good, then you need to kneel on the north side, in front of the purple candle."

"Shall I move elsewhere?" Cortez asked.

"Only if you want to."

"I'll sit back on the log and watch. If that bothers you, tell me and I'll get out of sight."

"Thanks."

When he went to take his seat, I cast a protective spell around us. Then I turned to Savannah.

"Before we start, I want you to know that I really want this to work. It's possible, though, that I might not have the power or the experience to do it properly. If it seems to fail, I'll keep trying, but—"

"It's okay," she said. "I'll know you tried. Thanks, Paige—for doing this, I mean. I know it's not what you had in mind for me."

"It's what your mother wanted. That's good enough for me." I laid my notes before me. "Okay, first the elements. If anything sounds wrong, stop me. Even if you aren't sure, don't be afraid to speak up. Better to restart partway through than repeat the whole thing later."

She nodded.

"Here we go, then. Air."

I slashed each athame through the air.

"Earth."

I poured grave dirt from the Baggie into each shallow clay pot.

"Water."

I uncapped the Evian bottle and filled both chalices.

"Fire."

I struck a match and lit the candles.

I paused then, closing my eyes and clearing my mind. When I opened my eyes, I focused straight ahead, seeing nothing. With a brief Latin invocation I called on the power of the elements to heed my will. Then I blinked, allowing myself to see again, and motioned for Savannah to watch carefully, since she'd need to repeat the next steps.

"Air to the north," I said, taking my athame and placing it before me.

"Earth to the east." I put my clay pot to my right.

"Water to the west." I moved my chalice to my left.

"Fire to the south." Taking the blue candle, I twisted, being careful not to fall, and laid it behind me.

I touched each in turn—the athame, the dirt, the water, and the flame. When it came to the last, panic darted through me and I hesitated, then gritted my teeth and forced my finger into the flame.

"Air, earth, water, fire. At their center I sit in balance. All nature in harmony."

I turned to Savannah and motioned for her to copy me. She did, intoning each phrase without faltering. When she'd finished, we repeated the last part together.

Then Savannah shifted onto her knees, lighting the candles as I resumed my place. Fingers trembling, I held the juniper branch over my candle's flame.

"With this offering I beg protection," I said in Latin. "Hecate, Selene, Artemis, goddesses three, hear my plea.

We ask this in your name. Grant this, your child, all the powers you can bestow." I looked Savannah in the eyes, lifting my hands and voice. "Grant her power without bounds. Give her the strength to wreak vengeance on her enemies."

The ground beneath me rumbled, but I held Savannah's gaze and kept going.

"Give her the power to overcome and the wisdom to do right by this gift. Give her all that you have to give."

The earth quaked, toppling the candles and igniting the cloth beneath. I raised my hands to the sky and stood, closing my eyes and pouring everything into the last few words.

"Hecate, Selene, Artemis! Hear my plea!"

For a split second all went still, preternaturally still and silent. I could hear nothing, feel nothing. No, I did feel something: I felt peace. Complete peace.

"It worked!" Savannah shouted, launching herself across the space between us and falling into my arms. "Can you feel that, Paige? It worked! You did it!"

"Yes," I said, smiling. "We did it."

Acknowledgements

With thanks,

To Helen Heller, my agent, without whom there would be no Women of the Otherworld series.

To Anne Collins, my editor at Random House Canada, who knew just the solution for all my manuscript crises.

To Antonia Hodgson, my editor at Time Warner UK, for her continued enthusiasm and great editing advice.

To Anne Groell, my editor at Bantam US, for taking an interest in this book, and for making the switch to Bantam absolutely painless.

Finally, to every reader who has e-mailed me with praise for the series. Your notes made a writer's day a whole lot brighter, and a day of writing a whole lot easier!

INDUSTRIAL MAGIC

Kelley Armstrong
Published in 2004

After the events of the previous summer, no one could blame Paige Winterbourne – ousted leader of the American Coven – if she just hid under her duvet for a few months and let the supernatural world manage without her. But fate, of course, has other plans . . .

A murderer is on the loose – someone with apparently superhuman skills. Whoever it is clearly has a grudge against the Cabals: all the attacks have been on Cabal family members. Paige wants nothing to do with the investigation, but when she learns that the killer is targeting children, she realises she has to get involved. Even if the cost turns out to be more than she can bear.

Facing the greatest threat of her life, Paige is forced to throw herself into a world of arrogant Cabal leaders, drunken necromancers, sulky druid gods and pretentious leather-clad vampires in order to protect those she loves. Luckily, she has a female werewolf and a certain renegade sorcerer on her side . . .

BITTEN

Kelley Armstrong

Elena Michaels is your regular twenty-first-century girl: self-assured, smart and fighting fit. She also just happens to be the only female were-wolf in the world . . .

It has some good points. When she walks down a dark alleyway, *she's* the scary one. But now her Pack – the one she abandoned so that she could live a normal life – are in trouble, and they need her help. Is she willing to risk her life to help the ex-lover who betrayed her by turning her into a werewolf in the first place? And more to the point, does she have a choice?

'A tasty confection of werewolves, sex and vendettas. Gory, sexy fun'

SFX

'Makes Buffy look fluffy'

Daily Express

'The most appealing heroine I have come across in ages. Clever, quirky, hip and funny. More please!'

Joanne Harris

STOLEN

Kelley Armstrong

Elena Michaels is a wanted woman. She hasn't done anything wrong. Well, not recently, anyway. But ten years ago her lover turned her into a werewolf: the only female werewolf in the world, in fact.

And now, just as she's finally coming to terms with it all, a group of scientists learns of her existence. They're hunting her down, and Elena is about to run straight into their trap. But they haven't reckoned on Elena's adoptive family, her Pack, who will stop at nothing to get her back. They haven't reckoned on Elena herself, either, and that's a very big mistake . . .

'A taut, sensual thriller that grips from the first page. Elena Michaels is at once sublime and sympathetic, a modern heroine who shows that real women bite back'

Karin Slaughter,
author of *Blindsighted* and *Kisscut*